The Schubert Club

125th Anniversary

Musings and Memories

The Schubert Club

125th Anniversary

Musings and Memories

CONTRIBUTING ESSAYISTS: MARY ANN FELDMAN / PATRICIA HAMPL
JUDITH KOGAN / MICHAEL STEINBERG / JANE JEONG TRENKA / MARGARET WURTELE

Editors: Sharon Carlson and Holly Windle

Contributing Staff Writers: Abbie Betinis / Max Carlson / Sharon Carlson / Rebecca Klein
Jason Kudrna / David Morrison / Richard Rames / Alison Scherzer / Holly Windle

Other Contributors: Mark Alpert / Paul Aslanian / Carol Barnett / J. Michael Barone
Ellie Bruner / Claire Colliander / Arlene Didier / Karyn Diehl / Mary Lynn Fixler
Margaret Gadient / Dana Gioia / Håkan Hagegård / Libby Larsen / Bruce MacCombie
Stephen Paulus / Christopher Dunn Raudenbush / Mona Lyn Reese / George Reid
Margaret Richardson / Paul Schoenfield / Jeffrey Siegel / David Evan Thomas
Joan Tower / Janika Vandervelde

NODIN PRESS

ISBN 10: 1-932472-52-5
ISBN 13 : 978-1-932472-52-3
Library of Congress Control Number: 2007936345
11 10 09 08 07 1 2 3 4 5 6

Acknowledgement: This book would not have been possible without the many people over the years who have sustained the organization itself: board members, committee members, staff, volunteers, musicians, donors, and, of course, our audiences.

Graphics editing and collages: David Morrison
Cover design: John Toren, Sharon Carlson, David Morrison
Cartoons: David Morrison
Book design and layout: John Toren

Photo Credits:
Philip Blackburn: 61 (Wild Music A-Go-Go)
Andrea Canter: 63, 72 (Jazz Piano winners)
Tom Foley: 56, 62 (after winners recital), 77 (2007 winners)
Minnesota Historical Society: 38 & background 38-39 (Ford Music Hall, Charles P. Gibson); 38 (People's Church, Charles P. Gibson); 38 (St. Paul Auditorium); 39 (Ford Interior & O'Shaugnessy); 39 (People's Church fire, A. Irber); 66; 67 (Carl R. Ermisch); 121; 124 (Charles P. Gibson); 125 (1935 Presidents, Kenneth Melvin Wright); 172; 173 (Charles P. Gibson); 174.
Beauty Queen photos, page 80 by: Fpvision (Nora Ali), Paula Preson (Nicole Swanson), and Miss America Organization (Dorothy Benham)]
Saint Paul Pioneer Press: 19, 61 (underwater concert by Joe Oden), 62 (1929 scholarship winners & 1944 Neighborhood House lesson), 75, 76 (Beatles or Bach), 81 (1970 winners by Neale Van Ness, St. Paul Dispatch), 81 (1964 winners), 178 (Progress cartoon), 201
Ben Saltzman and Richard Sorensen: 61 (Hot Notes)
Richard Sorensen: 40 (Ordway Interior), 91
Sharon Varosh: 111 (Music, Myth, & Magic)
Cover illustration: Moritz Von Schwind (1804 -1871)

Nodin Press is a division of Micawber's, Inc.
530 N. Third Street, Suite 120
Minneapolis, MN 55401

A Letter from the President

The Schubert Club was an outpost of classical music when it first appeared in the young city of Saint Paul in 1882. Much has changed since the time of new railroads and fast-growing cities in the west, yet The Schubert Club continues to present and nurture recital music of the very highest quality in our community.

This collection of essays and images is a remarkable offering of distinct remembrances and explorations of what The Schubert Club is, how it was shaped, and how it shaped others. The book has many voices, as befits an organization with a rich past and many fond friends. Finally it is an homage to the man whose ideas framed this book – The Schubert Club's steadfast and singular friend, the late Bruce Carlson. His voice will be remembered clearly.

Mary Probst
President, The Schubert Club Board of Directors

To Bruce Carlson, a major part of our history

Executive Director, 1968-2006

Contents

◈ Prelude ◈

◈ Concerts ◈

◈ Education ◈

◈ *Museum* ◈

◈ *Administration* ◈

◈ *Finance* ◈

◈ *Community Connections* ◈

The Schubert Club was founded in 1882. Here are a few of the other noteworthy events of that annis mirabilis*:*

MUSICAL PREMIERES:

– Wagner's last work, *Parsifal*, at Bayreuth
– Tchaikovsky's *1812 Overture*
– Bedřich Smetana's *Ma Vlast*
- Gilbert and Sullivan's *Iolanthe*

The Berlin Philharmonic Orchestra was founded in 1882. And a number of individuals who would later distinguish themselves in music, politics, or the arts were born that year, including Geraldine Farrar, Amelita Galli-Curci, Percy Grainger, Zoltán Kodály, Igor Stravinsky, Leopold Stokowski, Artur Schnabel, Sigrid Undset, Edward Hopper, Samuel Goldwyn, Joaquin Turina, Virginia Woolf, Franklin Delano Roosevelt, Anna Pavlova, Bela Lugosi, A.A. Milne, James Joyce, Georges Braque, and N.C. Wyeth.

The electric iron was patented in 1882, and also the Heinz ketchup bottle and the Janko piano keyboard (a key layout providing more notes within a hand span). The discovery of the bacterium responsible for tuberculosis was announced; Robert Louis Stevenson's *Treasure Island* first appeared in print. The publication that later became the *Wall Street Journal* also hit the newsstands for the first time, and the Standard Oil Trust issued its first shares of stock. The U.S. Congress passed the Chinese Exclusion Act, and Britain's Parliament passed the Married Women's Property Act, enabling women to buy, own, and sell property—and keep their own earnings. That same year British forces occupied Cairo, effectively making Egypt a British protectorate for the next forty years. And on the local scene, James J. Hill became president of the Saint Paul, Minneapolis & Manitoba Railway Company.

Walt Whitman's *Leaves of Grass* was banned in Boston in 1882, and the Hatfields and McCoys started up a feud that would last for six years. On January 2, 1882, Oscar Wilde arrived in New York City and began a lecture tour devoted to the aesthetic movement. On March 22, the U.S. Congress outlawed polygamy. On April 3, Jesse James was shot and killed by his cousin for a $5,000 reward. And in September the Saint Paul Public Library first opened its doors (with 8,051 books).

It was a good year for holidays. Labor Day was observed for the first time (on a Tuesday) and Edward Johnson (assistant to Thomas Edison) hung the first set of electric Christmas tree lights.

The Schubert Club: A Backward Glance

An anniversary is a time to look backwards; the galloping pace of modern life gives us few other moments for reflection. Where have we been? Where are we going? The Schubert Club's existence for 125 years—far longer than an average human life span—represents a period of enormous change: social, political, technological, artistic. It is a richly fascinating period, and a small book such as this can give it only a quick glance. But certain outlines can perhaps be discerned from the singular perspective of The Schubert Club, an organization that has held—for so long a time—to its particular mission of promoting recital music.

We usually date the beginning of The Schubert Club from that autumn afternoon in 1882 when Governor Ramsey's daughter Marion Furness and her friends organized themselves as the "Ladies' Musicale." But nothing grows from nothing. The roots go deeper. Apparently as early as 1873 a group of worthy ladies and gentlemen would gather together in one Saint Paul home or another for an evening of society including an hour or so of "good" music. Gradually the emphasis shifted from a "social club, with musical features" to a "musical club, with social features." When the meeting time was changed from evening to afternoon, the gentlemen were effectively excluded. The Ladies' Musicale was the result.

A few years later this same group re-styled itself as The Schubert Club.

Saint Paul was a very different town in 1882. Though a burgeoning center of commerce and transportation, the city was a rather rough-and-tumble place, still a new town, without the established seats of culture and learning that eastern cities boasted. Boston and Philadelphia each had its Athenaeum, and New York its Philharmonic Society. Saint Paul lacked similar amenities. Many of its residents, however, came here from the east, and had been raised in that "capital C" Culture, that was more sophisticated and "refined," to use a then-current term. They quite naturally wished to continue to enjoy the

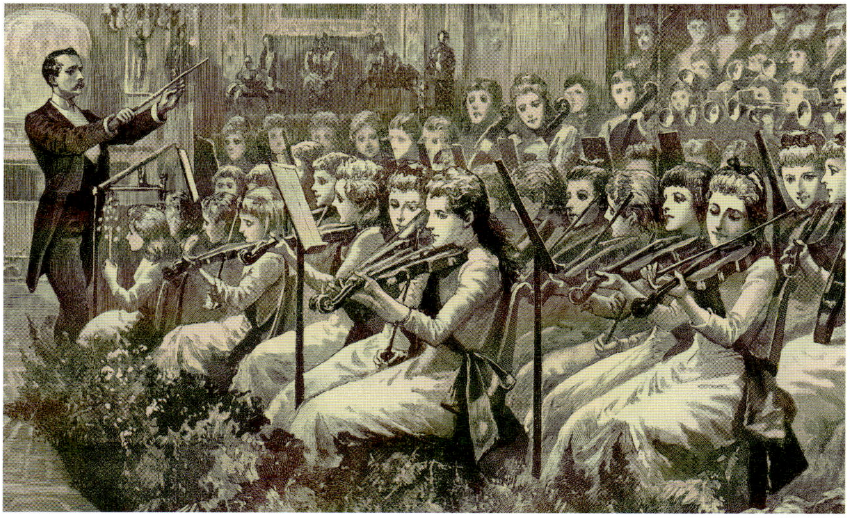

An idealized representation of a Ladies' Orchestra from an old print.

pleasures of the mind that "good" music afforded them.

And here is the nub, the essential thing that has kept The Schubert Club going for 125 years: an awareness that there is something especially good and worthwhile about a certain kind of music, and that the intellectual and emotional pleasures of understanding, performing, and listening to that music are worth cultivating in oneself and sharing with others.

That is the thread of continuity that we can see in The Schubert Club's activities throughout its long history. Club members performing for each other, sponsoring music lessons for young people, bringing gifted performers to Saint Paul to share their art, and establishing a student scholarship competition—all these things testify to a love of that "good" music. This music ranges across the centuries from works by Bach, Beethoven, and the club's namesake Schubert, to that of living composers—which in 1882 included Brahms still in his vigorous middle-age. Today The Schubert Club continues to promote good music, both old and new—witness the Pulitzer Prize-winning commissions by Dominick Argento and Aaron Jay Kernis.

In the organization's early days the members were themselves musicians, and The Schubert Club existed in part to allow them opportunities to perform. They gave individual recitals, a "ladies' chorus" was formed, and an orchestra was begun under the direction of Dr. Emil Oberhoffer. In addition to these Active members, the club also included non-musician, Associate members, and after 1900, a Student Section. The membership enjoyed lectures on musical topics by such luminaries as Frances Densmore, Alfred Dolmetsch and Walter Damrosch. In 1893 the club made its first student loan, which allowed Miss Ella Richards to study piano in Vienna. The club's altruistic work expanded in 1908 to include musical performance in orphanages and prisons. In 1911 musical classes for underprivileged children were started on the West Side of

Saint Paul. The annual student scholarship competition started in 1922 and is still going strong eighty-five years later. New technology was embraced: a Radio Committee existed as early as the 1930s. Concerts were broadcast in the 1970s, and "Live from Landmark," a weekly Schubert Club radio program began in 1980. In addition to all this, The Schubert Club from 1893 on has been engaged in presenting concerts in Saint Paul by national and international artists of the first rank: Leopold Godowsky, The Chicago Symphony Orchestra under Theodore Thomas, Ossip Gabrilowitsch, the Kneisel Quartet, Bidu Sayao, Percy Grainger, Helen Traubel, Gregor Piatigorsky, Tito Schipa. The list of legendary names goes on and on.

The changes in The Schubert Club's organization, from a club of amateur performer members to a 501(c)(3) non-profit arts organization, have been significant, but the idea at the core is the same. That is, in contradistinction to popular, folk, or dance music of the day—which thrives on its own—there is another sort of wonderful music, which takes a bit more effort to know, but repays that effort many times over. That The Schubert Club is still here, "still kicking" after 125 years, is a testament to the worthiness of its goal to promote that good music for one and all.

Ladies and gentlemen singing Gilbert and Sullivan's 1882 operetta *Iolanthe*. Members of The Schubert Club staged *Iolanthe* as a benefit for the Saint Paul Public Library, which was also established in 1882.

The Schubert Club Timeline

1882 – Founding of the "Musical Society," later called "Ladies Musicale"

1888 – "Ladies Musicale" changes to "The Schubert Club"

1892 – Official constitution and bylaws are adopted

1893 – First public recital at Ford Music Hall

1908 – "Altruistic Section" formed to provide musical performances for orphanages, workplaces, prisons, and other institutions

1911 – Schubert Club members begin providing music lessons for underprivileged children

1913 – Men are finally admitted, but only as special non-voting members

1915 – Officially incorporated as an organization

1915 – Fire at St. Paul Library destroys study sheets, music, scrapbooks and other Schubert Club documents

1916 – Composer and pianist Percy Grainger performs at the People's Church

1922 – Violinist Jascha Heifetz performs at the People's Church

1922 – Start of the annual Scholarship Competition

1928 – Pianist Vladimir Horowitz plays twice in the same year at the People's Church

1936 – Soprano Lotte Lehmann performs at the People's Church

1940 – The People's Church, beloved venue for The Schubert Club's main recital series, burns down

1942 – Pianist Artur Rubinstein gives a recital at Saint Paul Auditorium during The Schubert Club's 60th Season

1943 – Soprano Anne Brown (the original Bess from *Porgy and Bess* and The Schubert Club's first African American performer) sings at the Saint Paul Auditorium

1954 – The Schubert Club becomes a charter member of St. Paul Council of Arts and Sciences

1955 – Baritone Dietrich Fischer-Dieskau makes his American recital debut at the Saint Paul Auditorium

1958 – Officially becomes a non-profit, civic organization

1959 – Schubert Club music schools disband

1965 – An official Schubert Club office space is established at St. Paul Arts & Science Center

1968 – Bruce Carlson hired as Business Manager—the first paid man to work at The Schubert Club

1969 – Project CHEER, an after-school music lesson program, is formed

1970 – The main concert series is named "The International Artist Series" and is moved from downtown Saint Paul to O'Shaughnessy Auditorium at the College of St. Catherine

1972 – Acquisition of a Kisting fortepiano, the start of The Schubert Club Museum

1974 – Offices are relocated to Landmark Center (formerly known as the Old Federal Courts Building)

1975 – *From The Diary of Virginia Woolf* by Dominick Argento, a work commissioned by The Schubert Club, wins a Pulitzer Prize

1976 to 1983 – The Schubert Club shares its office space with the newly-formed Minnesota Composers Forum

1980 – The Schubert Club Museum opens in the Landmark Center (as the Keyboard Instrument Collection)

1980 – "Live from Landmark," a weekly concert series broadcast by Minnesota Public Radio, begins in Landmark Center

1984 – The Schubert Club Museum acquires the massive Kugler Collection of instruments and a collection of composer manuscripts donated by Gilman Ordway

1985 – Leontyne Price's Schubert Club concert opens the Ordway Music Theatre, and the International Artist Series returns to downtown Saint Paul

1987 – First official "Hill House Parlor Concert," a chamber music series in the historic James J. Hill House

1988 – "Authentic Instrument Series" starts – later called "Historical Instrument Series" then "Early Music Series"

1990 – "Courtroom Concerts," a new weekly series in Landmark Center replaces "Live from Landmark"

1995 – Indonesian gamelan instruments commissioned from Java arrive and The Schubert Club starts gamelan classes and performances

1996 – Keyboard Conversations™, a series of concert-plus-commentary with host Jeffrey Siegel is brought to Minnesota through Schubert Club sponsorship

1998 – Composer Aaron Jay Kernis wins a Pulitzer for his string quartet, *musica instrumentalis*, commissioned by The Schubert Club

1999 – Schubert Club wins Asian-Pacific Council leadership award

2002 – Grand opening of the Heilmaier Memorial Bandstand on Raspberry Island

2003 – Bruce Carlson is awarded the Sally Ordway Irvine Award for Commitment

2004 – Opening of second floor Gilman Ordway Manuscript Galleries; addition of Sunday hours for Museum

2004 – Scholarship awards exceed $55,000

2005 – Start of Jazz Piano Competition

2006 – Bruce Carlson inaugurates a new staff holiday, July 12, in honor of Alexander Hamilton

Concerts

Chatting with the artists is always a thrill — here it's Deanna and Rostropovich and ???

Governor and Mrs. Andersen in the audience at a Scholarship Competition Winners Recital

1934 recital artists included this matinee ide

Schubert Club Not in a Rut

The Ordway Center under construction — A new home for Schubert Club recitals

The Flonzaley Quartet performed three times under the auspices of The Schubert Club, in 1911, 1912, and again in 1913.

The Recital

Michael Steinberg

*Writer, lecturer, and musicologist, Michael Steinberg has been providing program notes for Schubert Club concerts since he moved to the Twin Cities in 1989. He has served as program annotator for many of this country's leading orchestras, including the San Francisco Symphony, the Minnesota Orchestra, the New York Philharmonic, and the Boston Symphony. His listener's guides (*The Symphony, The Concerto, *and* Choral Masterworks, *published by Oxford University Press) have been joined by* For the Love of Music: Invitations to Listening, *insightful and quirky reflections about music by Steinberg and Laurence Rothe.*

It's the concentration, the distillation of the artistic experience. The Vienna-born English critic Hans Keller maintained that if a symphony and a string quartet are equally good, the quartet is better—a pleasingly paradoxical insight instantly illuminating for some and forever unintelligible to others. Fewer is better. I love orchestras—the mountain climb to the last page of a Bruckner symphony and, no less, the sighs and whispers of Webern's Opus 10. I love opera and the possibilities, magnificent and mysterious, of the great choral machines. But a stage with just four or five musicians on it, or even fewer—now we're on the way to transfiguration and ecstasy.

A quartet, even a trio, is a mini-orchestra, a micro-team, a group with an intricate, carefully encoded system of mutually supporting and protective devices. But when you go down from three people to two you cross a border, and from two to one there is another frontier to traverse, a really daunting one. As the numbers get smaller, the vulnerability factor for the performers increases exponentially; at the same time, though, the intensity and precision of focus that the listener can lavish on just a singer and a pianist, a violinist or cellist with a pianist, or a pianist alone grows proportionally. We enter another world, and so it makes sense that we have a separate word to distinguish concerts given by two musicians, or just one: recital.

In the 1820s, when a concert meant a mixed grill with perhaps a pianist, a singer, some string players—and as recently as a hundred years ago orchestral concerts often featured the concerto soloist in a solo group of programmed encores, as it were—Franz Liszt was the first musician to dare produce events at which he was the sole performer. (Not unrelated, he was also the first pianist to set his instrument so as to display his profile to the audience.) And in London, in 1840, he also gave us a new term when he announced for Tuesday afternoon, May 9, in those Hanover Square Rooms where Haydn had enjoyed his symphonic triumphs in the 1790s, "RECITALS on the PIANOFORTE." Liszt had presented solo concerts before, but calling them "RECITALS" was new. That was in fact the brainchild of his friend Frederick Beale, a partner in the piano and publishing firm of Cramer, Addison, & Beale, and if we want to be really precise, we should note that the Oxford English Dictionary gives a citation for "recital" from the 1811 edition of Thomas Busby's *Complete Dictionary of Music*, "formerly the general name for any performance with a single voice." (Oddly, the *OED* tells us that "recital" is "a musical (now only instrumental) performance given by one person."

Liszt's 1840 "recitals" were in fact perceived as something new.

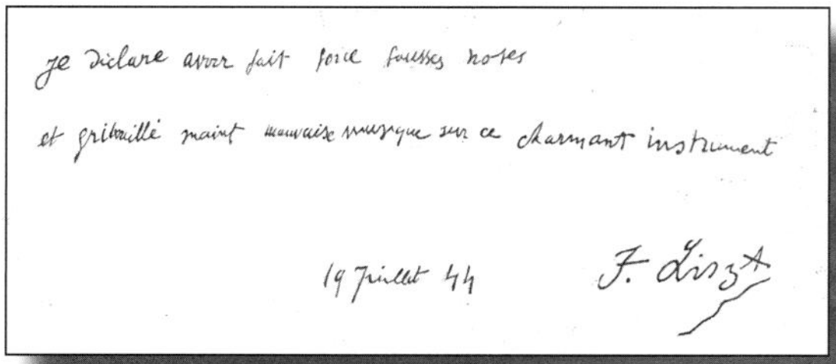

In an 1844 recital tour of France, Liszt performed on a small, charming Erard upright piano, now in The Schubert Club Museum. He made this inscription on its soundboard.

Note the plural "RECITALS" in the advertisement: each piece was to be thought of and heard as a separate recitation. What he "recited" is a program we would find most strange if Mr. Andsnes or Mr. Brendel or Ms. Hewitt were to offer it at the Ordway today: solo arrangements of two movements of Beethoven's *Pastoral* Symphony and two Schubert songs, the *Hexaméron* (variations on a Bellini march by Liszt himself and five of his most notable pianistic colleagues, Thalberg, Pixis, Herz, Czerny, and Chopin—actually a very engaging gallimaufry), and a few solo pieces of his own, ending with the *Grand Galop Chromatique,* with which he must have closed a thousand concerts in his traveling-virtuoso years. Equally strange for us, but perhaps not without a certain appeal, would be Liszt's practice—and this was something all his own—of descending from the platform between pieces and chatting with members of the audience.

Plural or singular, "recital" baffled people. How in the world do you "recite" on the piano? But the London public caught on, responding to the communicative and dramatic suggestions behind that word, and of course Liszt could realize those suggestions with incredible psychological force. The English critics had their doubts, finding Liszt's doings showy and ungentlemanly, but at least one of them, Henry Chorley in the *Athenaeum,* got the point when he wrote (as quoted in Alan Walker's Liszt biography): "We cannot call to mind any other artist, vocal or instrumental, who could thus, by his own unassisted power, attract and engage an audience for a couple of hours." It is still a marvel each time it happens.

Anyone who ever took music lessons will remember what it was like to be compelled into the recital experience. It is more than sixty years since I last sat on a stage by myself to play piano pieces, Chopin's *Minute* Waltz and some Gershwin and Poulenc, and far away as that experience is now, I can remember exactly the strange mixture of terror and power—the one because of realizing that I am out there all alone and there is no one to help me, the other because what I am doing is somehow getting all those people to be quiet, to look in one direction, and to pay attention only to me. (I was obviously thinking less about Chopin, Gershwin, and Poulenc than I should have been.) The terror part was compelling enough so that even now, as I write these sentences, I find myself working up a bit of a sweat. That essential part of the recital experience, the agon between the one and the mob, remains intimately and sometimes scarily familiar to me: I don't play in public now, but it all comes back to me each time I have to give a lecture.

Being on stage with another person, for example when I produced and participated in a series of concerts of four-hand piano music or took the reckless plunge of partnering a singer in Schubert's *Die schöne Müllerin,* was different. It removed the terror of being alone out there, although it introduced instead the jitters that came with knowing how much my partner's welfare—and the concomitant absence of the desire to strangle me afterwards—depended on my not screwing up.

When you have two people in musical partnership, ideally the two should both become one and remain two. The reasons for wanting the oneness are obvious: the partners are in pursuit of the same goal, bringing the Beethoven's D-major Cello Sonata or Schumann's *Dichterliebe* to clear and vivid life, revealing that music and that poetry as truthfully as they are able. I often think of the great bass Fyodor Chaliapin recalling recitals he had given with Rachmaninoff at the piano, saying it was never a matter of "I am singing" but always of "we are singing."

But remaining two? The two are more than the sum of their parts. Remaining two, that is for the electricity, the surprises, the friction (without which, after all, we could not move), for the sudden charge of knowledge and understanding that comes from another mind, another spirit, another heart. The room must have been alive with these currents when Schubert accompanied Michael Vogl in *Winterreise,* when Brahms played sonatas with Joseph Joachim or was partner to Julius Stockhausen in *Die schöne Müllerin,* or when Bartók played his music (and others') with Jelly d'Arányi, Zoltán Székely, or Joseph Szigeti. Performers, all these, who knew the music deeply, but who were ever receptive to that unexpected, unrehearsed spark vaulting across the stage.

Such things can also occur in the clearly non-intimate arenas of ballet and opera, the miracle being the ability of Fonteyn and Nureyev or, as I once experienced unforgettably with Tito Gobbi and Boris Christoff in *Don Carlos*, suddenly to shrink a huge theater at least for a moment so that no one is there except the performers and one's own ecstatic looking, listening self.

To witness and sense that is exciting and profoundly moving. The first time I was made aware of what partnership in music might mean was at a sonata recital by Adolf Busch and Rudolf Serkin in 1946. Theirs was a connection of long standing, and the sharing of ideals and ideas had come about because Busch had been a demanding mentor to the younger pianist, who had also become his son-in-law. Even when Serkin was a revered senior figure in his seventies, his awe of Busch was as alive as ever. I had somehow made my way into the hall—it was the McCarter Theater at Princeton—for their brief pre-concert warm-up, Serkin at the piano in shirtsleeves but with his black homburg still on, and what struck me as they touched passages in Beethoven's last sonata was the wordlessness of their communication: it was all grimaces, smiles, nods, and headshakes, and the occasional "hmmm." At the concert, forty-five minutes later, added to the depth of shared understanding that was the fruit of years of work together, documented on many recordings, was what one might call the fever of performance, and I recall vividly how amazing it was to witness the psychic power that emanated from the externally so quiet Busch as he both stimulated and restrained his all-nerve-endings partner.

Perhaps my most special memories—and lessons—are of song recitals. I think of Bruno Walter and Kathleen Ferrier, Walter's playing a bit all over the place, but definitely exerting an enlivening power over that sometimes pallid singer and himself obviously warmed and delighted by something she sent back to him. That, too, was essentially a mentor-mentee relationship. Very different was an electrifying recital of disturbing songs—Krenek was on the program and the sacred songs from Hugo Wolf's Spanish Songbook—by Eleanor Steber and Dimitri Mitropoulos. Here again the conductor-

Rudolf Serkin, "revered senior" recital artist, visits The Schubert Club Museum in 1977 while in Saint Paul for a piano recital. He was also engaged for recitals here in 1961 and 1969.

as-pianist was clearly the driver, but there was an almost harrowing sense of two great and by nature terrifyingly vulnerable musicians clinging to one another as they sought difficult artistic truth. Different yet again was the partnership of Leontyne Price and Samuel Barber, warmth blended with a touchingly old-fashioned courtesy and mutual awe. It was early in Price's career, and it was sad to learn that that elegant pair was unable to procure any significant number of concert dates. Grateful as I am to have heard those recitals, what meant most to me then—and still does, in retrospect—are the evenings in the presence of two partnerships grounded in the bedrock of years of working together but with fresh and inventive music-making that was all adventure and discovery: Pierre Bernac with Francis Poulenc and Peter Pears with Benjamin Britten. The two pairs could not have been more different with respect to temperament, stage presence, and even repertory, though I did hear both in *Dichterliebe,* but in each you had a singer with an extraordinarily personal, instantly recognizable, non-glamorous but to me stirringly beautiful voice and a pianist who brought to his task a combination of a composer's intelligence with unobtrusive, almost deliberately concealed keyboard skills of the highest order.

On stage, both those famous composers seemed as deferential as old-fashioned career accompanists to their partners. I remember how Bernac, for whom the word *"soigné"* might have been invented, introduced encore after encore with the words "Francis Poulenc," enunciated with a crisp precision that brought it just short of parody. Meanwhile, his eminent collaborator, who liked to speak of piano sound "bathed in pedal" and had all evening turned that ideal into a

Local newspaper coverage of English contralto Kathleen Ferrier's 1949 visit to Saint Paul for a Schubert Club recital.

ravishing treat to the senses, sat at the piano as though the words "Francis Poulenc" could not possibly have anything to do with him—nor for that matter the trifling matter of having composed "C'est ainsi que tu es" or "C." And did anyone ever look less like an important composer?

Britten detested performing, and often in later years needed to be literally pushed onto the stage, preferably with the fresh infusion of an ounce or two of brandy. Once out there, he seemed to strive only for utter invisibility. Could this man possibly have written "The Holy Sonnets of John Donne" or *Winter Words*? But from Poulenc and Britten alike, the playing of the one so seemingly carefree and dedicated to sensuous delight, that of the other as delicately chiseled and precise as some uncanny sculpture in ivory, there came music-making of rarely experienced authority and command as well as sheer sonorous beauty.

And what listeners they both were, deeply attuned to spontaneities of nuance, to colors of vowels, lengths of consonants, the unpredictabilities of timing that are at the heart of great singing. And great singing is what Bernac and Pears gave us, great singing founded on the understanding of poetry, of musical shapes, of color. And all four knew that the mysterious essence in a great song collaboration has everything to do with allowing the voice *seeming* dominance—it also of course has the possession of the words on its side—but creating *in fact* a partnership of equals, akin to an ideal marriage. The elegant Bernac and the more dramatic Pears, who also had a touch of British officer about him, were formidable presences, but each knew—without of course giving a hint of this to the audience—that he was only half himself without his pianistic other self.

And what about piano recitals, when one figure alone commands the stage and two thousand ears and eyes are trained on one human presence doing something that most of us cannot dream of doing? There the challenge to our power of concentration can become overwhelming. Two names are especially alive in my mind as examples, and if I confine myself to two it is not for want of gratitude to such musicians as the diabolic Michelangeli; Rudolf Serkin, who could appear angelic and possessed at the same time; and the warmly embracing Myra Hess.

"... when you went to hear Schnabel you went to be transported into those worlds that Bach, Mozart, Beethoven, and Schubert command." The Schubert Club owns an autographed copy of Schnabel's book *Music and the Line of Most Resistance*.

Artur Rubinstein was the first hugely, hugely celebrated musician I ever experienced in concert. It happened to be an orchestral concert at which he exulted in Rachmaninoff, but the pianist I encountered in recital soon after was clearly the same astonishing personality. He was so welcoming, so delighted we were there for him, no less delighted that he, on this evening, could be there for us. The stage always overflowed with extra seats; in halls where it was possible, he liked to enter not from the side but from the back, facing front and center. The crash of applause that always greeted the appearance of this compact figure was like no other concert hall sound I ever heard. But when he sat at the keyboard he was the embodiment of concentration, of avoidance of anything wasteful, of elegant economy of body use (except when, as an encore, he played Falla's *Ritual Fire Dance,* with hands flung higher than the top of his head). Aside from its musical pleasures, every Rubinstein recital was a demonstration, so natural to him and so easy, of what it means to be a host, of unconfined joy in the existence of great—or even just delightful—music, an equal joy in seeming to discover anew each time what might be done on a piano, and, so he made it seem, the greatest joy of all: sharing it with us.

A Schnabel recital was another sort of event. There was never a *Ritual Fire Dance* or anything remotely like it, not even a note of Chopin ("that right-handed composer," he said, unjustly), to say nothing of Liszt or Debussy. Mozart, Beethoven, Schubert, occasionally a little Bach or Schumann, were the centers of his musical world, certainly in those later years when I heard him. He once said that the typical piano recital program was like a tourist's day in Paris: Notre Dame in the morning, the Folies-Bergères in the evening. The difference between himself and other pianists, he remarked ironically, was that his recitals "were boring also after the intermission."

In other words, when you went to hear Schnabel you went to be transported into those worlds that Bach, Mozart, Beethoven, and Schubert command. When he was on, which was not always, he could take you to worlds of whose existence you had no idea. Even afterwards, as though after a dream, you could hardly credit that you had experienced something ineffable, something forever beyond words. I don't think I ever heard another musician who could do that in quite that way. The last time I ever heard him play he ended with Beethoven's Opus 111 Sonata, the final one, whose close is all that one could possibly mean by sublime music. (He never played encores, firm in his conviction that applause was "a receipt, not a bill.") There he sat, uncannily still in a domestic-seeming upholstered chair the like of which one normally never saw on a concert stage, another man who, with his gray brush cut, did not in the least suggest "artist." Nearly motionless, the energies flowing from that tired body caused the piano, through sounds granitic and limpid, to bear us out of ourselves. I remember afterwards thinking of the words from the Catholic burial service: "In Paradisum te deducant angeli—May angels lead you into Paradise."

It was the quintessential recital experience: one musician on stage, a listener, who knows how many feet away, and through the powerful, generous, and dedicated gift of the one, and the hunger and willing concentration of the other, distance dissolved into no distance.

Norwegian pianist Leif Ove Andsnes performed Mussorgsky's Pictures at an exhibition.

Dame Janet Baker sang the premiere of Argento's Pulitzer Prize-winning song cycle From the Diary of Virginia Woolf, which was a Schubert Club commission.

Mezzo-soprano Angelika Kirchschlager and soprano Barbara Bonney gave a dual recital.

Russian violin virtuoso Maxim Vengerov performed in 1996, 1999, and again in 2006.

American mezzo-soprano Frederica von Stade has appeared four times on the IAS.

Cellist Yo-Yo Ma has given six recitals for The Schubert Club, including unaccompanied recitals in 1992 and 1999.

Joshua Bell played a violin sonata by Eugène Ysaÿe in his 1990 recital. Ysaÿe also gave a recital here in 1895. Both Bell and Ysaÿe played music by Ysaÿe's teacher, Wieniawsky.

Cecilia Bartoli, operatic superstar, made her Saint Paul-Minneapolis debut at The Schubert Club with a program of songs by Haydn, Beethoven, Schubert, and Rossini.

Russian cellist (and conductor) Mstislav Rostropovich, a champion of artistic freedom during the Cold War, gave his first Schubert Club recital in 1963.

Pianist Mitsuko Uchida adored our attentive Saint Paul audiences.

Violinist Itzhak Perlman has given four recitals for The Schubert Club, 1970, 1980, 1988, 2003.

Jessye Norman, a true dramatic soprano, sang French and German art songs in her 1976 and 1993 recitals. In 1992 she sang Russian and Spanish pieces.

Pianist Alfred Brendel: 1977, 1979, 1985, 1989, and 2005.

Leon Fleisher appeared in recital here in 1955 and again fifty years later in 2005.

Soprano Renée Fleming arrived early, but her gown took a later flight.

Daniel Barenboim gave a recital of music of Liszt, Chopin, and Albéniz in 2001.

American mezzo-soprano Marilyn Horne, "probably the greatest singer in the world," according to Opera News in 1981.

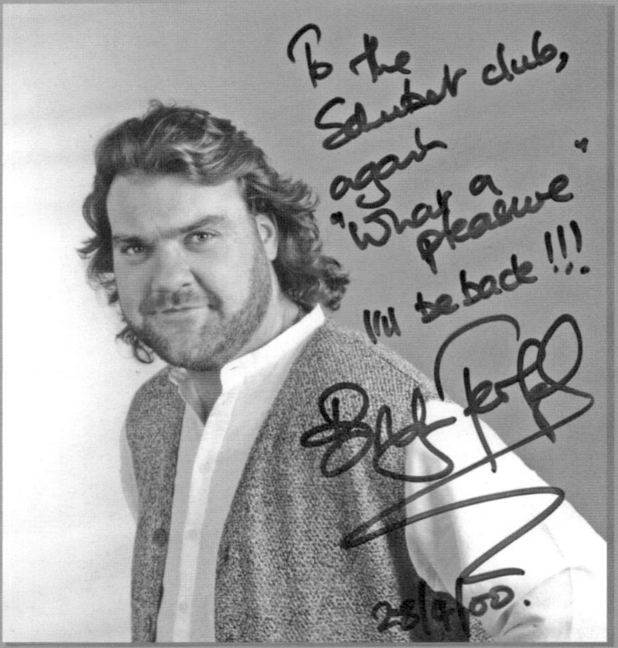

Welsh baritone Bryn Terfel had to cancel his February 2000 recital at the last minute due to illness, but came to sing for us in April.

James Galway, flute, performed on the IAS in 1984 and 1988. His encore, "Danny Boy," was surpassingly beautiful.

Claudio Arrau played two piano recitals on our series 31 years apart, 1953 and 1984.

Emanual Ax played solo piano here in 1983 and 2007. In 1997 we heard him in a recital with cellist Yo-Yo Ma.

Beverly Sills gave the first Schubert Club concert at O'Shaughnessy Auditorium, October 1970.

Emerson String Quartet: Lawrence Dutton, viola, Eugene Drucker, violin, Philip Setzer, violin, David Finckel, cello.

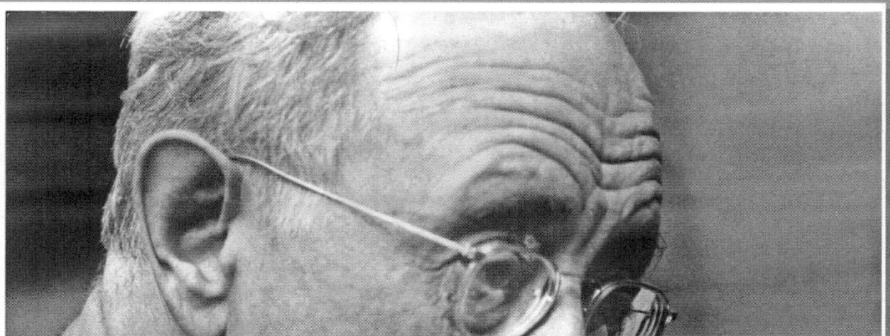

Rudolf Serkin, one of the great Beethoven interpreters of the 20th century, performed piano sonatas by that master in each of his Schubert Club recitals in 1961, 1977, & 1980.

Battling the Zipper

Sharon Carlson

In the days before unions made it impossible for someone to hang around backstage and help an artist, Bruce would sometimes call upon a member of his staff to be on hand to assist a performer. My turn came when Bruce asked me to be Kathleen Battle's 'lady-in-waiting' the night of Ms. Battle's Schubert Club concert at the Ordway.

Kathleen Battle, wearing THE DRESS, posed with the woman who zipped her into it and her nephew, 6-year-old Justin Stolpe, who had presented Ms. Battle with flowers at the end of the performance.

The four-page contract that brought Kathleen Battle to The Schubert Club for a recital in 1996 called for, among other things, a "female assistant" to be on hand backstage during her recital. The assignment seemed doable: remain backstage throughout the concert to help with errands, problems or emergencies. On the day of the concert Bruce learned that all she really needed was someone "to help zip up her dress at 10 minutes to 8." Bruce would simply fetch me from my hospitality table in the Ordway lobby, lead me back stage, and deposit me at Ms. Battle's dressing room door. There I would wait for her signal.

On the night of the concert, and at precisely the right minute, Bruce and I were at Kathleen's door. To let her know we were there, Bruce gave a good, firm knock, after which we both heard a reply from within that she'd let me know when she wanted me to enter. Then Bruce left.

I stood waiting for my cue when suddenly I heard someone yell "OKAY." I entered the room and immediately asked a stupid question. "Was that signal for me?" The beautiful Kathleen Battle was standing in front of her dressing room mirror having already done her hair and make-up. Suitcases and cosmetics were laid out on various chairs and shelves. She was facing the mirror, dressed in her gown and holding the bodice up to her with both hands—the back of it wide open...waiting for the zip-up to begin. When I entered and uttered my less-than-brilliant opening line, she looked at me with a faint smile on her face and said nothing.

I sized up the situation at once. This assignment was going to be a lot trickier than I thought.

With the palms of my hands already beginning to sweat, my eyes focused at once on the beautiful back of Kathleen Battle. It was her gorgeous skin that alarmed me. There was so much of it between the left and right sides of the zipper. The dress was a lovely blue, low-cut, form-fitting, short-sleeved gown, made out of fabric resembling a kind of spandex bathing suit. Almost at once the problems surfaced. First, the head of the zipper was so tiny I found it nearly impossible to grasp. I began by trying to hold the two sides of the dress together but needed both hands to do so, given the gaping width of the opening. A third hand would have been helpful to hold onto the zipper. Somehow I managed to juggle fingers and hands, take hold of the zipper head, and timidly inch it upwards, desperately trying not to let go. Meanwhile, Battle fiddled with the lining to make sure it was not shifting. A hook and eye at the top of the neckline escaped my notice completely as I charged ahead in a nervous hurry, not taking time to properly analyze how best to proceed. Suddenly she stopped me. "You should fasten the hook first," she said, "and it will be easier."

I went for the hook and eye, but soon realized that while it helped a little to close the top of the dress, a good four inches of skin still spanned that awful distance at the bottom. This time I grabbed a chunk of fabric on both sides of the zipper and clenched tightly, pulling them

A Recital fit for [a] Prince

Who would ever have thought that the renowned pop star Prince would attend a Schubert Club recital? Yet when Prince met Kathleen Battle at the 1987 Grammys and learned that in a few days she would be giving a recital in the Twin Cities (Prince's home town), he said he would make an appearance.

The recital was, of course, sold out, but Bruce Carlson, always eager to please, wasn't about to say no to Prince. Without hesitation Bruce generously offered him his wife Deanna's tickets. As promised, Prince arrived, rather flamboyantly dressed, and slipped into his seat, accompanied by his bodyguard and girlfriend, just moments before Battle walked out on stage. Battle opened with a set of Liszt songs, during most of which Prince fumbled through his program trying to figure out what exactly he was attending. Perhaps he was asking himself, *Is this all there is? Where are the fog machines and flashing lights? Why isn't she amplified?* In any case, he disappeared after the first cycle of songs, not even waiting for intermission.

After the performance Battle asked Bruce where Prince was, indicating that he had promised to visit her backstage. A disappointed Bruce replied simply, "He left."

toward me in an effort to squeeze the two sides closer together with one hand, at the same time forcing the zipper upwards with the other. "Is it okay to do it this way?" I asked feebly. No answer. I kept going. To my amazement, my efforts looked promising as the zipper slowly traveled to its destination, finally reaching the top. Hooray!

"It isn't sitting right," she said. "You moved the dress when you did that. You'll have to do it again." The zipper had to come down. Another look at all that skin. The second zipping session had Kathleen wiggling her hips this way and that, demonstrating how the dress was off-balance. Then more wiggling to try and re-adjust the dress so that it was back to its original position. By this time my heart was pounding. It was nearly 8:00 and she had to walk on stage at 5 after. There was no one else to help. My hands were wet. What if the zipper tears? Can this tight fabric really hold all of Kathleen? Where's Bruce? What am I doing here?

Carefully I started to undo the zipper and at the same time hang onto enough fabric so I could re-zip it quickly before too much expansion occurred if I let go. I knew if those same four inches of skin emerged between the zipper, I would be in the same awful pickle. I held my breath and repeated the process. Slowly the zipper moved upwards, the dress was fastened, the zipper held, and Kathleen was in her gown. After a brief analysis of my work, a barely audible "okay" emerged from the mouth of our evening's glamorous star. Relieved and wilting, I made a hasty exit and hid in the backstage wings where I stayed out of sight long enough to see Ms. Battle emerge from her dressing room, clothed in her beautiful blue gown. As she walked to the stage I overheard her comment to the stage manager, "That girl was so flustered."

Ninety years ago, Schubert Club concerts had already established a reputation for having an audience of good listeners:

The Schubert Club is one of the finest musical organizations in the country. I should know, because I have been an American for many years and have played in all the larger cities. Musicians are always glad to come to St. Paul, for they are assured of a cordial reception. Audiences here appreciate the best.

– Georges Barrère, Trio de Lutèce
Schubert Club performance, April 1916

International Artist Series Performers

1893 - 1900

Aus der Ohe, Adèle (piano)
Blauvelt, Lillian (soprano)
Chicago [Symphony] Orchestra, Theodore Thomas, conductor
Fergusson, George W. (baritone)
Ffrangcon-Davies, David Thomas (baritone), Schubert Club Chorus & Orchestra, Emil Oberhoffer, conductor
Gadski, Johanna (soprano)
Godowski, Leopold (piano)
Gordon, Katherine (soprano)
Greene, Plunket (baritone)
Hall, Glenn (tenor)
Hamlin, George (tenor)
Hay, Clarence (baritone)
Heinrich, Max (baritone)
Henri Marteau Company
Henschel, Mr. & Mrs. Georg (baritone & soprano)
Hofmann, Josef (piano)
Johnstone-Bishop, Genevra (soprano)
Linne, Range (soprano)
Marchesi, Blanche (soprano)
Marteau, Henri (violin)
Messiah Chorus & Orchestra, Emil Oberhoffer, conductor
Morgan, Geraldine (violin)
Perabo, Ernst (piano)
Perry, Edward Baxter (piano) with Agnes Staberg Hall (soprano)
Rosenthal, Moritz (piano)
Rubenstein String Quartet
Sauer, Emil (piano)
Scharwenka, Xaver (piano)
Shawe, Lewis (baritone)
Sherwood, William H. (piano)
Stein, Gertrude May (soprano)
Wilson, Genevieve Clark (soprano)
Yaw, Ellen Beach (soprano)
Ysäye, Eugene (violin)

1901 - 1910

Aus der Ohe, Adèle (piano)
Austin, Florence Muriel (violin) with Mrs. W. M. Thurston (contralto)
Bergh, Arthur (violin)
Bispham, David (baritone)
Blye, Birdice (piano)
Collins, Edward (piano) with Frances Vincent (soprano)
Cottlow, Augusta (piano)
Foster, Muriel (contralto)
French, Mrs. George Barton (voice)
Gabrilowitsch, Ossip (piano)
Ganz, Rudolph (piano)
Gordon, Katherine (soprano)
Hallock, Mary (piano)
Hamlin, George (tenor)
Hartmann, Arthur (violin)
Henschel, Mr. & Mrs. Georg (baritone & soprano)
Homer, Louise (contralto)
Kneisel String Quartet
Kubelik, Jan (violin)
Lütschg, Waldemar (piano),
Minneapolis Symphony Orchestra, Emil Oberhoffer, conductor
Miles, Gwilym (baritone)
Miller, Christine (contralto)
Minneapolis Symphony Orchestra, Emil Oberhoffer, conductor
Paur, Emil (piano)
Riedelsberger String Quartette
Ringen, Jessie (contralto)
Schumann-Heink, Ernestine (contralto)
Sherman, Blanche (piano)
Silber, Sidney J. (piano)
Sprotte, Berthold (contralto)
St. Paul Choral Art Society, Leopold G. Bruenner, conductor
Von Warlich, Reinhold (bass)
Witherspoon, Herbert (bass)
Zeisler, Fannie Bloomfield (piano)

1911-1920

Alexander, Arthur (tenor & piano)
Barrère Ensemble (nonet)
Braslau, Sophie (contralto)
Chilson-Ohrman, Luella (soprano)

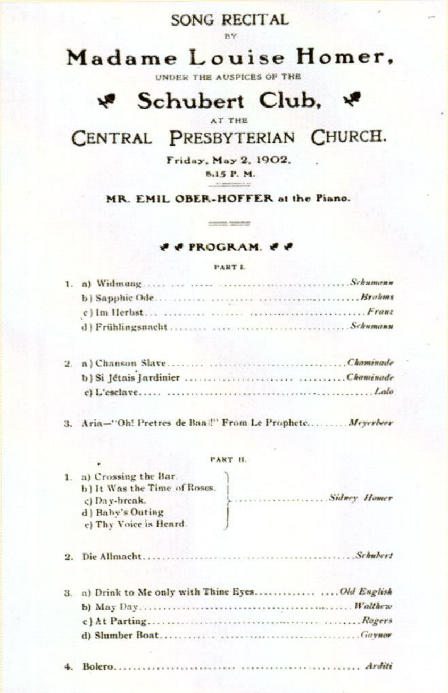

SONG RECITAL

BY

Madame Louise Homer,

UNDER THE AUSPICES OF THE

Schubert Club,

AT THE

CENTRAL PRESBYTERIAN CHURCH.

Friday, May 2, 1902,

8.15 P. M.

MR. EMIL OBER-HOFFER at the Piano.

PROGRAM.

PART I.

1. a) Widmung .... *Schumann*
   b) Sapphic Ode .... *Brahms*
   c) Im Herbst .... *Franz*
   d) Frühlingsnacht .... *Schumann*

2. a) Chanson Slave .... *Chaminade*
   b) Si Jétais Jardinier .... *Chaminade*
   c) L'esclave .... *Lalo*

3. Aria—"Oh! Pretres de Baal!" From Le Prophete .... *Meyerbeer*

PART II.

1. a) Crossing the Bar.
   b) It Was the Time of Roses.
   c) Day-break.
   d) Baby's Outing
   e) Thy Voice is Heard .... *Sidney Homer*

2. Die Allmacht .... *Schubert*

3. a) Drink to Me only with Thine Eyes .... *Old English*
   b) May Day .... *Walthew*
   c) At Parting .... *Rogers*
   d) Slumber Boat .... *Gaynor*

4. Bolero .... *Arditi*

Louise Homer

This great contralto, the aunt of composer Samuel Barber, selected repertoire that mixed classics with new music for both this concert and her later Schubert Club recital in 1913. Chaminade, Walthew, Rogers, and Gaynor were current composers at the time. Her 1913 program included the song "Eldorado" by Minnesota composer Leopold Bruenner. Both programs include a set of songs by her husband. Note that her accompanist for this recital is Emil Oberhoffer, who was, at the time, in between leading The Schubert Club Orchestra and establishing the Minneapolis Symphony.

Collins, Edward (piano)
Culp, Julia (contralto)
d'Arnelle, Vernon (baritone)
Edith Rubel Trio (piano trio)
Fanning, Cecil (baritone)
Flonzaley Quartet (string quartet)
Garrison, Mabel (soprano)
Gates, Lucy (soprano)
Goodson, Katherine (piano)
Grainger, Percy (piano)
Graveure, Louis (baritone)
Homer, Louise (contralto)
Lashanska, Hulda (soprano)
Leginska, Ethel (piano)
Menges, Isolde (violin)
Pelton-Jones, Frances (harpsichord)
Purdy, Constance (contralto)
Renard, Rosita (piano)
Robinson, Carol (piano) with
Mildred Langtry (contralto)
Schelling, Ernest (piano)
Shattuck, Arthur (piano)
Southwick, Frederick (baritone)
St. Paul Choral Art Society,
Leopold G. Bruenner, conductor
St. Paul Symphony Orchestra
w/180 boy soprano chorus,
Walter Rothwell, conductor
St. Paul Woodwind Quintette
Trio Aeolienne (piano trio)
Trio de Lutèce (chamber ensemble)
Werrenrath, Reinald (baritone)
Williams, Evan (voice)
Zeisler, Fannie Bloomfield (piano)
Zoellner String Quartet

1921 - 1930

Aguilar Lute Quartet of Madrid
Alcock, Merle (contralto)
Austral, Florence (soprano)
Bailey-Apfelbeck, Marie Louise (piano)
Bartlett, Ethel & Rae Robertson (duo piano)
Bauer, Harold (piano)
Bori, Lucrezia (soprano)
Breton, Ruth (violin)
Carpenter, Jean Vincent (contralto)
Chamlee, Maria (tenor) and
Ruth Miller (soprano)
Corigliano, John (violin)
Cortez, Leonora (piano)
Cortot, Alfred (piano)
Crooks, Richard (tenor)
Dux, Claire (soprano)
Elshuco Trio (piano trio)
Farbman, Harry (violin)
Farner, Bertha (soprano)
Garrison, Mabel (soprano)
Giannini, Dusolina (soprano)
Gordon, Jeanne (contralto)
Gradova, Gitta (piano)
Heifetz, Jascha (violin)
Hess, Myra (piano)
Hoekstra, Jurien (baritone)
Horowitz, Vladimir (piano)
Howell, Dicie (soprano)
Ivogun, Maria (soprano)
Kappel, Gertrude (soprano)
Kedroff Quartet (vocal quartet)
Kochanski, Paul (violin)
Kurenko, Maria (soprano)
Letz Quartet (string quartet)
Lindsay, William (piano)
London String Quartet
Lull, Barbara (violin)
Mario, Queena (soprano)
Mérö, Yolanda (piano)
Moiseiwitsch, Benno (piano)
Mortimer, Myra (contralto)
Mundy, Lota (violin)
Muzio, Claudia (soprano)
New York String Quartet
Niemack, Ilse (violin)
Nilssen, Sigurd (bass)
Olszewska, Maria (contralto)
Orloff, Nikolai (piano)
Rethberg, Elisabeth (soprano)
Roth Quartet (string quartet)
Rous, Marion (piano)
Samaroff, Olga (piano)
Schevill, Clara M. (contralto)
Schipa, Tito (tenor)
Schlusnus, Heinrich (baritone)
Schwarz, Joseph (baritone)

Seidel, Toscha (violin)
Stephens, Clyde (piano)
Thomas, John Charles (baritone)
Wilfred, Thomas (lute)
Woempner, Henry C. (flute) with
Henry J. Williams (harp)

1931 - 1940

Antoine, Josephine (soprano)
Averino, Olga (soprano)
Bampton, Rose (contralto)
Baromeo, Chase (baritone)
Bauer, Harold (piano)
Bonelli, Richard (baritone)
Brailowsky, Alexander (piano)
Casadesus, Robert (piano)
Cassado, Gaspar (cello)
Cherkassky, Shura (piano)
Coolidge String Quartet
Crooks, Richard (tenor)
Doe, Doris (contralto)
Eddy, Nelson (baritone)
Enesco, Georges (violin)
Evans, Wilbur (baritone)
Feuermann, Emmanuel (cello)
Frantz, Dalies (piano)
Garbousova, Raya (cello)
Ginster, Ria (soprano)
Gordon String Quartet
Hart House String Quartet
Hayden, Ethel (soprano)
Hubert, Marcel (cello)
Jagel, Frederick (tenor)
Kolisch String Quartet
Lehmann, Lotte (soprano)
Liège String Quartet
Mundy, Anne (piano)
Nicholson, Robert (baritone)
Piatigorsky, Gregor (cello)
Renardy, Ossy (violin)
Sayao, Bidu (soprano)
Schlusnus, Heinrich (baritone)
Sharnova, Sonja (contralto)
Smeterlin, Jan (piano)

≈

Horowitz Concert Thrills Audience

"So loath were the listeners to part from the slender young wizard that they refused to leave the spot even after two stalwarts appeared for the obvious purpose of removing the piano from the stage, with the result that the stalwarts retired, and Mr. Horowitz obliged once more."

from a review by
Frances Boardman,
Pioneer Press,
October 31, 1928

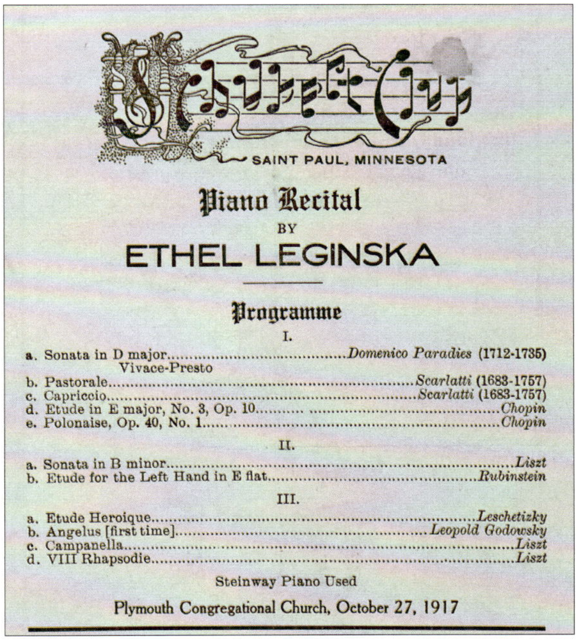

Schubert Club
SAINT PAUL, MINNESOTA

Piano Recital
BY
ETHEL LEGINSKA

Programme

I.

a. Sonata in D major........ *Domenico Paradies* (1712-1735)
Vivace-Presto
b. Pastorale........ *Scarlatti* (1683-1757)
c. Capriccio........ *Scarlatti* (1683-1757)
d. Etude in E major, No. 3, Op. 10........ *Chopin*
e. Polonaise, Op. 40, No. 1........ *Chopin*

II.

a. Sonata in B minor........ *Liszt*
b. Etude for the Left Hand in E flat........ *Rubinstein*

III.

a. Etude Heroique........ *Leschetizky*
b. Angelus [first time]........ *Leopold Godowsky*
c. Campanella........ *Liszt*
d. VIII Rhapsodie........ *Liszt*

Steinway Piano Used

Plymouth Congregational Church, October 27, 1917

Ethel Leginska, hailed as "the Paderewski of Women Pianists" by the *New York Herald*, later established herself as a composer and conductor as well. The first woman to conduct a major American symphony orchestra (the New York Symphony at Carnegie Hall in 1925), she also founded her own women's symphony. The *Pioneer Press* article about her Schubert Club appearance noted that she had bobbed hair and would not be wearing an evening gown. Her comment was that "women will never be really great, and never succeed in the work as men succeed until they stop devoting so much time, energy and money to clothes." Men wear a costume that is like a uniform, and so should women, she said, adding that "work must be the most important thing to her."

Nearly seventy years after the Schubert Club recital in 1938 of the remarkable young Russian cellist, Raya Garbousova, her grandson, pianist Jonathan Biss, became the third generation in his family to appear on our major series. In January 2005, he performed on the International Artist Series with his mother, violinist Miriam Fried. It was her second performance, as she and pianist Garrick Ohlsson had given a recital in December 1979, when the series was at the O'Shaughnessy Auditorium.

What a coup for The Schubert Club—presenting this baritone in his first U.S. recital! (We must confess that he had performed with the Cincinnati Symphony the week before in the Brahms Requiem, so it was not his first singing in the U.S.) The April 1955 concert opened with Beethoven's song cycle "An die ferne Geliebte" and included sets of songs by Schubert, Schumann, and Wolf. This promotional piece from his agent omitted the name of Gerald Moore, his long-time accompanist.

Spalding, Albert (violin)
Stradivarius Quartet
Stueckgold, Grete (soprano)
Szigeti, Joseph (violin)
Thomas, John Charles (baritone)
Traubel, Helen (soprano)
Vreeland, Jeanette (soprano)
Weissgerber, Andreas (violin)
Wysor, Elizabeth (contralto)

1941 - 1950

Bampton, Rose (soprano)
Bannerman, Lois (harp)
Bartlett, Ethel & Rae Robertson (duo piano)
Bel Canto Trio (Frances Yeend, soprano; Mario Lanza, tenor; George London, bass)
Bomar, Ann (mezzo-soprano)
Brown, Anne (soprano)
Budapest String Quartet
Busch Little Symphony, Eugene Istomin (piano), Adolf Busch, conductor
Carmalita Maracci Dance Group
Casadesus, Robert (piano)
Casadesus, Robert & Gaby (duo piano)
Collins, Robert Hall (baritone)
Curzon, Clifford (piano)
Duncan, Todd (baritone)
Ferrier, Kathleen (contralto)
Firkusny, Rudolf (piano)
Francescatti, Zino (violin)
Frantz, Dalies (piano) General
Platoff Don Cossack Chorus, Nicholas Kostrukoff, director
Gordon String Quartet
Graudan, Nicolai (cello)
Harrell, Mack (baritone)
Jonas, Marlyla (piano)
Kipnis, Alexander (bass)
Kullman, Charles (tenor)
List, Eugene (piano)
London String Quartet
Melton, James (tenor)
Moiseiwitsch, Benno (piano)

Morini, Erica (violin)
Nikolaidi, Elena (contralto)
Paganini Quartet (string quartet)
Rubinstein, Artur (piano)
Sayao, Bidu (soprano)
Shure, Leonard (piano)
Singher, Martial (baritone)
Spivakovsky, Tossy (violin)
Steber, Eleanor (soprano)
Stern, Isaac (violin)
Stewart, Reginald (piano)
Tinayre, Yves (tenor)
Traubel, Helen (soprano)
Travers, Patricia (violin)
Varnay, Astrid (soprano)
Vronsky, Vitya & Victor Babin (duo piano)

1951 - 1960

Albeneri Trio (piano trio)
Arrau, Claudio (piano)
Bachauer, Gina (piano)
Badura-Skoda, Paul (piano)
Bel Canto Trio (Gloria Lind, soprano; Leopold Simoneau, tenor; Theodor Uppman, baritone)
Curzon, Clifford (piano)
Davis, Ellabelle (soprano) with Lawrence Winters (baritone)
Dobbs, Mattiwilda (soprano)
Entremont, Philippe (piano)
Farrell, Eileen (soprano)
Festival Quartet (piano quartet)
Fischer-Dieskau, Dietrich (baritone)
Fleisher, Leon (piano)
Forrester, Maureen (contralto)
Gold, Arthur & Robert Fizdale (duo piano)
Graffman, Gary (piano)
Gulda, Friedrich (piano)
Hess, Myra (piano)
Hines, Jerome (bass)
I Solisti de Zagreb (orchestra), Antonio Janigro, conductor
Kallir, Lilian (piano)
Kraus, Lili (piano)
Lateiner, Jacob (piano)
Lipp, Wilma (soprano)
Little Singers of Paris (children's chorus), Fernand Maillet, director
Lloyd, David (tenor)
Loewenguth Quartet (string quartet)
London, George (bass)
Marshall, Lois (soprano)
Milstein, Nathan (violin)
Morini, Erica (violin)
Netherlands String Quartet
New York Quartet (piano quartet)
Novaes, Guiomar (piano)
Quartetto Italiano (string quartet)
Richter-Haaser, Hans (piano)
Roberto Iglesias Ballet Español
Rose, Leonard (cello)
Schwarzkopf, Elisabeth (soprano)
Seefried, Irmgard (soprano)
Societa Corelli (chamber orchestra)
Solomon (piano)
Souzay, Gérard (baritone)
Stern, Isaac (violin)
Vienna Octet (chamber ensemble), Willi Boskovsky, leader

1961 - 1970

Alvin Ailey American Dance Theater
Anievas, Agustin (piano)
Ashkenazy, Vladimir (piano)
Bach Aria Group (chamber ensemble)
Bach Collegium & Kantorei Stuttgart (chorus & orchestra), Helmuth Rilling, conductor
Browning, John (piano)
Casadesus, Robert (piano)
Chorzempa, Daniel (piano)
Curtin, Phyllis (soprano)
De Gaetano, Robert (piano)
de Larrocha, Alicia (piano)
Farrell, Eileen (soprano)
Finnila, Birgit (contralto)
Firkusny, Rudolf (piano)
Forrester, Maureen (contralto)
Gold, Arthur & Robert Fizdale (duo piano)
Hollander, Lorin (piano)
Istomin, Eugene (piano)
Janis, Byron (piano)
Johannesen, Grant (piano)
José Limon & Dance Company
Kim, Young Uck (violin)
Kuhse, Hannelore (soprano)
Lear, Evelyn (soprano)
Masselos, William (piano)
Moscow Chamber Orchestra, Rudolf Barshai, conductor
Nelsova, Zara (cello)
Netherlands Chamber Orchestra
New York Chamber Soloists
Novaes, Guiomar (piano)
Perlman, Itzhak (violin)
Price, Leontyne (soprano)
Ricci, Ruggiero (violin)
Roger Wagner Chorale, Roger Wagner, conductor
Rostropovich, Mstislav (cello)
Royal Uppsala University Chorus of Sweden, Eric Ericson, conductor
Schaff, Peter (piano)
Schickele, Peter (P.D.Q. Bach)
Serkin, Rudolf (piano)
Serkin, Peter (piano)
Sills, Beverly (soprano)
Snyder, Barry (piano)
Souzay, Gérard (baritone)
Szeryng, Henryk (violin)
Tureck, Rosalyn (piano)
Valletti, Cesare (tenor)
Verrett, Shirley (mezzo-soprano)
Virtuosi de Roma (orchestra), Renato Fasano, conductor
Vishnevskaya, Galina (soprano)

1971 - 1980

Ashkenazy, Vladimir (piano)
Bach Aria Group (chamber ensemble)
Baker, Janet (mezzo-soprano)

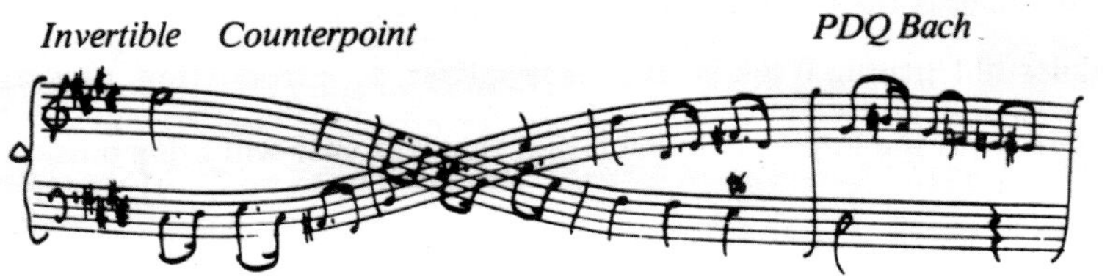

A P.D.Q. Bach concert by Peter Schickele (his second on the series) in October 1982 opened the 100th Anniversary Season of The Schubert Club. The program of works by this fictitious composer, performed with the Semi-Pro Musica Antiqua, included "Shepherd on the Rocks, With a Twist" for Bargain Counter Tenor and Devious Instruments, and the "Goldbrick" Variations.

Berman, Lazar (piano)
Bolet, Jorge (piano)
Bream, Julian (guitar/lute)
Brendel, Alfred (piano)
Buswell IV, James Oliver (violin)
Chamber Music Society of
Lincoln Center
Chorzempa, Daniel (piano)
Concentus Musicus of Vienna
de Larrocha, Alicia (piano)
de los Angeles, Victoria (soprano)
Entremont, Philippe (piano)
Fodor, Eugene (violin)
Fried, Miriam (violin) with
Garrick Ohlsson (piano)
Graffman, Gary (piano)
with Leonard Rose (cello)
Gregg Smith Singers
Gutierrez, Horacio (piano)
Haefliger, Ernst (tenor)
Harrell, Lynn (cello)
with James Levine (piano)
Horne, Marilyn (mezzo-soprano)
Horowitz, Vladimir (piano)
Janis, Byron (piano)
Juilliard String Quartet
Laredo, Ruth (piano)
Marlboro Festival Quintet
(chamber ensemble)
Moon, Ick Choo (piano)
New York Pro Musica,
George Houle, director
Norman, Jessye (soprano)
Orth, Peter (piano)
Paratore, Anthony & Joseph
(duo piano)
Perlman, Itzhak (violin)
Prey, Hermann (baritone)
Schub, André-Michel (piano)
Serkin, Rudolf (piano)
Shafran, Daniel (cello)
Sills, Beverly (soprano)
Spivakov, Vladimir (violin)
Swedish Radio Choir
Talvela, Martti (bass)
Tashi (chamber ensemble)
Valente, Benita (soprano)
von Stade, Frederica
(mezzo-soprano)
Waverly Consort
Zukerman,Pinchas&Eugenia(violin
& flute)

1981 - 1990

Arrau, Claudio (piano)
Ashkenazy, Vladimir (piano)
Ax, Emanuel (piano)
Baker, Janet (mezzo-soprano)
Battle, Kathleen (soprano)
Bell, Joshua (violin)
Blegen, Judith (soprano)
Brendel, Alfred (piano)
Davidovich, Bella (piano)
de Larrocha, Alicia (piano)
Demus, Jorg (piano)
Galway, James (flute)
Grimaud, Hélène (piano)
Guarneri String Quartet
Hagegård, Håkan (baritone)
Horowitz, Vladimir (piano)
Istomin, Eugene (piano)
Labèque, Katia & Marielle
(duo piano)
Lee, Eunice (violin)
Ma, Yo-Yo (cello)
Mendelssohn String Quartet
Noda, Ken (piano)
Perahia, Murray (piano)
Perlman, Itzhak (violin)
Prey, Hermann (baritone)
Price, Leontyne (soprano)
Ramey, Samuel (bass)
Rampal, Jean-Pierre (flute)
Rostropovich, Mstislav (cello)
Salerno-Sonnenberg,Nadja(violin)
Schickele, Peter (P.D.Q Bach)
Serkin, Peter (piano)
Söderström, Elizabeth (soprano)
Stern, Isaac (violin)
Stoltzman, Richard (clarinet)
Te Kanawa, Kiri (soprano)
Upshaw, Dawn (soprano)
Valente, Benita (soprano)
von Stade, Frederica
(mezzo-soprano)
Watts, Andre (piano)
Wild, Earl (piano)
Zukerman, Pinchas (violin)

1991 - 2000

Bartoli, Cecilia (mezzo-soprano)
with Andras Schiff (piano)
Battle, Kathleen (soprano)
Beaux Arts Trio (piano trio)
Bonney, Barbara (soprano)
Borodin String Quartet
Bronfman, Yefim (piano)
Bryant, Dinah (soprano)
Chamber Music Society of
Lincoln Center
Cherkassky, Shura (piano)
de Larrocha, Alicia (piano)

Elkina, Julia & Irina (duo piano)
Eroica Trio
Frank, Pamela (violin)
with Claude Frank (piano)
Glennie, Evelyn (percussion)
Goode, Richard (piano)
Guarneri String Quartet
Guarneri String Quartet
with Peter Serkin (piano)
Gutierrez, Horacio (piano)
Hagegård, Håkan (baritone)
Hampson, Thomas (baritone)
Horne, Marilyn (mezzo-soprano)
Hvorostovsky, Dmitri (baritone)
Kirchschlager, Angelika
(mezzo-soprano)
Kissin, Evgeny (piano)
Kremer, Gidon (violin) with
Vadim Sakharov (piano)
Lark Quartet with
Lydia Artymiw (piano)
Lin, Cho-Liang (violin) with
André-Michel Schub (piano)
Lupu, Radu (piano)
Ma, Yo-Yo (cello)
Midori (violin)
Mutter, Anne-Sophie (violin)
Norman, Jessye (soprano)
O'Riley, Christopher (piano)
Ohlsson, Garrick (piano)
Perahia, Murray (piano)
Pogorelich, Ivo (piano)
Rostropovich, Mstislav (cello)
Salerno-Sonnenberg, Nadja (violin)
Schiff, Andras (piano)
Solzhenitsyn, Ignat (piano)
Terfel, Bryn (bass-baritone)
Tomsic, Dubravka (piano)
Vengerov, Maxim (violin)
von Otter, Anne Sofie
(mezzo-soprano)
von Stade, Frederica
(mezzo-soprano)
Zimmerman, Krystian (piano)
Zukerman, Eugenia (flute) with
Shanghai String Quartet

2001-2007

Andsnes, Leif Ove (piano)
Andsnes, Leif Ove (piano) with
Christian Tetzlaff (violin)
Barenboim, Daniel (piano)
Bonney, Barbara (soprano) with
Angelika Kirchschlager
(mezzo-soprano)
Brendel, Alfred (piano)
Bronfman, Yefim (piano) with
Truls Mørk (cello) &
Gil Shaham (violin)
Bumbry, Grace (mezzo-soprano)
de la Salle, Lise (piano)
Emerson String Quartet with
Leon Fleisher (piano)
Fleming, Renée (soprano)
Fleming, Renée (soprano) with
Jean-Yves Thibaudet (piano)
Fried, Miriam (violin) with
Jonathan Biss (piano)
Graves, Denyce (mezzo-soprano)
Hahn, Hilary (violin)
Hampson, Thomas (baritone)
Hewitt, Angela (piano)
Lang, Lang (piano)
Lieberson, Lorraine Hunt
(mezzo-soprano)
Mattila, Karita (soprano)
McDermott, Anne-Marie (piano)
McDermott, Anne-Marie (piano)
with Phyllis Pancella
(mezzo-soprano) &
Paul Neubauer (viola)
Moravec, Ivan (piano)
Mutter, Anne-Sophie (violin)
O'Riley, Christopher (piano)
Perlman, Itzhak (violin)
Podles, Ewa (contralto)
with Garrick Ohlsson (piano)
Quasthoff, Thomas (bass-baritone)
Terfel, Bryn (bass-baritone)
Uchida, Mitsuko (piano)
Vengerov, Maxim (violin)
von Stade, Frederica
(mezzo-soprano)
with Samuel Ramey (bass)

Preferring ground transport to air travel, soprano Cecilia Bartoli arrived at the depot in Saint Paul for her 1996 concert. Her recital, accompanied by pianist András Schiff, was her premiere performance in Minnesota—another triumph for The Schubert Club!

The Schubert Club International Artist Series:

Venues

The Ford Music Hall 1893 – 1912

Located at the intersection of Sixth, St. Peter, and Market Streets, this hall was the home of The Schubert Club's first public recital on March 4, 1893 featuring German pianist Adéle Aus der Ohe. Concerts were held in the building's luxurious third floor auditorium which, over the years, was also known as Conover Hall, Raudenbush Hall and The Odeon. This multipurpose building was also the setting for board meetings, music lessons and other Schubert Club events. The structure was torn down in the 1970s and Landmark Plaza, a small park next to Landmark Center, has taken its place.

The People's Church 1894 – 1940

With its supreme acoustics and generous-sized hall, this church, located at Pleasant Avenue and Chestnut Street, was the city's musical center throughout the 1920s and 1930s. It remained a favorite spot for Schubert Club recitals until 1940 when the building was destroyed by fire.

The Saint Paul Municipal Auditorium 1940 – 1969

Twice the size of The People's Church, with 2,651 seats, this auditorium was The Schubert Club's central locale for thirty years, hosting over 145 concerts. Unfortunately, the hall was generally considered tasteless and unattractive. Its administration was often unpredictable with scheduling, and gave more profitable attractions priority over Schubert Club events. In 1982 most of the structure was torn down to make way for Ordway Center. What remains is now known as Roy Wilkins Auditorium.

The interior of the Ford Music Hall

Fire takes the People's Church in 1940

O'Shaughnessy Auditorium 1970 – 1984

After eighty-eight years of concerts in downtown Saint Paul, The Schubert Club relocated its main concert series to the campus of The College of Saint Catherine. The brand new 1,700-seat O'Shaughnessy Auditorium served over seventy-five Schubert Club International Artist Series concerts and was also home for The Saint Paul Chamber Orchestra, The Minnesota Orchestra and occasionally The Minnesota Opera. The move to O'Shaughnessy coincided with the renaming of the concert series to The International Artist Series.

Ordway Center for The Performing Arts 1985 – present

Ordway Center first opened in January, 1985 when it was called Ordway Music Theatre. It was soprano Leontyne Price's Schubert Club recital that first welcomed the audience to this new hall. From the beginning The Schubert Club has comfortably been established as one of Ordway Center's resident arts organizations. The 1,900-seat classical and contemporary hall has seen more than 125 Schubert Club International Artist Series concerts.

Ordway Music Theatre Opening Night

Tuesday, January 8, 1985, Leontyne Price, the great Metropolitan Opera soprano, and her longtime collaborator, pianist David Garvey, appeared in recital on The Schubert Club's International Artist Series. The venue? The new Ordway Music Theatre on Rice Park in downtown Saint Paul. This was in fact the opening concert at the Ordway, beating out The Saint Paul Chamber Orchestra by one day and The Minnesota Opera by three. Talk about excitement!

The new hall had been eagerly anticipated. Designed by Saint Paul's own Benjamin Thompson, the Ordway harkened back to older models, with more glamour and sumptuous decoration than Minnesota audiences had seen in a long while. Gleaming brass, polished mahogany, glittering lamps and chandeliers were everywhere. The main hall had tiers of curving balconies, and (gasp!) even some boxes! How classy! How "European"!

And what a contrast with the former location of the International Artist Series concerts. Comparisons are odious, of course. But the trials

During her stay in Saint Paul, Leontyne Price was accompanied by her brother, Brigadier General (Ret.) George Price, who became her personal manager after his retirement from the military.

of navigating the endless, aisleless rows of seats in that singularly graceless example of late-twentieth century concrete-bunker style architecture must have been fresh in the Ordway audience's memory.

The audience that night was very stylishly turned out. Seeing and being seen at intermission in the soaring, beautiful foyer was everyone's delight. So much so, in fact, that the signal for the audience to return to the hall was ignored, if even heard over the roar of conversation and the general ooh-ing and ah-ing.

Mix-ups can happen at the beginning of any enterprise. And, in this case, somehow, it happened that Miss Price strode out on to the stage to begin the second half of her program, only to find the lights up and almost all of her audience still out in the lobby. Panicked murmuring was soon heard throughout the place, "She's back on stage!" The great diva, although known for her tart tongue, merely shrugged and smiled. "I can't blame you for wanting to enjoy this beautiful new building." So saying, Miss Price swept off stage to await the return of her audience. And return they did, somewhat sheepishly—and gave her a hearty ovation.

The View from the Left

David Evan Thomas

David Evan Thomas was The Schubert Club's composer-in-residence from 1997-2005, where, among many other activities, he was Accompanist's Associate (i.e. page turner) for the International Artist Series.

Page-turning blends stage management, library science and meditation. The main requirements: stand up; don't turn early; don't turn late; don't turn two pages at once; sit down.

And one more: be invisible.

One of my first jobs was for Jessye Norman. After adjusting the lights and moving the piano back and forth on the Ordway stage, she was gently introduced to me by pianist Ann Schein. "Hollo, David Thomas...." She addressed me as if I were Aeneas, floating her eyes into the fly space.

Some pianists are something of a terror to turn for. Anne-Marie McDermott removed the music rack from the piano and placed the score flat on the pins. Try reading Copland's meter changes like that!

An hour before her recital, I found Renée Fleming alone onstage, accompanying herself in a newly-faxed arrangement of "God Bless America," which she was to sing two days later at the White House. Her accompanist, Jean-Yves Thibaudet hadn't yet arrived, so I was pressed into service. Bruce Carlson, always alert to a photo-opp, snapped her singing over my shoulder, pages cascading onto the keys.

What a privilege to witness the late Lorraine Hunt Lieberson's intense partnership with Peter Serkin, in which Serkin played Handel's *La Lucrezia* from a ragged scrawl of a score while

Lieberson's Lucrezia dissolved before our eyes; or to sit beside the redoubtable Leon Fleischer, who seems to wield implements rather than fingers in his dystonic right hand, yet whose ear imagines a most lovely legato, which the hand obeys.

Sitting at their sides, I found these performers to be even better than the audience knows, and more diligent, but at the same time, more human. When I tried to gush over Bryn Terfel, he grabbed me by the throat...and straightened my tie.

Accompanists

Accompanists are crucial artistic collaborators in recitals, even if Schubert Club concert publicity—and summary lists of stars on our series—often omit them. A few, like Martin Katz and Warren Jones, appear so regularly on recordings and on Schubert Club concerts as to be well-known to the audience.

In the first two decades of Schubert Club concerts, local pianists Katherine Hoffman or Emil Oberhoffer (later conductor of the Minneapolis Symphony) accompanied many of the visiting performers. In the 1950s and '60s, Leon Pommers accompanied violinists five times. Sam Sanders performed here multiple times from 1969 through the 1980s; Lambert Orkis, specializing in string accompaniment, played with cellist Mstislav Rostropovich and with Anne-Sophie Mutter (twice). Warren Jones, in addition to his many accompanying performances over the past twenty years, also led a master class for the 2007 Summer Song Festival, coaching singer and pianist combinations.

Soprano Renée Fleming promotes David Evan Thomas, briefly, to accompanist.

Pianist Martin Katz has reached the double digits for his International Artist Series appearances over more than three decades, having accompanied Marilyn Horne (three times, first in 1974), Kiri Te Kanawa (1985), Kathleen Battle (1995), and, most recently, Karita Mattila (2007).

"My first task was to take charge of the white linen runner that protected the gowns of the singers when they walked onstage."

– Pianist Thelma Hunter, remembering her early service to The Schubert Club in the late 1950s and early 1960s

A Greeting from Håkan Hagegård

Swedish baritone Håkan Hagegård has appeared with The Schubert Club many times since first coming to our attention in the early 1980s. Håkan has premiered several important works commissioned by The Schubert Club, including The Andrée Expedition *and* A Few Words About Chekhov, *both by Dominick Argento. Through the years under Schubert Club auspices, Håkan has given recitals and master classes, and twice appeared on the Saint Paul Summer Song Festival.*

To the 125th anniversary book:

"I don't know what I would have done, or where I would have been without The Schubert Club. My memories are so closely connected to Bruce and Sharon but also to all the people around the organization who believe in the lifesaving necessity of a healthy culture in the society of today—Nick Nash, Stephen Paulus, Linda Hoeschler and many, many more!

Thea Dispeker, my North American manager who brought me to the U.S., pointed out The Schubert Club as number one on the list of important organizations where I could go and sing. She spoke with enormous respect about Bruce and The Schubert Club.

Many are the works that have been commissioned for me and many are the works that I have been given the opportunity to perform in Saint Paul. And I want to mention Dominick Argento who has become one of the most important people in my professional life, thanks to The Schubert Club and Bruce Carlson.

May The Schubert Club live forever, and through many brilliant artists offer an alternative to a sometimes troubled world!

With deep appreciation and gratefulness!

– Håkan

Rehearsing in a Landmark Center courtroom for the premiere of *A Few Words About Chekhov* in 1996, pianist Martin Katz plays for singers Håkan Hagegård and Frederica von Stade while composer Dominick Argento listens.

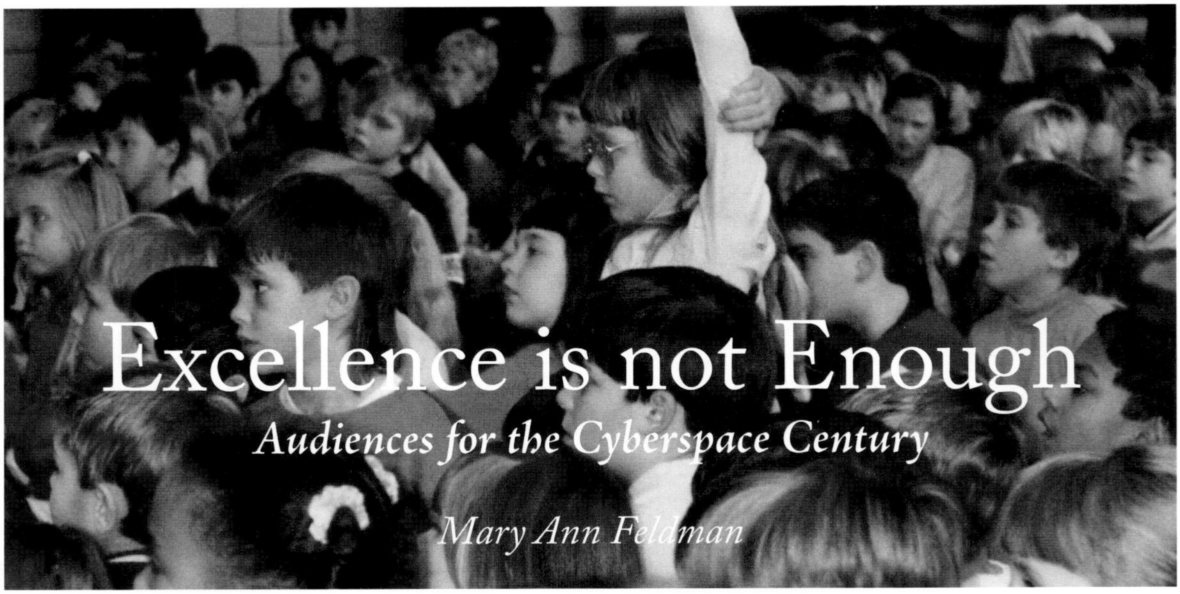

Excellence is not Enough

Audiences for the Cyberspace Century

Mary Ann Feldman

An advocate for music education, Mary Ann Feldman served on The Schubert Club Board in the 1970s. A writer, lecturer, and historian, she holds degrees from Columbia and the University of Minnesota, including a Ph.D. in musicology. In addition to having written for Opera News *and* The New Grove Dictionary of Music and Musicians, *she worked for thirty years as program annotator for the Minnesota Orchestra. She wrote a key essay for* Song Above the Land, *The Schubert Club's centennial history of the International Artist Series in 1993.*

A 17-year-old called me to share his passion for music: total number of tracks on his iPod: 3,460. All throb with the beat of heavy metal and industrial rock, plugged-in music representing yet new descendants of hard rock dating back two generations. The first rock-n'-rollers nowadays are retiring, and the words "You rock, Grandma," are sweet to their ears. "Let's rock!" resonates as the imperative for fun.

Fueling a megabucks music business worldwide, these sturdy progeny descend from bands like Aerosmith and the iconic Elvis Presley, who was gyrating in his "Blue Suede Shoes" exactly a half-century ago. The genre's physicality served the post-war society of the drug scene and the sexual revolution. Before long, Leonard Bernstein would cite Elvis as the most important figure in American music. Most concertgoers might have nominated Lenny himself, above all because he revealed the world of classical music to a vast public on network television.

My young friend, aspiring scientist and son of an orchestral musician, explains the easy access to his music: he simply inserts a CD into his computer, and soon the music is in his pocket, a companion wherever he goes. "The sounds consume me," he enthuses, noting that he'll worry about hearing-loss when he's 80. Medical specialists predict that otorhinolaryngology will be the thriving practice of the future, serving at least three generations who've come of age as rockers while music in American schools declined.

When Bruce Carlson invited me to choose a topic for this celebratory book, I instantly shot back, "Audiences! And it won't be an entirely blue-skies piece."

"Write it anyhow," he replied. That was Bruce, the best of listeners, even if he didn't like what he was hearing. A calm, reassuring leader, he had the grit to carry on, with his Board and staff, when others reported cultural clouds. And across three decades when recital series have declined nearly everywhere across America—the lament of New York managers who are conduits for the best in the world—The Schubert Club International Artist Series did not erode. Amplified by numerous free and low-cost events, from noontime Courtroom Concerts to Hill House Parlor Concerts, widespread collaborations, underwritten inner-city music lessons, museum collections, Keyboard Conversations™, the annual Summer Song Festival and more—The Schubert Club continues to flourish in high-tech times of instant gratification.

Of all my brain-storming dialogues with Bruce across decades when I worked Upriver on the orchestral scene (writing for Minnesota Orchestra audiences, talking to them, visiting classrooms, collaborating on expanding

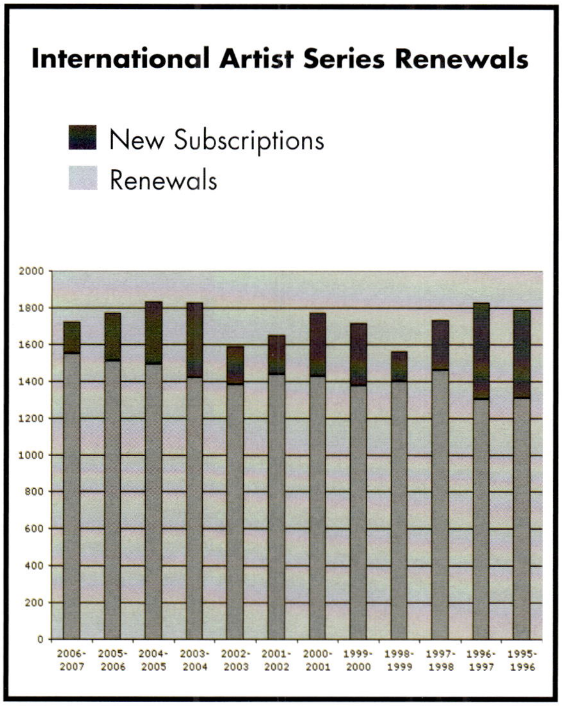

This graph shows the consistently high level of subscribers for The Schubert Club's International Artist Series. (The total seating capacity in Ordway Center 1906.)

How has the audience changed over the years?

written by a Musical Friend

Fading memory recalls the picture of grey-haired ladies, dressed with the conservative, fashionable taste of over 50 years ago, quietly gathering in the hall, eager to hear the current offering. It must be this same vision that today makes us undistinguishable from those distant listeners—behold, we have become them! But while the older clientele seems representatively constant, many more young people have discovered the joy of quality programming, creating the truly diverse audience of today. It must also be recognized that the bygone days of attendance required serious money and a social position high enough to separate that audience from the general population; the exclusivity of those days is gone forever.

marketing efforts), few explored the nagging audience problem: "Not on our radar screen," to quote youth's explanation. The Schubert Club, especially after the 1985 Ordway opening, never faced a box office crisis nor required a marketing department. Its renowned International Artist Series not only holds its own, but by sheer excellence and appeal makes it difficult to purchase single tickets or transfer to different seats. Providing the best, rather than relying on extravagant promotions, fills the hall, mostly with a mature audience.

Patrons typically are around 55 or 60, pushing towards retirement and beyond, like audiences everywhere in times when 40-50 is considered young. They embody the word "elite," not as in wealthy or prominent, but as the best of something considered collectively as a group. Such a class of listeners will never disappear if it is replenished by succeeding generations who sustain the nation's cultural values.

Classical music in China today is a growth industry fueled by its neophyte capitalist passion for everything Western. In booming America the scene is not so rosy. Consider this: On a Washington, D.C. street corner one morning last spring, Joshua Bell, busker-style, tucked his Stradivarius under his chin and played music of six great composers. Few passersby paid attention, no doubt because rapper verse and thundering shopping mall beat of the past 50 years were absent. Excellence was not enough.

Talking with Schubert Club regulars illuminates consensus. In this age of super-abundance, what they appreciate is the compact series of five stellar events—*world-class*, in the jargon of our times. Nearly everyone echoes the same thought: "Even if I haven't encountered an artist's name before" (like the phenomenal pianist Lise de la Salle in the '06-'07 season), "I am confident that this will be someone I want to hear." In short, credibility, trust, reasonable number of events, affordable pricing, pre-paid parking, sparkling city venue—all these generate loyalty. "The Ordway feels like a clubhouse," they observe, emphasizing the friendliness of an experienced congregation of genuine music lovers.

One issue brings them up short: the matter of their children and grandchildren. On this discomforting topic assurances do not abound. Will offspring be filling the seats 25 years from now? There is more hopefulness than certainty among their progenitors.

Many of today's concertgoers grew up when families from Brooklyn to Natcogdoches, Texas, and beyond, gathered around Philco radios to hear Toscanini conduct the New York Philharmonic; some purchased sets of shellac records before the age of the LP, contemporaneous with the birth of rock. They became what broadcaster Tom Brokaw has dubbed our "Greatest Generation": they fought World War II, then came home to rebuild the nation's economy as well as support athletics and the arts in America. Their generosity underwrote sports arenas and performance venues across the land, and they continue to fill them—witness crammed-to-the-rafters events in Florida's retirement cities.

Those who have music in their lives, loyal also to public radio and television, do not always like to ponder the live music challenge. They console themselves that websites may help out. Like hard-working arts managers and marketers, they subscribe to the hopeful "menopause" theory, a complacent notion that "when they grow older, and the kids are gone, they will come..." Not necessarily true. Moreover, the accelerated pace of these techie times is fundamentally at odds with the concert hall, for it conflicts with new perceptions of time. We live in an age of sound-bytes rather than unfolding masterpieces which cannot be condensed or accelerated.

Time is music's element. Like Beethoven's *Eroica*, Schubert's C Major Symphony, known as *The Great*, spans nearly 50 minutes. And Richard Strauss's *Alpine* Symphony arches across a similar span as it displays the extravagantly big modern orchestra to produce a virtual trek, dawn to nightfall, in a mountain paradise. "Grand Teton music," I call this work in classrooms I invade with a CD player and a message: "These are stressful times, and before long most of you will be chained to technology in this global economy, confined to working at a computer in your padded-cell office, hoping your job won't be outsourced to Bangladesh. No generation more deserves the freedom of the unspoiled outdoors as well as the euphoria of listening to live music—no drugs necessary."

Local singers greet baritone Bryn Terfel after his recital in 2000.

Raised on high-energy music cast in short segments, will new generations absorb the legacy of the past? Mercifully, when they hear classical fragments, they usually ask for more—this very generation which would not recognize the name Beethoven had it not been for Schultz's "Peanuts" cartoon. Will they consume entire pieces in instant-messaging, coded times? For their parents, too, the problem often is the time-span of classical repertoire. Surveyed by concerned marketers, lapsed concert patrons report their love for orchestral experiences, especially with a "fun conductor" on the podium. Yet many express surprise that "so many pieces last 24, 35, or even 45 minutes or more!" Right on—some are known as symphonies, concertos, tone poems. Length is the alienator.

The Achilles heel of the music scene may be both denial and a reluctance to implode its own propaganda. Nor will provocative cleavage and hip attire automatically entice young listeners to be participants.

Habits, good and bad, are formed early. Would any self-respecting baseball club count on fans-in-the-stands without Little League teams to grow them? Not all is cloudy on the international scene: live music flourishes in Finland, a little country with a mighty tradition of music education in the schools—exactly the process from which the United States has retrenched.

When we honestly confront a problem we usually find an answer. There *is* a solution to the audience dilemma facing both top-ranking institutions and the abundant smaller-budget organizations with which the country abounds, big cities and small. This key to audience-building is participation: for nearly every child, the major predictor is music-making, just as garage rock bands have bred ongoing rockers. The Schubert Club, like orchestras everywhere, finds its audience among people who sang in a choir, tootled a 17-pound tuba in the town band, or attended a Suzuki violin class. Music is life's supercharged vicarious experience. Has anyone ever observed a string quartet without sensing vibrations of their own fingertips?

In 1994, pianist Awadagian Pratt, performing on the stage of Penumbra Theatre on a battered upright piano, played pieces by Beethoven, Bach, Schumann and Rachmaninoff for about 75 children from The Schubert Club's Project CHEER program. Questions from the audience afterwards included, "How many hours a day do you practice?" and "How many songs do you know?"

Just when we most need it, a document has appeared to debunk myths and point a way: *The Search for Shining Eyes* (September 2006), Dr. Thomas L. Wolf's persuasive summary of the John S. and James L. Knight Foundation's $13 million investment in a "Magic of Music" initiative involving 15 symphony orchestras. Its evidence summarizes what a lifetime of audience-building has taught me: that youth must make music in order to feel the need for it in their lives, even if only as consumers. No addiction is more benign than the great music habit.

The Knight conclusions prompt reconsideration of many half-truths: that free concerts generate more ticket-buyers; contemporary music will lure young people; new concert formats and enhancements may solve all problems. All the current panaceas, including cross-over works, come under scrutiny.

Most disappointing is the class field trip to youth concerts, which in pre-rock times often triggered an epiphany—that sudden awakening to something fascinating and essential for life. Ironically, when students this year lobbied the Minnesota State Legislature for additional funding for after-school programs, they showcased hip-hop music to argue their case—this in a week when rapper misogyny was the subject of a national telecast.

In short, the Knight study forces an overdue test of shaky assumptions, including the credo that aging has everything to do with becoming a music lover. Discarding outdated myths opens the way for fresh ideas.

Above all, the "Shining Eyes" report concludes that participatory music-making is the key to becoming a music lover. Amateurs are priceless. Without entering the realm of performance on whatever level, a person may always remain a foreigner in the concert hall, easily seduced by the drugs-and-sex clamor of the dominant pops world. The competition thrives as Big

Business, independent of philanthropy, and its idiom is enduring: Sting, for instance, started out as a singer/bass player back in the '70s and still holds fast on the charts.

Classical music is in no danger of dying, but younger audiences are hard to win. Ironically, never in history has there been a bigger crop of gifted musicians and this not only in the Western hemisphere. Some 17,000 students in America earned music degrees in 2006; only 1200 snared full-time music jobs by the following fall. Competition is merciless when excellence and audience-growth are out of sync.

The goal is a vested audience like that of The Schubert Club, along with music in every child's life—even though that *may* raise our taxes. Encounters with great music are no longer a given in this society, as they were in the pre-television years of booming Hollywood. Not only did a study of three decades of films (1927-1957) reveal compelling symphonic soundtracks, but even more significantly, in them I found great music exhibited in the lives of ordinary Americans. Story-lines featured musical people, and classical performers often turned up in films shown to GIs in wartime.

Music-making is the mantra. Everything else is supplementary—valuable but not primary in assuring that vacant seats will be filled. No one lives by Blackberry, cell phone or any other electronic pulses alone. We are not robots but emotional beings who understand our own humanity better through the power of music in the concert hall.

Visiting with retired University of Minnesota professor Robert T. Laudon, we reminisced about school days. He grew up as a boy from White Bear Lake who rode the Randolph-Mahtomedi trolley to downtown Schubert Club events; not long after, I was boarding the same line at its western fringe, initial link of a multi-transfer adventure to Northrop Auditorium, where my friends and I experienced the likes of Artur Rubinstein, Jascha Heifetz and John Cage.

Both of us became concertgoers through cumulative musical experience, above all by playing the piano, singing in the classroom, and listening to the best. Music gave us something essential for a happy life: discipline, self-esteem and a circle of friends.

The audience challenge of the cyberspace century is by no means hopeless, and the Internet may be a big help if excessive communication doesn't devour too much discretionary time. Since excellence of performance falls short as the primary route to a joyful goal—full houses—the solution remains clear: participatory music-making in the life of every child. Ultimately, it is impossible not to enjoy what we love and understand.

Clear the skies . . . Onward!

A Variety of Concerts

This glamour image has been used for several of the Summer Song Festivals, with the sophisticated foreground couple in different concert locations.

The International Artist Series is both the flagship and the anchor (if that's not too mixed a metaphor) of each Schubert Club season, but there have always been other concerts to provide more musical options. In the first seventy-five years, there were regular member (later "Active Artists") and student recitals. In the 1960s and '70s, there was a Daytime Concert Series and later a Morning Series. A Chamber Music Series comes and goes periodically. For a while in the 1980s, there was a Debut Series to launch up-and-coming stars. Many excellent musicians performed on the Metro Area Artist Series that existed from 1988 to 2000. "Concerts for Youth" at the McKnight Theatre took place for two seasons in the early 1990s, and the Elizabeth Willett Musser New Music Series in Landmark Center was a four-year adventure later that decade. Some other past and current concerts appear in the Museum section of the book, notably the Early Music Series with its long roots in the past.

The Schubert Club Summer Song Festival

Four years of discussions and planning took place before the inaugural presentation of The Schubert Club's first Saint Paul Summer Song Festival in June 2004. Bruce Carlson, Executive Director of The Schubert Club, brainstormed over many breakfasts with Ecolab Executive Jack Forsythe. Over cups of coffee and plates of Swedish pancakes, they engaged in some lively talks while tossing around a variety of possible formulas, eventually coming up with a template that, with some variation, has now been in place for four years.

Why have a summer song festival?

The Schubert Club has been in the recital business for 125 years. Our major recital programs are usually kept within the academic year, leaving summers open for vacations, cutting back on season ticketed events, and, at least from Bruce's point of view, going up to the cabin on weekends! Several decades ago The Schubert Club produced a ten-day Summer Vocal Festival, engaging baritone Gérard Souzay, soprano Elly Ameling, and master pianist/accompanist Dalton Baldwin. Over a ten-day period recitals and master classes were programmed. Then we had a lull until now.

While our musically-rich cities of Saint Paul and Minneapolis provide fertile ground that yields loads of musical choices, we had a hunch that a week-long series of musical events during the first part of June may not appeal to the masses. Still it was hard to resist the opportunity to explore the programming of a small festival devoted to the world of song literature. Who could tell? An idea like that might take root among some of the enthusiastic folks still in town, eager for quality musical events in summer.

And so in June of 2004 our Festival began. With first-class headliners like Håkan Hagegård, Susanne Mentzer, Sharon Isbin, and Nathan Gunn, Mayor Randy Kelly hoped it would become "an annual celebration of the beauty and power of words and music."

The Saint Paul Summer Song Festival has attracted many lovers of song, offering a little something for everyone—master classes, picnics, lectures, noontime and evening concerts, films, even an art song competition. Downtown venues have included the beautifully renovated SPCO Center in the historic Hamm Building, the McKnight Theatre at Ordway Center, St. Paul's old Central Presbyterian Church on Exchange Street, and various courtrooms at Landmark Center. Sunny days have brought families to Raspberry Island for picnics and song—with the musical portion presented on the stage of The Schubert Club's charming bandstand, with

The weather was perfect for the bandstand performance by The Singers—Minnesota Choral Artists at the 2006 Summer Song Festival.

the co-sponsorship of Minnesota Public Radio.

And so as with all musical series, the future of the Saint Paul Summer Song Festival awaits a verdict dictated by the support of friends and donors. For the present, The Schubert Club is pleased to continue this new version of an old idea—celebrating the beauty and power of words and music.

The Hill House Parlor Concerts

The Schubert Club's affection for old Saint Paul began with its founding in the late 1800s. The historic mansions lining Summit Avenue, as well as homes throughout the neighborhood, figured prominently in the early days when the women who began the Ladies Musicale—one day to be renamed The Schubert Club—were holding concerts in their homes.

That was in 1882, the same year James J. Hill purchased two lots on the eastern end of Summit Avenue where construction would later begin on the impressive mansion that is now the location of one of The Schubert Club's longest running series, the Hill House Parlor Concerts.

The origins of this Series came about some twenty years ago when a group of Twin Cities musicians approached Bruce Carlson with an idea. Would The Schubert Club be interested

Members of the original Hill House Chamber Players gather around Bruce Carlson's desk in Landmark Center to discuss some details in the early days of setting up the Series. Along with soprano Maria Jette—a frequent guest artist, are Tanya Remenikova (cello), Julie Ayer (violin), Jeffrey Van (guitar), and Rees Allison (piano).

in co-sponsoring a regular series of chamber music with the Minnesota Historical Society? The plan was to hold an evening recital four times a year in the music room of the historic James J. Hill House on 240 Summit Avenue. Bruce loved new ideas, and he had a knack for making them work. He said yes, and the Series was launched.

The early players were musicians with rotating members, but soon a permanent quartet was established and when the foursome presented its first program in 1987 the newly-christened Hill House Chamber Players officially took up residence in the James J. Hill House on four evenings each year, presenting innovative programming that brought a larger audience with each season. The Players themselves added members. In subsequent years the quartet became a quintet and then a sextet, then back to a quintet. Depending on repertoire, guest artists were featured and included singers, instrumentalists, and occasionally a narrator. Soon the ever-enlarging audience assembled in the mansion's cozy music room necessitated adding a second recital so that each program was performed twice, increasing the four-concert season to an eight-concert season.

Today, the Hill House Parlor Concerts continue to draw record crowds. A hundred folding chairs are occupied at each performance as music lovers congregate in one of Saint Paul's oldest and most historic mansions . . . just as they did more than a century ago when the homes along Summit Avenue were alive with the sounds of music.

Keyboard Conversationalist

Jeffrey Siegel

It has been more than twenty years since The Schubert Club first featured pianist Jeffrey Siegel and his Keyboard Conversations™. Since then, the location of the concerts has shifted, but there is always a dedicated audience. In 2006, The Schubert Club, in partnership with Twin Cities Public Television's Minnesota Channel, produced a DVD of Keyboard Conversations on Chopin and Mozart. Brief segments filmed in The Schubert Club Museum show letters from these composers and pianos associated with them.

After a concert as part of a Minnesota Orchestra Sommerfest many summers back in which I was soloist in a Beethoven concerto with this superb orchestra, two ladies from The Schubert Club came backstage to introduce themselves: Gloria Sewell and Thelma Hunter. Due to mutual musical friends in the Twin Cities I knew both names very well and was honored to see them. They mentioned that they had heard a great deal about my Keyboard Conversation programs, a series of solo piano programs, concerts with commentary, in which I speak about the music before performing each composition in its entirety. Would I be interested in presenting such a program under the auspices of The Schubert Club? Would I?! The Schubert Club is known

Jeffrey Siegel and Bruce Carlson share a breakfast planning session.

to all classical musicians as an absolutely top-notch concert presenter of high quality musicians, and their programs have one of the most discriminating audiences in this country. Thus Gloria and Thelma brought the idea to Bruce Carlson, twisted his arm until he said, "OK, let's try this talking pianist" and three solo programs were arranged at the McKnight Theater in the 1985-86 season. I cannot say that the programs immediately drew a large audience but Bruce continued to present them over the years as long as the "Artist" did not cost him too much money! We have now passed our twentieth season.

It remains a joy and an honor to present Keyboard Conversations to the Twin Cities audiences, now under the joint sponsorship of The Schubert Club and Hamline University. Bruce is, and always will be, very much missed and I shall never forget his support and appreciation of these "concert with commentary" programs. The Schubert Club staff is, and remains, one of the finest group of people with whom it has been my pleasure to work, both

The cover of this 2006 DVD, "Keyboard Conversations," features items from The Schubert Club Museum which pianist Siegel included in his presentation.

professionally and personally—and I have worked with many in my career!

All best wishes to The Schubert Club for the next 125 years—I hope Keyboard Conversations remains on The Schubert Club's roster for many years to come.

New York Concerts

Throughout the past thirty years, The Schubert Club has made possible a number of opportunities for local artists to be presented in New York. In some cases, these occasions have served as an important debut concert—introducing an artist to the New York public; in others, the recitalist may already be an established artist.

Before their New York concert, Jorja Fleezanis and Cyril Huvé performed in Saint Paul at Sundin Music Hall, Hamline University, using the Schantz fortepiano copy from The Schubert Club Museum.

One memorable performance took place in April of 2000, when Jorja Fleezanis, concertmaster of the Minnesota Orchestra, performed with French fortepianist Cyril Huvé under Schubert Club auspices in New York's Merkin Concert Hall. They played portions of the double-CD recording they made of Beethoven's complete violin sonatas (which The Schubert Club also supported). Other New York concerts sponsored by The Schubert Club include violist Cynthia Phelps, pianists Julia and Irina Elkina, and the baroque ensemble Belladonna.

Meanwhile, here's what New York thinks of us:

Good recital series in the US are few and far between. It was much different 20 years ago. The Schubert Club takes the considerable risk to put on the very best artists and hopes the audience will come. They seem to. The finest artists love to go to Saint Paul. They often have even better houses there under your auspices than in New York. We honor The Schubert Club series greatly. Keep it up. Hold out the light. The Schubert Club is what we want to think of to help carry out the tradition.

– Mark Alpert, Manager,
Columbia Artists Management

I'd like to take this opportunity to let you know how much you and your very distinguished series mean to those of us managing concert artists. Recitals, both instrumental and vocal, are hard to come by these days, the demand for some having dropped off precipitously over the years. However, The Schubert Club continues presenting the highest quality artists available season after season... There are a very limited number of viable and independent recital presenters still active, and I'd like you to know that I consider you and your series the leader, and a model for the industry.

– Mary Lynn Fixler,
Vice President,
Herbert Barrett Management

"Live from Landmark" and The Courtroom Concert Series

Wander into the beautiful Landmark Center in Rice Park on a Thursday afternoon between October and April, and if your meanderings take you near the high-ceilinged, wood-paneled courtroom on the third floor at the north end of the building you are likely to hear performances of some of the finest musicians in the Twin Cities. On some days you might even happen upon a celebrity guest artist.

A worthy, albeit humble, successor to its predecessor (the long-running popular "Live from Landmark Series" co-sponsored with Minnesota Public Radio), the Courtroom Concert Series came into existence in 1992 as a response to Ramsey County's request that Landmark Center make available for the general public some free events in the building. The timing was good. MPR was making changes in its programming format, reassigning priorities: which programs to keep, which ones not to. When the decision by radio executives was made to cancel "Live From Landmark," some hearts sank, but almost as quickly a remarkable recovery materialized with the County's interest in providing free concerts in the building.

Only a few changes were necessary. First, the programs would not be broadcast. Secondly, the venue was changed from the Weyerhaeuser Auditorium in the lower level of Landmark Center to the Ramsey County Room on the third floor. Next, a change of hosts. Randall Davidson filled that role and became our weekly commentator. Performers would be tapped from our musically-rich community, and to get our first season rolling we set about contacting orchestra players, teachers, student scholarship winners and other performing musicians. Our small budget enabled us to offer a modest honorarium. All that was needed was an audience.

While some early attenders might recall a few empty seats in the first years of this newcomer series, it didn't take long for word to spread that here was a little concert worth coming to. And why not? In addition to the rows of green-upholstered chairs lining the room in traditional concert fashion, a few café tables were added with white table cloths for those wishing to bring a lunch—and a sprig of fresh flowers was set out to brighten each table. Complimentary coffee continues to be served each week, and there is no admission charge. Best of all, an interesting and varied program featuring superb performers has remained the Series centerpiece throughout the years. A broad mixture of programming is the norm and this formula seems to suit a wide spectrum of musical tastes. No wonder the numbers grew! After more than a decade in business, we sometimes fill the courtroom with more chairs than a vigilant fire marshal might approve!

Long-time host Randall Davidson clowns with frequent guest artist Maria Jette, as they check their calendars to mark a date for a Courtroom Concert engagement.

Today, the Courtroom Concert Series takes its place among other innovative concert offerings The Schubert Club has created over the years, filling an important niche for our wonderful friends and patrons who favor a daytime hour for attending a Schubert Club concert.

Distant Disasters

In so many decades of concerts, there have been dramatic episodes of cancellations and other harrowing losses. In most cases, time has provided enough distance that the event no longer creates a sinking feeling in the pit of the stomach. Subscribers who recall recent weather- and illness-related substitutions and postponements presumably are not still brooding on the inconvenience and disappointments. Here are a few crisis moments from the past to add even more perspective:

The influenza pandemic of 1918 made large public gatherings (such as concerts) inadvisable and, in October 1918, illegal as well. Soprano Mabel Garrison's performance was put off until February of 1919. She proved so popular that she was invited back in May of 1921.

March 22, 1940, the People's Church, which had served for more than forty years as the concert venue for Schubert Club visiting artists, was destroyed by fire. Tenor Richard Crooks was scheduled to give a recital there in two and half weeks. The mad scramble to find a replacement venue resulted in booking the Saint Paul Auditorium (a space not nearly as good acoustically or aesthetically) not only for that night, but also for the next thirty years.

At their January 1948 concert, the Paganini Quartet was the victim of an elaborate scam by a well-dressed, middle-aged man who greeted them at the stage door when they arrived and showed them around the concert hall, even giving instructions to the electricians about spotlights. Schubert Club organizers assumed he was the Quartet's manager, but it turned out he was aiming to take his own bow for the concert. Or, as it turned out, four bows—that is, four bows taken from the cases of the players, worth about $1,200. He was last seen, making his getaway on the streetcar after the concert, the bows carefully laid across his knees. After this episode, The Schubert Club took out liability insurance.

A more tragic loss occurred in October 1949. Violin virtuoso Ginette Neveu was killed when her airplane crashed in the Azores

THE SCHUBERT CLUB
ST. PAUL, MINN.

MABEL GARRISON
of the Metropolitan Opera of New York

THE AUDITORIUM
Tuesday Evening, October 29, 1918

Annual Dues admitting to all concerts $3.00 and $5.00.
Apply to Mrs. C. A. Guyer, 676 Summit Avenue

Garrison tickets for benefit of Musicians in France $2.00 and $2.50,
and war tax

Seat reservations at Dyers' beginning Saturday, Oct. 26th.

POSTPONED
ACCOUNT OF EPIDEMIC SITUATION

en route from France to her United States performance tour. Her brother Jean-Paul, who served as her accompanist, was also killed. In 1935, at the age of fifteen, she had won the Wieniawski violin competition (where David Oistrakh came in second). She had been scheduled to perform in January 1950 for The Schubert Club. There was enough time to schedule another violinist, Erica Morini, to replace her in the season, but there was no way to make up for the loss to the music world of this brilliant young violinist.

The loss of soprano Irmgard Seefried, on the other hand, turned out to be only temporary. The evening before her 1952 recital, the welcoming committee from The Schubert Club waited at the airport until midnight, meeting all the planes from Chicago with growing concern. No Miss Seefried. The next day, she telephoned from her Minneapolis hotel to explain that she had mistakenly assumed that train and plane tickets were interchangeable. Unable to fly from Chicago, she had simply taken the train.

Two years later, in 1954, another soprano gave the concert organizers a scare. En route to the Chicago airport, Elisabeth Schwarzkopf was delayed by a slow freight train and missed her plane. The next flight would get her into town with very little time to spare. Axel von Bergen, husband of Schubert Club President May Morrill von Bergen, asked the Saint Paul chief of police for help. The von Bergens met the plane at 7:45 (in Minneapolis territory), hoping to make the 8:30 performance. At the Fort Road Bridge near Fort Snelling (the Saint Paul border), the police met them. Sirens blaring, the escort took off for downtown. Schwarzkopf, comfortably ensconced in the back seat of the von Bergens' car, asked, "Do you mind if I vocalize a little? I won't have time when we get to the hall?" And so, the duet of vocalizing soprano and police siren continued down West Seventh. Unflustered throughout, Schwarzkopf remarked that the escort made her feel like the Queen Mother. Her dress, of the new nylon net, didn't need ironing, so she walked out on stage only ten minutes late—and gave a fine recital.

In the summer of 1975, The Schubert Club scheduled a vocal festival with Gérard Souzay and Elly Ameling as the featured artists. After Ameling was booked, she was asked to sing at the wedding of her friend Princess Christina of Holland. For a while, things looked bad for The Schubert Club, but the Royal Family changed the wedding date so that Ameling could go to Saint Paul.

In 1978 Finnish bass Martti Talvela had perhaps grown too accustomed to operatic engagements where the costume is waiting backstage. He neglected to pack a white shirt for his Schubert Club recital. Board President Jeanne Shepard knew there was trouble when she heard her son say over the telephone, "But I'm not as big as you are!" The burly 6'7" singer ended up being delighted by the roomy white turtleneck bought for the occasion.

There will always be unanticipated setbacks–sometimes even true disasters. An organization that has produced as many concerts in its time as The Schubert Club might well take as its motto: "L'imprévu est toujours possible" (the unforeseen is always possible). But in spite of everything, The Schubert Club has kept the music ringing out for 125 years, and promises to continue for many years to come.

Concert Oddities

Unusual concerts have punctuated the Schubert Club season from time to time. The occasional foray into unexpected waters (sometimes literally, as you will read) shows the versatility of the organization. Sometimes an entire series provided a jolt, or perhaps there was just a single surprise performance.

On four occasions over the years, the main concert series departed from the standard recital by presenting dance companies: the Carmalita Maracci Dance Group in 1941, the Roberto Iglesias Ballet Español in 1959, José Limon & Dance Company in 1961, and the Alvin Ailey American Dance Theater in 1969. There were also eight large choral presentations on the main series. These included General Platoff's Don Cossack Chorus in 1944, the boys of the Little Singers of Paris in 1957, the Roger Wagner Chorale twice in the 1960s, and the Swedish Radio Choir in 1975.

Off the main concert series, there were more surprises. For instance, in the summer of 1969, The Schubert Club sponsored a locally written and produced rock musical called *House of Leather*, composed by Dale Menten, scripted by Fred Gaines and performed by the Blackwood Apology. Set during the Civil War, the story is an attack on greed, war, hypocrisy, and racism. The Brechtian character of Mrs. Grimm operates a versatile establishment where upper-class children receive training in deportment, defective guns are manufactured for sale to both Union and Confederate armies, and the offspring of her prostitutes are sold to the slave trade. Whew. Directed by H. Wesley Balk and performed at the Crawford Livingston Theater in Saint Paul, *House of Leather* was praised by the *St. Paul Pioneer Press* as "a brilliant piece of theater, absolutely bursting with vitality." When the show got to Broadway, however, it only lasted for one performance.

New musicals and new music can take the audience to new places, figuratively or literally. On December 31, 1970, some New Year's Eve celebrants opted to attend a concert sponsored by The Schubert Club—in an unusual venue. The audience called ahead for reservations in either the shallow or deep end of the Midway YMCA Swimming Pool. Ushers were replaced by lifeguards, and evening gowns with swimsuits and goggles. Percussionist Max Neuhaus composed an underwater musical experience called "Water Whistle," where the best auditory experience involved being submerged under water. Sound was controlled by pumping water through miniature whistles, varying the pitch with valves. The concert was part of a series entitled "Nobody's Old Favorites," featuring music of the avant-garde.

Another series ventured into new waters, with concerts using MIDI piano. *Hot Notes: The Future of the Piano* was a series of concerts co-sponsored by The Schubert Club and The Science Museum of Minnesota. Libby Larsen served as artistic director with pianist Alexander Braginsky performing "compositional realizations." Several new works were premiered, combining piano and electronic sounds.

Saint Paul Pioneer Press critic John Harvey once referred to "The Schubert Club's Janus-headed nature—with a benevolent gaze on tradition and a lively interest in the present." He was reviewing a 1971 concert that included traditional harpsichord music by Handel and Scarlatti as well as avant-garde vocal music by Berio and Bussotti. But his description applies equally well today.

In March 2007, The Schubert Club, the Science Museum of Minnesota, and the American Composers Forum presented *Wild Music A-Go-Go* in conjunction with the "Wild Music" exhibit at the Science Museum. The performance opened with a fanfare for conch shells—"The Call of the Sea" by Philip Blackburn—played on thirty shells from The Schubert Club Museum's Kugler Collection. Two pieces on the program featured The Schubert Club's lithophone (a Vietnamese set of tuned stones). One was a world premiere by Steve Heitzeg, commissioned by The Schubert Club. Soprano Maria

Carmalita Maracci, 1941

The best seats for this 1971 concert!

For the Hot Notes Series of the 1993-94 season, technological innovations were obvious in the publicity photo as well as the MIDI instruments.

Jette sang words by naturalists Rachel Carson, Jane Goodall, and Terry Tempest Williams, accompanied by the lithophone and other sounds, including seed rattles, whale bones, and recorded bonobo apes. Another segment of the program included the option for the audience of putting Mexican jumping beans in their ears for the aural experience.

Organizational longevity does not mean stodginess.

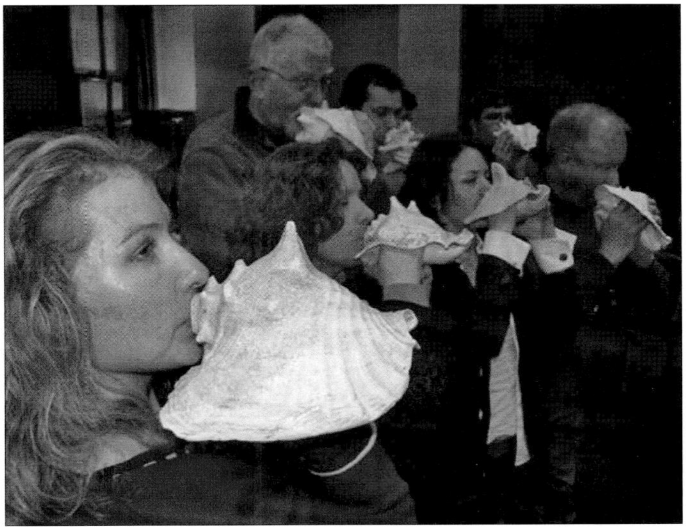

Percussionist Heather Barringer started off in the winds section with the opening fanfare for the 2007 *Wild Music A-Go-Go* performance.

Education

Schubert Club To Give Final Students' Tea

Musical Program Will Precede Social Affair to Take Place Saturday at the House of Hope.

MRS. GEORGE B. PIERCE AND Mrs. W. H. Kindy will be hostesses at the last students' tea of the season to which all members of the Schubert club are invited. They will be assisted by Miss Dorothy Langen, Miss Eloise Holterhoff, Miss Dorothy Vernon, Miss Betty Cornell and Mrs. P. J. McGinn.

The tea will follow a musical program beginning at 3 P. M. Saturday in the parish house of the House of Hope Presbyterian church.

The program will be given by Miss Emily Raudenbush, Miss Ruth Lenox, Miss Harriette Richardson, Miss Agnes Thro, Miss Emma Birkmeier and Miss Grace Buyer.

Schubert Club piano students

The Schubert Club, Inc.
SAINT PAUL
STUDENT MEMBER'S TICKET
Good until February 20 1930
Miss Agnes Thro
NOT TRANSFERABLE. $3.00
IN CASE OF LOSS, THIS TICKET WILL BE DUPLICATED ONLY UPON PAYMENT OF 50 CENTS
This Ticket must be presented at Dyer's when seats are reserved

Agnes attended all the concerts!

The SCHUBERT CLUB
LECTURE-RECITAL
"Wagner and the Bayreuth Festival"
(Musical and Stereopticon Illustrations)
By MRS. CHARLES W. RHODES
Assisted by HERR ADOLF GLOSE
At The Odeon, cor. Sixth and St. Peter Sts.
Monday, February 9th, 1903, 8:15 p. m.
Tickets $1.00. To Club Members @ their Guests, 50c.

Wagner was all the rage!

FREE PIANO LESSONS at the Neighborhood House have started many a young student on his or her way to fame. Here Miss Virginia Hoeltje is teaching Angelita Hernadez, left and Esperanza Ruiz.

WINNERS OF SCHUBERT CLUB MUSIC SCHOLARSHIPS

Four persons were given scholarships at noon Saturday in the annual award made by the Schubert club to those persons who, after an audition, were considered by the judges worthy the free tuition. They are, left to right, Earl Rymer of Superior, Wis., piano; Ruth Cornell, Minneapolis, violin; Clarice Christopherson, Minneapolis, and Edward Marriott of St. Paul, voice. The voice award resulted in a tie. The awards are made possible by the Fortieth Anniversary scholarship fund of the Schubert club. Three sums of $100 each are given to the winners of competitive trials in the divisions of voice, piano and violin. This is the seventh year such awards have been given and the final test followed preliminaries February 23, conducted by Mrs. W. M. McClintock, 2225 Langford avenue, for the club.

Earl won a scholarship in 1929

After the Winners Recital 2007

The Schubert Club's Educational Programs

Jane Jeong Trenka

Micah Fitch performed at the piano with Dakota Jazz Club musicians as part of the first Jazz Piano Competition in 2005.

For several years, Jane Jeong Trenka administered The Schubert Club's Musicapolis program of after-school music classes, while also performing and teaching piano. A magna cum laude graduate of Augsburg College, she holds degrees in music performance and English literature. She is the author of The Language of Blood: A Memoir *(a winner in the 2004 Minnesota Book Awards) and* Fugitive Visions. *She is also one of the editors for* Outsiders Within: Writings on Transracial Adoption.

THE PROGRAM IS NOT BACH, Beethoven, and Brahms, but Thelonius Monk, Miles Davis, and John Coltrane; the setting not a concert stage, but the intimate Dakota Jazz Club and Restaurant, with its warm atmosphere of brick and wood, accented by one slim line of pale blue light tracing its way around the balcony. In the minutes before the music starts, waiters rush to serve the entire audience at once: ice cubes clink against clear heavy glasses, and the aroma of an inventive Minnesota cuisine fills the dining room: grilled fish tacos in soft lefse, chicken salad with wild rice, walleye and crab salad with grilled asparagus.

The occasion is the First Annual Jazz Piano Scholarship Competition Finals, presented by The Schubert Club and The Dakota Foundation for Jazz Education. Students were invited to submit recorded entries to the competition, and then the top three were chosen to perform at the Dakota for three scholarships: The Marie Froelich Memorial Award, The David Paulus Memorial Award, and The Schubert Club/Dakota Foundation for Jazz Education Award.

It's not what you would expect from The Schubert Club—and former board member Jane Matteson would have loved it. After her husband passed away, Jane—often dressed in reds, sporting her latest hat, and a jeweled dragonfly inevitably adorning her jacket—could be found almost nightly at the Dakota. The best table in the house was hers, and there, silhouetted against the bright lights of the stage, she was surrounded by friends, her companion patiently waiting to drive her home. Jane's infectious enthusiasm for jazz and young people brought The Schubert Club together with the Dakota in a co-sponsorship called the J Train, an afternoon program giving high school students the opportunity to hear legendary jazz musicians play music, talk about their craft, and give master classes.

Jane Matteson, jazz-lover and creative spirit.

Of course, master classes are not new to The Schubert Club. Six to ten times a year, the organization sponsors performers visiting the Twin Cities in master classes for students. These classes are held at various universities, where the students can easily attend. Classical masters have included Yo-Yo Ma, Yefim Bronfman, and Christopher Hogwood.

What could be more exhilarating than to take a lesson from a master—often a long-admired musical idol? The student who performs obviously benefits, but the nature of the master class is that everyone can discover something. We see remarkable learning unfold right before our eyes—what a gift for students, teachers, and music enthusiasts. Amazing things happen when a flexible, daring student is paired with a charismatic master who acts as a link between past and future musical traditions.

Because master classes are not concerts, we hear music in a new way. Freed from the order of beginning-to-end, we hear a passage this way, then once more in another. Music becomes lively, open, filled with choices. The player might interpret a passage with more or less legato, a different bowing, or with the counter-melody brought out more. What aspect of the musical idea does the player really love, really want to highlight?

"I'm an inner voices man myself," said Abbey Simon, exuberantly springing up from one of the two pianos during a master class. Mr. Simon had played along with a student in a master class, at one of the two black Steinways placed side-by-side, then energetically moved about the stage at Ferguson Hall, as if the stage were not large enough to contain him, his musical ideas, his desire to share. He spoke not just to the student next to him, but to the students sitting in the furthest row of the audience.

In his brown suit and neatly combed hair, the angular and restless Simon was exactly the opposite in appearance of another great musician in a Schubert Club master class, Jorja Fleezanis, dressed in flowing garments and punk rock streaks of purple highlighting her naturally silver hair. Of a violin concerto commissioned especially for her, she remarked that the composer had pushed her to the edg es of her technical limits—how gratifying to hear the concertmaster of the Minnesota Orchestra confess that even she has to practice the hard parts! And how wonderful it is to see our most cherished musicians revealed in a way that we cannot know them on the concert stage—their intelligence and charm laid out so intimately, the mysteries of grand musical interpretation discussed so honestly, accessibly, and so refreshingly without mystery.

The Schubert Club's earliest records are housed in the archives of the Minnesota Historical Society. Opening the boxes filled with papers submitted for annual meetings—brittle notebooks, financial records, and programs and brochures impressed by metal type—a musty yet sweet aroma pervades the workspace, the scent of a grandmother's lavender perfume. The emotion that pervades is sweet, too, the kind one might have when rummaging through grandmother's old treasures in the attic—a happiness and satisfaction with the past, because one's own relationship to it is so palpable today.

My own work in music education for The Schubert Club, through Musicapolis and Project CHEER, was indeed a descendant of the musical work that had been set in place such a long time ago. The idea was—and still is—to bring music directly to the people: at the 1923 annual meeting, Mrs. Briggs, President of The Schubert Club, reported that there had been "many programs carried to those who could not come to us."

Florence L. C. Briggs: it is her graceful cursive and her distinctive taste in fine-tipped fountain pens that I can now recognize at a glance.

Master Classes

For more than a century, professional musicians have given presentations or provided coaching through Schubert Club programs. The 1960s brought a more regular pattern where performers from the International Artist Series (though it was then called the Evening Concert Series) were invited to do master classes.

(Top) Baritone Thomas Hampson encouraged singer Kathleen Humphrey in this 1993 master class held in the Ordway's Drake Room.

(Above) While in Saint Paul for his performance with The Schubert Club in 1981, flautist Jean-Pierre Rampal led a master class at Macalester.

Two years after The Schubert Club made its first educational grant—a loan in 1893 to Miss Ella Richards in order for her to study piano in Vienna—Mrs. Warren Briggs became chairman of the Chorus Class study group, where "good instruction and good accompaniment is provided." Seven years later, Mrs. Briggs was elected President of The Schubert Club. Her tenure as President lasted from 1902-1905, and she was re-elected again shortly thereafter, serving from 1908-1930.

Mrs. Briggs, Schubert Club Board president.

It is not known if the impetus for her work at The Schubert Club was informed by an early illness (as an unmarried woman, she had come from New England to Minnesota "for her health"), or her marriage to a physician and a consequent proximity to people in need, but what is very clear is that, during an era of tremendous disparities between the wealthy and the poor, Mrs. Briggs had entered into the refinement of one of Minnesota's most exclusive social clubs, yet had saved a steadfast place in her heart for the less fortunate.

In a photograph dated 1923, Mrs. Briggs perches on a windowsill in a three-quarter pose, her gaze directed not at the photographer and not through the window, but somewhere in between, perhaps over the viewer's shoulder. Immediately one notices the texture, the contrasts: both the taffeta and the wool of her matronly yet elegant dress; the shining smoothness of her string of black pearls; the gleam of a white pendant on a chain, the miniature sparkles of beads stitched to fabric; the rough solidity of the brick wall behind her; and the gossamer fabric of the lace-edged curtains at the open window. Mrs. Briggs clasps a sandalwood fan, half-opened, in her rather muscular hands. The fan points toward her knees; through the shine of her dress, they are also thick and muscular. Her hairstyle is simple, pulled back loosely, away from a face that could not be any plainer. Her nose is too large to be beautiful, her mouth unshapely. Change her into rougher clothes, substitute a different background, and a worse photographer—and she could be a common farmwife, a factory laborer, an immigrant.

But she is not. Note the expression. Her left eyebrow is raised slightly above the right, her head tilted just slightly to the left. See the crooked wrinkle above her nose. The edges of her smile. Her enormous eyes. In this slightly asymmetrical portrait of Mrs. Briggs, we see her character, the depth of her generosity.

If one looks with an imaginative eye at what is contained within a portrait, one can also turn the imaginative gaze towards what lay outside the edges of it: the Jazz Age, electric streetcars, women's suffrage, Sinclair Lewis, F. Scott Fitzgerald, Lindbergh's solo trans-Atlantic flight, World War I, and masses of European immigration—all this during Mrs. Briggs's long tenure at The Schubert Club.

It was a time of enormous social upheaval, when "progress" often resulted in disastrous consequence for some. Mrs. Briggs was not content to concern herself solely with her own social milieu; it was under her watch that The Schubert Club Music Schools were begun in 1911. Soon teachers were busy at places that reflected the needs of Saint Paul at the time: the West Side Neighborhood House, the Protestant Orphan Asylum, the State Hospital for Crippled Children.

European immigrants comprised the bulk of pupils for The Schubert Club Music Schools. In 1926, 266 pupils—56 Americans and the rest other "nationalities" such as French, Italian, Irish, Greek, and Jewish--took lessons in voice, piano, and violin in private studios and in ten different locations throughout Saint Paul. "The Schubert Club Music School is a most interesting channel

Dancing at Neighborhood House, ca. 1920. In 1910, the Philanthropic Committee reported that it had presented thirteen programs in the following locations: Neighborhood House, Woman's Christian Home, Soldiers Home, City Hospital, Old Ladies Home, Bethel, and the Home for the Friendless. "In addition to these programs, beginning with Nov. 16, a pianist has gone to the Neighborhood House every Tuesday afternoon to play for the games and dances of the Children. The total number of musicians responding to the invitation for this good work has been fifty-two. This number, however, allows for repeated visits on the part of a number of those who have rendered services."

SCHUBERT CLUB

ACTIVE MEMBERS' SECTION

1914-1915

—

MUSIC IN AMERICA

December 9. Music Schools, Conservatories, and Musical Industries.
At the residence of Mrs Benjamin Sommers, 628 Fairmount Avenue.

January 6. American Composers.
At the residence of Mrs. Chas. O. Krieger, 793 Goodrich Avenue.

February 3. Operas.
At the residence of Mrs. J. W. G. Dunn, 1033 Lincoln Avenue.

March 3. Orchestras.
At the residence of Mrs. A. B. Stickney, 288 Summit Avenue.

March 31. Eminent American Performers.
At the residence of Mrs. Oliver Crosby, 804 Lincoln Avenue.

For subject matter read current musical papers.
The programs will begin promptly at 3:45 P. M.

The Schubert Club offered educational activities to all of its members, not just to students. Regular study sessions provided opportunities to listen to, learn about, and discuss music and musical issues.

for music development among the masses. By the opportunity given many of musical training at a nominal sum, the club is helping to create an intelligent and appreciative musical public, besides enriching the lives of those who otherwise would not have the advantages of music," wrote Mrs. Briggs.

Every so often, one finds evidence of mild disgruntlement within the archives—a teacher reports that her student has terminated lessons because he could not pay the 25 cent tuition for want of shoes, or, conversely, a board member believes that the Music School families could afford to pay more for tuition, and don't you think people are taking advantage?

Yet Mrs. Briggs pressed on. Beginning with the self-education and betterment of its own members through Chorus Class and lectures, meetings, manuscript studies, and practices, The Schubert Club expanded its circle of human relationship through sharing music with the immediate community.

During Mrs. Briggs's tenure, other programs were instituted for the benefit of students, including the following enlightened way to give performance opportunities to students: The Students' Professional Bureau, created "for obtaining remunerative engagements without cost to the student." Through the Bureau, students were employed as performing musicians for weddings, funerals, banquets, receptions, and conventions.

Other inventive programs for students included The Schubert Club Student Ensemble, which sang at churches and clubs. Competitive music scholarships were given, and free single admission tickets for concerts were given to public school students. During the 1933-1934 Season, music met with the art of writing: all students attending free concerts were required to enter a 150-word essay on "My Impressions of the Schubert Club Artist Concert I Attended." The best essay received a 1-year associate membership in The Schubert Club. And to commemorate the Club's 75th anniversary year (1957-58), the Maude Taylor Hill Scholarship in Music Fund was established with a $10,000 gift.

Under Mrs. Briggs, the Club constantly sought ways to bring new musicians into the fold, to give to the cultural life of Saint Paul, and to educate students. Wrote Mrs. Briggs: "The outstanding features of The Schubert Club have been its…musical standards and their urge through the many and organized contacts of human relationship—the functioning of a divine spark, if you please, through the desire to share."

The Schubert Club Music Schools faithfully continued serving the community's underprivileged children, 47 years in all. Then, in 1958, the music schools were closed, as the services were considered no longer necessary.

So, during the next season, the sections of The Schubert Club directly affecting students were listed as Student Section, Altruistic Section, Concert Series, Junior Hostessing, and Scholarship. Also significant in 1959 was The Schubert Club's offering of a "Salute to Youth." For only $2.75, members were provided with luncheon and a program on "how to understand and teach teen-agers." The program must have worked. In 1960, five Student Section Teas were organized, students purchased over 500 tickets, and many others were donated to students through the generosity of Mr. I.A. O'Shaughnessy.

Fast-forward to 1968: the Music Schools are revived under Executive Director Bruce Carlson and given a new name: Project CHEER (Creative Help through Enrichment and Educational Resources). Mrs. Robert J. Harris, along with several teaching assistants, gives lessons in piano, violin, and guitar at the Hallie Q. Brown / Martin Luther King Center near University and Dale.

(Top) Prentice Harris, originator of the CHEER name.

(Bottom) Long-time CHEER director Joanna Kirby at work.

Today, under the leadership of program director Joanna Kirby, Project CHEER offers lessons year-round. Students study piano or guitar, as well as participate in a music activities class, where music literacy is enhanced by playing rhythm instruments or using interactive

A CHEER Mother

Nearly 10 years ago I was asking around, hoping to find an affordable way for my kids to learn piano. A friend and fellow single parent told me about Project CHEER, and the rest is history! Each of my five children has had the opportunity to take piano and guitar and music theory lessons over the years. It has been a terrific experience, not only for them, but also for me and my extended family that loves to come to every recital possible. I have steered a number of friends and co-workers toward Project CHEER and have been able to keep in touch with them through the program. It has been a good connection to the community. In fact, when Joanna (director of Project CHEER) was a little girl, I would see her run under her grandparents' piano during my lesson from her grandma, Irene Titus. I didn't know until her grandpa passed away recently that she had grown up to be my own children's wonderful teacher. Our lives would be very different and much less enriched without Project CHEER. I know I could not have provided my family with such great quality music instruction anywhere else. I am very grateful for everyone who makes Project CHEER possible!

- Margaret Richardson

Students paint the wall in the new Musicapolis studio at Sabathani Community Center.

computer programs. Mrs. Briggs's original, inspired idea of carrying programs directly to the people is readily apparent at Project CHEER: children come to the MLK Center after school, and these eager children can be seen all afternoon, traversing the hallway between Project CHEER and the daycare center, reminding their friends that it's time for lessons. Musical study becomes part of the fabric of children's after-school activities that already exist—a convenience for busy, working parents, and an integral part of the life of the community center.

The Schubert Club's education programs have been diverse, inventive, and far-reaching. Recent collaborations with Minneapolis public schools such as Howe, Bancroft, Cedar-Riverside, and Seward Montessori have provided children with supplemental music instruction when budget cuts threatened music in the schools. The Schubert Club has created ingenious partnerships with organizations such as the Public Housing Authority Project, the Minneapolis and St. Paul Public Libraries, Meet the Composer, the Ordway Center

Norbert Augustine and some of his steel drum students.

for the Performing Arts, and 3M—just to name a few—in order to share music with students in memorable, accessible ways.

In the 1990s, after-school educational programs and summer music camps were offered at the Sabathani Community Center and the Tapestry Folkdance Center in Minneapolis. These educational programs not only provided a musical training for students, but also offered a livelihood and a chance to expand networks for the musicians who live and work in our community. Immigrant and minority musicians such as steel drummer Norbert Augustine, pianist and vocalist Li Lei, and Indonesian gamelan orchestra instructor Joko Sutrisno have shown us more ways to nurture human relationships, expanding both our ears and our hearts, through the limitless world of music.

One cannot end this chapter without a brief mention of The Schubert Club Museum of Musical Instruments located at Landmark Center, which includes the Kugler Collection of Musical Instruments from Around the World, the Gilman Ordway Manuscript Collection, and the Keyboard Instrument Collection, spanning six centuries of keyboard craftsmanship.

Weighing in at close to 1,000 pounds, measuring nearly 9 feet long, and strung with over 45,000 pounds of tension, the modern Steinway D is a magnificent, powerful machine—the ideal instrument upon which piano students are trained to play all the keyboard literature. Yet, the instruments upon which many of our beloved composers did their composing are quite different things, in sound, touch, and character. The demure fortepiano of Mozart, the harpsichord and clavichord of Bach, and even the Pleyel piano of Chopin—when a pianist plays these keyboards, one experiences in an instant what years of training on a modern instrument may not have revealed: the true sound of the music, as the composer heard it.

At Landmark Center, pianists may enjoy playing copies of historical instruments, and even some original instruments. The benefit of

Jill Dawe, assistant professor of music at Augsburg College, on a fieldtrip to The Schubert Club Museum with some of her piano students.

Author Jane Jeong Trenka with a Musicapolis student.

being able to actually play and hear these instruments instead of just looking at them in a darkened room (as is the standard practice in many museums) cannot be overstressed. What a thrill to play the music of Schubert on an instrument that he himself would have played, with a tuning that would have sounded natural to him. How amazing to touch the delicate, impeccably sanded keys of the 1726 Cristofori fortepiano copy. And what sheer fun it is to use the bassoon pedal on the Streicher when playing Mozart's Rondo alla Turca. A pianist can gain important insight into technique and phrasing as the result of playing an historical instrument at The Schubert Club, which he or she can bring back to the modern Steinway D upon return. These kinds of experiences, for a serious pianist, are rare and priceless.

Opening a museum that musicians can actually use is just one creative way that The Schubert Club nurtures Minnesota musical talent and contributes to the artistic vigor of the community. The Club's many-faceted education programs currently include master classes, grants for music therapy, grants for special projects, scholarships for young composers, and the ongoing scholarship competition. From a pool of about 250 applicants each year, The Schubert Club currently awards a total of $50,000 in prizes to 30 contest winners in classical music. Anyone who has come to a Winners Recital at Luther Seminary in the springtime can attest to the amazing breadth and depth of musical talent in the Twin Cities, which The Schubert Club has helped foster with its dedication to musical education programs over the past 125 years—most recently, with the Jazz Piano Scholarship Competition.

Micah Fitch sets his wool fedora on the desk of the Dakota Jazz Club's piano and launches into a solo "Blue in Green," then "Bouncin' with Bud." Soon Jacob Siegel, sixteen years old and mostly bony shoulders and fast-tapping left foot, plays his arrangement of "Naima" in

Winners in the 2005 Jazz Piano Competition: Jacob Siegel, Elizabeth Stoiaken, and Micah Fitch.

close harmony, followed by "Armando's Rhumba" alternating nimble triplets with fierce parallel octaves. Finally, Elizabeth Stoiaken, in skin-tight black slacks and high heels, plays a cool, classy "Black Orpheus" with a blonde fringe of hair swinging over her face.

The judges, wowed by these performances, decide on three equal awards of $500 each. Such sums of money would have shocked the earliest Schubert Club scholarship winners, but the goal is still the same: increasing opportunities for students, nurturing a musical community, and creatively responding to the challenges and opportunities of the times. In our aural tradition of music, passed from teacher to student, one musician to the next, it is the fellowship that counts—the time shared learning, practicing, and creating music together.

Wrote Mrs. Briggs for her Annual Meeting address on April 18, 1923, "We find great joy in the sincere and living student within arm's reach, testifying that it is the dream that counts in his estimate of values…To such as he, would we hold ready the strength of our organization."

In 2007, the Scholarship Competition was renamed the Bruce P. Carlson Student Scholarship Competition. A plaque commemorated the change, which looks to the future while honoring the memory of a vital long-time leader.

Early Educational Presentations

Schubert Club

CONOVER HALL, DEC. 4, 1895.

The Music of the American Indians.

LECTURE, WITH PIANO ILLUSTRATIONS,

BY

MISS FRANCES DENSMORE.

..OUTLINE...

SOCIAL SONGS, - Songs of the Hæthuska Society
Songs of the Poogthun Society

INDIVIDUAL SONGS, Songs of the Warpath and Battle
Songs of Love.

RITUAL SONGS, The Tribal Prayer.
The Wa-wan, (or Calumet Ceremony)

Frances Densmore (1867- 1957) was a classically trained pianist from Red Wing, Minnesota who became legendary for her work in preserving and transcribing the music of Native Americans. Using a wind-up phonograph to record the music of thirty different tribes, she made wax cylinders that are now part of the Smithsonian's collection. Most of her work was still ahead of her at the time of this presentation for The Schubert Club—made the year that she first began lecturing.

Schubert Club

ST. PAUL, MINN.

Student Section

Music of the Olden Time

ARNOLD DOLMETSCH

assisted by

MRS. MABEL DOLMETSCH
MISS KATHLEEN SALMON

PROGRAM

Two Dance Tunes for the Lute
a. Cascarda - - - - - - - - - - - *Anon 1600*
b. Canaries - - - - - - - - - - - *Anon 1600*
MR. DOLMETSCH

A Song accompanied by the Lute
"O Mistress Mine" - - - - - - - - - *Anon 1550*
MISS SALMON

A Piece for the Virginals - - - - - - - *Anon 1600*
"The Lark, with Divisions"
MR. DOLMETSCH

An Old English Ballad for Viola d'Amore - - *Anon 17th Cen.*
MR. DOLMETSCH

"La Forlana" for the viola d'Amore, Viola da Gamba and Harpsichord - - - - - - - - - - *Anon 1660*
MR. DOLMETSCH, MRS. DOLMETSCH, MISS SALMON

Musette for the Viola da Gamba accompanied by the Harpsichord - - - - - - - - - - *Delaise d'Hewelois 1717*
MRS. DOLMETSCH

Sonata in G minor for the Harpsichord - *Domenico Scarlatti 1715*
MISS SALMON

Song accompanied by Harpsichord
Gia il Sole - - - - - - - - *Alessandro Scarlatti 1690*
MISS SALMON

Sonata for Violin accompanied by Harpsichord *G. F. Handel 1710*
MR. DOLMETSCH

Troisieme Concert for Viola d'Amore, Viola da Gamba and Harpsichord - - - - - - - - - *J. P. Rameau 1720*
Toccata for the Harpsichord . - . - - - *J. S. Bach*
MR. DOLMETSCH

Prelude in B flat for Clavichord - - - - - - *J. S. Bach*
From 1st Volume of "Das Wohltemperite Clavier"

PARK CONGREGATIONAL CHURCH,
Saturday evening, February 17th, 1906.

Special Notice. The members of the Schubert Club are invited to a Reception tendered by the Local Biennial Board to Mrs. Sarah Platt Decker, Mrs. Phillip N. Moore and Mrs. Country Ward at the Aberdeen on Monday afternoon, February 19th from three to five o'clock.

The next regular Musicale will be a Song Recital by Mrs. Jessica DeWolf in The Odeon, Wednesday afternoon, February 28th, 1906.

A pioneer in the early music revival, Arnold Dolmetsch was a musician, historian, and instrument-maker. On this program from 1906, it is difficult to determine exactly who played what. Dolmetsch, though proficient on both violin and harpsichord, seems unlikely to have played both simultaneously. His third wife, Mabel, after studies with both Arnold and his eldest daughter, was noted for her skill with the bass viol. At the time of this performance, Dolmetsch was working for the Chickering factory in Boston, superintending the building of harpsichords, clavichords, lutes, and viols. Later, back in England, he perfected the first modern recorder made to Baroque specifications. The early music center he established at Haslemere attracted scholars and musicians. With its annual festivals, it also developed a growing audience for early music and fostered an interest in historic performance practice. Dolmetsch's son Carl, a virtuoso recorder player, in addition to taking over the supervision of his father's general instrument building, developed the inexpensive plastic recorder. The Schubert Club Museum owns a couple of the latter, along with a Dolmetsch harpsichord from about 1970.

Scholarship Competition

The Student Scholarship Competition began in 1922, as part of celebrating the fortieth anniversary of The Schubert Club. It started modestly, but significantly. Three winners, representing the categories of Voice, Violin, and Piano, each received $150. By the time of the 84th annual Competition in 2007, there were thirteen different categories, most of them with both a first and second place winner, and top prizes of $2,000.

Some aspects of the Competition that were established that first year have lasted over the decades. There has always been a preliminary round as well as a final one, and, aside from the final recital, the audience is restricted to the judges and the timekeeper. On the other hand, the "five points of judgment" that were laid out that first year for the preliminary round have disappeared. Originally, the key elements were to be "for piano—rhythm, tone, technique, pedaling, and interpretation. For voice and violin—the same with the exception of intonation in place of pedaling." Now, individual judges may consider and rank all aspects as they wish, giving an overall score.

Initially, competitors had to be student members of The Schubert Club or, if male (and thus ineligible for membership), certified as students. For a time, competitors were required to have had three years of study, and to be residents (or attend school) in Ramsey County. When application fees were instituted, student membership (which existed through 2003, long after official Club memberships had vanished) granted a free or discounted application fee for the Competition. By 2007, the fee was $45, with no offsetting membership possibility. Over eighty-some years, rules change.

The four winners from 1947 included Paul Freed (right) who taught piano at the University of Minnesota for 35 years and also served as president of the Minnesota Music Teachers Association.

Why are these men smiling? The preliminary round of the competition may last as long as four hours in some divisions, and the judges, in addition to scoring the contestants, must write their critiques—clearly, helpfully, and speedily. Here are the three judges for the Junior High Strings division in 1998: Sachiya Isomura, Korey Konkol, and Michael Sutton, performers on cello, viola, and violin respectively.

In the late 1940s, students were required to select repertoire from two eras, including works by both an early composer (Haydn, Bach, Mozart, Beethoven, or others) and a later composer (Schumann, Brahms, Chopin, or modern composers). Now there can be up to five repertoire categories in a division. Piano competitors, for example, select among Baroque, Classical, Romantic, Impressionistic, and Composers born after 1880. (Renaissance is an option for other divisions.) What categories will be added in another eighty years?

Year after year, photographs of the Scholarship Winners appeared in the *Pioneer Press*. The newspaper also ran announcements about the Competition in advance and ran a short story about the Winners Recital, sometimes even listing the entire program.

Mrs. R. E. Van Kirk, Chair of the Competition Committee in the early years and underwriter of a discretionary award, pointed out the camaraderie of the competitors, something still sensed by those who work at the Prelims and the Finals. In 1925, she wrote:

> *Many who enter do not expect to be winners but say quite frankly they are glad of the experience. One of the finest things about the contest is the splendid cordial interest the students show in each other. There is no petty rivalry or ill will, just the right sort of comradeship. It is quite heart-warming.*

SATURDAY, OCTOBER 10, 1964

SCHUBERT CLUB SCHOLARSHIP FINALISTS QUIZZED

Which Long Hair Is Better: the Beatles or Bach?

Marcia · Jeanne · Mary · Norman · Barbara · Kathryn · Anita

For the first half century or so, there was regular press coverage for the Competition and for the winners. In October 1964, photographs of seven students, ages 16 to 20, ran under the caption: "Schubert Club Scholarship Finalists Quizzed – Which Long Hair is Better: the Beatles or Bach?" Two of them dismissed the Fab Four as not particularly musical, but the other five made a place for both. One young woman explained, "Friday night at the dance, Ringo captures my heart, but on Monday night when I sit down at the piano, I prefer good old Johann Sebastian."

(Above) Most of the first and second place prize winners in the 2007 Student Scholarship Competition joined in for this engaging photo taken at The Winners Recital. Their happy smiles might also reflect their pleasure in being a part of the joint Schubert Club/Twin Cities Public Television documentary about the competition, filmed for release on public television in The Schubert Club's 125th Anniversary Year.

(Left) An enthusiastic timekeeper took this photo of Byron Stripling during the Competition of 1978. Byron won first prize in the Brass division that year and went on to become a trumpet virtuoso with the Boston Pops. His Carnegie Hall debut was with Skitch Henderson and the New York Pops, and he has been a featured soloist on PBS television, with many orchestras, and at jazz festivals worldwide. An actor, singer, and conductor, he currently directs the Columbus Jazz Orchestra in Ohio.

Award amounts dropped as the Depression cast its shadow, and the number of contestants increased. In the 1930s, the award was $75, and the Voice category was divided into men's and women's categories. There was also a special "discretionary award" of $200. In the late 1950s, the piano division acquired some age categories, and Voice returned to including both genders. The Strings division morphed into "instrumental and organ" for a while in the '50s and '60s. In 1970, second place winners also received an award, and the number of instrumental and age categories blossomed. Voice and Piano had three age divisions and Strings had two. For a while, perhaps driven by the numbers of competitors, Woodwinds and Brass were separate categories.

And award amounts grew. In the thirty years since 1977, total awards have gone from $8,000 to $50,000 annually. That's a long way from the $450 of that first year.

Competition Winners

Celius Dougherty, from Glenwood, Minnesota, won the piano prize in 1924, the second year of the competition. He went on to establish himself as a composer, accompanist, and half of a piano-duo. After studies at Juilliard, he toured as an accompanist with Ukrainian-American bass Alexander Kipnis. Dougherty missed returning to Saint Paul for Kipnis's 1944 Schubert Club appearance, having formed a duo-piano team with Vincenz Ruzicka that toured extensively. The duo premiered many new works for two pianos, including pieces by Hindemith and Stravinsky. Dougherty's own compositions include a piano concerto, various sonatas, a one-act opera for children, and about two hundred songs, many of which were in the repertoire of renowned singers Marian Anderson, Povla Frijsch, and Roland Hayes. Bass-baritone George London included Dougherty on his Schubert Club concert in 1951, as did Leontyne Price—in 1983 and also in 1985 for the opening concert at the Ordway. Schirmer recently published two volumes of Dougherty's music—one a collection of art songs and the other "folksongs and chanties."

One of Iceland's most prominent composers was a Schubert Club winner. **Thorkell Sigurbjornsson** had studied violin and piano at the Reykjavik School of Music before coming to the United States where he earned his B.A. at Hamline University and a Master's from the University of Illinois at Champaign-Urbana. The Schubert Club gave him a discretionary award in the 1958 Competition and then first prize in Senior Piano the following year. Back in Iceland in the 1960s (having married a Minnesota woman he met at Hamline), he established himself as a composer and pianist. He has held positions as composition teacher, moderator of New Music with Iceland National Radio, festival director, and Chair of the Icelandic Society of Composers. He has written more than 300 pieces, with an emphasis on chamber music and choral music for church settings.

Daniel Chorzempa began studying piano at the age of four, violin at seven and organ at twelve. In 1960 he won first prize for Junior Piano in The Schubert Club Scholarship Competition, what was to become the first of many awards from The Schubert Club Piano category. In 1962 he won first prize in both Organ and Senior Piano. The Schubert Club also granted

him two discretionary scholarships for post graduate studies.

At the age of seventeen Chorzempa became instructor of music at the University of Minnesota where he later earned a Ph.D. in musicology. He pursued his studies in Europe, where he also began a career as a concert pianist. Chorzempa earned international acclaim for his performances as keyboard soloist on all five keyboard instruments—piano, clavichord, harpsichord, fortepiano, and organ. For his organ playing he was awarded the Bach Prize of Leipzig in 1968. In 1971 The Schubert Club brought Chorzempa back to the Twin Cities to perform for The Schubert Club Evening Concert Series. The *Minneapolis Tribune* called his performance a "solid display of musicianship and sensitive interpretation." His concert was the last of that series before it was renamed the International Artist Series. Chorzempa has been a member of Studio für Elektronische Musik in Cologne, Germany since 1970 and is an active composer of electronic music.

In 1972, before there was a separate category in The Schubert Club Student Competition for guitar, **Sharon Isbin** won first prize in the strings division. Six years and many awards later—including the International Guitar Competition in 1975—she performed on a Schubert Club concert. In a newspaper interview at that time, she referred to The Schubert Club Competition and noted that "my main goal in entering competitions is developing a style of preparation and gaining confidence in myself that could carry through any kind of situation." Versatile in her repertoire and her collaborations, she has made more than 25 recordings, winning a Grammy in 2001. In addition to performing 60 to 100 times a year, she chairs the guitar department at Juilliard, which she created in 1989.

Sharon Isbin was greeted by guitarist Jeffrey Van (her former teacher), following her performance with mezzo-soprano Susanne Mentzer at The Schubert Club's Saint Paul Summer Song Festival in 2004.

Beauty and Brilliance

Many Schubert Club competition winners, not surprisingly, continue with successful careers in renowned musical institutions. Somewhat more unexpected is a recurring pattern of Beauty Queens gracing the competition and then going on to receive illustrious titles in the pageantry world. In 1976 soprano Dorothy Benham was awarded first place in the Intermediate Voice category. She went on to become Miss America in 1977. In addition to serving on The Schubert Club board in later years, she has sung for several events, including the groundbreaking of the Schubert Club's Raspberry Island Bandstand. Violinist Gretchen Carlson won first place for Intermediate Strings in 1980. Nine years later she became the third Minnesotan and first classical violinist to win Miss America. Gretchen later went on to pursue a career as an anchor with Fox News. Violist Nicole Swanson earned multiple first and second place awards from 1998 to 2003. In 2006 Nicole won the title of Miss Minnesota. She has performed several times on The Schubert Club's Courtroom Concert Series. Pianist and violinist Nora Ali, who won first prize in junior high piano in 2002, was crowned America's Junior Miss in 2007. The Schubert Club is honored to have sponsored these young talents, who have continued to share their gift of classical music with the world.

From the top:
Dorothy Benham
Nicole Swanson (with violin)
Gretchen Carlson
Nora Ali

Winners Then & Now

In April 1970, the *St. Paul Dispatch* ran a photograph of the scholarship winners in The Schubert Club's Student Scholarship Competition (above). The young man second from the right is Michael Antonello, violinist. His sisters Michele and Cara Mia, flute and violin respectively, also became Schubert Club winners, and his family later established the Antonello Performance Award for string players in the Competition.

(As an aside, the young man on the far left of this picture, Richard Rames, winner in senior high piano, currently works part-time for The Schubert Club.)

Another photograph (above right) was taken after a recent Courtroom Concert that featured Michael Antonello, playing his 1720 Stradivari violin. No prize this time, but he certainly won his audience.

Thirty-five years later, we're still hearing his music.

The crop of Competition winners in 1964 included two local pianists who have continued to enrich the Twin Cities: Hiram Titus (fourth from the left)—a composer widely known for his work with theatre, television, and film, and Christine Dahl (far right)—who performs as a soloist and accompanist in addition to teaching at Macalester.

Artists as Judges

The Schubert Club Student Scholarship Competition judges are generally made up of local musicians and teachers. On occasion, however, The Schubert Club brings in internationally renowned artists from across the nation to participate in the final judging—many of whom have performed for The Schubert Club. Celebrated sopranos Evelyn Lear and Benita Valente, both Met Opera regulars and Schubert Club International Artist Series veterans, have judged the competition's vocal finalists. Mezzo-soprano Cynthia Munzer, opera and oratorio specialist, judged in 2005 and two months later hosted a master class at The Schubert Club Saint Paul Summer Song Festival.

Mezzo-soprano and opera diva Shirley Verrett judged the vocal finalists 39 years after her Schubert Club recital in the Saint Paul Auditorium in 1964. New York pianist Ursula Oppens, famous for pioneering the classical and contemporary recital, was the judge for the piano finals in 2000. Violinist virtuoso Pamela Frank judged the string finalists five years after her performance for The Schubert Club in 2000. Trombonist and Minnesota Orchestra conductor Henry Charles Smith judged the 2005 brass/woodwind finalists. Pianist Erika Nickrenz and cellist Sara Sant'Ambrogio, both members of the Eroica Trio, judged the string and piano finalists in 2006, eight years after their International Artist Series debut.

Shirley Verrett conferring with a student at the Competition in 2005.

Competition at the Competition

Ellie Bruner

Former Board President Ellie Bruner continues to volunteer for the Annual Student Scholarship Competition.

My fondest memories of The Schubert Club revolve around the Student Section, which culminated annually with Student Competitions. Board members handled most of the details including scheduling the performers, the volunteers and the judges, designing and printing up of all the score sheets, performer, volunteer and judges' schedules, providing refreshments and lunch, tabulating the scores, mailing the results and the critiques to the students, etc. Our committee of volunteers met often and the camaraderie that ensued resulted in lifelong friendships.

One year we had worked particularly hard on making sure everything was organized to the smallest detail, and the day was running very smoothly until around 11:00 a.m. Unbeknown to us, the Scottish Festival at Macalester was scheduled on the same Saturday as Competitions, and the sound of bagpipes drifting in through the open windows of the music studios made it difficult for judges to hear the student performers. The next year we made sure to check the Macalester schedule before setting the date for competitions.

I have many precious memories of my years in The Schubert Club. It was always a pleasure and a privilege to serve as a board member and as president of an organization that does so much for the musical community.

Volunteering at the Competition: A Convert

Paul Aslanian

Having served more than twenty years as chief financial officer at Macalester College, Paul Aslanian's work on the Finance Committee of The Schubert Club Board has been invaluable. And now that he has experienced the excitement of the Competition, so is his work at the registration desk during the Preliminaries.

I have served on The Schubert Club Board, off and on, for about seventeen years. For the first 15 of those years, I hid when the call went out for volunteers for the Student Scholarship Competition, thinking I had dodged another bullet. A couple of years ago I gave in, telling myself, "It's only one Saturday morning." Well, that Saturday morning had an amazing impact on me. I have become the Schubert Club cheerleader for the annual competition. The program consists of a preliminary competition in early April; two weeks later, the finals; and about two weeks after the finals, we have the winners' recital.

If you ever find yourself slipping, as I do from time to time, into the position of thinking that America's youth have all been attracted away by bright lights, glitter, and instant gratification, volunteer for the Student Scholarship Competition and plan your life around the date of the winners concert. I'm serious. The tonic of seeing these young people who have taken the very long-term view of life is palpable. As they show up for competition, they are about as nervous as their parents. To see a little guy—competing in junior high piano—wearing gloves on a warm April Saturday to keep his hands warm for the challenge, gives you some idea as to the seriousness of the day. The day is serious, the competition is stiff, and the rewards to all of us connected with the Student Scholarship Competition are immense, valuable, and reassuring.

Enthusiastic volunteers: Karen Kremer, former Schubert Club staff member who continues to help on Competition days, and Paul Aslanian, with his clipboard at the ready.

A young singer (Joan Phalen) performs in 1978 in the home of Board member Arlene Didier, who hosted many of these events.

Student Section Concerts

Until student memberships were discontinued in 2003, there were regular Schubert Club student performances in area homes. Throughout the 1990s, these recitals became increasingly problematic due to a declining interest among the students—and last-minute cancellations because of their busy lives. Karyn Diehl, who was president of The Schubert Club Board in the mid 1980s, recalls the earlier days of the home recitals. She remembers the proud parents, the rearranged furniture, and the houses where some of the audience had to sit on the steps going up to the second floor. Her warmest memories are of the students themselves and their youthful musical enthusiasm.

Music students, parents, teachers, friends and neighbors would gather in private homes on Sunday afternoons for student section concerts. The purpose of these two-hour musical gatherings was to give young performers recital experience in a very friendly and comfortable performance setting.

Each student presented approximately five minutes of music. Programs included a variety of performers ranging from upper elementary to college age students with piano, vocal, string, brass, and wind instrument performances. Selections from Bach to Bartók were enjoyed.

After the musical portion of the program was completed, everyone would gather for refreshments and conversation. All would then go their separate ways to continue their study, performance, and love of music.

Today, there are musicians in major orchestras, recording artists, and many with solo and ensemble careers who, in their youth, performed in Schubert Club Sunday afternoon student concerts.

– Karyn Diehl

My Experiences in the Student Section, 1971 – 1982

Arlene Didier

In addition to her work on a number of Schubert Club committees, Arlene Didier served as Board president in the early 1990s. She is currently a member of the International Artist Series Committee.

I was comfortably seated at my first Schubert Club Board Meeting in June, 1971, when the Nominating Committee Chair, Marge Porter, began reading off our responsibilities. I was assigned to chair the Student Competitions.

Dorothy Alshouse, seated across the room, noted the shock registered on my face. Since she had previous experience in the Competitions, she volunteered to co-chair with me. Dorothy hauled the boxes of disorganized materials home with her and brought beautiful order out of chaos and thereby began at least nine years of successful Competitions with her at the helm and with me assisting. She completely overhauled the ways and methods, and her re-designed judging critique forms are still in use.

Margaret Day, a long-time member of the Board, arranged our move from the Arts and Science Building at Tenth and Cedar to Macalester College. Not only had we used the Arts and Science Building for Auditions and Competitions, our Schubert Club office was tucked into a narrow hallway near an outside door on the lower level. When students auditioned for membership, we promised to present them in recitals during the year. In those days, it was the custom to arrange their recitals in the auditorium in the Arts and Science Building. That was not a pleasant experience with only a few parents and a teacher or two attending. It was then that Marie Brabeck and I took it upon ourselves to open our homes on Sunday afternoons, making up our own guest lists for better attendance in a better setting. The home recitals were wonderfully well attended, and the tea tables were enjoyed by students and guests alike. This form of Home Recitals continued into the mid nineties.

My association with the Student Section continued well into the eighties. While scheduling the young musicians, there was much delight in watching them progress. There was one very unusual ensemble that formed out of the membership. A young 12-year-old violinist auditioned before the Judge who was Romuald Tecco, the new Concertmaster of the SPCO. Paul Huppert received a perfect score of 15, and Mr. Tecco said to me, "I may as well pack my bags and go back to Paris with that kid around." Paul was joined by pianist Michael Ching, age 13, and cellist Laura Sewell, age 14. This same Laura founded The Lark Quartet after she finished her studies at Juilliard. The impression these young people made on their audiences was phenomenal.

Boys & Noise

The Schubert Club Boychoir

1970 – 1981

IN THE EXPERIMENTAL 1970s The Schubert Club adopted a Catholic boychoir that had been foundering for lack of funding. The choir was originally created for the Cathedral of Saint Paul in 1964 by Gerhard Lang, a former member of the Vienna Choir Boys. The Schubert Club took it under its wing in 1970. The choir ranged, over the years, from 20 to 40 members, ages 8-14. They rehearsed twice a week focusing on theory, vocal technique and recorder instruction. In the early '70s they gave about 12 performances a season. In 1975 they received numerous requests from schools, churches, business and social organizations, putting them in such high demand that they expanded to over 25 concerts for that year. One of the highlights of their time with The Schubert Club was when the choir traveled to New York with The Minnesota Orchestra to perform Benjamin Britten's *War Requiem* and Mahler's Third Symphony.

(Above Left) The Schubert Club crest that adorned all the bright blue blazers

(Above) 1981 photo of three choir members

Halama Wind Octet in the Schools

In the mid 1990s, The Schubert Club supported a residency program where the Halama Wind Octet worked with local high school bands. In each school, the Halama players were paired with an octet from the band (two each of oboe, clarinet, bassoon, and horn), providing one-on-one coaching and lessons. The combined student-professional ensemble also performed together under the direction of Halama's conductor, Marlene Pauley (on the left in the photo above).

These residencies presented a superb opportunity for younger musicians to see the discipline, commitment, and enthusiasm that the Halama performers brought to their music. Marlene Pauley, a former Schubert Club Scholarship Competition winner (clarinet), has also played with The Saint Paul Chamber Orchestra and conducted their family concerts.

Fostering Young Composers

In 2004, The Schubert Club's composer-in-residence, David Evan Thomas, selected the first young composer in the newly-established Composer Mentorship Program. The following year, when Edie Hill became one of two composers-in-residence for The Schubert Club, she expanded the program to two composer apprentices, and in the 2006-2007 season, she increased it to three.

To apply for the position, high school students send in an application form and up to three of their compositions. Activities for those selected include composition lessons, attending open rehearsals and meeting musicians, complementary American Composers Forum membership for one year, and the opportunity to have a piece performed on a Schubert Club Courtroom Concert.

The Schubert Club provides another opportunity for young composers by offering scholarships for students to attend the summer Junior Composers Institute, a week-long residential program offered through the National Federation of Music Clubs. The scholarship is offered to winners of the Minnesota Music Teachers Association Composition Contest.

Both of these programs are fairly new initiatives for The Schubert Club, but they are logical outgrowths of the organization's commissioning history—with echoes of the more distant past when the Manuscript Study Group of The Schubert Club invited composer Ernst Krenek, then teaching composition at Hamline, to bring some of his students to their meetings.

Schubert Club Special Grants

Margaret Gadient

A long-time member of the Special Grants Committee, Margaret Gadient chaired the committee for many years and helped considerably to refine and professionalize the selection process.

In addition to the annual Student Scholarship Competition, The Schubert Club offers grants to serious, talented music students in need of financial assistance to further their musical development. Most grants are used for special music education projects such as music camp, workshops, or other similar venues. The Schubert Club's history of making special grants goes back to the Educational Loan Fund of the 1890s, where money raised by these concerts provided loans for young musicians to study in Europe. In the 1920s, there were "discretionary scholarships" that supplemented the Competition awards. Eventually, the committee handling those awards developed into the Special Grants Committee, which shows up first under that name in the early 1970s.

Stories have been told of how committee members were so committed to providing young students with the opportunities they were requesting that they would supplement the budget with money out of their own pocketbooks to ensure the students would be able to participate in these life-impacting musical experiences.

In more recent times, recognizing that the grants application to The Schubert Club is often the first grant request made by many of the younger students, the committee realized that the application process itself was a significant teaching moment for students. After working with a member of the Minnesota Foundation staff about eight years ago, the committee reworked the application process and forms. They established and defined clear criteria for evaluating the requests, and they revised the system for awarding the grants. An evaluation piece was also added for the benefit of the committee, as well as for the student. For several years now, the process has been used and refined. It gives students a realistic idea of how to go about applying for a grant without being overwhelmed.

The Special Grants program gives The Schubert Club an opportunity to make awards based on both talent and financial need. The committee's greatest challenge is balancing the number of applicants and their needs, against the limited budget it honors. It is a small but wonderful program that helps to provide special opportunities in the musical development of many students.

Mozart Mania!

Jason P. Kudrna

Jason Kudrna currently works as Community Programs Manager for The Schubert Club.

I came to The Schubert Club in March 2006 after ten years of teaching high school. I came armed with energy, experience, education and a desire to work quietly in administration away from the day-to-day emergencies of ninth graders and corridors crowded with adolescents. My first week was a blessing. I was enthralled to be working in a historical office in the Landmark Center, surrounded by an 1830s Pleyel piano, an early 20th century Victor phonograph and shelves of books about composers and music. I was on my way to becoming one of those rarified intellectuals who work for the advancement of our culture through non-profit organizations. Week two found me at the Guthrie costume shop trying on tights, frock coats and powdered wigs. Week three found me in rehearsal for a play about the life of Mozart as a child. I soon learned that variety is not only the spice of life but the essence of employment at The Schubert Club.

Schubert Club staff members Holly Windle, Jason Kudrna, and David Morrison find a place as servants in the Mozart household.

Mozart Mania was born out of a Schubert Club collaboration with the Minnesota Opera and the Saint Paul Chamber Orchestra to celebrate Mozart's 250th Birthday. The Opera supplied a troupe of young singers who performed Mozart's opera, *Bastien and Bastienne*. The SPCO supplied a string quartet, their Music Hall as a performance space, and bus loads of elementary school students who arrived for multiple daily performances over the course of a week. The Schubert Club contributed a replica of an eighteenth-century Stein fortepiano, two gifted sibling pianists (Lillian and Erik Nordahl) to play the young Wolfi and his sister, and three staff members (Holly Windle, David Morrision, and I) in a dirndl, wigs, and tights to play the Mozart family servants.

The play, commissioned from playwright Beth Gilleland, told the story of Mozart in word and song. Erik and Lilly played a duet and acted out Mozartian sibling rivalry. Local actress Vera Mariner starred as *mutti* Mozart and brought a light hearted comedic touch to the role. The SPCO quartet was first rate and the small troupe of teenaged opera stars wowed the crowds with their portrayal of young love. Two *Mozart Mania* performers went on the next year to win first prize in their respective categories at the 2007 Schubert Club Scholarship Competition—Erik Nordahl for Junior High School Piano and tenor Daniel Segura for Intermediate Voice.

Tights and wigs aside, *Mozart Mania* turned out to be a positive and definitive experience for a new Schubert Club employee. The collaborative aspect of the performance exemplified how The Schubert Club works with and for the greater community. The hundreds of students and families who saw our small program experienced a taste of the dedication to education The Schubert Club promises. The Schubert Club is steeped in history, not only its own but that of the greater musical world. *Mozart Mania* brought the 18th century to life through performances on historical instruments and through three Schubert Club employees who made superb Austrian servants. Collaboration, education, history—values The Schubert Club holds dear and values that made me glad to have played a small part in *Mozart Mania*.

Museum

Holly and David were a little punchy by the time all 29 crates of gamelan instruments were unpacked

Fiske circular cornet made in America, mid 19th century

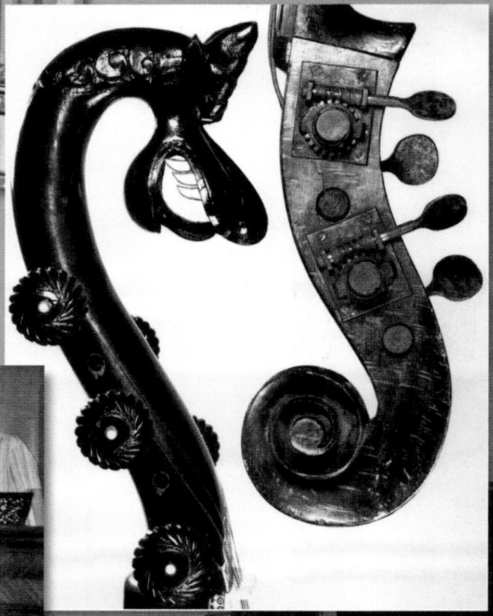

East meets West in the Kugler Collection

The young composer leading a tour, the visitors all smiles

The Gilman Ordway Manuscript Collection has three letters each from these two!

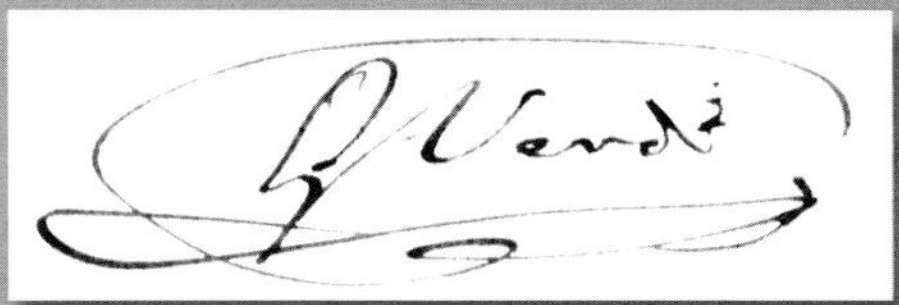

Mother and child and Beethoven letter

These are two of the remarkable instruments made by Arthur Ferris in the 1920s and '30s that are now part of the Kugler Collection. On the inside of the belly and back of these instruments, Ferris wrote ramblingly about their construction and the angelic visions that inspired him.

The Schubert Club Museum of Musical Instruments

The Museum is one of the newest additions to The Schubert Club. At thirty-five years old, this Johnny-come-lately has been in existence for less than a third of The Schubert Club's history. The public concerts that became the International Artist Series had been going on for eighty years and the scholarship competition was over fifty years old before the first historical piano arrived in 1972 to start the Museum. Now, however, the Museum is one of the three pillars of Schubert Club activity: Concerts, Education, Museum.

Origins

The Schubert Club's Museum began serendipitously, with the almost casual acquisition of a stunning nineteenth-century fortepiano that came with an impressive historical provenance. As Bruce Carlson, former executive director, explained:

It started with Dayton's. This great department store had a Senior Executive, Joe Wright, who was responsible for putting together in their 8th floor auditorium an elaborate holiday show every Christmas. One season, in the early 1970s, Mr. Wright developed a big fancy exhibition based on the theme of "A Dickens Christmas in London." Joe Wright somehow secured an authentic 1830 Kisting grand piano for this project. After the show closed, the piano was offered to The Schubert Club. I accepted this gift, stored the piano temporarily in my office, and—behold—a musical instrument museum was hatched with just one splendid gift, a beautiful fortepiano on which Brahms and Clara Schumann had often performed.

At that time The Schubert Club's offices were in the Saint Paul Arts and Sciences Center and space for keyboard storage was minimal. Instruments that were acquired in those first years were often stored in the homes of Schubert Club Board members until the time when a physical museum space could be developed.

The acquisition of instruments was varied—some instruments came by way of referrals from other museums; others were acquired by Schubert Club Board or Museum Committee members who located treasures (like the 1768 Zumpe piano that came up for auction at Sotheby's). Others were offered by owners who liked the idea of helping this new museum of keyboard instruments.

How It All Began

(Above) The donation of this Kisting fortepiano started the Museum. It had been purchased in 1835 for the Berlin home where the painter Adolf von Menzel lived with his sister and her husband, Musikdirektor Hermann Krigar. As the center of social evenings for the family's artistic and musical friends, the piano was played by Robert and Clara Schumann and later by Johannes Brahms.

(Below) Bruce Carlson stands proudly by one of the wall signs for the new museum. The signs incorporated a special font designed for the new museum by Philip Larson.

Anne Voglewede, here playing the double-manual Pleyel-Moór piano, served as museum guide and noon-time performer during the first years of the Museum.

Students from The Schubert Club's Project CHEER in 1984 explore the Museum instruments.

Bruce Carlson continued the saga:

> *The next acquisition was a rare eighteenth-century clavichord from the Moravian communities of Pennsylvania, which The Schubert Club purchased from the Edina harpsichord maker Brad Benn. Soon after that, the Science Museum of Minnesota de-acquisitioned in our direction an ancient French serpent, a fascinating wind instrument. The ball was rolling. A few mid-19th century Steinway square pianos arrived on our doorstep.*

The Schubert Club moved to new offices in Landmark Center, and in 1980 restoration work was completed for the new Keyboard Instrument Museum in the building's basement level. The space, used previously as a lunchroom by post office employees, was painted in gold and dusky rose to resemble a 19th-century drawing room. Iron gates from the old elevator were re-used as the entry gates to the museum. For the opening reception, Helen Hollis of the Smithsonian gave a greeting. Mary Briggs Sadovnikoff, a fortepiano maker and one of the proponents of the growing interest in historical instrument performance, played on the Kisting fortepiano and on another replica brought in for the occasion.

The Museum was now open. A staff member was assigned to be on duty in the Museum during the work week, and to give an informal performance every day over the noon hour. Hearing the sound of these early keyboard instruments, not just seeing them, became part of the museum experience for visitors. For pianists of any age or skill level, playing and hearing these old instruments can be a revelation. However, it takes restoration work and replacing of old parts to keep an antique instrument in playing condition, and those "improvements" often obscure the historical evidence of the original construction. Even gentle playing will eventually wear down the keys and hammers and loosen the action parts. Over centuries, the tension of the strings can pull the case out of alignment.

Surrounded by original instruments in what was then the workroom for the Keyboard Instrument Museum, Dick Sorensen worked on the keyframe of a fortepiano he made for The Schubert Club in 1982. His copy of a 1784 fortepiano by Johann Andreas Stein is the kind of instrument Mozart played.

In the Freeport, Maine workshop of Rod Regier, Holly Windle looks over the beginnings of the Museum's copy of a six-and-a-half-octave Viennese fortepiano with four pedals. Fourteen years later, Rod got to meet his instrument again, when he lectured on fortepiano construction for the 2007 Midwestern Historical Keyboard Society annual conference hosted by The Schubert Club in Landmark Center.

REPLICAS

In order not to lose the value of hearing and playing old instruments, The Schubert Club started commissioning playable replicas of historical instruments. That way, the genuine old instruments retain their historic validity by not having to be refurbished, and the new versions replicate the sound and feel of the past instruments for concerts and demonstrations.

The first copy was commissioned in 1982 from the Museum's conservator, Dick Sorensen. More instrument replicas arrived throughout the 1990s, providing pivotal examples in the evolution of keyboard instruments. Visitors can now test knee levers that sustain the notes and hear for themselves how a moderator or a bassoon rail changes the sound.

As the playable copies increased, so did the visits of music teachers. Sometimes private piano teachers bring students; sometimes a college or university class schedules a session in the Museum. On occasion, The Schubert Club offers special hands-on opportunities like the Historical Piano Workshops introduced by James Callahan in 2007. At these workshops, students play compositions appropriate to each keyboard's historical era.

1984: A WATERSHED YEAR

The Museum never aimed to bring in thousands of visitors a day. Instead, it became an oasis for music lovers, a resource for music teachers, and an inspiration for those captivated by the subtle delights of the fortepiano and the bright

Holly Windle, The Schubert Club Director of Museum Education is taught by builder David Sutherland in how to set up his copy of a 1749 fortepiano by Gottfried Silbermann.

The Schubert Club owns another Sutherland instrument—a copy of a 1726 piano by Bartolomeo Cristofori, the Italian credited with inventing the piano. (That instrument was for a time on loan to the Smithsonian Institute after they extended their *Piano 300* exhibit and had to find a replacement for the original Cristofori that had been loaned from Italy.)

Museum Associate David Morrison installs a letter from Beethoven in one of the free-standing cases. In this letter from 1815, Beethoven is arranging the purchase of a fortepiano by Johann Schantz. This letter provides a link between Museum collections because our Museum has a playable copy of a Schantz fortepiano!

charm of the harpsichord. The creation of the Keyboard Collection signaled more possibilities, as Bruce Carlson explained:

> *Bill Kugler, a big time musical instrument collector, former bandleader and musical jack-of-all trades called and said he was donating his collection to either the Smithsonian or the Metropolitan Museum of Art. Wanting to keep this vast treasure trove in Saint Paul, Schubert Club President Mildred Ellerbe, prominent arts patron Betty Musser, the Mayor, the Governor, and I (and some lawyers) leaped into action and convinced Bill Kugler and his wife Ida that they should donate everything to The Schubert Club.*

The year 1984 brought significant developments: two major donations that altered the focus of the Museum. First was the Kugler Collection, with its mixture of mundane and exotic, homegrown and international, dilapidated and pristine. It presented a fascinating look at the history of music around the world.

The second major development was the gift of a batch of twenty-three manuscripts, mostly letters, donated by Gilman Ordway—every piece a stunning link to a famous musician. Like the Kugler donation, this was to be another tremendous expansion of The Schubert Club Museum. The first manuscripts ranged alphabetically from Beethoven to Wagner. One item of particular significance to The Schubert Club was a musical manuscript written by Schubert himself, *Jägerlied* (Hunter's Song) arranged for "two voices or two horns," with text by Theodore Körner.

Gilman Ordway's donation coincided with the construction of what was then called the Ordway Music Theatre, the new home of the International Artist Series. The Schubert Club installed four cases on the theater's lobby walls for the purpose of displaying items from the Manuscript Collection. Later, Museum Conservator Dick Sorensen constructed beautiful, free-standing oak cases for additional display of the composer letters in the Museum space.

The Gilman Ordway Manuscript Collection has expanded considerably, through additional donations from Gilman Ordway himself and others, and through occasional purchases. In addition to letters, there are also signed photographs—some of them of early Schubert Club performers such as Percy Grainger and Eugène Ysaÿe.

Gilman Ordway stands beside the newly-installed manuscript cases.

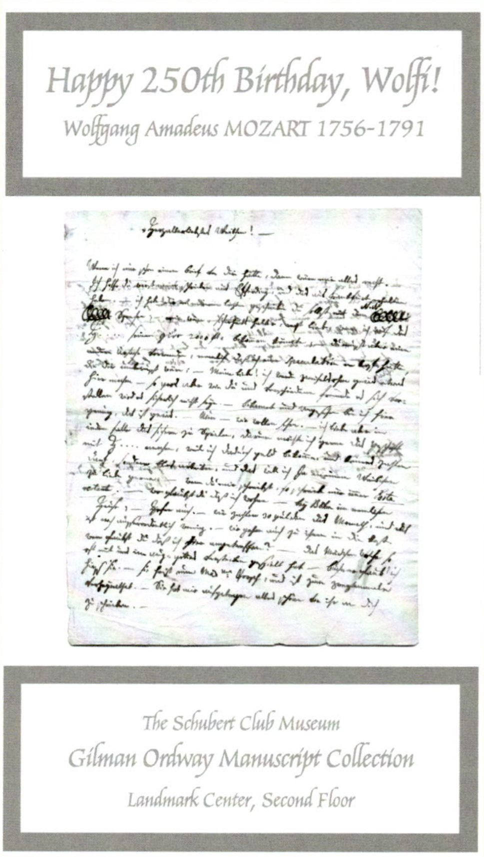

Seeing a letter from Mozart on display during his big anniversary year was an added thrill for visitors to the Gilman Ordway Manuscript Collection in 2006. The Schubert Club created a big poster directing people to the galleries where they could stand just inches from Mozart's actual signature.

Video Tour of the Manuscript Gallery

In April 2005, a video crew from Twin Cities Public Television took over the second floor galleries of The Schubert Club Museum. The result was a program about the Museum still broadcast periodically on TPT. Soprano Maria Jette comments engagingly on the letters and instruments as she moves through the Gilman Ordway Manuscript exhibits on the second floor of Landmark Center. A DVD version of The Schubert Club Museum *Composers Tour* is available through The Schubert Club.

Making Connections

Visiting musicians continue to be encouraged to tour the collection. Flautist James Galway even played one of the Museum's late 18th-century English flutes for his concert encore. Philip Blackburn of the American Composers Forum made a recording using a couple of the unusual stringed instruments made by Arthur Ferris that are part of the Kugler Collection (pictured on page 91). Brass and woodwinds from the Museum were on display in Northfield, Minnesota for the vintage Band Music Festival and Conference in the summer of 2006. Each year, the Minneapolis Institute of Arts borrows an 18th-century harpsichord as part of its period room holiday display.

Because of the Internet, The Schubert Club's collections have become internationally known to scholars and researchers. The Museum has provided detailed digital images of our Mendelssohn letters for a researcher in Leipzig and of our Liszt letters for a researcher in New York. We have taken photographs of nameboards and interiors of several of our early pianos to aid scholars from around the world. Laurance Libin of the Metropolitan Museum of Art in New York came to Saint Paul to spend a day photographing and measuring an early clavichord in our collection. Scholars from the Hardanger Folk Museum in Norway have visited to register one of the Museum's Hardanger fiddles.

And The Schubert Club hosted the 1990 American Musical Instrument Society conference and the Midwestern Historical Keyboard Society conference in 1994 and 2007.

ANOTHER WATERSHED

In 2004, The Schubert Club took over a string of five galleries on the second floor of Landmark Center, allowing the Museum to show more of the Gilman Ordway Manuscript Collection, supplemented with instruments from the Keyboard and Kugler Collections. The Museum also started to be open on the weekend for the first time, making the exhibits more available to the general public. Although it sometimes seems that visitors from elsewhere are more likely to know about The Schubert Club Museum of Musical Instruments than local residents, Landmark Center's frequent Sundays at Landmark events bring serendipitous (and enthusiastic) visitors.

NOW

The Schubert Club Museum of Musical Instruments includes nearly a hundred keyboard instruments, thousands of musical instruments from around the world, and several hundred items in the Gilman Ordway Manuscript Collection. As with many museums, the bulk of the collection is in storage where it awaits the opportunity for restoration, exhibition, research, or performance.

The Museum strengthens Schubert Club educational and concert activities. It makes sense for a recital-centered organization to be able to recreate the sounds of historical performances. It makes sense for an organization that draws on the repertoire of great composers to honor their genius by displaying documents that they wrote. It makes sense for a music-oriented institution to celebrate the amazing diversity of human musical expression.

A young performer who plays a Mozart sonata on a copy of an instrument from 1784 learns at once that Mozart was not writing for the modern piano. When *Die schöne Müllerin* is performed with an early 19th-century fortepiano, we hear how Schubert was able to make the forte-

In 1999, the Museum Committee (Ruth Donhowe, Charlotte Drake, Jane Matteson, Mildred Ellerbe, Bruce Carlson, Terry Hoffman) looks over the viola d'amore, recently restored by Andrew Dipper. The instrument, made by Paul Aletsee, dates from about 1760.

A young visitor to the second floor galleries admires the plaster cast of Chopin's hand resting in the case with a letter he wrote.

Nell Slater shows off the *Tanzbar*, an automatic accordion that operates with a paper roll.

piano sound like water rippling in a millstream. A museum visitor who gazes at Chopin's handwriting on a letter written in 1839 is reminded of the humanity of a mythic composer. Someone who looks at the fanciful dragon carved on a Javanese gamelan gong rail may reflect on the connection between visual and musical arts.

Six days a week visitors are free to browse the exhibits on their own or to take advantage of a personalized tour from one of the docents. Scholarly inquiries are always welcome, as is the help and expert assistance that scholars can offer as the Museum continues the on-going process of cataloguing, restoration, and preservation. Opportunities for growth abound, and with generosity from donors and the enthusiasm of visitors, The Schubert Club Museum will maintain its position as a treasure trove of musical history.

Searching for a Museum

George Reid

George Reid first became acquainted with The Schubert Club in the 1970s when he was head of the Education Department at the Minneapolis Institute of Arts. After a concert collaboration in the galleries that involved Schubert Club musicians, George was invited to serve on The Schubert Club Board of Directors. His museum background was needed as The Schubert Club began figuring out how to create a museum. He has continued, on and off for thirty years, to serve as a Board member and on the Museum Committee.

He recalls how he and Schubert Club Executive Director Bruce Carlson discussed the possibility of broadening the Museum's scope beyond just keyboard instruments. They knew that Bill Kugler was looking for a home for his vast collection, and Bill was happy to talk with them about his vision. However, he wanted to do more than talk; he wanted to show them a museum he liked. So one day the three of them set off.

We left Bill's house in his huge old station wagon that gave off the feeling of the old horse leaving the stable for another familiar trip through the countryside. We traveled on the minor roads in Wisconsin. Bill knew this territory, having been a leader of a touring band for years and also having tracked down many instruments for his collection in farmhouse attics, barns, and forgotten musical places throughout Minnesota and Wisconsin.

We passed slowly by a "museum" that featured a monstrous snake and a camel, among other oddities. We were afraid we would have to go in, but Bill put us at ease, saying that wasn't the kind of museum we were interested in. Several hours into the trip, Bill stopped at Dairy Queen for a break. He made a recommendation that we all have the kind of ice cream that came out of a spigot. I can taste it still.

In time we arrived at the museum Bill had in mind. The House on the Rock is a building on top of a curious geological formation in the middle of Wisconsin. The haphazard-looking building sat on or seemed to hang on top of these rocks. Bill led us with confidence up to the collection. I don't remember the visit as a big help to our thinking about the Schubert keyboard collection, but I do remember two things. We passed through a room that featured a string quartet set-up. The four chairs, music stands, sheet music, and instruments were in place, but there were no performers. All the instruments were mechanically fitted out to be played by motors and pulleys. Bill said he would get them to turn it on for us, but we insisted that wasn't necessary. Instead, he explained in more detail than necessary how it worked.

The second thing I remember was when we finally left this mechanical musical wonder and turned the corner into another room. Waving his hand at the impressive display of Lepidoptera, Bill said with his continuing enthusiasm, "Here we have the butterflies, you see!" What we saw was that there would be no limitation of scope for Bill's ideal museum.

We returned to Saint Paul. Later, Bruce and I visited other museums, including the Yale Collection of Musical Instruments in Connecticut, the Shrine to Music Museum in South Dakota (now renamed the National Music Museum), and the Stearns Collection at the University of Michigan in Ann Arbor.

Eventually, we got the Kugler Collection. Fortunately, there were no butterflies.

This sweet portrait of Charlotte Ordway hangs in the lower level museum with the following inscription:

In recognition of the generous support of Polly Ordway Wallace to The Schubert Club Keyboard Instrument Museum given in memory of her mother Charlotte P. Ordway and her Schubert Club Friends.

I assist Shirley Kysilko, Tom Kysilko, Dick Sorensen, and a mostly-obscured fifth worker in loading a Seeburg automatic piano onto the truck.

I Rode with the Wurlitzer Gang: The Kugler Move

Holly Windle

After having written a few program notes for The Schubert Club in the 1980s, Holly Windle signed on for the memorable caper described below. Four years later she came to work officially for the organization.

IN 1984, WHEN BILL and Ida Kugler agreed to give their collection of musical instruments to The Schubert Club, I was one of the crew that helped to transfer the instruments to the warehouse space in Minneapolis. Bill Kugler was still strong and wiry—and intensely interested in musical instruments. His collection had taken over their home. There was no room to acquire any more instruments, and hardly any space for the instrument-building and repair Bill used to do. More unfortunately, though, as his wife Ida could see, his growing mental confusion meant that it was time to pass on the stewardship of his collection.

Most of the people working on the move were music-lovers, recruited for what we had been told would be a couple of days of work. As it turned out, the moving went on for weeks, as we laboriously uncovered the treasures that had accumulated over the years. A small cadre stuck with the work throughout, while others came and went.

Most of the time during the move, Bill understood that he had given the collection to The Schubert Club. Sometimes, though, he would forget and be horrified to see his treasures going out the door. Once he turned the light out on us and locked us in. We took to referring to ourselves as the Wurlitzer Gang, a reference to the manufacturer of some of the automatic musical instruments we were moving and a rueful acknowledgement of Bill's variable attitude toward us.

"I understand there was a robbery here?" a voice asked tentatively. With a sinking heart, I realized that Bill, in an effort to prevent his collection from disappearing into our moving truck, had telephoned for help.

"Yes, officer," I was tempted to say. "Take me into custody." Instead, Ida and I explained the situation. The policeman left and Ida once again reminded Bill that we were moving the instruments to a better place. The Schubert Club was even planning to set up a workbench for him in the warehouse so that he could continue his instrument-making and repair. He was mollified for the time being, but we decided to quit work for the day.

The Kugler move was dirty, though fascinating, work—challenging to body and mind. Substantial physical labor was punctuated by the excitement of our discoveries, as we practiced the important discipline of moving along to the next item without undue gawking (or, heaven forbid, playing the instruments).

The huge room that held most of the instruments had gradually filled up over the years. The collection had started against the outside walls and then accumulated in subsequent vertical stratifications until there was only a narrow trail or two through the center of what had been a large dance studio addition to their Roseville home. Boards fastened together with C-clamps stretched across old pianos or boxes of instruments to provide makeshift shelving for more boxes of instruments and instrument parts. We would disassemble one layer, pack and load its harvest of brass instruments or old phonographs on to the truck, and then move on to the next layer of c-clamped shelving on top of orchestrions or a crate of ukuleles. There was also a network of tall, rolling pegboard panels with instruments fastened to them. These panels, having long ceased to have rolling room, were wedged among the music boxes, supplies from a dismantled brass instrument factory in Pennsylvania, African drums, and accordions. We filled several boxes with C-clamps over the course of the move.

I was astounded at the scope of what Bill Kugler had collected, from quirky vaudeville instruments to Civil War over-the-shoulder horns, from Chinese stringed instruments to American Indian drums and rattles. How difficult it must have been for him on those days when he did

"I was always music crazy. I'd sooner do that than eat."

– Bill Kugler, interview, 1978

Instruments in The Schubert Club warehouse.

Billie Kugler's dance band toured the country and performed locally at the Saint Paul Hotel, the Saint Paul Auditorium, and the Wildwood Amusement Park on White Bear Lake.

Bill and Ida Kugler stand under the exhibit sign made from an old band organ plaque.

not understand why his collection was dwindling before his eyes. However, I sometimes pictured him wandering through the suddenly more spacious room at the end of each day, after we had left, noting with pleasure a newly-uncovered player piano or carved vina that he hadn't seen in years.

Bill Kugler grew up a South Dakota farm boy, then played violin and saxophone before becoming a bandleader in the 1930s. After settling in the Twin Cities, he ran a violin shop, later owned a music store, and then operated a music and dance studio with his wife. Throughout his long career, he collected instruments. Once they were established in Roseville, his wife's education background helped him make his museum an exciting tour destination for students. Tours of fascinated schoolchildren visited the crowded aisles, gawked at the unfamiliar instruments, and listened to Bill Kugler talk about the history of music. He let them play conch shells as part of the tour, then bugles, and finally (illustrating the evolution of brass instruments) trumpets. Eventually the acquisitions reached a point where the fire marshal put a stop to the tours. Bill and Ida still wanted their instruments to educate and enthrall, and in their new home with The Schubert Club, they would.

At some point, we brought Bill over to the new warehouse, to see where the instruments were being put on racks of sturdy metal shelving. He wandered through the rows, shaking his head. "I used to have one just like this," he would say. "No, Bill," I explained over and over, "this is yours." He never did come and use his workbench in the warehouse.

A year later, Bill and Ida Kugler came to the opening of The Schubert Club's special exhibit "Bill Kugler: Music Man and Collector." Bill may not have understood exactly what all the fuss was about, but he realized that many people were grateful to him for having preserved and passed on so many interesting instruments. And many of the items on display were old friends to him.

The interior of the Mills Violano, a coin-operated automatic piano and violin with no keyboard.

Keyboard Curiosities from The Schubert Club's Collection

The Schubert Club Museum has quite a variety of keyboard instruments on exhibit, but there are many more which are rarely shown to the public, either because they are in need of restoration, or because there just isn't room for them. Some are stored in Landmark Center, and some in a nearby warehouse. The range and scope of the collection is a fascinating mix of the historical and curious.

At the humble end of the spectrum is a reed organ from around 1900 in the shape of a tall upright piano. It has what looks like piano pedals but which are really the pumping pedals for the bellows. It was designed to appeal to those who wanted their home to be graced by that symbol of middle-class status, a piano, without the expense. Reed organs were much cheaper than pianos.

There are more normal-looking unashamed reed organs as well, including one with beehive decorations stencilled on it, and even a transposing reed organ (the Museum also has two transposing pianos). There are portable reed organs from India, with a bellows at the back which is squeezed with one hand while playing the small keyboard with the other. Indian music does not use chords, so two handed-playing isn't necessary. The Indian harmonium does have, however, drone stops that provide a continual note. A more familiar and more ergonomic bellows-driven instrument is the accordion and the Museum has no fewer than seventy-six of those!

When is a piano not a keyboard instrument? That sounds like a riddle, but player-pianos designed for use in bars and cafes often had piano actions, but no keys. While this made it a challenge for the piano-tuners, it did prevent patrons from striking up their own tunes. Our collection has a Mills Violano, which plays a violin and piano. It is controlled by a perforated paper roll, and powered by electricity. This is especially novel, since electricity was not widely available in 1905 when it was made. It is also unusual in that the lowest notes (the longest piano strings) are in

(Above) The surprising Dolcette.
(Right) On a visit to the Museum in the 1980s, pianist Peter Serkin gets a demonstration of the Hupfeld player piano from Museum Conservator Dick Sorensen.

the middle of the "harp," with higher notes ascending alternately right and left. If you've played a kalimba or "thumb-piano" you'll be familiar with that arrangement. (The Schubert Club has several of those, too.)

In addition to the pianos with no keys, there are the pianos with nothing but the keys: the practice keyboards. Nowadays, people who don't want to disturb their neighbors can play an electronic keyboard and listen to themselves on headphones. But in earlier days, serious pianists used a keyboard which had an adjustable "touch" but which made no sound. One such keyboard, which was used by Rachmaninoff on his travels, has been on display in the second-floor gallery of our Museum.

Then there's the "street piano" which has no keyboard but is played by a large pinned cylinder, like a music box. The Schubert Club has at least one of these instruments and multiple parts for others. They were outdoor devices subjected to the elements, and not very highly regarded even when new, so many have not survived intact.

The Schubert Club's collection has several conventional pneumatic player-pianos, but more unusual is the completely mechanical player mechanism of our Hupfeld upright piano, made in Leipzig around 1900. This uses a loop of stiff perforated cardboard which moves laterally, under the keybed, propelled by a crank. Little levers under the cardboard are twitched when a hole passes by, and push the appropriate rods against a long rotating rubber-covered spindle, which provides the force to strike the notes. We have only one cardboard loop, and it's not in very good condition. But that doesn't really matter, since the mechanism probably never worked very well anyway.

Another oddity is the Dolcette, which is shaped like a delicate upright piano, but has the strings visible above the keyboard, rather like a large upended auto-harp. When a key is struck and held, a hammer repeatedly thrums against the string. It is like a cross between a mandolin and a hammered dulcimer.

One of the historic keyboards which has not yet been on exhibit is a Nannette Streicher fortepiano from around 1820 which has a large drum and bells built in for the special effects needed for the Turkish or Janissary music which was an exotic fad among European musicians of the late 18th and early 19th century.

A visit to the Museum makes it clear that the piano changed rapidly in the early 19th century and there was much experimentation with the mechanism at that time. Such experiments continued into the 20th century, but most failed to catch on. There is a Pleyel grand piano in the collection which has two keyboards, much like a double-manual harpsichord or organ. This was an invention from the 1920s, of the Swiss musician Emanuel Moór. The upper keyboard played an octave higher than the lower, and could be coupled to the lower. Where the two keyboards meet there is a kind of overlap or common area, so notes from the two keyboards could be played more easily with one hand. This piano was championed by a few pianists, but the practical aspects of getting manufacturers to make them, and then haggling with concert-presenters over who would pay the cost of transporting them on tour, proved to be too daunting.

Another unusual Pleyel grand piano in the collection is a double grand, for two pianists, with the two keyboards facing each other, and the strings sharing one large cast-iron plate. This also proved not to be successful, either commercially or technically–the one we have has a broken plate, presumably due to its experimental design not having had a chance to be refined over the years. Commercially it must have been a hard sell, since it would be unwieldy to move, and probably not any cheaper than two ordinary and more versatile grand pianos.

With such a large collection, there is always something unusual and fascinating that is not on public display. But the Museum's collection stands ready for more restoration, more visits by scholars, and more chances for exhibition. It is the hope of many that someday, these instruments will be able to be appreciated by museum visitors.

The Kugler Series

A few years after the acquisition of the Kugler Collection, The Schubert Club created a concert series inspired by that collection's variety of instruments from around the world. From 1991 to 1996, concerts representing different classical (and non-classical) music traditions were given in a number of different locations, often as co-sponsorships: Vietnamese folk and art music, Macalester's Chinese Music Ensemble, Taiwanese music, Iranian santour music, Javanese gamelan music and dance, Indian sitar and sarod, and Lakota flute player Kevin Locke.

Performers might have local, national, or even international fame, and the audience size ranged from a couple dozen in The Schubert Club Museum to full houses at Macalester College's Janet Wallace Fine Arts Center. Sometimes a playful streak would enter into the title, as with the "Gaga for Raga" performance of Indian music or "Piping Hot," an array of bagpipers assembled by local Northumbrian piper Dick Hensold.

Kevin Locke, with the 28 hoops from his Lakota hoop dance on his shoulder (and the sweat from his impressive exertions still glistening on his face), greets Mrs. Kugler and other fans after a performance in Landmark Center.

The Schubert Club had been involved with non-Western music earlier, starting with study sessions in the beginning of the last century that included learning about classical and folk music traditions from other parts of the globe. In 1967, The Schubert Club presented a Latin American Music Seminar and Festival. The increasing emphasis on diversity in the 1970s brought a significant number of world music programs. African instruments were played at one of the season's "impromptus" in 1970, and there was a pipa and chin concert by Tsun-Yuen Lui, head of Chinese music studies at the Institute of Ethnomusicology at UCLA. A collaboration with the Performing Arts Program of the Asia Society presented "Chinese Skin Shadow Plays" by Tech-cheng Chang at Macalester College and the Topeng Dance Theatre of Bali in the O'Shaughnessy Auditorium at the College of St. Catherine. The Schubert Club co-sponsored a North Indian dance performance with the University of Minnesota. In 1979, there was a Schubert Club program in Saint Paul high schools called "Ethnic Influences on our Musical Heritage" with the following topic areas: Japanese, Black, Spanish-Mexican, Balkan, and Scandinavian.

When The Schubert Club acquired a full set of Indonesian gamelan instruments in 1995, the growth of gamelan-related programs (classes, workshops, and performances) absorbed most of the non-Western focus of the organization. Indonesia was also the source of the words

The poster for the Piping Hot performances (of which there were two over the years) featured a border of bagpipes. Despite taking place at Macalester College with its long Pipe Band tradition, the concert did not include the Great Highland pipes, opting instead for an assortment of bagpipes deemed more suitable for an indoor performance.

Harpsichordist Frances Pelton-Jones usually performed in costume suitable to the era of the music.

stenciled on the door of one Schubert Club office: "Aneka ragam musik sedunia"—different kinds of music in the world. Most of the gamelan activities have now been spun off to another organization, but the wealth of Kugler instruments in the Museum testify to the diversity of human musical expression.

Early Instruments in Concert and Recording

Long before The Schubert Club had its own harpsichords, clavichords, and fortepianos in the Museum, the organization put on concerts with these instruments. Arnold Dolmetsch, a principal figure in the revival of interest in the harpsichord, performed for The Schubert Club in 1906. One of his most famous American pupils, Frances Pelton-Jones, gave a concert fourteen years later. Harpsichords continued to be heard periodically throughout the decades, and The Schubert Club Collection of Keyboard Instruments (as it was first called) brought a surge of activity for early keyboard instruments in particular. Performers on Schubert Club instruments have included Malcolm Bilson, Gustav Leonhardt, Melvyn Tan, Joan Benson, Robert Levin, Penelope Crawford, Roger Goodman, and Christopher Hogwood. Sometimes other instrumentalists and singers—like cellist Anner Bylsma and baritone Sanford Sylvan—were involved. The Smithsonian Chamber Players with pianist Lambert Orkis were on the Chamber Music Series, and in the 1984-85 season, The Schubert Club presented a Festival of Visiting Baroque Orchestras with Tafelmusik, the Academy of Ancient Music, Ars Musica, and the Orchestra of the 18th Century.

When Belgian pianist Jorg Demus performed on the International Artist Series in 1982, he used two instruments from The Schubert Club Museum in addition to a modern piano. One was a recently-completed copy of a 1784 by Johann Andreas Stein (built by Schubert Club conservator Richard Sorensen), and the other an 1824 fortepiano attributed to Conrad Graf of Vienna. Around that time Peter Serkin recorded Beethoven sonatas and Schubert dances on the Graf. (These recordings, out of print for some time, are now going to be re-issued by Vanguard Classics.)

After the Museum was established, there were variously-named concert series that used Museum instruments or other early instruments.

This informal picture, taken during the recording session, shows a dressed-down version of both performer Peter Serkin and the fortepiano (where the less-attractive wood on the flat side of the instrument is in contrast to the beautiful veneer on the "audience side").

At first, focusing on the Collection, the series was called the Authentic Instrument Series—but not for long. The Historical Instrument Series (1990s) became the Early Music Series by the end of the decade, after The Schubert Club had co-sponsored concerts with the St. Paul Early Music Series, a local group that was happy to pass on the programming to The Schubert Club.

In the past fifteen years, the series has included excellent local musicians as well as internationally-renowned individuals and ensembles: King's Noyse, the Baltimore Consort, Piffaro, violinist Andrew Manze, recorder player Marion Verbruggen, lutenists Paul O'Dette and Hopkinson Smith. Sometimes the presentation has been entirely vocal, as with the Tallis Scholars and Anonymous 4—with no reference to the Museum instruments at all. There have been co-sponsorships with the Bach Society of Minnesota and the Lyra Baroque Orchestra. Belladonna baroque quartet has become the artists-in-residence for the series, performing each of the past seven seasons.

Belladonna performers, in their customary high spirits and white outfits: Barbara Weiss (harpsichord), Margaret Humphrey (baroque violin), Cléa Galhano (baroque recorders) and Rebecca Humphrey (baroque cello).

Herb Scherer with the Kugler Collection's Victor XXV—the "Schoolhouse Victor" manufactured from 1913-1925, with a lockable cover and a state-of-the-art acoustic sound system.

Musical Horn of Plenty

In 1992, The Schubert Club presented a series of three concerts in a small wood-paneled courtroom in Landmark Center. *Musical Horn of Plenty: Historic Recordings from the Golden Age* was the brainchild of Herb Scherer, longtime art librarian at the University of Minnesota. Using a handsome oak phonograph from the Kugler Collection, he shared music from his pristine collection of 78-rpm phonograph records.

The first revelation to the audience was that "old records" could sound beautiful—clear and loud—if they have been properly cared for and are played on a good phonograph with a new needle. One presentation, entitled "Looking Back: Instrumental and Vocal Selections from Past Schubert Club Performers, 1900-1925," featured recordings by Schubert Club artists, including soprano Lucrezia Bori, violinist Jascha Heifetz, the Flonzaley Quartet, pianists Alfred Cortot and Percy Grainger, and tenor Tito Schipa.

The second revelation was the thrill of hearing these long-ago performers through a wooden horn, as many people (not fortunate enough to attend their Schubert Club concerts) would have heard them.

Museum Outreach

The Schubert Club offered educational programs from the beginning—first for its members and later for the wider community. A century later, the resources of the Museum opened up new possibilities. And, because Museum exhibit space is limited, sometimes those educational activities go beyond the walls of the galleries.

In its first decade, the Kugler Collection inspired a "Museum on Tour" program that used instruments from a variety of cultures in classroom or assembly presentations. The most popular topic was "Music in the Environment," exploring how people have made music from the materials at hand. The presentation showed how gourds, bamboo, and animal skins became part of rattles, flutes, and drums, and how found objects like conch shells or discarded steel drums become transformed into musical instruments.

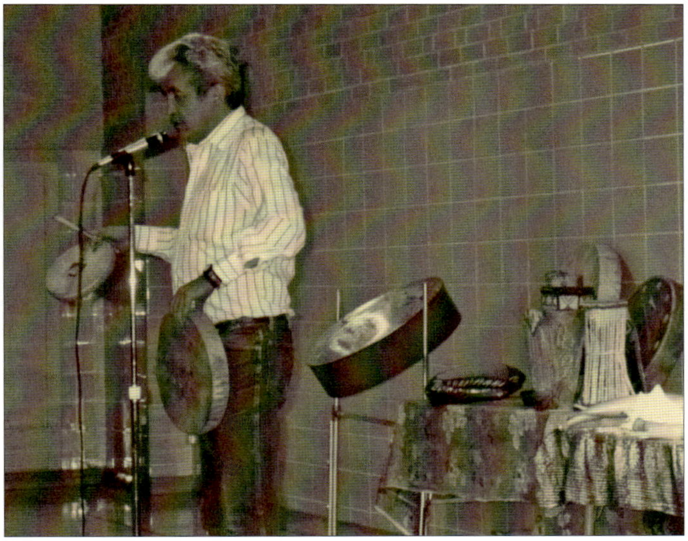

(Above) "Music, Myth, and Magic," with Miriam Gerberg and John Munzer, toured schools and libraries in the 1990s.

(Right) In a "Museum on Tour" school program in the 1990s, Native American musician Johnny Smith explains the symbolism of the painting on a drum.

In 1994, The Schubert Club commissioned two talented performers, composer/musician Miriam Gerberg and choreographer/actor John Munzer, to create a touring program for children that incorporated musical instruments from the Kugler Collection into stories. The multicultural program blended story telling, world music, theatre, and dance. "Music, Myth, and Magic" dazzled audiences at libraries and community centers, while introducing children to instruments that included the Japanese koto, an Arabic oud, and a Mexican guitarrón.

After the acquisition in 1995 of a full set of gamelan instruments from Java, The Schubert Club was able to offer longer-term residencies, as well as performances, in the music of another culture. Currently, most of the gamelan outreach activities are handled through the Indonesian Performing Arts Association of Minnesota. (See the gamelan article to learn how these activities evolved.)

The Museum also occasionally arranges for educational loans and special exhibits outside of the Museum.

The Schubert Club Gamelan Program

One of the most ambitious—and perhaps least likely—of The Schubert Club Museum's programs was centered on the classical music of Java. The specialized instruments of the gamelan orchestra that the music is performed on are mostly percussion, including huge hanging gongs, ranks of kettle gongs, and bar metallophones. In 1995, when The Schubert Club commissioned a complete hand-forged bronze gamelan set from a respected maker in Java, there was no gamelan in Minnesota, although there were already almost two hundred gamelan ensembles elsewhere in North America.

There was apparently a good deal of pent-up demand for gamelan music in the area. The Schubert Club's community classes in gamelan music, led by a talented musician from Java, Joko Sutrisno, quickly filled three nights a week. By 1996 a performing ensemble had been established. After a year, the instruments had revealed their character to the extent that a traditional naming ceremony was held. The Schubert Club's gamelan was christened *Kyai Medharing Madu*, or the Venerable Blossoming of Honey. The word "medharing" means spreading out like ripples emanating from the center of a pool or the radiating scent of a flower, and it reflects the expansion of the gamelan program.

Demand grew for elementary school residencies, and The Schubert Club bought a set of "traveling" iron gamelan instruments for school programs. A second bronze set was bought and lent to St. Cloud and Winona State Universities. Soon The Schubert Club was helping other schools, individuals, and institutions with the purchase of their own gamelan instruments. Normandale French Immersion School, the Bloomington School District, St. Cloud Public Schools, the National Music Museum, and others all own their gamelan instruments thanks to The Schubert Club's efforts.

(Above) The Schubert Club brought the exotic beauty of Indonesian gamelan music to thousands of area students in hands-on workshops and residencies.

(Below) In 2001 The Schubert Club Gamelan Ensemble released a recording of traditional music from Java.

With its classes, workshops, residencies, and performances that included traditional Javanese dance and shadow puppet plays, the gamelan program was a wonderful educational outreach. However, by 2002 it was apparent that it really had grown far beyond The Schubert Club's core mission of promoting western classical recital music. In addition, the amount of staff time and effort diverted into running such a complex and wide-ranging program was huge. Consequently, a new, independent non-profit organization, the Indonesian Performing Arts Association of Minnesota (IPAAM) was created to take over administration of the gamelan program with The Schubert Club's blessing. With the loan of some of The Schubert Club's gamelan instruments, IPAAM has continued the excellent work of bringing the music of this venerable Asian tradition to Minnesota schools and audiences.

One completely unintended, but happy, consequence of the Schubert Club's acquisition of these exotic Asian instruments is the creation of a body of new, contemporary music for gamelan orchestra. A group of former students from the Schubert Club gamelan program have been meeting weekly—for over four years—to rehearse their original compositions of mostly western-influenced music. Under the name "International Novelty Gamelan" they perform occasionally, and are releasing a recording. The ripples keep expanding.

Exhibits

For the Museum's first decade or so, keyboard instruments were the focus of the exhibits, because the Gilman Ordway Manuscript Collection and the Kugler Collection had not yet been added to the Museum's collections. Two early exhibits, *Composers and their Pianos* and *The Piano in American Life*, highlighted items from the Keyboard Collection. Later, in the 1980s and '90s, the exhibit galleries drew on the expanded collection. *Incredible Music Machines: History of the Phonograph*, for example, was a popular exhibit that showed the shift from home-made recordings on wax cylinders to celebrity performers on disks.

Henry Steinway, great-grandson of the founder of the Steinway piano industry, has visited the Museum several times over the years and given advice about the Steinway instruments in the collection.

(Above) Sean Farley has been tuning Schubert Club instruments for twenty-five years. Here, he works on the copy of a 1726 piano by Bartolomeo Cristofori.

(Left) The *Song of India* exhibit included instruments Bill Kugler had collected in the 1970s—as well as a gourd to show the raw material from which some of the resonators were made.

Meanwhile, the newly-installed cases at the Ordway provided a place for The Schubert Club to begin displaying Gilman Ordway's remarkable collection of letters. After the first Kugler-oriented exhibit in Landmark Center, the Museum collaborated with local violin expert Claire Givens to create an exhibit (and book) about *Violin and Bow Makers of Minnesota* in 1988. Instruments made by fifteen living and fifteen past makers were displayed.

With the advent of playable keyboard copies, a more structured tour evolved in the Museum to give visitors an understanding of the evolution of the piano. This historical focus (often with a hands-on component) has supplanted the gallery-wide themed exhibit, though the back gallery can still be used for targeted displays.

One exhibit, *Song of India*, was inspired by a comment from a visiting scholar that he hadn't seen such a collection of Indian instruments outside of Bombay. Sitars and vinas were hung on the wall, with panels of sari material behind them. Local painter and sitar player Bill Stille created beautiful illustrations that showed how the instruments would be played. He also did restoration work on many of the instruments and wrote about them for the exhibit's booklet. The variety of drums included one made from a jackfruit log, a large kettledrum, and also a beautiful five-headed drum. A typical two-foot tall *sarangi* (a bowed instrument) was displayed next to one nearly seven feet tall. Other surprises included a vina in the shape of a crocodile, and a sitar made with an ostrich egg as the resonator.

The Gilman Ordway Manuscript Collection now has two display cases in the Saint Paul

Public Library, as well as cases at Ordway Center and in the Museum's second floor galleries in Landmark Center. The Library cases sometimes include sheet music or an instrument from the Kugler Collection along with a composer's letter. A letter from John Philip Sousa was displayed with a cornet, and one from Percy Grainger with a glockenspiel. Often the exhibit commemorates a significant birthday, like Mozart's 250th in 2006, where a plastic "action figure" of Mozart was included in the case. *Hand of the Master*, in the second floor galleries, juxtaposed a letter from Chopin with an actual plaster cast of the composer's hand. Cases with letters from Tchaikovsky, Mendelssohn, Mozart, Haydn, Beethoven and others broadened the exhibit into a comprehensive look at a very personal side of legendary, world-famous composers.

Bellezza d'Italia Exhibit

IN 2003, THE SCHUBERT CLUB MUSEUM mounted the exhibit "Bellezza d'Italia" (Beauty of Italy), which highlighted letters from the Gilman Ordway Manuscript Collection. Italian keyboards from the Museum's collection were also featured, as well as large watercolor paintings on Italian themes by acclaimed regional artist Mary Rice. Several of the paintings included representations of manuscripts and instruments from the Museum's collections, among them "Rasina's Afternoon Delight" (*above*) which includes a Puccini letter. The instruments on display represented six centuries, from the 16th century Rossi pentagonal spinet to the 21st century GEM *pianoforte digitale*. Letters chosen were from composers inspired by the beauties of Italy, such as Mendelssohn, Berlioz, and Argento, and from Italy's native sons, Puccini, Rossini, and Verdi.

The Spiering Papers: A Life in Music

The Manuscript Collection, established through the generosity of Gilman Ordway, has become a magnet for gifts from other donors. Foremost among these is a remarkable collection of material relating to the German-American violinist and conductor Theodore Spiering (1871-1925). Letters, photographs, and other memorabilia—including a signed commission by President Lincoln—donated by Spiering's daughter Wilma Guyot open a window on American cultural life of the late nineteenth and early twentieth centuries.

Theodore Spiering, American violinist, conductor, educator.

Spiering, a violin prodigy, was born in Saint Louis into a highly cultured and politically active family, whose patriarch had fled Europe in the wake of the failed liberal revolutions of 1848. Young Spiering's musical schooling took him to

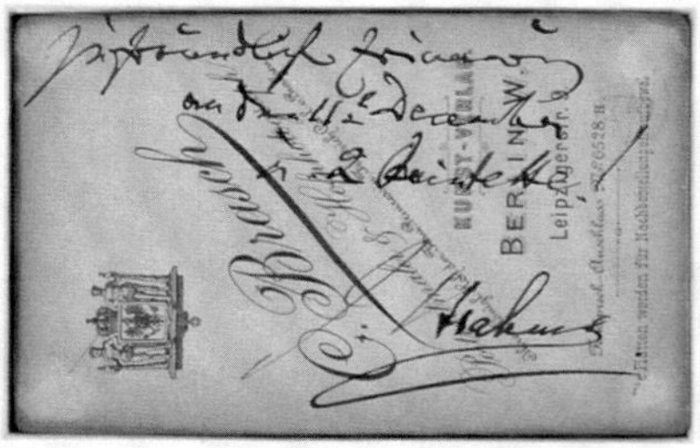

Carte-de-visite autographed by Johannes Brahms (with the composer's photo on the other side) when young Spiering performed a new quintet for the maestro.

Europe where he studied under famed violin virtuoso Joseph Joachim, and made the acquaintance of Johannes Brahms.

Back in Chicago, Spiering's quartet played an informal premiere for Antonín Dvořák of the composer's "American" quartet. Spiering's musical career kept him active on both sides of the Atlantic and reached a highpoint when Gustav Mahler, assuming the leadership of the New York Philharmonic, engaged Spiering as concertmaster. Spiering subsequently took over the helm of that orchestra during the Maestro's final illness, conducting seventeen concerts.

Signature of Gustav Mahler from one of five letters in the collection written to Spiering by the great Austrian composer.

From the many fascinating pieces of the Spiering collection, a picture comes into view of a once vibrant, now vanished German-American culture. It is a significant testimony to a world that changed utterly with World War I and its aftermath.

A Musical Tribute to Gilman Ordway

Using a tune by one of the composers in the Gilman Ordway Manuscript Collection, Holly Windle of The Schubert Club created a musical tribute to Gilman Ordway and to the many superb letters from composers that he has given the Museum over the years. The song was performed at a reception held at the home of Ford and Catherine Nicholson in June 2006, during one of Gilman Ordway's periodic visits to Minnesota.

Maria Jette, having just performed a song in praise of Gilman Ordway (right), makes a point of introducing him to her (off-camera) accompanist.

To the tune of Gilbert & Sullivan's "I am the very model of a modern Major-General"
from *The Pirates of Penzance*

He is a major model of a man of generosity:
A fan of words and letters, but not given to verbosity.
In 1984, he changed The Schubert Club's long history
By giving us some manuscripts – of that there is no mystery.

That crucial batch of twenty-three fine letters that he gave to us
Began a new direction that makes visitors now rave to us.
From Beethoven to Wagner, also Brahms and Grieg and Debussy—
Material for showing off and putting on the web, you see.

And so the Schubert Club increased its pattern of exhibiting
Because of all the manuscripts that Gilman was distributing.
He's fond of words and letters, but not given to verbosity.
He is a major model of a man of generosity.

And through the years, more letters. The collection grew progressively.
The roster of musicians he's augmented most impressively.
The cases at the Ordway bear his name and show variety,
But we can never show it all in glorious entirety.

There's Sousa and Stravinsky, dear Franz Schubert and Sibelius,
Two Strausses (Richard and the one with "Waltz King" as his alias),
The man who wrote the music to Mikado and this very song.
Berlin, Cole Porter, Herbert – men who well could write a merry song.

For opera buffs: Puccini, Verdi, Weber, Donizetti too,
And Mozart who gets accolades and, in this year, confetti too.
For all of these, in letters that compete in fabulosity,
He is a major model of a man of generosity.

And that is why the Schubert Club expanded to new galleries
And hired some new docents (but at reasonable salaries).
Now visitors who come to see Chopin, Tchaikovsky, Mahler too
Include some great performers and occasion'ly a scholar too.

When teachers bring their students for a field trip educational,
Informative museum tours are also inspirational.
For Mendelssohn has handwriting that's neat and full of curlicues,
While Beethoven's is bad – a scrawl you wouldn't of a churl accuse.

The Gilman Ordway Manuscript Collection has sublimity,
And all is due to one man's very thoughtful magnanimity.
So we express our gratitude with musical velocity:
He is a major model of a man of generosity.

Administration

Temporary offices were at 5th and Wabasha—second floor, on the corner—while waiting for Landmark Center renovations

A fine demonstration of staff teamwork

Letterhead from the early days

Schubert Club
of
St. Paul, Minn.

Annual meeting notice from 1901

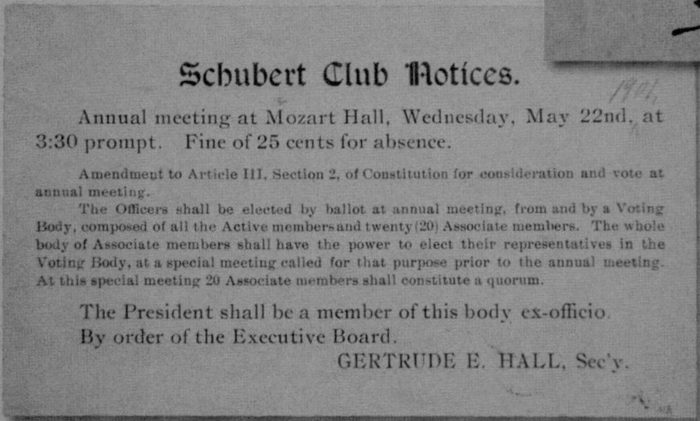
Schubert Club Notices.

Annual meeting at Mozart Hall, Wednesday, May 22nd, at 3:30 prompt. Fine of 25 cents for absence.

Amendment to Article III, Section 2, of Constitution for consideration and vote at annual meeting.

The Officers shall be elected by ballot at annual meeting, from and by a Voting Body, composed of all the Active membersand twenty (20) Associate members. The whole body of Associate members shall have the power to elect their representatives in the Voting Body, at a special meeting called for that purpose prior to the annual meeting. At this special meeting 20 Associate members shall constitute a quorum.

The President shall be a member of this body ex-officio.
By order of the Executive Board.
GERTRUDE E. HALL, Sec'y.

Florence Fairchild designed our logo in 1892

Nine Schubert Club presidents pose for a snapshot

All in a day's arts administration

The Executive Board, 1910. Not all of their meetings were indoors.

The March of Time

THE WOMEN WHO CREATED and ran The Schubert Club in the early days of the twentieth century were remarkable. This was a powerhouse organization almost from the beginning, with a network of committees that met regularly and divided up the work to make the organization run.

Executive Committee members held meetings every two weeks, reporting on their activities since the last meeting and determining the next actions. In the first seventy years, there were fifteen to twenty-five subsidiary committees that carried out specific duties and met regularly. The Secretary's Books are a chronicle of "motioned," "seconded," and "carried" that reflects incredible dedication and wide-ranging concern about the musical life of Saint Paul.

In addition to the regular concerts and lectures by members and visiting musicians, there were free concerts in factories and orphanages. (The Philanthropy committee supplied fifty-two such programs in 1921.) Teas

The Schubert Club Board in 1935. Did they all agree to tip their hats the same way?

were held to recruit or welcome new members. (The Hospitality Committee hosted 23 in the 1909-10 season.) Schubert Club members ran the annual Scholarship Competition, wrote weekly press releases, sold ads, found paying engagements for student members, supported civic projects (like the municipal organ in 1920 for which they raised money), and provided music lessons. In 1936, the 25th anniversary of The Schubert Club Music School program, there were twelve different locations and 17 teachers, providing more than 4,500 lessons annually.

The shortened story of The Schubert Club often emphasizes the huge change that took place with the hiring of an executive director in 1968, and the subsequent growth of a staff to replace the work that had originally been carried out by volunteers. It was the gender of the person hired, rather than his position that was the real break with tradition. Bruce Carlson's original title of "business manager" had been used back in 1914 when the Board first authorized Mrs. Briggs to hold that position for $500 a year.

The shift to paid staff was significant, but we should recognize the impressive number of volunteer hours that were being devoted to the planning and activities of The Schubert Club in, say, 1920. At times, it may not have been much less than is covered now by the full-time equivalent of nine employees and our current schedule of events.

Many Schubert Club activities from the pre-WWII era gradually disappeared and never were replaced. Some of the social activities (afternoon teas, for instance) lost ground as more women took paying jobs. Saint Paul reached a cultural level where there no longer seemed such a need for The Schubert Club's regular lectures and demonstrations about various aspects of music, with papers presented to the members by musicians and scholars in the organization. The availability of excellent live classical music increased dramatically as the Twin Cities grew.

And after World War II, music education in the schools had made the network of Schubert Club Music Schools less necessary.

On the other hand, recent decades have brought new areas of activity for the organization. The Museum, visited by thousands of people each year, has galleries on two floors of Landmark Center that are staffed and open twenty-four hours a week. In addition to the annual scholarship competition (which has grown hugely since its inception), The Schubert Club now offers other scholarships and grant programs for young musicians. The leaders in the early years did not envision that the organization would be involved also in commissioning new music, publishing books, producing recordings (both CDs and DVDs), and maintaining a website. All of these activities rest on the grounding of commitment to music and a belief in civic outreach that was established by the hard-working leaders and members of the early days.

As past president Florence Briggs said in her President's Report of 1910, "In looking backward, we would bow in reverence to the works of many days that are gone, take to our hearts the lessons to be learned from the gathered up experience of the past and summon our courage for the look forward."

Anita Furness, the daughter of Marion Ramsey Furness (one of the organization's founders) joined The Schubert Club in 1910, when she was 32 years old. She served on the General Membership Committee, chaired the Reception Committee and later the Printing and By-Laws Committees. She was on the Board as a vice president, eventually holding an honorary vice presidency. When she died in 1964, she had served The Schubert Club for 54 consecutive years.

The Organization's Evolving Purpose

Constitution, 1892
Article I.
The name of this Association shall be THE SCHUBERT CLUB, and its object the study and practice of the best music and the promotion of a refined taste among its members.

Constitution, 1900
Article II. THE OBJECT
The object of this Club shall be:
First—to study and practice the best music.
Second—to advance the interests and promote the culture of musical art in the City of St. Paul.

Season Booklet, 1964
The purpose of the Schubert Club is to stimulate interest of music in St. Paul and to encourage the talented musician.

100th Anniversary Year booklet, 1982

The Schubert Club
Purpose

To promote the art of music, particularly recital music, through education, performance and museum programs—and to maintain a high standard of artistic excellence.

This last statement remains the mission of the organization today.

Board Presidents, Past & Present

Florence Miller Raudenbush and The Schubert Club

CHRISTOPHER DUNN RAUDENBUSH

Florence Raudenbush had the second longest term of a Board president, serving ten years to the first Florence's (Mrs. Briggs) twenty-five. Her tenure might have been longer had she not resigned in a war-related move to accompany her husband, Webb, a US Naval Commander-retired, to Illinois in 1943. She had faced some serious challenges on her watch. She had brought the Club through the Depression, maintaining membership, morale, and high musical standards, while continuing the music schools and scholarship program, which had become even more important amid the economic pressures of the time. It was also during her leadership that the venue for the main recital series, the People's Church, was destroyed by fire just two and a half weeks before a major performance in 1940. A sudden shift to the Saint Paul Auditorium enabled the concert to go on, and Schubert Club recitals continued there for nearly thirty years.

Her grandson, Christopher Raudenbush, carries on the musical interests of his family, raised as he was with his father's memories of this remarkable woman and of the family's piano business.

My late father, Webb Russell Raudenbush Jr., shared many recollections related to his mother and my grandmother, Florence Miller Raudenbush, and her involvement with The Schubert Club.

Before she was thirteen years old, Florence Miller, who was raised by her grandmother Bergen in Brooklyn, New York, had crossed the Atlantic Ocean seven times by steamship to be educated in Weimar, Germany. Here she established life-long friendships with her classmates, friendships that would last a lifetime through correspondence in German. By the time she reached adulthood, Florence was considered an authority in German classical music, opera, and culture, as well as a gifted pianist and teacher.

Florence married Webb Russell Raudenbush Sr., the first Minnesota graduate of the United States Naval Academy at Annapolis, in about 1900. They lived at 791 Linwood Avenue in Saint Paul. Webb was the president of the Raudenbush and Sons Piano Company, founded in Saint Paul by his father, Samuel Wesley Raudenbush, in 1883, one year after the founding of The Schubert Club in 1882. By the time the company closed its doors in 1936, more than 40,000 pianos had been manufactured, according to the founder.

The company had its store on the first floor of the Raudenbush Building at 6th and St. Peter, located just east of what is now Landmark Center. For many years, Raudenbush Hall, located on the second and third floors, served as a Saint Paul recital venue for the music students of Mrs. Raudenbush and others. It was also used for Schubert Club committee meetings. Before the turn of the century, as the Ford Music Hall, the building had been used for Schubert Club concerts.

My grandmother was the tenth woman to head The Schubert Club, serving as Board president from 1933 to 1943.

In addition to her ongoing activities with The Schubert Club, Florence Raudenbush was closely involved in other aspects of the cultural life of the Twin Cities. My father recalled many occasions as a teenager going to Union Station in downtown Saint Paul to meet international artists arriving by train, including Pablo Casals, Robert Casadesus, Yehudi Menuhin, Jascha Heifetz, Nelson Eddy and many more. My dad said he routinely brought artists to the family home to visit, some overnight. Some artists were Schubert Club performers. Others, such as Pablo Casals, performed for other local events.

Florence Miller Raudenbush, who passed away in 1961, regularly provided piano accompaniment for her friends and students including, among others, soprano Maud Moon Weyerhaeuser, another Schubert Club member. Today, many of my grandmother's former students continue to be active leaders in the Twin Cities music scene.

I never knew her as Florence Raudenbush, though. To me, she was always Nana Boo. She started me on the piano when I was four years old in 1954. She continued as my teacher until she passed away in 1961, when I was ten. Now, forty-six years later, I play the piano every day. What kind of piano is it, do you ask? Why, of course, it is a Raudenbush! I have three, one for each daughter.

A sliver of The Schubert Club's current building, Landmark Center, is just barely visible to the right of the Raudenbush Building (where Schubert Club meetings were held).

(Above) In about 1935, past Schubert Club board presidents surround the current president, Mrs. Webb Raudenbush (center). The others (identified as they were then) are Mrs. Warren Briggs, Mrs. Charles Guyer, Miss Gertrude Hall, and Mrs. Charles Furness. Marion Ramsey Furness, one of the founders of the organization, was about 80 at the time of the photo.

(Below) Presidents Luncheon at the Grill in the St. Paul Hotel, October 12, 2004. Back row: Arlene Didier, Dee Ann Crossley, Terry Hoffman, Shirley Kartarik, Anna Marie Ettel, Barbara Rice; Front row: Mildred Ellerbe, Carolyn Collins, Bruce Carlson, Ellen Bruner.

(Left) Arlene Didier at a Metro Area Artists Concert the year before she assumed the Presidency.

(Above) Pianist Vladimir Ashkenazy (on one of his four appearances on the International Artist Series) is surrounded by Schubert Club women (Nancy Weyerhaeuser, Catherine Neimeyer, and Julia MacGregor) at a post-concert reception in 1990.

Reflections on My Time as Schubert Club President

Arlene Didier

When I assumed the Presidency of The Schubert Club in 1990, I asked my immediate predecessor, Ellie Bruner, to provide some timelines just to help me keep on track for board actions, etc. She graciously responded with a "President's Manual" that I passed on to the office for staff use and for future presidents.

It quickly became apparent to me that not much recent history was known to either new or old board members. So I began the "Note From the Past" presentations at board meetings. The first person I invited to speak to us was Catherine Neimeyer, President in 1948-51. In the course of my four years, we heard some wonderfully rich stories from some very gifted women, including Virginia Olson who had rejoined our board after an absence of 25 years.

When I moved to Saint Paul in 1970, I was fortunate to meet such women as Julia MacGregor, Catherine Neimeyer, Margaret MacLaren and Ethelwyn Power. They learned of my musical training and experience and proposed me for membership on the board of The Schubert Club. So I began my long relationship with one of the most fascinating organizations one could hope for. It seems that each musical organization I had been associated with was made up entirely of women. It wasn't until

Board Presidents

Mrs. Charles McIlrath	1882-1886
Mrs. Charles E. Furness	1886-1887
Mrs. Charles McIlrath	1887-1888
Mrs. Lyman D. Hodge	1888-1893
Mrs. Russell R. Dorr	1893-1900
Miss Elsie M. Shawe	1900-1902
Mrs. Warren S. Briggs	1902-1905
Mrs. Gertrude E. Hall	1905-1908
Mrs. Warren S. Briggs	1908-1930
Mrs. Charles A. Guyer	1930-1933
Mrs. Webb R. Raudenbush	1933-1943
Mrs. Julian S. Gilman	1943-1948
Mrs. John C. Neimeyer	1948-1951
Mrs. Charles E. Porter	1951-1954
Mrs. Charles H. Loomis	1954-1957
Mrs. Seigel A. Anderson	1957-1959
Mrs. William H. Abbott	1959-1961
Mrs. S. Axel von Bergen	1961-1963
Mrs. Knight Pryor	1963-1965
Mrs. Leonard G. Olson	1965-1967
Mrs. Kenneth O. Johnson	1967-1969
Mrs. Henry Kartarik	1969-1971
Mrs. Thomas F. Ellerbe, Jr.	1971-1973
Mrs. John A. McNeil	1973-1975
Mrs. Gordon Shepard	1975-1979
Mrs. Donald Sell	1979-1983
Mrs. John Diehl	1983-1985
Mrs. Marshall Blomquist	1985-1988
Mrs. Philip Bruner	1988-1990
Arlene Didier	1990-1994
Anna Marie Ettel	1994-1997
Carolyn Collins	1997-1999
Dee Ann Crossley	1999-2001
Barbara Rice	2001-2003
Terry Hoffman	2003-2005
Marsha Hunter	2005-2006
Mary Probst	2006-

Ethelwyn's nephew, George Power, joined the board as investment chair that we relinquished that female requirement. We expected that board members were either musicians or shared a passion for music since, from the beginning, solo recitals were our major interest, the centerpiece of our organization. Such a recital series was almost too good to be true.

Soon after I joined the board, I was elected to serve as the voting delegate to the Arts and Science Council. The largest issue before us at the time was the question of what to do with the Old Federal Courts Building. I followed the lead of Betty Musser as she led the move to pay the price of one dollar to the U. S. Government for the building. Betty never slipped a stitch in her knitting (literally as well as figuratively), and we fought long and hard to spare the building from destruction. The Schubert Club had to detour to another available space above the Fifth Street Bootery for a short time, but eventually we moved into our choice third-floor corner offices of the newly-named Landmark Center.

During my presidency we had to deal with the terms of office one could serve on the board. We introduced the three-year rotation in use today. My association with a major organization that had practiced this rotation system over a period of years gave us our model. I used to tell the board that if they kept saying such nice things to me, I might stay on for 22 years as Mrs. Briggs did from 1908 to 1930. That threat may have hastened our adoption of the rotation system.

I was asked, as president, to host a lovely pianist from Ohio who was visiting St. Paul. A wonderful friendship developed with Margaret Baxtresser, and we arranged for her to perform a recital at the Minneapolis Institute of Arts to coincide with a Monet exhibit. Her choice of music was all Debussy accompanied with slides of French Impressionist paintings. When Margaret died in 2005, she bequeathed her 1878 Bechstein piano to The Schubert Club. The gift to our Museum was celebrated with a concert on the instrument performed by Thelma Hunter, who was joined by Margaret's daughter, Jeanne Baxtresser, a flutist, and soprano Maria Jette.

There were particular women who have held special places in my Schubert Club life. There was Elizabeth Dorsey who always referred to pianist Daniel Chorzempa [a Schubert scholarship winner who went on to a major career as a performer] as "Danny." And Ethelwyn Power who furnished a history of the club for me to help me decide whether or not to join. When I asked Ethelwyn if she had known Mrs. McIlrath in whose Summit Avenue home the first meeting of the club was held in 1882, Ethelwyn said, "Oh, yes. You see, she was my aunt."

Elizabeth Dorsey is shown here with pianist Daniel Chorzempa, one of the young Schubert Club artists in whose career she took an interest. Her long participation on the Board of The Schubert Club lasted from 1921 until her death in 1978. The special Maria Ewing concert at the Arts and Science Center Auditorium in September 1974 was a surprise tribute for her many years of service to the arts in Saint Paul.

I also spent some years on the Concert Committee, and my work involved arranging and hosting Special Concerts. One of those concerts included a young, exciting mezzo who went directly from our stage, singing a more than acceptable performance of varied songs and arias, to the Metropolitan stage in New York where she danced a Salome like no other. The critics went wild. Her name is Maria Ewing.

We celebrated our 100 years of the International Artist Series in 1994. At a dinner just before the Mstislav Rostropovich concert, Bruce Carlson walked around the tables distributing a shiny black book to each person, instructing each to open to page 2 where was written: "Dedicated to Arlene Didier." What a wonderful way to cap my four years as President. The introductory phrase of the book was taken from one of Rilke's *Sonnets To Orpheus*. The last line cites a benediction, "Song above the Land."

Committees

Over the years, the work of The Schubert Club has been advanced by a plethora of committees. Committees still play an important role in the organization, but in the years before there was an office staff, committees *were* the organization. The Secretary's book from 1916-1917 included year-end reports from the

President, Treasurer, Recording Secretary, Corresponding Secretary, Programs, Active Section, Students Section, Associate Section, Students Bureau, Active Membership, Philanthropy, the Music School, Education, Press, Auditing, and Advertising.

In May 1945, the Executive Committee reviewed reports from the following committees: Active Section, Auditions, Altruism, By-laws, Unused tickets, Finance, Hospitality, Inter-Club Council, Manuscripts, Scholarships, Music School, Membership, Press Records, Radio, Section of Artists, Discretionary Scholarships, Student Section, Ticket Sales, Promotion, Printing, Director of Fall and Spring Programs, and the Guarantor's Fund.

Board and Committee members often experience two sides of Schubert Club activities: the behind-the-scenes, hands-on work that makes things happen and also the more glamorous mingling with the musicians.

Pat Hart does the hands-on work of setting up refreshments in a Landmark Center Courtroom, probably in the 1980s. A woman who makes things happen, she has been involved with Museum acquisitions and the bandstand on Raspberry Island.

Epitomizing the glamour side, former Board president Helen Blomquist hobnobs with pianist Peter Serkin in 1988. (Behind-the-scenes her work has included providing The Schubert Club with a wall-sized bookcase for its reference library.)

Thirty Years of Office Observations

A light-hearted look at the goings-on in a busy arts organization

SHARON M. CARLSON

Sharon Carlson served as Executive Director Bruce Carlson's secretary and assistant for more than thirty years. Her office observations began in 1975 when the staff consisted of just three people. Over the course of three decades the number grew to 9, and increased even more throughout the years when composers-in-residence, artists-in-residence and museum docents were added. Since 2006 Sharon has been The Schubert Club's Interim Director.

CLOSE YOUR EYES AND imagine sitting in the main theater of Saint Paul's beautiful Ordway Center waiting for a Schubert Club recital to begin. Or if you like, imagine a concert hall anywhere in the world—the Musikverein in Vienna, Carnegie Hall in New York City, Wigmore Hall in London, the Sydney Opera House. Among many thoughts and impressions coming easily to mind, one of them must surely be the thrill of experiencing in person the performance of a musical genius heard only thus far on a treasured recording. Indeed, that very thrill of experiencing a live performance in a beautiful concert hall is precisely the hoped-for reward The Schubert Club wishes to bestow on its music-loving audience.

So for the concert-goer who has checked his coat in the lobby, climbed the stairs to the hall and handed his ticket to an usher, a number of pleasurable thoughts are likely to come over him. Even more so once he has been handed a program and been directed to the aisle and seat number matching his ticket stub. Because it is just now, sitting comfortably in his chair, browsing through the program and waiting for the dimming of chatter and lights that anticipation starts to build, waiting for the artist to emerge from the wings and take center stage.

Now for someone who works in an arts organization and is involved with the multiple tasks that are essential to the planning of such concerts, a slightly different set of thoughts is likely to emerge—some even crowding out the peaceful, restful kind just mentioned. This chapter takes the reader on a tour of what goes on behind the scenes in a small arts office like ours. It gives you a glimpse of some of our many tasks, a few of our stresses, but also the many joys that follow the completion of a successful musical event. Participating in the mixture of duties necessary to accomplish this result is where I come in. The following pages contain a compilation of memories garnered over three decades working as the secretary and assistant to Bruce Carlson, Saint Paul's master concert presenter, arts administrator, and The Schubert Club's beloved, long-time executive director.

Though Bruce is no longer with us, and we do not have the pleasure of hearing him call out our names or see him sitting at his big oak desk dishing out our assignments, his presence in our office has naturally shaped my observations over many days and hours spent working by his side. So even though he is missing in our beautiful rooms at Landmark Center, you will find him on these pages as I share some of my recollections of what it's like participating in and observing the daily goings-on in The Schubert Club office. Quite naturally, into some of my narrative about Bruce a variety of tenses is woven into descriptions and stories, as the present tense still seems so appropriate. But that fits nicely into the way our staff thinks of him.

Bruce was with us, isn't now, but always will be!

Our Boss, Bruce

Born on a mountain top in Tennessee
Greenest state in the land of the free . . .

That's Bruce in his office singing Davy Crockett's Theme Song while sitting at his iMac going over the morning e-mails. Bruce has already gotten a jump on his electronic letter-writing before the rest of us get there, arriving at his office somewhere between 7:30 and 8. Weather doesn't matter much, he still comes early. Bruce often says that he likes to be "the first one in and the last one out." Even when his days start and end with meetings that take him out of the office, he stops in first before heading to an early appointment, and oftentimes returns to the office following a late one.

A typical start to the day once the doors open to The Schubert Club office, is hearing the sound of Bruce tapping his computer keys while listening to Minnesota Public Radio or a classical CD. Staff members start trickling in around 8:10; starting time is 8:30. By the time we turn the lights on and take off our coats, Bruce has already gotten some of his e-mail correspondence out of the way and is now moving on to the newspapers. Holly brings in the *St. Paul Pioneer Press* and the *Wall Street Journal*, and I show up with the *Star Tribune*. *The New York Times* can be viewed on-line, though Bruce often has the Arts and Leisure section tucked inside his briefcase. Articles, reviews, news items—local and national—are gone over and sometimes discussed. Soon it's time for the mail, and once a bundle of miscellaneous parcels is deposited on Bruce's desk, another stretch of time is taken up looking over letters, bills, contracts, and so on.

. . . then, more Davy Crockett, same lines

Born on a mountain top in Tennessee
Greenest state in the land of the free . . .

In between these verses are lots of phone calls, so he usually doesn't sing more than a few lines at a time. Friends, board members, other arts administrators, concert managers, ad reps, local artists—various people call him throughout the day. Then somewhere in there is the conclusion to Davy Crockett.

Davy, Davy Crockett,
king of the wild frontier.

My day mirrored Bruce's day. When I arrived at the office around 8, he was already either sitting at his computer or talking on the telephone. He'd hear the sound of my key turning in the door, followed by footsteps. As I entered, the familiar sound of his voice brought me to the archway of his office. It was not unusual to see him at his desk with one hand on the telephone and another on the handle of an outboard motor. A collector of boats and motors, Bruce kept one Johnson outboard on a stand by his desk, and another bolted to the wooden table in the middle of his office, with brass holders on either side for the oars! He'd glance up; I waved, then he waved, and so our day began. No two days were alike. Projects on a wide variety of subjects crossed our cluttered desks—material for planning concerts, creating advertising, writing press releases, conducting Board business. Bruce loved every aspect of his job, and he had the knack for making projects fun and interesting.

Bruce loved his staff, and he had a special relationship with each of us. He was a voracious reader and a great debater and he loved to engage in conversations about politics, government, religion, education, world events, and so on. We all got ribbed a lot, and most of us were teased daily, but he hardly ever scolded. Instead, he piled lots of assignments on us, and we went off on our projects, making sure to keep him posted on our progress. Bruce had very few rules (when I was hired we didn't even have a personnel manual!) and he basically operated on three principles he developed after reading an article in the *New Yorker* about the first Music Director of the Cleveland Orchestra. The players had to be on time, love their work, and keep their eyes on the conductor. Bruce crafted his motto along the lines of an arts manager, altering the list only slightly:

- Be on time
- Love your work
- Check with me

From time to time we would have a staff meeting. While it's true most organizations have regular staff meetings, ours, under Bruce's management, were infrequent and haphazard. This drove some of us crazy. Our staff meetings could be any day of the week, and there was no set hour. The way they usually came about was I would hear stirrings among staff members that a meeting would be helpful in order to share important information about each other's jobs, particularly as they pertained to upcoming events. I would then prompt Bruce to arrange one. He usually winced at the suggestion and said, *"Today?"*

A response like this most likely meant that Bruce wasn't wild about being interrupted from the tasks he loved, and he probably had a hunch

Bruce's hobbies usually found their way into his office. Outboard motors near his desk kept him company until the weekend, when he headed north to his cabin on Bay Lake where the ones attached to boats awaited him!

some of us would gang up on him and pressure him about office issues he preferred to avoid. We needled him about things like getting a new phone system and other matters—some of which he tended to, some he did not. (Lists of that sort don't appear in this essay but can be found somewhere in staff members' notebooks.) So after obtaining a suitable time from Bruce, say 10 AM, I would email the staff, clear the conference table, and wait for our staff to assemble. Once in a while if people didn't come on time, he blew his trumpet, but that signal was generally reserved for birthdays or other celebrations. Soon staff members began showing up carrying pads of paper, coffee mugs or teacups; occasionally we had snacks. Bruce sat at the head of the table, and, unaware of how *real* businessmen conduct staff meetings, it seemed perfectly normal to me that Bruce began his by reading a poem.

Classic poets such as Rilke or Sandburg were usually chosen, but oftentimes Bruce favored more current ones such as Billy Collins, Joyce Sutphen, or Dana Gioia. After the reading, a brief period was spent reacting to Bruce's poem, and then the meeting would begin.

The agenda varied. We usually tackled issues pertaining to our major departments: Education, Museum, and Concerts. These might include such topics as upcoming concerts, who should do what, and so on. Following some discussion on these matters, Bruce would adjourn—whether we were finished or not—so he could get back to making phone calls, and we would disperse to our respective offices. It would usually be quiet on the staff meeting front for a week or so, until I heard murmurings from people wanting another meeting. Then the whole procedure would happen again with me asking Bruce if we could have a staff meeting and hearing him answer *"Today?"* while wearing the same pained expression.

Bruce worked awfully hard. Weekdays, weeknights, lots of Saturdays and Sundays—he was always out and about doing Schubert Club things. A lover of boats and water, Bruce seemed in some ways like the captain of a small ship as he sat comfortably at the helm of the organization he loved, steering its course with grace and certainty—and always with a considerable dash of humor. He never took his work more seriously than was necessary. When other bosses were giving their secretaries advice on how to be a more effective employee, Bruce was telling me, "Don't work too hard on being organized. Part of our charm is that people think we don't know what we're doing." How's that again? In

Every once in a while Bruce pulled out a Santa Claus hat whether it was Christmastime or not. Here it came in handy when he worked on The Schubert Club Strategic Plan.

his later years, when many of his duties were shifting to me, he tried to explain what he did so that I might pick up the mantle and carry on his work. But instead of giving me helpful lists, he shrugged and said, "You know, I don't really do too much. I make some calls, open the mail, and then I walk around the halls talking to people."

Undoubtedly one of the most effective arts administrators in the business, I once heard Bruce tell someone, "I think it's a good trait not to know what's going on. The important thing is to give the impression you're on top of things." Now there's a line you're not likely to get from your average CEO. But with a successful 38-year tenure as The Schubert Club's executive director under his belt, there was never any doubt that Bruce, in his own unusual way, was definitely on top of things! But how about those wacky impressions he gave? Last summer he put on a Santa Claus hat while working at his desk on The Schubert Club's Strategic Plan. I never figured out how that fit into his theory, but perhaps a comical gesture like that helped put a little zip into an otherwise ho-hum assignment.

Our Amazing Staff

Current Office Staff: Abbie Betinis, Max Carlson, Sharon Carlson, Rebecca Klein, Jason Kudrna, David Morrison, Richard Rames, Tessa Retterath, Kathy Wells, Holly Windle

Our staff is a happy bunch. Musical, multi-talented, brave and enthusiastic, we soar through the day accomplishing a myriad of tasks. All our positions share one basic requirement: "Check your job description at the door." Translation: Always be prepared for an unusual assignment.

Bruce asked a lot of us, no question about it. And like real troupers we always came through. We have dressed up like Mozart, wheeled fake palm trees to the Ordway, hauled piano benches to concerts, posed with cows, uncrated instruments, chauffeured artists, transported musical instruments from other states, written limericks, performed limericks, participated in turn-of-the-century style shows, acted as photographers, presented bouquets to performers, taken artists to doctors, ushered at concerts, and turned pages for pianists. The men have built, varnished and

(Left) Our staff worked at the opening of The Schubert Club Bandstand on Raspberry Island and wore the tee shirts we had specially designed for the occasion. (Right) Piano benches on the move. (Above) A group of skaters in the 21st century enjoy the skating rink constructed outside of the 19th-century Landmark Center. Hey, that's The Schubert Club staff on ice skates!

painted things, and the women have cleaned, scrubbed and dusted things. Or is it the other way around? Gender doesn't matter in our office. We've all done crazy things and each of us has had to pitch in to perform duties not found in a normal job description. As long as muscles and stamina hold out, we are unstoppable. And on top of all that we are full of other talents as well! Some of us sing, some play instruments, a few write music, and a couple are in plays. One former receptionist did cartwheels!

But in addition to all the unusual gifts I have just mentioned, each of us has a real job description containing specific duties we were hired to do: mounting museum exhibits, managing concert series, coordinating the student scholarship competition, writing grants, producing CDs, running the box office, answering the phone, balancing the books, producing ads, brochures, and concert programs. And oh, so much more! But ask any of us if working for The Schubert Club is worth it and the answer is always Yes! After all, where else can you come to work thinking you might have just another ordinary day and suddenly James Galway drops in and you get your picture taken with him!

After office hours—that is, if we are not too exhausted from doing all the things I just mentioned—we sometimes get together and do fun things. This winter we put on ice skates, hung onto each other for safety, and tried figure skating!

Our Offices in Landmark Center

Now let's take a look at the beautiful, castle-like building where we work—that historic landmark in downtown St. Paul. It's a mammoth structure covering a whole city block between Fifth and Sixth Streets, recognizable by its granite stone, clay tiles and green turrets … and the big clock tower that watches over Rice Park. Home to several arts organizations, Landmark Center has a rich history dating from the turn-of-the-century when it was constructed. It is especially notable for the years when it functioned as the Old Federal Courts Building when such notorious gangsters as John Dillinger walked its halls during the criminal trials in the early 1920s. The FBI had an office here, too. In its present era, this magnificent building is home to various theater and musical organizations including The Schubert Club, whose office and museum space now spreads out over nine rooms on two floors giving us various views of the Saint Paul Hotel, the Saint Paul Public Library and the Ordway Center for the Performing Arts. On the lower level is where we proudly display our treasures in the Museum of Musical Instruments.

Constructed in 1891 in the Richardsonian Romanesque style of architecture, Landmark Center's historical origins are special to us because this building became a prominent part of Saint Paul's developing landscape just around the time The Schubert Club's early beginnings were making their mark on Saint Paul's musical landscape.

It was still known as the Old Federal Courts Building when I went to work for The Schubert Club over thirty years ago. Our offices were on the second floor in those days, but only briefly. Although the building escaped the wrecking ball in the 60s and early 70s thanks in large part to Saint Paul civic leader Betty Musser and a team of dedicated women who succeeded in saving it from that fate, the Old Federal Courts Building was deteriorating and in need of repair when Minnesota Landmarks acquired ownership in 1972. A few arts organizations trickled in as tenants, the first being The Schubert Club. An old organization but newly under the leadership of Bruce Carlson, The Schubert Club was already outgrowing its tiny office in the St.

Flautist James Galway made a surprise visit to our office one day, and Bruce snapped our picture.

Box Office Manager Tessa Retterath worked at her computer in the lobby of the Ordway the night of the Maxim Vengerov concert in 2006. Lauren Viner assisted in processing season renewals.

Paul Arts and Science Center on 30 East 10th Street. Bruce eagerly accepted Mrs. Musser's offer to come on board and relocate. "This was the most beautiful building in Saint Paul," Bruce remarked at the time. "It was fun being here. It was spooky. . . Things did not work quite right. That was part of its charm. Everyone loved coming to work everyday just because the building was so beautiful."

Bruce's enthusiastic assessment notwithstanding, the building needed a lot of restoration by then, and it wasn't long before a massive three-phase renovation was being planned that necessitated The Schubert Club vacating its offices and finding temporary office space elsewhere during the restoration's two-year process. So The Schubert Club's headquarters moved to an office building nearby at Fifth and Wabasha Street. From this location we watched the renovation of our building. We monitored its progress and prepared for the grand reopening in 1978 when the newly-christened Landmark Center was finally ready to welcome back its tenants, while taking its place among other buildings in cities across America which were similarly saved from demolition and restored to original grandeur. The inaugural ceremony brought Vice President Walter Mondale, his wife Joan Mondale, and other dignitaries to Saint Paul for the public reopening when it was officially named a National Historic Monument.

Preparing for a Concert

Remember the concert-goer I described earlier—that quiet soul sitting in a beautiful concert hall with calm, peaceful reflections flooding over him? Well, that lucky devil could afford to relax because he didn't work in our office, and browsing through 16 pages of a program booklet for him is meant to be a pleasurable, pre-concert experience. Not so for the frazzled employee whose responsibility it is to prepare that booklet! This important task is included in my job description, so by the time an usher hands me a program and I find my concert seat, an entirely different set of thoughts begins to sweep over me.

For example, as I scan the sea of nearly 1800 patrons reading the program I put together, I immediately fear there might be typographical errors in the copy that were not caught by several rounds of diligent proofreading prior to printing. Simple ones come first: Is the date correct? Are the pieces listed accurately? Then more serious ones: Had I used the most recent version of notes and texts sent to me by the artist's manager? Did I look at the contract closely enough so that the font sizes of the artists and accompanists are the proportions requested? Did I include the proper credits? Do the texts follow in the proper order? How about mistakes in the foreign languages? (Count on a brilliant scholar out there to catch the most minor error and telephone our office the following day to report a goof.) On the other hand, reporting a mistake by telephone pales compared to an artist pointing one out from the stage! The year PDQ Bach appeared on the opening concert of The Schubert Club's 100th Anniversary Year in 1982, Peter Schickele asked the house lights to come up so he could draw attention from the podium to an error he found in the program! Lucky for me O'Shaughnessy Auditorium did not have a spotlight that could identify the culprit.

The most recent ohmygoodness happened this year when preparing the program for The Schubert Club's recital featuring Frederica von Stade and Samuel Ramey. I had identified Samuel Ramey as a bass-baritone rather than a bass and discovered the error after the program had gone to the printer—despite much proofreading, including by the artist's management! First, an urgent call to Mr. Ramey's manager to get a reading on my blunder. I expected to hear "it's probably okay" but instead I got "It's very serious and has to be fixed—Mr. Ramey is very particular about that." Oh dear! Next, a frantic call to the printer. A mixture of disheartening news gave way to a speck of hope. The programs had all been printed but not stitched, so the decision was quickly made to fix the error and re-run the first page. Whew! What a close call!

So you get the picture why someone behind the scenes approaches these concerts with caution. So much work happens prior to watching that artist walk out on stage. No wonder I quickly stuff my program in my briefcase upon taking my seat in the theater. Much safer to peek at a neighboring patron's program page and applaud when everybody else does, rather than open my own and give in to the urge to scrutinize the copy after it's too late to correct an error.

Cancellations

Even a nasty weather forecast on the night of a concert isn't as dreadful a prospect as news that an artist has cancelled a performance. Almost any problem a concert manager faces brings with it a variety of creative solutions. Bad weather? If the artists are already in town, the show goes on—a skimpier audience may be the unfortunate result, but stormy weather would rarely shut down the show. Concerts not selling well? Paper the hall. Artists need more rehearsal time? Roll in a piano and give them a few more hours. How about a last minute repertoire change a performer sometimes springs on us? Xerox an insert, or announce the switch from the stage. Even gowns lost in airline luggage can be replaced by a search of local dress shops. When Renée Fleming landed in St. Paul for her International Artist Series recital in 2001, her baggage missed her flight, and Bruce phoned me to ask if I had any Oscar de la Renta gowns in my closet! Okay, that was a long shot! But even that problem disappeared when Ms. Fleming's dress bag arrived hours later on another flight. And if it hadn't, some serious shopping would definitely have been in the offing.

These and other ups and downs are not uncommon in the course of a concert year. On the other hand, artists that don't show… now, there's a headache for you. While The Schubert Club has been extraordinarily fortunate to have faced this dilemma few times in its long history of bringing in hundreds, perhaps thousands, of artists from many places across the globe—we have on occasion been the recipient of alarming news that an artist cannot fulfill an engagement. Oh, the hair-pulling at such times. And it's usually a phone call from an apologetic manager bringing us this distressing news.

Bruce never wastes time when he gets a call like that. A deep breath and he's on the phone looking for a replacement. Who's available? Who's ready? Who got good reviews in a recent performance? Who can get here in time?

One of The Schubert Club's most disheartening cancellations came the day before our much-anticipated recital featuring Welsh bass-baritone, Bryn Terfel. A telephone call came in at 9 AM from Terfel's London manager, informing Bruce that Bryn had suffered a terrible attack of sciatica in New York where he was appearing in *The Tales of Hoffman* with the Metropolitan Opera. He was unable to walk or even stand up. The doctor's orders? Stay in bed for four to six weeks. So upon canceling all of his opera performances, a heavily-sedated Bryn was placed on a stretcher, transported onto an airplane and flown out of New York and back to Wales where he underwent a laser operation through a small hole in his back. Recovery included swimming therapy in the Pantglas, Wales Municipal Swimming Pool, and, much to our delight, a slightly-limping Bryn came back to St. Paul for a re-scheduled Schubert Club recital in April where he received a rousing greeting complete with a bright red "Welcome Back Bryn" banner and a standing ovation from the audience.

Now back to Bruce's office and the grim news that came in at 9 AM. Our staff learned of this immediately, resulting in lots of long faces. But with no time to spare, Bruce was on the phone within minutes and soon urgent phone calls were made between Saint Paul, New York, and London. Thomas Hampson was almost able to step in but couldn't; Samuel Ramey was willing to fly out here but was unable to get released from a rehearsal at the Met. By 11:30 AM, however, Bruce had miraculously secured a re-scheduled date for Bryn's recital! What a coup! And so, with news like that to announce, it was decided that in this case a substitute would not be pursued. Instead, the hall would remain dark, program booklets would stay in their unpacked boxes in the Ordway's basement, and calls would be made to our subscribers and ticket-holders informing them personally of this sudden cancellation.

Twelve people began telephoning non-stop throughout the day and evening hours, as we slogged away at our goal of reaching nearly 2000 ticket-holders by evening. Around dinner time, pizza boxes and other refreshments began appearing as the telephoning continued. Radio stations and newspapers were called and Minnesota Public Radio began communicating our news. This marathon continued into the next day. Then around 7:30 PM a few weary staff members were dispatched to stand at the front doors of the Ordway and explain to any patrons who trickled in why the lights weren't on.

Bryn's case was unusual, and normally it is preferable to pursue any avenue necessary to replace an ailing star with a non-ailing star. At least there's someone on the stage! This is what happened when one of our long-time favorite mezzo-sopranos—Frederica von Stade—cancelled her February 14th concert in 2002. Suffering from some kind of digestive problems that had plagued her for months, Ms. von Stade found it necessary to cancel her Schubert Club engagement, and she personally called to convey her sorry-ness to her old friend, Bruce. That news brought a flurry of discussions and a full day of phone calls which ended with Bruce making the

Bruce and Grace Bumbry outside the Saint Paul Hotel, following her Schubert Club recital in 2002.

superb choice of engaging mezzo-soprano Grace Bumbry! The crowd-pleasing Ms. Bumbry gave a fabulous concert and the headline from the newspaper review the next day prompted some well-deserved high-fives: "In von Stade's stead, Bumbry is masterful." Now that's what I call a great save!

Health problems of varying degrees can easily fall into the "Cancellation Alert Category" because any uncertainty in an artist's health carries with it this alarming possibility—even after an artist has landed in St. Paul. Maladies of varying descriptions have plagued some of our finest artists, requiring differing and sometimes creative solutions. Alfred Brendel needed a chiropractor; Peter Serkin had a headache; Jonathan Biss an earache. Still, the shows went on.

But in 2002 we found ourselves in a pickle when a hint of a medical dilemma accompanied Håkan Hagegård upon his arrival to St. Paul for an appearance on our Summer Song Festival. The beloved Swedish baritone was to sing Schubert's *Wintereisse* on one of the evening recitals. Håkan's warm telephone greeting to our office put Bruce on notice that a potential problem was brewing. Håkan was having trouble with his throat (not good for a singer) and asked Bruce to find him a doctor. Immediately the assignment was given to me: find an ear, nose and throat specialist and get a quick appointment. So the next day Håkan sat in my Volvo as I drove him to the Otolaryngology Department at the University of Minnesota where he was examined by one of the University's top physicians. I sat in the waiting room while the inside of Håkan's throat got inspected, photographed and diagnosed. Images of his arytenoid cartilages revealed "microhemorrhages in the vocal folds"—medical lingo for a situation that required resting the voice. Thankfully the doctor permitted our popular baritone to fulfill his engagement on the Festival before returning to Sweden to complete her prescription for recovery.

CONCLUSION

These are just a few of the recollections that came to me as I tackled my chapter and jogged my memory for details about the office and other events that reveal a little of the drama that goes on behind the concert scene. These snippets focus on the thirty-year period of Schubert Club history that span the years of my employment. And they naturally include a portrait of the man I worked for—that amazing and amusing impresario who left an indelible mark on this organization.

Many other stories exist from earlier periods that are part of The Schubert Club's long and dignified history. Scrapbooks and diaries from those years contain memories of the wonderful individuals who helped shape this remarkable organization. Undoubtedly those who come after me will add volumes of their own to its fascinating archives.

The rewards have been great. My office colleagues and I have had the good fortune of being part of the history of one of the finest musical gems in the world.

Thank you, Schubert Club!

"One of my most poignant memories of The Schubert Club is Sharon Carlson from the front office. Whether it is her slight build, quickness of eye, imperceptible movements, or all three—she was far and away the best page-turner I've ever had."

– Paul Schoenfield,
pianist and composer

Finalist for the 2003 Pulitzer Prize in composition, Paul Schoenfield is a pianist, composer, and scholar. Schoenfield himself, once a student of Rudolf Serkin, has often appeared as soloist on Schubert Club recitals. His commissioned work has been premiered on the Ordway stage by Christopher O'Riley and Anne-Marie McDermott.

Bruce with the young reporter (his son, Max)

Interview with Bruce Carlson

A young reporter from a Minnesota college conducted the following interview with Bruce Carlson, the Executive Director of The Schubert Club late in 2005.

Young Reporter: What do you like most about The Schubert Club?

Bruce Carlson: Its age—begun in the nineteenth century and now it's the twenty-first. Three centuries is a lot of time for good music in the US... or anyplace.

YR: Anything else?

BC: Yes, its focus on recital music, which is endangered. So, as a conservative, I like the idea of helping to save something very rich and beautiful from the potential dustbin of history.

YR: What's your average day like?

BC: I get up early, check a blog or two and the *New York Times* on the web, and often meet someone for breakfast connected with the local arts, well, "industry," if that's the right word. Who knows what might come out of that? Maybe an angle on a foundation grant or an idea for an interesting recital.

YR: But aren't there already too many concerts around town?

BC: True, but I believe there can be room for something exquisite such as a high-quality recital. We don't always need to fill thousands of seats, and we're really quite happy with small recitals—say, 75 people in a lovely little concert hall. We've got one. It's perfect.

YR: No kidding?

BC: There are lots of great musicians around who have been beautifully educated at Juilliard or some other music conservatory, who are loaded with talent and looking to present and share their art. . . to be appreciated. They find us. We find them. It's not only the audience that interests us. We are pro-artist.

YR: What's the smallest audience you've ever had?

BC: Oh, three or four or five hardy souls who turned out for a Joan Benson clavichord recital during a blizzard twenty years ago on a dark January midweek night. And Benson was great. She was magical like Wanda Landowska pulling it right out of heaven.

YR: The biggest?

BC: Probably when we set the Ordway record with a Cecilia Bartoli recital in 1996. There were well over two thousand thrilled people in the house including the fullest possible configuration of seats, plus stage seats, plus standing room. The works.

YR: So is your average day over after breakfast?

BC: Pretty much so. There is a great staff at The Schubert Club and from nine to six I wander around chatting with everybody and talking about music and projects. One of our employees has an MBA and she read a book entitled The Four Styles of Management. Mine, she concluded, was not structural, political, or personnel; it was the fourth, symbolic. I don't know what it means, but I don't disagree either.

YR: Is that it? Your day?

BC: Oh, the phone rings, so I have a fair amount of calls. And much to my amazement I'm on the computer quite a bit. Soon it's 1 PM, time for lunch. I've been a big regular at the Saint Paul Hotel Grill. Mike Anthony, the music critic for the *Star Tribune*, wrote that the Grill was "my office." Here I like to talk with composers, musicians, patrons, board members, and anyone else in the local classical music world who will join me. Dominick Argento, our great Pulitzer Prize-winning composer and George Reid, long time Schubert Club board member, have been two of my most frequent lunchtime companions. We are all old enough to enjoy martinis and fortunately have missed out on the newer luncheon habits of eating yogurt and working out at a health club.

YR: It sounds good.

BC: It's a wonderful life. Sitting in the Grill, chatting with someone about mutual artistic interests, and looking out the big glass windows across lovely Rice Park at the magnificent Ordway Theater. I love it. And then at night quite often I go to concerts. That's very enjoyable. Everything else leads up to the aesthetics, the epiphanies of a great concert.

YR: How did you land such a gravy-boat job?

BC: I was lucky to be in the right place at the right time back in the summer of 1968 when The Schubert Club was looking for a professional manager, and just happened to select me out of a field which included no other applicants.

YR: So you've had the same job for almost 40 years?

BC: I know it sounds long but there are others who have stuck with the same thing over the years. Carl Drake, the former CEO of the Saint Paul Companies, retired a few years ago after about 40 years with that historic company, which even predates The Schubert Club in Saint Paul history. Carl, whose wife Charlotte has been on The Schubert Club Board for many years, has an office just above mine now in Landmark Center and he is a big hero of mine. He was Chairman of the Ordway Board when that was being built in the 1980s. And wasn't someone named Weston Noble the director of the Luther College Choir for 57 years?

YR: What are some of the highlights of your career?

BC: Certainly when Dominick Argento won the 1975 Pulitzer Prize in Music for writing "From the Diary of Virginia Woolf," a great piece The Schubert Club had commissioned. Dame Janet Baker sang it both here and in Carnegie Hall. The *New Yorker* magazine's music critic, Andrew Porter, called it "a masterpiece." There were exciting festivities in New York with Miss Alice Tully herself, a "Mrs. Rockefeller" and others hosting post concert parties and dinners.

YR: Anything else?

BC: The Schubert Club opened the Ordway in 1985 with a gala concert featuring Leontyne Price. That was fun. And I just love the new Gilman Ordway Manuscript Galleries we established a year or so ago in Landmark Center. We have five of the most beautiful rooms imaginable overlooking Rice Park filled with some carefully selected musical treasures such as letters from Mozart and Beethoven and a manuscript by Schubert himself. Plus the oldest harpsichord in the United States which dates back to 1542. Strolling through these quiet, magical galleries gives me a great thrill.

YR: Isn't there a small concert hall in those galleries?

BC: I'm glad you asked. Indeed, it's Wigmore Hall West in the largest corner gallery, just kitty-corner from the Ordway. We've informally named it Wigmore West recognizing and honoring the distinguished Wigmore Hall in London. Ours is truly an elegant space and probably my favorite concert hall anywhere.

YR: What about music education?

BC: We are for it, and in it, big time, and have pushed it along for decades. Our annual scholarship competition is probably the oldest and the largest in the country. By 2007 we will be making annual awards totaling $125,000 to about forty or fifty of the most talented young musicians in Minnesota. Some winners go on to distinguished careers in major orchestras and opera companies around the world. Others stay in the Twin Cities teaching music, performing, buying tickets and going to concerts. We think this huge scholarship program, which dates back to 1922, has done a great deal in nurturing our local musical culture. It's beautifully run and I'm very proud of it.

YR: What's the financial picture at The Schubert Club?

BC: We would probably have a triple A bond rating and have never had an annual deficit. This is due to responsible management by the Board and myself. And after all, I took Negotiable Instruments in law school. (Never mind at the time I thought I'd signed up for a course on buying pianos.) We have also built up over the years a very solid endowment fund.

YR: How did this endowment fund get started?

BC: About 25 years ago someone suggested that we sponsor a master class with the great cellist Janos Starker. Starker's fee was $500. So to pay for this class I had to figure out how to raise $500. It then dawned on me that if fifteen or twenty times $500 were raised we could use the interest or income from that larger amount and present a master class every year in perpetuity. This is the principal behind endowments. It's much harder at first, but down the road the dividends are remarkable. So we have used this principal and developed endowment underpinnings for many of our ongoing program categories.

YR: Where does the money for this endowment fund come from?

BC: Well, I must say that I've seen some very generous pledges and checks over the years passed across the white table cloths in my direction while sitting around having coffee after a nice luncheon or dinner in the Saint Paul Grill. That, for sure, has been the vast bulk of it—probably almost 95 per cent. Fund raising is important and can be quite pleasant, too.

YR: Are you quite interested in the business side of running an organization?

BC: Yes. For example, I've always enjoyed reading the *Wall Street Journal* and not just for its excellent music and arts reporting. If the money isn't there—and well-managed—we can't engage Renée Fleming and the other artists who perform at the highest level. And we cherish our reputation for artistic excellence that sometimes is very expensive.

YR: Do you follow the trends in recording classical music?

BC: Yes, I do. We have had our own classical label called 10,000 Lakes for over twenty years. We started out on Long Playing 33⅓ rpm vinyl discs. Our first LP was the pianist Liz Woolf playing Rachmaninoff. Soon after, we made several splendid LPs with Peter Serkin playing Schubert and Beethoven on early nineteenth-century pianos that are part of our Museum collection. Gradually we moved into cassettes and then CDs. We have produced about thirty recordings and are just now getting our feet wet with DVDs.

YR: I've heard of Sony, but do enough people know about your company?

BC: Yes. What is by far the best classical music magazine in the world, *Gramophone*, published in England, gave a wonderful review recently of O Bell' Alma, a great new 10,000 Lakes CD of flute and harp music performed by two outstanding players in the Minnesota Orchestra, Michele Frisch and Kathy Kienzle. This CD is selling very well.

YR: Isn't the CD business changing?

BC: Certainly. CDs may soon be obsolete and people will just download music from the web. But we are looking into new web possibilities and recently have even made some small ventures in podcasting.

YR: What period of classical music do you specialize in?

BC: Only the Baroque. No, just kidding. I guess most of our concerts encompass the time frame from Mozart and Haydn down to the present. We are very interested in the front edge of music and in fact have two composers in residence on our staff. Over the years we have commissioned scores of new works including two that have won Pulitzer Prizes. And we reach back into early music and in fact have a separate series that particularly explores that repertoire.

YR: What about jazz?

BC: We have under-weighted it, almost ignored it for years. But two things happened in the last decade that put jazz back in our programming. One was the Wynton Marsalis/Ken Burns film series on PBS about jazz in America. I watched all ten shows and came away believing that jazz was indeed the great American contribution to serious music. And there was a woman on our Board, Jane Matteson, who was really bitten by the jazz bug late in her life. Every night she went to the Dakota Jazz Club. Many times I went with her. We became great friends and when she died a Jane Matteson Jazz Fund was established in her memory. So now we offer several jazz scholarships every year.

YR: Do you sponsor any jazz concerts?

BC: We have done a few at the Raspberry Island Bandstand we built several years ago on this lovely island in the Mississippi River in downtown Saint Paul. But with traditional Western classical music itself on the endangered list we can't spread ourselves too thinly. The same holds true for world music. Some years ago we had a big Indonesian Gamelan Orchestra program that we have radically scaled back so that we can really concentrate on, and tend to, our (traditional Western European) knitting. We want to be focused and we are way too small to try to do everything. The traditional classical recital is our life-blood and our first priority.

YR: What about the future of classical music in America?

BC: It will never disappear because its intrinsic merits are too beautiful, powerful and strong. It may go sort of underground or be more cultish for awhile. Who knows? Shakespeare has been dropped as a subject in favor of some trendy nonsense even in very distinguished universities, but it will recover. But The Schubert Club would never give up on classical recitals even if the audience dwindled down, for a few years, to just a handful. The endowment should carry us through any lean years when and if ticket sales might plummet.

YR: So you are optimistic?

BC: About classical recitals, of course I am! They are so sublime, so rooted in the heart of the finest aspects of our culture that they just have to be imperishable.

YR: Thank you very much.

BC: You're entirely welcome. It was a pleasure.

Dana Gioia in the Museum.

Remembering Bruce Carlson

Dana Gioia, Chairman
National Endowment for the Arts

Dana Gioia was the featured speaker at The Schubert Club's Annual Meeting in 2004. His visit to Saint Paul at that time included touring The Schubert Club Museum and talking with Executive Director Bruce Carlson about music, poetry, and the arts in society.

"Bruce Carlson possessed a remarkable combination of charm and erudition. Certainly I am not the only person who could say that within minutes of first meeting him I knew we would be friends. He spoke with enormous knowledge about music, musicians, and musical instruments, but he did so in a way that made you feel the irreplaceable human importance of the arts. Through his vision and leadership, the Schubert Club has made a genuine contribution to the field of music. He is much missed."

Lunch with soprano Dorothy Benham

Lunch with Bruce

Margaret Wurtele

A long-time Schubert Club subscriber, Margaret Wurtele held positions with the Walker Art Center and the St. Paul United Arts Fund before serving as managing director of the Dayton-Hudson Foundation. She was co-founding publisher of Hungry Mind Press (now Ruminator Books Press), served as chair of the Guthrie Board, and is the author of Taking Root: A Spiritual Memoir *and* Touching the Edge. *She divides her time between Minnesota and California where she and her husband Angus own Terra Valentine, a vineyard in the Napa Valley.*

I'm steaming down the Tenth Street exit ramp off Highway 94. It's noon, and I'm about five minutes away from the Grill at the Saint Paul Hotel—late for lunch. Normally five minutes wouldn't bother me, but I know Bruce will already be there, sitting coolly in the booth, his fingers wrapped gingerly around the stem of a Manhattan, patiently waiting. I know, because we've been doing this for thirty years. It's always the same.

Bruce and I met in the early 1970s when I was in charge of publicity and membership at Walker Art Center. As Executive Director of The Schubert Club, he often co-sponsored concerts with Sue Weil, the gutsy, flamboyant impresario of Walker's performing arts program. Because I wrote the press releases for those events and my office was next to Sue's, Bruce often stopped at my door to chat on his way to meet with her.

He was, even in his early thirties, professorial. Rumpled and bespectacled, he would lean against the doorjamb, arms folded, a bemused expression on his face. His voice was tight and high, its Midwestern drawl a product of pure Minnesota Swedish heritage. Those of us on the museum's staff were acolytes of cutting edge art, and we all took it very seriously. Bruce, who was a fierce proponent of the new in music, was more wary when it came to the visual arts. He would mention that he had just come through the latest exhibition, and—just as an aside— point out that the emperor had no clothes. His unabashed expressions of everyman's take on the latest installation were good comic relief.

Breathless, I'm shown to a booth at the Grill, and sure enough, there he sits, imperturbable. "Oh. Hi, Margaret." He's wearing a rumpled cotton sport coat, a no-iron button-down shirt, and a pastel Liberty print tie that is way too narrow for the fashion of the times. "Gee, it's good to see you." Balding on top now, he has a slicked, slightly frizzed comb-over that starts just above the left ear and reaches all the way over to the right one.

"Sorry I'm late," I say, smiling, as I slide into the booth opposite him. "It's good to see you too."

I left Walker in 1973 to have a baby, and two years later, driven by a divorce and the need to make money, took a job in the development department at the Saint Paul Arts and Science Council. Our principal mission was to conduct the annual United Arts Fund, raising money each year that was divided among Saint Paul cultural organizations, among them The Schubert Club.

In the three years I worked there, I saw Bruce nearly every day. The Schubert Club was a star among our affiliates: efficiently run and financially stable, it offered up a variety of programs that appealed to the full range of donors: the diva-studded International Artist Series of recitals; new music concerts co-sponsored with the Walker; classes for children; master classes and exposure opportunities for talented young musicians. Bruce was good company. We had the same take on our co-workers and shared a low tolerance for inflated egos or administrators who took themselves too seriously. When I felt bad, he held my hand.

But as Bruce's friend in those Saint Paul years, I was learning more important things than how to raise money. I began to develop my own taste in music, for example, listening to him rave about a talented tenor or a newly commissioned song cycle.

I learned to read from him as well. I was already a book lover when we met, but by imitating him, I learned to pick an author—Edith Wharton, say—and read everything she wrote. I learned to read the books in chronological order, purchased in dusty, yellowed editions scrounged from the crowded shelves of local used book stores. Bruce knew all the dealers and taught me how to prowl the aisles, searching for a first edition. He encouraged me to buy the best Wharton biography and compare her life to mine. I planned, as a result, to make my own "little motor trip through France," as soon as I

(Top) At the Saint Paul Grill with Minnesota composer Dominick Argento

(Middle) Lunch with longtime supporter and museum contributor Gilman Ordway

(Bottom) At the Grill with mezzo-soprano Jennifer Larmore

(Top) Breakfast with son Max Carlson

(Middle) At À Rebours with Schubert Club board member George Reid

(Bottom) Drinks with violinist Itzhak Perlman

could put together the time and money, and I too began using initials in my diary to identify friends.

Bruce modeled his own journal-keeping habits on those of Henry James, one of his heroes, and his enthusiasm inspired me to chronicle those months and years of single motherhood with a kind of faithfulness that I am deeply grateful for now.

The waitress is standing over us, pen in hand. Bruce studies the menu briefly, then decides on the Mediterranean chicken pasta and a glass of cabernet sauvignon. I join him with the pasta, but—as usual—not the wine. He never seems to mind. His wife Deanna has mentored him for years on good nutritional habits. He regularly avoids high fats and often goes for the fresh grilled fish. He's good—that is, until dessert. He can't seem to resist a slice of lemon tart or even a profiterole.

Bruce laughs, fingering a torn piece of paper. "Believe it or not, I brought a list of things to talk about. You know I always do that, because I'm just so afraid I'll forget the stuff I want to cover when I get here." I am aware, as he's talking, that I am focusing on just the one of his eyes that sees. At five, Bruce lost his right eye to the snap of a fishing line. The good eye—the left one—bulges just a little, muscular and prominent from overuse, and it's a riveting presence. One on one with him, I've always felt especially focused on and attended to. He doesn't have the luxury of a distracting peripheral vision.

He reaches under his coat and pulls an envelope out of the inside pocket. "I brought a couple of photos to show you." An inveterate shutterbug, Bruce is armed nearly every time we meet with a small stack of snapshots: of his daughter Vanessa and her children, of his son Max, of him with Deanna at some music event, of a smiling donor posed in front of The Schubert Club's current installation in the Ordway Center lobby.

But today I'm not interested in his kids or his weekend. Uppermost on my agenda is to hear the latest on the leukemia: the results from the latest blood test, how he's tolerating the Gleevac, when he'll have to be retested. He looks good—a little pale maybe. I think I notice a swelling around the eyes, but it's hard to tell if it's really new. So far, so good. But how long will it keep working?

Month after month, Bruce has been consistently upbeat about his disease. "I feel fine," he says. "I have energy. I don't know what will happen, but the drug's working now, and that's enough for me. It won't forever, but maybe they'll come up with something new when this one has run its course." He cackles in his inimitable way. "You could pray for me, though."

I grew up in a secular household, and—in the early days of our friendship—I paid little attention to Bruce's interest in religion. He was rooted in the Swedish Covenant tradition, a graduate of North Park College, a small church school in Illinois. Unlike so many products of Christian households, he never seemed to throw it off. To the contrary, he read, he pondered, he probed. Like me, he majored in philosophy in college and was consumed by the allure of ultimate questions. His odyssey, unlike mine, took an early theological turn. He's always loved Kierkegaard, and he's a true believer: not one to wear religion on his sleeve, but one deeply rooted in the spiritual life.

As I reached the end of my thirties, a mid-life shift awakened in me a hunger for spirituality and a voracious appetite for theological discourse. I don't credit Bruce with its inception—he had never tried to convert me—but he was supportive and enthusiastic from the start. He read my writing on the subject with glee and shared with me some of his own meditations, published in issues of a Swedish Covenant periodical he edited and contributed to on a regular basis.

After three years at the Arts and Science Council, I left in 1978. I married again and took a new job

(Top) Drinks at the Saint Paul Hotel with Pianist Alfred Brendel

(Middle) Breakfast with friend Carl Johnson

(Bottom) Lunch with Schubert Club friend Peggy Hawks

administering arts grants for the Dayton Hudson Foundation. It was a dream job, offering me the financial security and structure of a corporate setting and the bliss of spending my days observing and channeling support to the local arts scene.

Those were the days when "non-profit management" was emerging as a *bona fide* career track, complete with internships and its own master's degrees. Bruce was a refreshing antidote to all that. When we met to discuss his annual Foundation grant, we talked less about the ratio of earned to unearned income and more about commissions, or the music therapy program he was developing. His instinctive, casual style just got the job done, simply and well. He befriended his board members—mostly female and of a certain age—paying regular visits to them in their homes for tea and lively conversation. He loved local history and reveled in their stories of family and the subtle intricacies of Saint Paul society. Somehow it worked, without all the trappings. The Schubert Club was lean, flexible, and enviably secure. Bruce was slowly building up an impressive endowment and amassing a world-class collection of antique keyboard instruments.

One of the tools for survival for a non-profit arts organization is "earned income," the revenue it can pocket from ticket sales, bookstores, or restaurants. The Schubert Club could easily sell the likes of Frederica von Stade or Garrick Ohlsson—and it did—but Bruce took it one step further. He became a musical and literary entrepreneur. He published books, helping to revive several works by his beloved friend, Minnesota author Brenda Ueland. He produced CD recordings of works by favorite Minnesota composers or newly commissioned pieces that needed exposure. I've never been sure whether any of these projects actually broke even financially, but they have done a lot of good in the process.

As we dig in to the steaming bowl of garlicky penne with chicken, olives, and tomatoes, Bruce launches into a series of anecdotes about the latest developments in the Saint Paul arts scene: who's leaving what job; how the disparate performing groups are working together (or not) to share the Ordway Center spaces; what his favorite musicians, composer and writer friends are up to. Bruce relishes gossip, but it's never mean spirited. He's secure in himself and doesn't need to put others down to feel good. He revels in the successes of the talented, the generous, the quick-witted, and he shakes off with humor (and forgives) the self-aggrandizers, the overly ambitious, the inconsiderate among his colleagues. Live and let live are words he survives by.

Though Bruce is a loner and maybe even an introvert at heart (he goes to concerts and movies by himself, spends hours reading, listening to music or writing), he is a stalwart and loyal friend. I know many of the others, the personal leitmotifs in his life: friends like me who have been constant for years, even decades. The heart of his life as an impresario is the relationships he's developed, the friends among his panoply of performers. He meets them personally at the plane, keeps up with their lives, eats meals with them, and puts up cheerfully with their peccadilloes.

"Hey, check this out," he says, leaning to one side and fishing another scrap of paper out a pocket that I imagine to be bulging with the crumpled detritus of a working day. It's another photograph, a creased one—this time of an antique boat motor. I glaze over, as usual. I only

half listen, between mouthfuls, to his enthusiasms about the year it was built or its horsepower or the condition it's in. Bruce is a true collector: of the boat motors he stores up north near their cabin, of the antique pianos, harpsichords and rare ethnic instruments he keeps polished and beautifully displayed in The Schubert Club's museum in Landmark Center. Along with those are the original musical manuscripts, the signed letters and other memorabilia, and of course his own personal collection of first edition literary works.

Producing performances is his real business, and that is essentially an ephemeral phenomenon. A particular note hit just so today, this phrase beautifully executed, and all of it gone tomorrow. I wonder if the collecting, the amassing and preserving of hard objects, is his own subconscious effort to preserve the moments of beauty he enables that soar briefly and are too soon gone. "Oh, Margaret," he'll groan, rolling his eyes, telling me about a concert. It was just sooooo beautiful,"

(Left, Top to Bottom) Breakfast at the Saint Paul Hotel with daughter Vanessa Johnson; Lunch at the Grill with friend Don Franklin; Lunch with Schubert Club board member Paul Aslanian; Coffee with Judy Dayton (note singer Renée Fleming's book *The Inner Voice* on the table)

(Below) With the author (and friend) Margaret Wurtele, June 2006

as if he'd never heard anything like it before. Bruce is a true connoisseur, a man of appetite, of passion, hungry for the well-turned phrase, the pitch-perfect note, the exquisite interpretation of a favorite song. He's channeled his energy, his life force into creating those rare moments for performers and their audiences again and again.

"It's my turn, Margaret," he says, grabbing the check as he does just a little too often. "I love getting together with you." *And I, you*, I think, *my long time, dear, old friend with the boundless vision. I, you.*

Management Style

Claire Colliander

Working for The Schubert Club for nearly ten years (1994 to 2003) gave Claire Colliander a chance to observe organizational—though perhaps idiosyncratic—management in action.

While I was the accountant for The Schubert Club, I went back to school to get an MBA. As part of my studies, I read books and articles galore about management theories—*Six Sigma, Total Quality Management, The Seven Habits of Highly Effective People*. By the time I got my degree, I was armed with every current management theory except the one that I witnessed daily at The Schubert Club: good instincts.

As the long-time executive director of The Schubert Club, Bruce Carlson could write a very entertaining management manual. The section on corporate culture would recommend that a manager regularly indulge in a bit of trumpet playing during employee functions. The chapter on negotiations would include tips for disarming the other person with theological questions, poetry, or witty limericks. There would be a lengthy section on the outboard motor as a metaphor for leadership.

Although a good read, there would be very little in Bruce's manual that an aspiring manager could imitate. Bruce's devotion to The Schubert Club's mission and his ability to attract resources are gifts that can't be faked. His disinterest in blowing his own horn contradicts most management treatises I've read. Ultimately, Bruce's management style comes down to following his instincts and not worrying about what the other guys are doing. I think that may be the best example of leadership I've come across.

Bruce Carlson, High Commissioner

Bruce called me up on the phone to tell me I'd received a commission. He had a great sense of humor. This is an exact quote. I will never forget it:

"Is this Mona Lyn Reese? This is Bruce Carlson from The Schubert Club. I want to commission you for the big money."

I was completely surprised when I was asked to write a work for harpsichord (I knew ZIP about harpsichords!), but a few weeks later there I was working on a new piece, a tombeau in the style of Couperin, with Roger [Goodman] in his Chicago studio. He was great and had such good ideas. It was wonderful fun.

– Mona Lyn Reese, composer

Minnesota native Mona Lyn Reese wrote "Tombeau for Michael Collins" for solo harpsichord in 1987 before serving as composer-in-residence with the Minnesota Opera from 1991-1999. Nominated for a Pulitzer Prize in 1995, she now works as a professional composer in California.

Bruce Carlson always seemed larger than life, and had quirky ideas that, once implemented, were so right. How exciting, then, to be commissioned by Bruce/The Schubert Club in 1988 to write a piano piece for Anthony De-Mare, and what an honor to be included on the same program as Meredith Monk and Frederic Rzewski. I still remember sitting in a Chinese restaurant with Tony on a bitterly cold March evening, going over the score. And hearing "Apparizioni" done, the next night, with Tony's typical panache.

– Carol Barnett, composer

A charter member of the American Composers Forum, Carol Barnett has received commissions from, among many others, the Minnesota Orchestra, Saint Paul Chamber Orchestra, and Children's Theatre of Minneapolis, and major grants from the Camargo, Jerome, and McKnight Foundations. For nine years, she served as composer-in-residence with the Dale Warland Singers, and now teaches at Augsburg College in Minneapolis.

Inspired by the 1957 photograph of Schubert Club Board members (Mrs. Frank Lightner, Mrs. Louis Hill, and Mrs. William Dorsey), Schubert Club staff members Sharon Carlson, Raenay Rock, and Nell Slater donned hats of their own thirty-some years later.

Finance

PEOPLE'S CHURCH - St. Paul

Thursday Evening, 8:15 o'Clock

OCTOBER 15th

Auspices of THE SCHUBERT CLUB

Fees: Initiation . . . . $5.00 Annual Dues, $3 and 5.00 Season Guest Ticket 5.00	Seats Reserved at DYERS beginning Wednesday, October 14th

Hartsook Photo

QUEENA MARIO

Lyric-Coloratura Soprano

Management: Metropolitan Musical Bureau
33 West 42nd Street
New York City

"She sings as though she had a thrush in her throat."—*N. Y. Eve. Post.*

Schubert Club tickets have long been a great bargain, as this 1925 promo shows

The fund for the annual scholarship awards got off to a great start in 1922 & 1923!

SCHUBERT CLUB SEEKING FUNDS FOR SCHOLARSHIPS

The Schubert club is making plans to establish a permanent scholarship fund.

Temporary funds contributed by interested individuals have already been used in awards recently made to three students who won in competitive trials in the departments of violin, voice and piano. The sum of $450 was thus awarded.

The aim now is to make this an annual event with a two-fold purpose in view—encouragement to students for higher accomplishment and financial aid necessary in many cases to continued music study.

The fund, now being solicited by Mrs. Frank Williams and Mrs. Edwin Ames Jaggard, will be called "The Schubert club's 40th anniversary scholarship fund."

SCHUBERT TREASURY SHOWS BIG BALANCE

Crowning Work for Year Is Means Provided for Annual Scholarship.

The Schubert club finished its fortieth year with its annual meeting held in the Women's City club Wednesday. The business was preceded by a luncheon at noon, attended by 115 members, after which were heard reports from twenty-five officers and chairmen of committees, with the election of officers for 1923-1924 following.

The distinguishing feature of the closing year was held to be the accumulation of a permanent fund of money, amounting, to date, to $2,300, the annual yield from which will be offered each year as a Schubert Club Fortieth Anniversary scholarship. This amount has been contributed in sums ranging from $1 to $100 from 480 persons. While it is not the intention to solicit repeatedly, according to the report written by Mrs. E. A. Jaggard and read by Mrs. F. D. Williams, the fund will remain open

20

Season of 1894-95.

Nov. 1st. Xaver Scharwenka, pianist.

Dec. 6th. Miss Lillian Blauvelt, assisted by Rubinstein String Quartette.

Jan. 15th. Miss Adele Aus der Ohe, assisted by Mr. A. DeC. Madeira.

April 29th. Mr. Eugene Ysaye, violinist, assisted by Mr. Aime Lachaume, pianist.

Net proceeds $628.64.

Total net proceeds for all three seasons, $1,528.96.

1945 Budget summary — Concert expenses sure went up in the first fifty years!

Miss Punderson, chairman of the Budget Committee submitted the following tentative budget:

```
    Expense of the evening concert course----$7225
       "     "   "  Active Section Program---- 220
    "  "     "   "  Student     "     "         60
    General Expense-----     ----------------276
                         Total              $7781
```

She also presented figures for ann " Income Goal" which, if achieved, would relieve the club from all financial worries. It was moved by Mrs. Paetzold, seconded by Mrs. Beebe, that the budget as presented be approved. Motion carried.

Single seat sales

Increase parquet center from $2.40 to $3.00
" " sides " $2.40 to $2.40
1st 4 rows in balcony from $1.80 to $2.40
Rest of 1st balcony....$1.80
All second balcony.....$ .90

Season memberships

All downstairs the same prices as this year.... $8.40 and sides $7.
1st balcony:
1st 4 rows increase from $5.40 to $6.60
Next 4 rows " " $4.80 to $5.40
Next 3 rows " " $3.60 to $4.30
2nd balcony the same price as this year.... $2.40

(Right) Emanuel Ax was 33 when he made his first performance on the Schubert Club series. He has come back once each decade since then. (Above) Price increases in 1951 for the Saint Paul Auditorium.

Emanuel Ax
Sunday, March 27, 1983
"With his dream technique, he is a virtuoso who glories in being one."
H. Schonberg, New York Times
with Richard Killmer, oboe, and John Miller, bassoon

Ticket Prices

Each year when Schubert Club season tickets go on sale, the office gets at least one telephone call from someone double-checking that the season price is for *all five* of the concerts, not just one. A person who has recently moved here from New York City, where $100 for a single ticket is possible, could easily wonder. For instance, in spring 2007, top-price tickets to hear soprano Karita Mattila's recital at Carnegie Hall were $84, more than twice the cost of the best Schubert Club tickets when she sang at Ordway Center a week later.

On the other hand, the $40 you might have spent for the best ticket to hear pianist Emanuel Ax in March 2007 would have bought you prime balcony seats for The Schubert Club's entire 100th Anniversary Season (1982-83) at O'Shaughnessy Auditorium twenty-four years earlier—including Ax's performance then (see above).

Naturally, ticket prices have risen over the years as production costs and artist fees have gone up. Season tickets for The Schubert Club's 125th Anniversary Season (2007-2008) range from $90 to $160 ($40 for students). That lowest $90 subscription is twice the price of the top subscription ($45) from the 100th anniversary season twenty-five years earlier. If we go back even further for comparison, the 125th season highest subscription amount is a whopping 1600% increase over the $10 top-price subscription in the 75th Anniversary Jubilee Year (1957-58). The bargain lowest-price seats that year were only $3.00 (for a five-concert subscription!) but were in distant corners of the huge St. Paul Auditorium.

The remarkable thing is that ticket prices stayed incredibly low for decades.

Until the 1940s, dues of $5 would admit members to all concerts (though they sometimes had to wait in line ahead of time to claim reserved seats). That annual $5 membership fee included admission to performances by other Schubert Club members as well as by the leading musicians of the day: Jascha Heifetz, Myra Hess, Louise Homer, and Vladimir Horowitz. It is a shock to realize that a single parking pass now costs more than an entire five-concert season once did.

Nevertheless, International Artist Series tickets are still a bargain. What's more, men no longer have to come only as guests of the women members. And, thankfully, the rule (from the 1890s) that only non-residents could buy single tickets has been dropped. (Of course, it is a sensible idea that local residents have no excuse for not being Schubert Club members—or, in the present day, subscribing.)

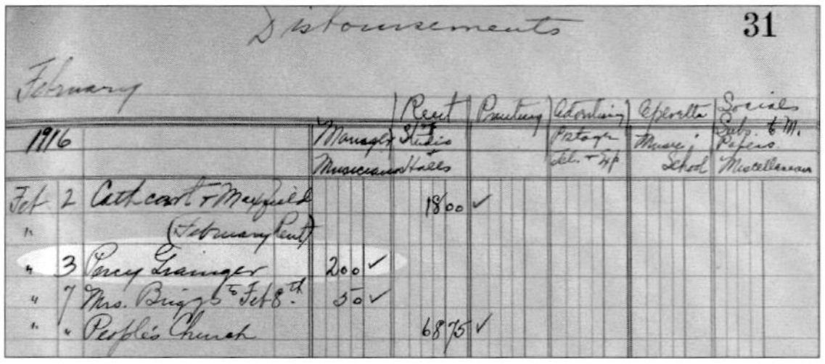
Disbursements 31
February
1916
Feb 2 Cathcart & Maxfield (February Rent) 18.00
" 3 Percy Grainger 200
" 7 Mrs. Briggs 5th Feb 8th 50
" " People's Church 68.75

(Top) Composer/pianist Percy Grainger's fee was $200. His interesting program included works by Grieg, Ravel, Debussy, Franck, and several pieces of his own: "Mock Morris" Dance, "Colonial Song," and "Shepherd's Hey."

Artist Fees

With an eye on the bottom line of the budget, Schubert Club leaders over the years have sought the best artists at the best price. In hindsight, we might now wish that they had engaged opera stars Geraldine Farrar or Emilio de Gorgoza rather than the bass

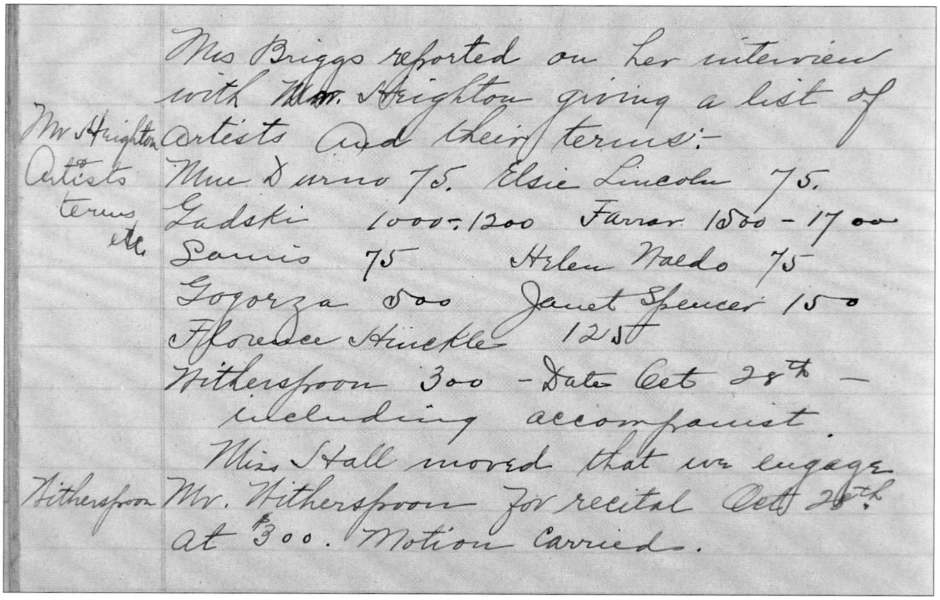
Mr Heighton Artists terms etc
Mrs Briggs reported on her interview with Mr. Heighton giving a list of artists and their terms:-
Mme Durno 75. Elsie Lincoln 75.
Gadski 1000-1200 Farrar 1500-1700
Sannis 75 Helen Waldo 75
Gogorza 500 Janet Spencer 150
Florence Hinckle 125
Witherspoon 300 - Date Oct 28th - including accompanist.
Witherspoon
Miss Hall moved that we engage Mr. Witherspoon for recital Oct 28th at $300. Motion carried.

(Bottom) The minutes from 1908 show proposed artists and their fees, with the executive committee settling on baritone Herbert Witherspoon.

ARTISTS.Mrs.Porter reported that they had met with Columbia's representative,Mr. Fox,and that the committee was considering the following:a joint program by Serkin and Adolph Busch,Elena Nikolaidi,George London,Primrose,and a pianist, Istomen.Columbia will give us Serkin and Busch,Nikolaidi,London,and Primrose for $4500.in series;and the same artists plus Istomen for $5000.in series.

Columbia offered a package deal for the 1950-51 season. From this list, only the singers Nikolaidi and London came that year.

Herbert Witherspoon in 1909, but it seemed like the right choice at the time. (Wagnerian soprano Joanna Gadski, also on the Executive Committee's prospect list that year, had performed previously—and probably at a lower fee—in 1899.)

Of course, it is not necessarily true that the best artist is always the highest paid. Not to pick on the picturesquely-named Witherspoon, but his fee was $50 more than Vladimir Horowitz received twenty years later in 1928. (Another fifty years after that, when Horowitz performed for The Schubert Club in 1979, his contract was for 80% of the house, which ended up being about $45,000. His contract also stipulated that his accommodations include a two-bedroom suite "with one bedroom having its own bathroom self-contained in the bedroom, plus a working kitchen with

EVENING CONCERT ACCOUNT.

Receipts:

Advertising		$ 492.00
Single Admissions Sold		292.50
Rebate Garrison Concert		67.50
		$ 852.00

Disbursements:

Artists	$ 4000.00	
Rent	375.00	
Printing	335.75	
Advertising	86.80	
Express and Telegrams	23.22	
Carriage Man	12.00	
	$ 4832.77	
Total Cost Account		$3980.77

By 1922, the artist fees for the evening concerts were up to $4,000 (from only $1,000 in 1917) in a total budget of about $10,000. Note the fee for the "carriage man," a line item that no longer exists on Schubert Club budgets.

Driving a Hard Bargain

"Mrs. Briggs reported that Madame Homer's price was Three Thousand Dollars for three engagements. Mrs. De Wolf moved that Madame Homer be offered $800 for single engagement. Carried."

– Executive Committee meeting, May 24, 1913

The bargaining strategy appears to have paid off, as Mrs. Briggs was able to report back that Louise Homer, who had already performed once for The Schubert Club in 1902 (accompanied by Emil Oberhoffer) would sing in October.

ST. PAUL, MINN.

Song Recital

Madame Louise Homer

Program

a. Dem Unendlichen - - - - - - - *Schubert*
b. Von Ewiger Liebe - - - - - - - *Brahms*
c. Meine Liebe Ist Grün - - - - - - *Brahms*
d. Mit Deinen Blauen Augen - - - - - *Strauss*
e. Des Kindes Gebet - - - - - - - *Reger*
f. Der Elfentanz - - - - - - - - *Wolf*

a. Sing to Me—Sing! (new) -
b. Boats Sail on the Rivers - -
c. Ferry Me Across the Water - } - *Sidney Homer*
d. The Stormy Evening - - -
e. The Song of the Shirt - -

Aria from "Orfeo"—"Che Faro Senza Euridice" - *Gluck*

a. Eldorado - - - - - - - *Leopold Bruenner*
b. Down by the Sally Gardens - } *Old Irish*
c. A Ballynure Ballad - - } *arranged by Herbert Hughes*
d. A Ballad of Trees and the Master - - - *Chadwick*
e. Wings (Mss.) - - - - *B. Sherman-Merriman*
f. Festal Song - - - - - - - *Bantock*

Mrs. Edwin N. Lapham at the Piano.

People's Church, Friday, October 10th, 1913 at 8:15 P. M.

Steinway Piano Used

As the cost of Issac Stern will be $400 and the Auditorium $200 making a $600 expense and with only $554.64 in the General Fund - Mrs. Dorsey moved, seconded by Mrs. Clayton, that $200 be taken from the Savings Acc't. and put into the checking acc't. --leaving $27.67 in the Savings Acc't. Motion carried.

a dishwasher and an oven.") Witherspoon was also paid a third again as much as composer Percy Grainger on his Schubert Club recital in 1916.

In the late 1940s, the great Wagnerian soprano Helen Traubel received $2,000, while contralto Kathleen Ferrier a few years later was paid only $1,400. The entire Paganini Quartet received $750 in the same season that Traubel sang.

Schubert Club management has always hunted—or negotiated—for a bargain. In the early days, there was sometimes a reduced fee when a performer would be scheduled in Minneapolis during the same period. Later on, artists' managers would present possible performers to the Minneapolis Symphony, the University Artists Course, and The Schubert Club as part of their regular circuit, and the presenters would cooperate as they put together their seasons.

In the 1950-1951 season, artist fees accounted for half of The Schubert Club budget. The 75th Anniversary Season of 1957-58 reached a record high of $8,700 on artist's fees—out of a total budget of $15,000. The next year, when there was less of an attempt for the splashiest artists, the fees subsided a bit to $6,700. Artist fees, which hovered at around half of the budget for several decades in the middle of the century, are currently closer to one-fifth of the budget.

Individual fees in the 1970s generally ranged from about $2,000 to $10,000 and may seem paltry considering the big time stars they're attached to. Take, for instance, pianist

CONTRIBUTION APPEAL LIMERICK 1990S

As our Schubert Club programs have grown,
We can't manage through tickets alone.
But we find the solution
In each contribution.
And at least we're not asking by phone.

Byron Janis, whose 1975 Schubert Club payment was a mere $4,000 or French pianist Philippe Entremont's bargain fee of $1,750 in 1972 (presumably a negotiation of some sort). Even soprano Beverly Sills went for $6,000 in 1970 —yet over the course of the decade her rate had escalated to $15,000 for her fourth and final Schubert Club performance in 1979. Isaac Stern, who performed four times for The Schubert Club went from $400 (in 1943) to $22,500 forty years later. In the 1980s fees generally spanned from $10,000 to $25,000. One of the highest during this time was Leontyne Price's $30,000 fee to sing at the opening of the newly built Ordway Music Theatre in 1985.

Schubert Club leaders watched uneasily as artist rates increased over the years. In just one decade the added total of International Artists Series fees went from approximately $40,000 in 1980 to $95,000 in 1990. Naturally inflation plays a role in the rising expenses, but so too does the demand of the artist. Kathleen Battle, in the midst of her rising stardom during the '80s, sang for a modest fee of only $15,000 in 1987. Eight years later the opera diva's International Artist Series rate skyrocketed to a whopping $60,000, though audience members present at her 1995 recital would agree that she was well worth it. Current artist rates range from $20,000 to $75,000, and while they may put a dent in The Schubert Club's ever resilient budget, the results are always a series of first-rate musical experiences.

The Schubert Club's bookkeeper, Kathy Wells, is grateful that computer accounting systems have replaced hand-written ledger books like the one reproduced above.

Always looking forward ... by endowing the future

Why is The Schubert Club one of the most fiscally sound organizations in town? Perhaps it's because, since our earliest days, the stewards of The Schubert Club have had the foresight and discipline to spend little, and save lots. Over time, their generosity and prudent frugality have built an endowment that is the financial bedrock of the organization. Long-term saving has allowed short-term spending—every year the endowment generates annual funding that allows us to grant music scholarships, implement new programs, and present the very best international and neighborhood musicians.

One stellar example of early stewardship is the Hill Family, who, in 1957, established the *Maud Taylor Hill Scholarship in Music Fund* with an initial gift of $10,000, augmented with an additional $30,000 in 1974. By investing for the long-term in endowment, that gift today is now worth $158,000! And it generates more than $7,500 annually towards The Schubert Club's scholarship programs.

Many other donors have taken similar steps to ensure the future of The Schubert Club and its outstanding programs. The *Maud Moon Weyerhaeuser Sanborn International Artist Series*, the *Gilman Ordway Manuscript Collection*, the newly created *Bruce P. Carlson Student Scholarship Competition Fund*, and the many other named scholarships and funds are all prime ex-

A Schubert Club scrapbook clipping from 1927 shows the singer in whose honor the organization's major recital series was renamed The Maud Moon Weyerhaeuser Sanborn International Artist Series.

ANNUAL SCHOLARSHIP

Receipts:		
Interest and Coupons	$ 309.98	
Balance from 1929	27.50	
	$ 337.48	
Disbursements:		
To three Scholarships	$ 300.00	
Balance . . .	$ 37.48	
TOTAL BALANCE		$ 5,899.10
On Deposit -- First National Bank, Savings Department		$ 37.48
40th Anniversary Bonds		5861.62
Balance . . .		$5899.10

The 1930 Treasurer's Report shows the use of the 40th Anniversary Bonds to create an endowment for the Scholarship Competition awards.

> *"That women today can handle more than $10,000 annually without going into the red isn't surprising. But that women, with no help from the other sex, have had the care and spending of similar amounts for more than 70 years, without once overspending, is something of a miracle."*
>
> From an article in the *St. Paul Pioneer Press*, November 7, 1954, "After 72 Years – Schubert Club Still is Growing" by Amy Birdsall

amples of endowments created by families and friends who care about the future of our music and our community.

The Schubert Club remains true to its early principles. We spend our donations wisely, and invest for the future. And we proudly acknowledge the foresight and generosity of our patrons.

Piano Expenses

Pianos have been useful at Schubert Club concerts—in fact, often essential. And for most of The Schubert Club's history, the organization has relied on renting them. In the 1960s, thanks to a bequest from former Board President Gertrude Loomis, the organization finally purchased its own piano, a Steinway grand. Now that Ordway Center has two 9-foot Steinway Model D pianos (one selected by Peter Serkin in time for the first concert in 1985), The Schubert Club no longer has one there. In Landmark Center, however, The Schubert Club keeps two Steinway B (7-foot) grand pianos (used regularly for Courtroom Concerts) as well as some other special pianos, like the 1878 Bechstein in Gallery 205, and an assortment of playable Museum instruments.

Because there are many concert series and a variety of venues on The Schubert Club season, piano rentals continue, as of course do tuning and maintenance expenses. Starting in the 1970s, the acquisition of keyboard instruments for the Museum added exponentially to the upkeep costs, as wood-framed harpsichords and fortepianos require more frequent tuning.

Expenses from a century ago now seem laughably minor. The Treasurer's report from 1900 shows a line item of $5 for piano tuning and drayage. In the 1921-22 season, piano rental costs were $57 and insurance on the piano $1.00. By 1960, piano rental (including tuning) had risen to $68 per concert.

Sometimes special pianos have to be brought in, adding to the cost. Some performers, even in the early days, make a commitment to a specific piano manufacturer. At one concert in 1912, the

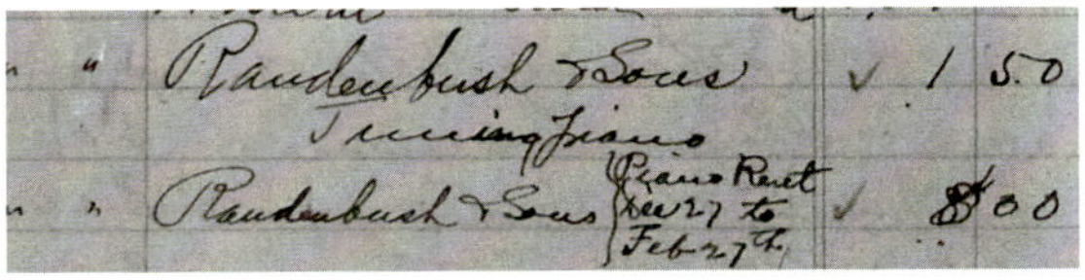

The Raudenbush & Sons Piano Company, based in Saint Paul, provided a piano at a cost of $8 for three months. Twenty years later, Florence Raudenbush—the wife of one of the "& Sons" (Webb Raudenbush)—became president of The Schubert Club.

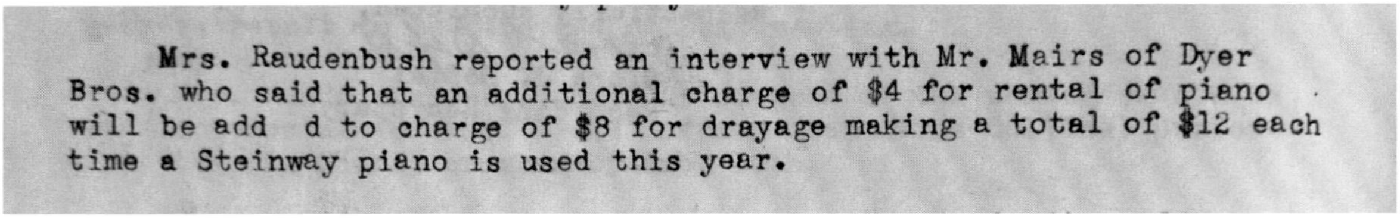
Mrs. Raudenbush reported an interview with Mr. Mairs of Dyer Bros. who said that an additional charge of $4 for rental of piano will be add d to charge of $8 for drayage making a total of $12 each time a Steinway piano is used this year.

Mason & Hamlin piano had already been delivered when the Board realized that the artist was "under contract with the Steinway people." A switch had to be made at the last minute.

An artist may require not just a Steinway, but a Hamburg Steinway (that is, one made in Hamburg, Germany, not the U.S.). Krystian Zimmerman in 1999 traveled with his own, but The Schubert Club had to send to New York for a Hamburg Steinway for Daniel Barenboim in 2001. Artists may also have requirements about bringing their own piano technician (as Horowitz did and, more recently, Mitsuko Uchida in 2003).

To some performers, the piano tuner is an invisible taken-for-granted element of a concert performance, while others may hover over the shoulder of the tuner, asking for a different sound quality. Mark Bunker, as Ordway Center's piano technician, has been tuning for The Schubert Club International Artist Series since 1988. He has stories (but you won't read them here) about how some performers are notoriously idiosyncratic about the tuning or voicing of the piano. Having to spend a long time doing (and later undoing) a peculiar voicing can add to the cost of piano preparation.

Some pianists also insist on more on-stage rehearsal than others, which for concerts at Ordway Center, where the hall is closely scheduled, can add considerably to the cost. Evgeny Kissin required extensive on-stage practice before his recital in 2000. The cost of a touch-up tuning was nothing to the cost of the space.

In addition to the planned-for costs, there is always a possibility of unanticipated expenses, as in this post-concert report presented at a Board meeting in December 1949:

"Mrs. Porter reported that Wylie Piano Co. called re the Baldwin piano used at the Ann Bomar concert. It was a new piano and the top had been badly scratched probably from the bouquets of roses. Mrs. Porter talked with the manager and he asked if the Schubert Club would pay $10 to help cover the cost of refinishing the top. A motion was made by Mrs. Loevinger and seconded by Mrs. France that we pay the $10 if their insurance doesn't take care of it. The motion carried."

Hungarian pianist Yolanda Mero (who made her Minnesota debut in 1921 with The Schubert Club) was one of several artists committed to Steinway.

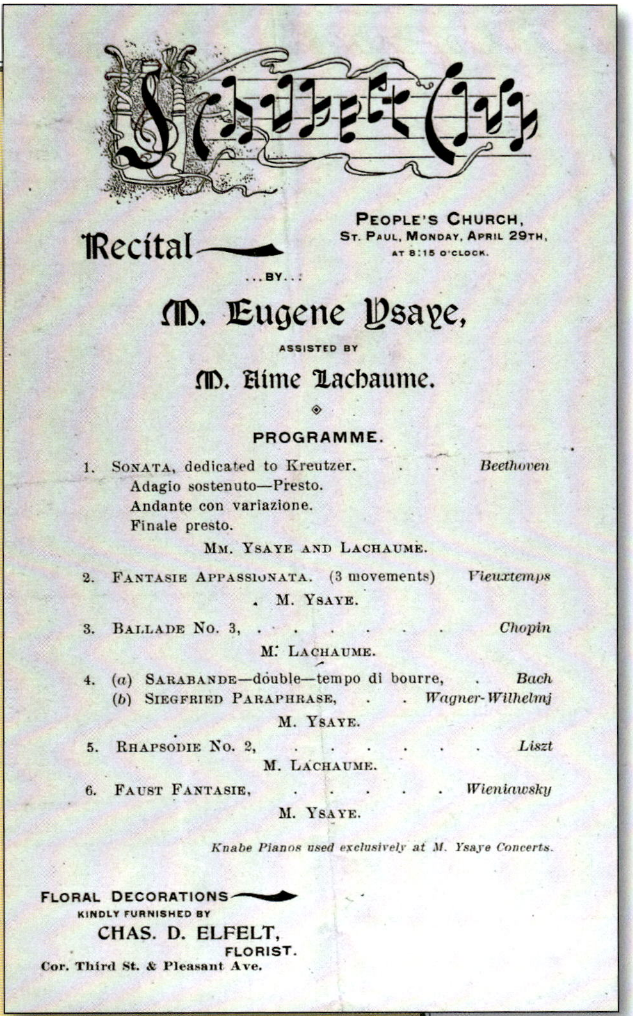
Schubert Club

Recital —— ...BY...

PEOPLE'S CHURCH,
ST. PAUL, MONDAY, APRIL 29TH,
AT 8:15 O'CLOCK.

M. Eugene Ysaye,

ASSISTED BY

M. Aime Lachaume.

PROGRAMME.

1. SONATA, dedicated to Kreutzer. . . . *Beethoven*
Adagio sostenuto—Presto.
Andante con variazione.
Finale presto.
MM. YSAYE AND LACHAUME.

2. FANTASIE APPASSIONATA. (3 movements) *Vieuxtemps*
M. YSAYE.

3. BALLADE NO. 3, ... *Chopin*
M. LACHAUME.

4. (a) SARABANDE—double—tempo di bourre, . *Bach*
(b) SIEGFRIED PARAPHRASE, . . *Wagner-Wilhelmj*
M. YSAYE.

5. RHAPSODIE NO. 2, ... *Liszt*
M. LACHAUME.

6. FAUST FANTASIE, ... *Wieniawsky*
M. YSAYE.

Knabe Pianos used exclusively at M. Ysaye Concerts.

FLORAL DECORATIONS
KINDLY FURNISHED BY
CHAS. D. ELFELT,
FLORIST.
Cor. Third St. & Pleasant Ave.

NOTICE ABOUT CONCERT BY GREAT BELGIAN VIOLINIST EUGÈNE YSAŸE, APRIL 1895:

"The Committee has shouldered a very heavy burden in this enterprise, and it must have your earnest and united help in carrying it. The expenses are enormously heavy, and outside attractions numerous, but so great is the desire to hear this splendid artist that we are sure a little effort on your part will insure us a full house... Enclosed are four tickets, each one of which is worth 25 cents when presented at the box office at Howard, Farwell & Co.'s in exchange for reserve seats. Seats are $2.00, $1.50, $1.00 and 75 cents, according to location, with a reduction of 25 cents to anyone presenting one of the enclosed tickets.

It is desired to make this a gala event, and we hope that the members and their friends will so far as possible come in evening dress."

Ysaÿe's managers had offered two performances in the two cities for $900. The Schubert Club latched on to the St. Paul performance. At the same time, the group rejected American soprano Lilian Nordica's $600 fee as being "too great a risk for the club to undertake."

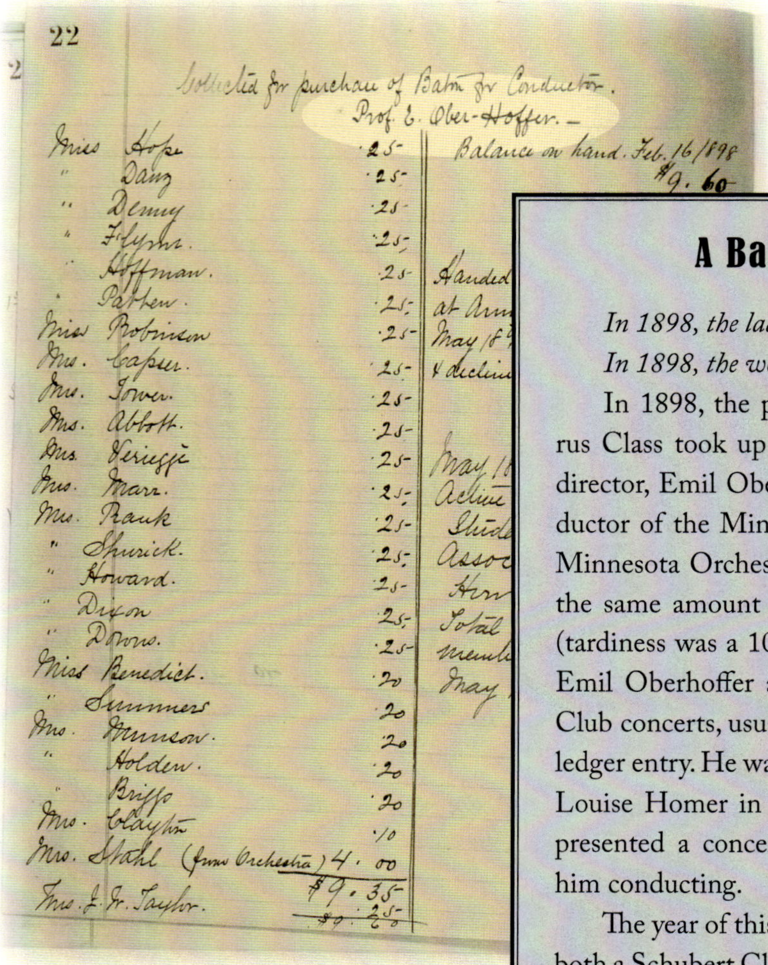
22

Collected for purchase of Baton for Conductor.
Prof. E. Ober-Hoffer.—

Miss Hope	.25	Balance on hand. Feb. 16/1898 $9.60
" Dainz	.25	
" Denny	.25	
" Flynn	.25	
" Hoffman	.25	
" Patten	.25	
Miss Robinson	.25	
Mrs. Capser	.25	
Mrs. Tower	.25	
Mrs. Abbott	.25	
Mrs. Veriggi	.25	
Mrs. Marr	.25	
Mrs. Rank	.25	
" Shurick	.25	
" Howard	.25	
" Dixon	.25	
" Downs	.25	
Miss Benedict	.20	
" Summers	.20	
Mrs. Munson	.20	
" Holden	.20	
" Briggs	.20	
Mrs. Clayton	.10	
Mrs. Stahl (from Orchestra)	4.00	
	$9.35	
Mrs. J. W. Taylor	.25	
	$9.60	

A Baton for Their Leader

In 1898, the ladies of the Ladies Chorus . . .

In 1898, the women of the women's chorus . . .

In 1898, the participants in The Schubert Club Chorus Class took up a subscription to buy a baton for their director, Emil Oberhoffer, who later became the first conductor of the Minneapolis Symphony Orchestra (now the Minnesota Orchestra). The common 25¢ contribution was the same amount as the fine for those who skipped class (tardiness was a 10¢ fine, and missing a performance 50¢). Emil Oberhoffer appears several times on early Schubert Club concerts, usually with his name hyphenated as on this ledger entry. He was an excellent accompanist (including for Louise Homer in 1902), and in 1906 The Schubert Club presented a concert by the Minneapolis Symphony, with him conducting.

The year of this subscription, Oberhoffer was director of both a Schubert Club chorus and orchestra. Alas, the following season, the orchestra was "relinquished with great regret on account of the expense of maintaining it." Oberhoffer consoled himself by developing the Minneapolis Symphony Orchestra, which held its first concert in 1903. Did he perhaps use the baton he had been given five years earlier?

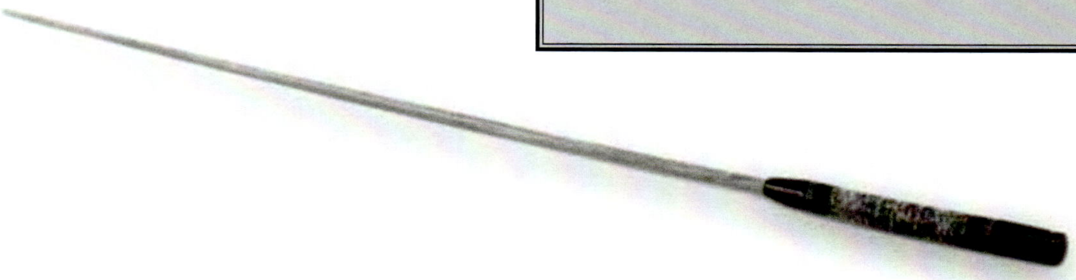

Carrying on through the Depression

"Faltering not at all, in the face of the most disastrous and terrifying economic conditions the wide world has ever experienced, that gallant body of women, the Executive Board, took up the banners and marched forward—each member a conspicuous unit in the mobilized forces, arrayed for mortal combat, against the ravages of circumstance. That ideals and solvency have been preserved; that standards have been upheld and perhaps surpassed, (certainly this is evident in the activities of the students' section); that the caliber of the evening concerts has not been sacrificed, either in quality or quantity, is scarcely short of a miracle; —but the kind of a miracle that is manifested by dint of unwavering energy and application to a purpose well-grounded in the hearts of its believers."

- Mrs. Guyer, President's Report, 1933

"Mrs. Briggs reported that the Homer Programme would cost $37.00 for 2000 programs and that the last page had been sold for an ad to the Scranton Coal Co. for $37.00."

Executive Committee meeting,
October 6, 1913

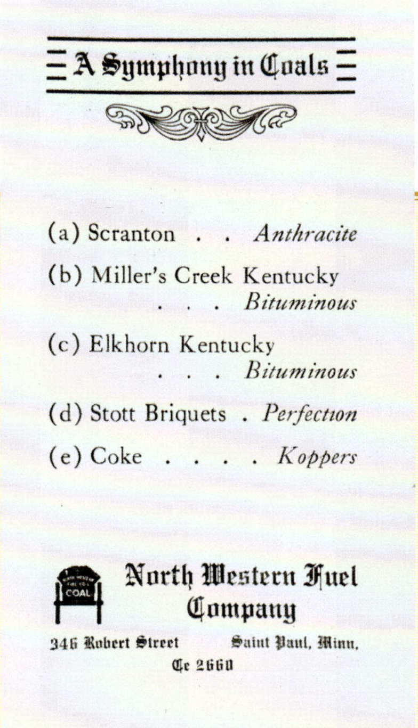

Coal advertising, as shown in this one from a 1927 program, fueled many early Schubert Club concerts.

Community Connections

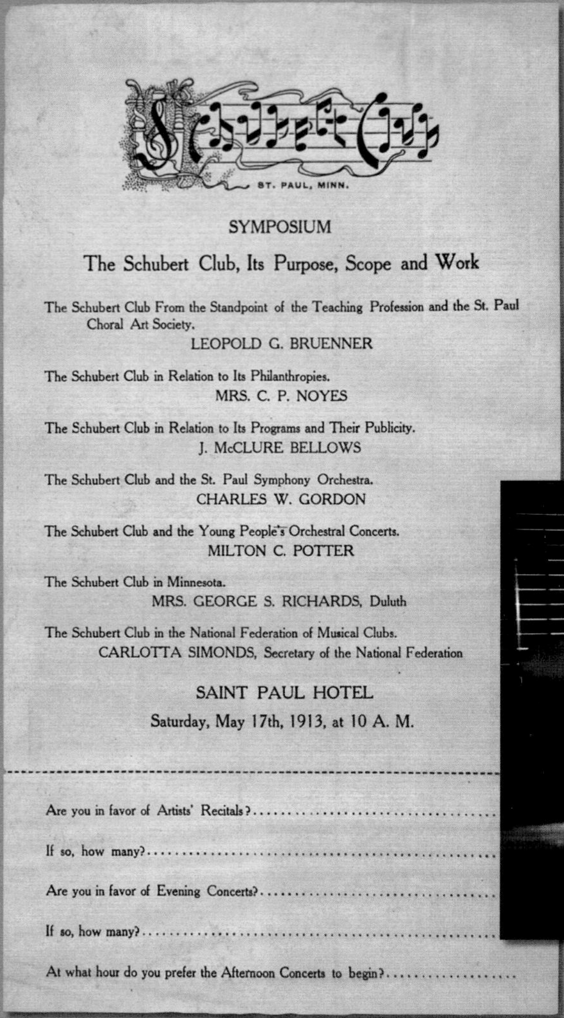

Schubert Club
ST. PAUL, MINN.

SYMPOSIUM

The Schubert Club, Its Purpose, Scope and Work

The Schubert Club From the Standpoint of the Teaching Profession and the St. Paul Choral Art Society.
LEOPOLD G. BRUENNER

The Schubert Club in Relation to Its Philanthropies.
MRS. C. P. NOYES

The Schubert Club in Relation to Its Programs and Their Publicity.
J. McCLURE BELLOWS

The Schubert Club and the St. Paul Symphony Orchestra.
CHARLES W. GORDON

The Schubert Club and the Young People's Orchestral Concerts.
MILTON C. POTTER

The Schubert Club in Minnesota.
MRS. GEORGE S. RICHARDS, Duluth

The Schubert Club in the National Federation of Musical Clubs.
CARLOTTA SIMONDS, Secretary of the National Federation

SAINT PAUL HOTEL
Saturday, May 17th, 1913, at 10 A. M.

Are you in favor of Artists' Recitals?..........

If so, how many?..........

Are you in favor of Evening Concerts?..........

If so, how many?..........

At what hour do you prefer the Afternoon Concerts to begin?..........

A period room at the Minneapolis Institute of Arts graced by our 1765 harpsichord

Backstage at SPCO Cente during "Mozart Mania" — everyone wanted to try on the wig!

Future percussionists outside our tent at the Children's Festival

Young turks from the Minnesota Composers Forum around 1980

Pioneer Music

Patricia Hampl

A Regents' Professor at the University of Minnesota, Patricia Hampl teaches in the English Department. She has written three memoir books that were listed as New York Times *Notable Books of the Year, as well as poetry, fiction, travel pieces, and* Spillville*—a history of Dvořák in Iowa. Her most recent book,* Blue Arabesque *was published in 2006. She wrote essays for two of The Schubert Club's previous anniversary publications:* Saint Paul's Schubert Club: A Century of Music *and* Song Above the Land, *a centennial history of the International Artist Series.*

MID-MARCH, A KILLER BLIZZARD HOWLING down Linwood Avenue, and out the window of the stucco bungalow, I see two delivery men stagger, hatless, their open parkas snapping in the wind as they desperately cleave to the zaftig torso of a grand piano they're struggling to haul up what is ordinarily our front staircase but now is a sheer face of packed snow. Except for them, the world has disappeared. Out there *the real snow, our snow* is falling, as Fitzgerald says at the end of *Gatsby* of the profound winter storms of the Midwest.

Something likewise *real*, likewise *ours* that I couldn't name at the time, a half century ago, attached itself to these figures clasping their broad-hipped burden. A solemn valor attended that embrace. They bore the piano up, two working guys alone and anonymous in the lost world, straining to bring something monumental—music in its unwieldy body—to us.

To me, in fact. For it was my ninth birthday and this massive wooden object making its way through the snow was to be mine. I'd been promised a piano. And blizzard or no blizzard, I must not be disappointed: my father's thought.

The piano was also a kind of marital triumph for him. My mother had finally caved: all right, he could buy a piano, but just an upright, no grand piano—we couldn't afford one, and where on earth would we put it? But he, Sunday violin player and passionate proponent of domestic music-making, was possessed by a vision of stagy father-daughter piano-violin duets. He easily forgot the no-grand-piano part of the deal.

My mother and I stood at the front window as the heroic action played out before us. "That thing," she said with weary resignation, "it's going to hog the whole living room." She regarded with regret the diminutive green velvet settee, her pride and joy. "The loveseat," she said, "will be just *swallowed up.*"

True. For the rest of my girlhood and well beyond, the chestnut brown Whitney, a piano of no particular repute, was our 800-pound gorilla, claiming more space than any other piece of furniture in the house. But over time, except for my brother's inaptly named collie, Champ, it became our most beloved possession. In any case, the piano long outlasted Champ who spent his dispirited days curled up beneath it, fixing his urban keepers with a guilt-inducing gaze from his born-to-be-free eyes. The piano sent out no such malcontented vibes. It filled the room unapologetically, radiating the serene self-regard of a fat woman who thinks people stare because *there's just a lot of me to love.*

But it isn't the piano itself or even the excruciating piano-violin duets from the red Schirmer books (My father's voice: *Count, Patricia, count!*) that pulls me back. That's common nostalgia, the syrupy homebrew everyone loves to sip, though it's without savor to anyone else—if you're lucky enough to have that kind of sweet family elixir bottled up.

No, the snow still sweeping my mind, the fascination that still dazzles my eye, isn't the personal white-out of family memory. That's another story, another storm. The storm swirling around our old chestnut Whitney is wholly civic as it comes laboriously up the staircase. It's a picture lodged in the heart, though, an indelible freeze-frame from mid-century Saint Paul. I see it clearly: my knees, covered by the blue serge of my Saint Luke's uniform, feel the scorch of the radiator as I lean toward the cold window, my not-persuaded mother next to me, frowning. Outside, in the obscuring whirlwind, two men I will never see again valiantly take on the elements in order to bear civilization—for what else is that piano to us?—to our narrow door.

It may be difficult for us to comprehend what live music meant 125 years ago to a proud provincial town rising on the edge of the disappearing prairie near the newly-razed boreal forests of the north. Make that a touchy, insecure, but madly optimistic provincial town. And lose the phrase "live music"—all music was "live." It was largely homemade, singing around the piano. Or it was church business, warbling in the choir. For the emerging social and intellectual elite there were also musicales, home concerts for an invited audience to hear a serious pianist or a trained voice.

Or—rare big town pleasure—to sit, lights lowered, in a hired hall where a singer or violinist "of renown" took the stage for a single night, a breathless Saint Paul stop on the Great Northern route before hitting Omaha on one of the improving concert circuits of the nineteenth century that swept across the plains. This was music as missionary work, the grand stars of Vienna and New York conveying art (that is, Art) to the "wilderness." Adelina Patti and Ole Bull, Jenny Lind ("the Swedish Nightingale"), itinerant opera companies, marching bands, even Antonin Dvořák came to town.

The inhabitants of the wilderness—or former wilderness—could take this chance to prove to themselves they weren't wild at all. They were people of culture. It's no mere coincidence that the greatest musical novel in our literature, Willa Cather's *Song of the Lark*, features a girl from a Nebraska prairie town who becomes a great international soprano, Cather's heroic model of the true artist. With a novelist's cunning, she knew only a solitary, art-starved child of the lost Midwest could carry the weight of all that romantic urgency about what music can mean in a life.

The history textbooks of my own mid-twentieth century grade school always stressed the *hard work* that Midwestern pioneers of the second half of the nineteenth century endured to "clear the wilderness." They made their own soap, they butchered hogs, they sewed their own clothes. Busy,

". . . to sit, lights lowered, in a hired hall where a singer or violinist "of renown" took the stage for a single night . . ."

busy, busy. Not much was said in our textbooks about what—or whom—had been "cleared." But the defensive point was made: There was no *time* for writing books and making art or attending concerts. What more could be expected of people contending by turns with floods and draughts, hordes of grasshoppers and ferocious wildfires?

We were encouraged to think of the frontier, with a thrilling shiver, as a raw place that needed to be "settled." The saloon came before the salon. Our teachers liked to pass along as a mild scandal that the village that became Saint Paul was first called Pig's Eye, named for a disreputable whiskey runner with a bad eye who set up business on the river's edge near Lambert's Landing after he'd been forced away from his clientele near Fort Snelling. With a pedigree like that we should understand that Art, for the likes of us, was bound to show up "later."

Presumably *later* was our own time, the 1950s and 1960s, though it wasn't entirely clear if the golden age of culture had now arrived or was still, at least in Saint Paul, floating off somewhere just beyond reach. A deep insecurity about anything touching on art or culture remained the birthright of the Midwest, as it does of any provincial place, deep into the post-War period of my school years. Real art happened elsewhere, as did all great things. We accepted our sidelined status in a vaguely wounded way, even as we pressed on with our piano lessons. We understood that *Main Street* was a Minnesota book. Its faults were, somehow, our faults, a little like Original Sin. You just had to accept it and soldier on.

The point was driven home again and again in history class: life for the pioneers was dead serious—and it was utterly exhausting. We were shown period photographs in which farm families, dressed either in ramrod starched garments or in sagging wrinkles, posed stoically for the slow shutter speeds of the age. We were encouraged to see these stern souls as heroic but almost feral. A lank woman in a dark weedy gown stood before the hovel of a sod house, her mouth a thin line, the featureless landscape spreading in all directions around her like hopelessness. No concert-goer, she. No Whitney in her living room. Well, no living room.

All you had to do was read Laura Ingalls Wilder to know what a tough time they had, how threadbare, if intense, their pleasures, how endless their chores. I couldn't quite fathom it, and during our grade school pageants celebrating pioneer life, confusedly imagined these frontier forbearers laboring mightily by day, and then collapsing at night, dropping off in front of the

"The snug immigrant enclaves closer to the river—the Czechs near Schmidt Brewery on West Seventh . . ."

TV as the laugh track of *I Love Lucy* blared away. Wasn't that exhaustion?

Yet somehow in this cracked kiddie version of pioneer history the idea also surfaced that absence and denial made the cultural heart grow not only fonder, but more determined. *We made our own fun*—another article of pioneer life as it was purveyed to us. Which meant, it almost went without saying, *we made our own music*. In the *Little House* books, from time to time Pa did manage to tune up his violin and fiddle by the firelight.

Having a piano in the house was a talisman of the ideal life, life as it should be, as it might be. The snug immigrant enclaves closer to the river—the Czechs near Schmidt Brewery on West Seventh, where my father had grown up and where I was born, and the Italians on the levee—were devoted to music.

By the mid-Sixties the children of these tight, tender old ethnic neighborhoods were taking to the urban margins, to what we would come to know years later as sprawl. Sometime around 1965 the Italians departed in a more drastically biblical way, flooded out.

Think of the pianos! My mother cried, looking up from the *Pioneer Press* the morning after the river had crested. Dismaying pictures of drowned houses filled the front page. John-boats with outboard motors plied the suddenly Venetian streets, pausing at the stop signs of submerged intersections.

Women on the levee sang opera music as they hung out the wash, my mother claimed. *Every house down there had a piano!* Her dismay seemed to center on the notion that this cultural refinement should have saved them if there was any fairness in the world.

"*Think of the pianos!* My mother cried . . ."

The piano was partly about music, partly about creating a social world—"making our own fun." But it also represented the platonic ideal of all that should be held valuable not only in home life but in civil society. This lofty vision of *the good* was not indulgent. It assumed discipline—lessons, practicing, the formal commitment of time and effort. It assumed that music, highest of the arts, was not only a communal value. It was the civic hearth and it was tended, typically, by women.

No wonder so much ardent effort went into the music societies that sprang up in towns and cities across the country, especially in a "provincial capital" like Saint Paul in the boom years of the 1880s and 1890s. These music clubs upheld the vision of public life that acknowledged what Walt Whitman called the "democratic vistas" inherent in American art. Around this hearth of music-making the city could gather like a family, not only for fun and fellowship, but to pledge allegiance to a nobler life perhaps more imagined than real.

Years later in college, I read Whitman's great notebook essays, written in the 1870s and 1880s—the very years when these music clubs were being founded. I recognized dimly the cultural idealism of my father and my town in his wonderfully bombastic, romantic claim that art alone could be trusted as the assurance of American democracy.

His was a prophet's oracular fire: America could only hope to survive any "mortal crisis" by relying "neither [on] the written law, nor... self-interest, or common pecuniary or material objects—but [on] the fervid and tremendous *Idea*..."

What, exactly, this *Idea* was he went to long, tortuous paragraphs to explain. Whatever it was, he felt it must be based on "the love of comrades." It required a vision of the best possible imagined national self—a vision that could be articulated and understood only by the nation's artists and their faithful audiences.

In "Democratic Vistas," his visionary manifesto of America, Whitman acknowledges the materialistic faith of his age, a faith in Progress that ignored the depredations of the land and of native populations. Perhaps "worldly prosperity and...all life's material comforts, is the main thing, and is enough." He even allowed that "it may be argued that our republic is...really enacting today the grandest arts...by beating up the wilderness into fertile farms, and in her railroads, ships, machinery, etc."

Fertile farms and railroads—the very "arts" being "enacted" in Saint Paul and across Minnesota as he wrote those words. "It may be asked," he goes on in his faux-Horace Greeley way, "are these not better, indeed, for America, than any utterances even of the greatest rhapsode, artist, or literatus?"

He even admits (or rhetorically allows), "I too hail those achievements with pride and joy." But this is a man who calls a musician a *rhapsode* and a writer a *literatus*. His faith is elsewhere: It is not by beating the wilderness into fertile farms or by tracking the continent with railroads that "the soul of man will…be finally satisfied," he says. The citizen soul needs rhapsodes, people who will not only beat swords into plowshares, but plowshares into parlor pianos.

Whitman's "*Idea*" translates the pursuit of happiness into something more than a march across the geographic expanse of the frontier, more even than a victor's celebration of the triumph, less than twenty years in the past, of "the Union." Like Lincoln, Whitman saw the war's outcome not as a victory, but as the very survival of the republic. Now, in the aftermath of that national bloodbath, he urges, against the wild speculative greed of the post-war boom, a fervent civic solidarity that puts its faith and future in what art and music and literature have to offer.

Pretty crazy. And though Whitman, everyone agrees, is a great poet, that doesn't stop people from thinking he was a bit cracked. Or simply a cloudy dreamer adrift in an essentially materialistic (we would say, "consumer") society. Because who believes that anything as airy as his grand *Idea* of a republic of rhapsodes could take hold in our grab-what-you-can culture?

Still, that indelible blizzard of a half-century ago refuses to fade. I see it now for what it is: a graphic illustration of Whitman's idea that the job of culture is not simply to make beauty but to "indicate the path between reality and men's souls."

And there, in the pristine frame of total recall, are those two working men, their red faces chapped by stinging snow, straining against common sense and safety to deliver a Whitney grand up the slippery staircase to the little house of a man determined to pass along to his child what he believed—what he knew—was nothing less than civilization in a big shiny wooden box.

But not civilization as a package deal, but a way of *being* civilized, of living the participatory dream of Whitman's democratic vistas. And that March day nobody thought it was crazy, nobody denied its rightness—not the delivery men who could have called the whole thing off, not I gazing at a storm straight out of *Giants in the Earth*, not even my mother who stood at the cold window, regretting her green settee, but knowing that some furniture is not just stuff. It's an ideal, and you have to give it all the room it needs.

The Schubert Club was—and remains—a herald of this buoyant Whitmanian spirit. It was founded in 1882 by ardent, intelligent women who were humble enough to take their intentions seriously. It was an auspicious year:

Bedřich Smetana's great romantic tone poem, *Ma Vlast*, received its first full performance in Prague that November, articulating in wholly musical terms the urgent longings of a nation for its own cultural identity. Whitman would have approved.

Virginia Woolf, James Joyce, Igor Stravinsky, and Leopold Stokowski were all born that year, and also my Czech grandmother. And it was the year Darwin and Emerson died. Passionate idealists coming and going.

More to the point for the civic life of Saint Paul, the 1880s were the period when James J. Hill established his massive transportation empire. In a historically tidy convergence, the final spike of the Great Northern Railway, uniting Saint Paul and Chicago and "the East" to the West Coast and "the Orient," was driven in January, 1893, just weeks before the debut recital in what became The Schubert Club's International Artist Series, on March 4, 1893 at the Ford Music Hall in downtown Saint Paul.

In the spirit of the parlor musicales where so many nineteenth century music societies—including The Schubert Club—had their roots, the first artist in the International Series was a pianist, Adele aus der Ohe, who had studied with Franz Liszt. It was Liszt, in fact, who first used the term "recital" to promote his wildly popular solo concerts. The lineage was solid—from Liszt, the greatest recitalist of his time, radiating a rock star's aura, to one of his star pupils on stage in downtown Saint Paul. The Schubert Club staked its claim to greatness from the start.

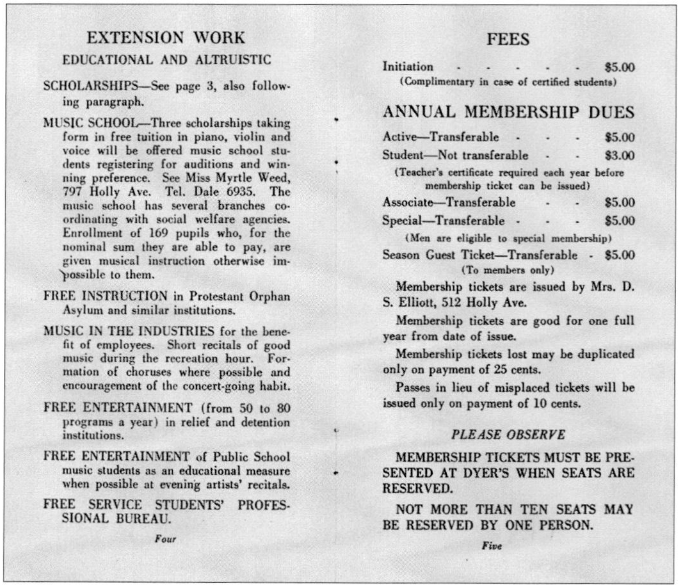
EXTENSION WORK

EDUCATIONAL AND ALTRUISTIC

SCHOLARSHIPS—See page 3, also following paragraph.

MUSIC SCHOOL—Three scholarships taking form in free tuition in piano, violin and voice will be offered music school students registering for auditions and winning preference. See Miss Myrtle Weed, 797 Holly Ave. Tel. Dale 6935. The music school has several branches coordinating with social welfare agencies. Enrollment of 169 pupils who, for the nominal sum they are able to pay, are given musical instruction otherwise impossible to them.

FREE INSTRUCTION in Protestant Orphan Asylum and similar institutions.

MUSIC IN THE INDUSTRIES for the benefit of employees. Short recitals of good music during the recreation hour. Formation of choruses where possible and encouragement of the concert-going habit.

FREE ENTERTAINMENT (from 50 to 80 programs a year) in relief and detention institutions.

FREE ENTERTAINMENT of Public School music students as an educational measure when possible at evening artists' recitals.

FREE SERVICE STUDENTS' PROFESSIONAL BUREAU.

Four

FEES

Initiation - - - - - $5.00
(Complimentary in case of certified students)

ANNUAL MEMBERSHIP DUES

Active—Transferable - - - $5.00
Student—Not transferable - - $3.00
(Teacher's certificate required each year before membership ticket can be issued)
Associate—Transferable - - $5.00
Special—Transferable - - - $5.00
(Men are eligible to special membership)
Season Guest Ticket—Transferable - $5.00
(To members only)

Membership tickets are issued by Mrs. D. S. Elliott, 512 Holly Ave.

Membership tickets are good for one full year from date of issue.

Membership tickets lost may be duplicated only on payment of 25 cents.

Passes in lieu of misplaced tickets will be issued only on payment of 10 cents.

PLEASE OBSERVE

MEMBERSHIP TICKETS MUST BE PRESENTED AT DYER'S WHEN SEATS ARE RESERVED.

NOT MORE THAN TEN SEATS MAY BE RESERVED BY ONE PERSON.

Five

". . . a club to sustain their own musical life and to encourage the musical education of the next generation . . ."

There's something wholly Saint Paul about all of this, though, not "international" at all. Something about choosing to focus on the solo form, the chamber setting—the recital instead of the symphony orchestra—comes straight out of the unconscious core of this place. Deep in the glinting fissures of its reticence and rectitude, Saint Paul is a lyric town. Even its greatest writer—Scott Fitzgerald—though a novelist, was essentially a poetic writer, a man whose sense of the line was all rhythm, all voice. Even more than a storyteller, he was a singer.

The women who banded together to found The Schubert Club in 1882 didn't initially found an international series. That came later, in 1893, as part of their growing sense of mission and audience. In 1882 they started a club to sustain their own musical life and to encourage the musical education of the next generation, mostly girls as they themselves had been girls who had been given lessons and become "musical." Even in that early domestic version of the club they meant business: annual membership was two dollars and carried a commitment to perform at least twice at club gatherings. If you failed to keep up your two-recital performance contract, you were fined a dollar. Serious money for an infraction of the club's serious code.

The International Artist Series put Saint Paul on the musical map—and still does. But the root of The Schubert Club burrows deeper, right under the nineteenth century parlors of women who did not yet have the vote. They moved the big cultural furniture into this doughty river town, and staked a claim—an *Idea* that has proved to be more enduring than the railroad tracks of the great empire emerging along the river's edge that same year.

You feel all this when you cut across Rice Park from the Hotel garage on a weeknight in November, the night of the first International Artist Series recital of the season. Passing by Michael Price's statue of Fitzgerald, his bronze topcoat slung over his arm, you head out of the bitter cold into the woody glow of the Ordway, and this city sends its dart as usual, its Cupid-arrow tenderly nicking the civic heart: Look who we got to come play for us this time—year after year they come.

Bruce Carlson, heir to all this ardor and determination bequeathed by the ladies of the nineteenth century musicales to us, stands in the lobby, an unflappable impresario, his red bowtie slightly askew, a sign that all is well. My hero: Only a few months ago he solved yet another musical dilemma in my life. What to do, finally, with the old Whitney grand now that my father's gone, and my mother after him, and the piano no longer makes sense for me to keep.

Just what he could use, he said—a perfect example of a mid-twentieth century family piano for The Schubert Club Keyboard Museum. So all that effort—mine to keep time with my father's violin, and the piano movers' struggle in the midst of that wild March blizzard—all that strenuous effort has finally found a home, its modest self wedged in with the eighteenth century harpsichords and the pianofortes Peter Serkin bends to touch.

Several times a year The Schubert Club sponsors chamber concerts in one of the grand parlors of the James J. Hill mansion on Summit Avenue. Intimate audiences, exquisite programs. These aren't part of The International Artist Series. The artists who perform here are local, though they often have international careers.

You walk down the great hushed avenue of the old neighborhood toward the big brownstone across from the Cathedral. Maybe it's deep winter and so the streetlamps are glowing in their

"But here you are on the doorstep of this old house, the abandoned castle of a Midwestern king."

ineffectual way but the banks of mounded snow make up the difference, casting the great funereal house in moony light.

You are enacting a historical moment and you know it. You're going to an evening musicale in one of the stolid family houses on the supreme street of your proud old city. You're not entirely here in this new century, even though you wouldn't be anywhere else. You never wanted to be a pioneer, you're no hero, and you want the vote.

But here you are on the doorstep of this old house, the abandoned castle of a Midwestern king. And of course you're also on the doorstep of the twenty-first century.

You have your ticket which is to say your invitation. You open the heavy resistant door and let yourself in. A rush of warm air meets you. Someone, smiling, hands you the printed program, and points the way. There will be a piano quintet. Later you will be offered something to drink, a cookie, cheese on a saltine. It will all be uplifting—that magnificent lost adjective of the nineteenth century. It will be just what the ladies of The Schubert Club had in mind.

Civic Progress

In 1908, the *Pioneer Press* ran this cartoon celebrating the many points of pride in the City of Saint Paul, including, of course, The Schubert Club. The Institute of Arts and Sciences had just been incorporated earlier that year—and would later become The Science Museum of Minnesota. The St. Paul Symphony Orchestra had been founded in 1906 but would last only until 1914. (The Schubert Club, trying to support another cultural endeavor and do what would be best for the local music community, had suspended evening concerts that first year of the new symphony in order to "give the orchestra full sway.")

When is a Club not a Club?

The Schubert Club is a name with impressive historical roots. Unfortunately, the name also brings some confusing associations. No, the organization was never devoted exclusively to Schubert (and is no relation to the entrepreneurial theater-owning brothers Shubert). Yes, it was a club at one time, with various kinds of memberships. But for many years its membership has been a legal classification, referring only to the "corporate members" who vote for incoming Board members.

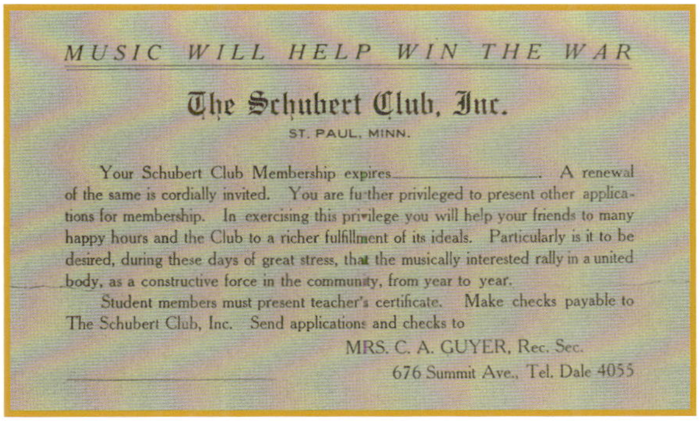
MUSIC WILL HELP WIN THE WAR

The Schubert Club, Inc.

ST. PAUL, MINN.

Your Schubert Club Membership expires__________. A renewal of the same is cordially invited. You are fu-ther privileged to present other applications for membership. In exercising this privilege you will help your friends to many happy hours and the Club to a richer fulfillment of its ideals. Particularly is it to be desired, during these days of great stress, that the musically interested rally in a united body, as a constructive force in the community, from year to year.

Student members must present teacher's certificate. Make checks payable to The Schubert Club, Inc. Send applications and checks to

MRS. C. A. GUYER, Rec. Sec.
676 Summit Ave., Tel. Dale 4055

Why this name, Schubert Club? In the nineteenth century, it was fashionable to name clubs after admired figures in music or literature. Boston's Handel and Haydn Society (founded in 1815) is the oldest performing arts group still flourishing in the United States; New York and Boston still have Browning Societies. There are currently a number of Mendelssohn Clubs and Beethoven Clubs across the United States, even a Schumann Club (originally the Clara Schumann Club) in Mobile, Alabama, and a former Schumann Club that changed its name to the MacDowell Music Club in 1912. Some of these have evolved into professional arts organizations; some have remained clubs. Their main activities may be choral, educational, or social. They each carry the weight of their historic name.

The Schubert Club of Saint Paul is not the only Schubert Club still around. The one in Fairfield County, Connecticut goes back nearly one hundred years and is still a club, annually presenting a Young Musicians Festival. The Schubert Club of Kenosha, Wisconsin, also about a century old, is still a club and focuses primarily on encouraging young musicians. They give away nearly $4,000 in scholarships and continue to be involved with the National Federation of Music Clubs (which was itself founded in 1898—and our Schubert Club was a charter member). The Schubert Club of Grand Rapids, Michigan, operating since 1883, has evolved into mainly the Schubert Male Chorus. And the one in Jonesborough, Tennessee seems as interested in gardening as music. At one time, other Schubert Clubs existed in Iowa, Rhode Island, Illinois, and California.

The name "club" brings with it an implication of membership, which may be why, even now, Schubert Club subscribers sometimes refer to themselves as members.

And no wonder they're confused. Even after the complicated categories of membership had been dropped and concerts were open to the general public (which happened in the 1940s), subscribers continued to be referred to officially as "members." This holdover from the past continued through the 1950s and early 1960s, when the organization brochure stated, "The purchase of a season ticket to our Concert Series entitles you to a membership in The Schubert Club and admission to all other club activities." Finally, in 1968, the word membership dropped out of that section, but the sense remained the same: "Purchase of a season ticket entitles the holder to participate in all Schubert Club activities." And subscribers were referred to as "members" in the organization handbook until 1988.

Originally, The Schubert Club was indeed a club. Concerts and other events were restricted to members. Members could bring guests, but only out-of-town visitors could purchase individual tickets. There were various kinds of members. "Active members" were those who performed. They were expected to contribute at least two "numbers" in Club performances during the season. They were also the people from whom the leadership of the organization was drawn. "Associate members" did not have an obligation to perform—and also lacked voting rights. However, membership entitled them to attend the biweekly matinees (October through April) and other activities of the organization, which included periodic study sessions and social gatherings. "Honorary members" were those who paid higher annual dues (in 1892, this meant $5, instead of the usual $1).

Participation from Active members was so important that in 1893, the Executive Committee decided that all vocalists (with a few exceptions) were required to attend chorus class rehearsals. There were fines of ten cents for tardiness and twenty-five cents for unexcused absences. That was the same year that auditions were instituted for the "Active members."

Commitment and quality were both important. In the minutes of the Executive Committee for September 6, 1893, the following comment was entered:

"In order to raise the standard of the club it was decided to have the active members examined yearly by a committee of competent musicians outside of the club. Those unable to take such an examination to go on the associate list. This rule to go into effect next fall, thus giving all members ample time to prepare themselves."

Active membership meant performing for other Schubert Club members.

I got through at The Schubert Club very well, I was a little frightened but that didn't entirely rob me of my voice, which Mrs. Selmes & cousin Katie told me sounded very well. Mrs. DeWolf stopped me afterwards & told me how much she enjoyed it. "She was tired," she said, "of hearing these young greenhorns sing, and for her part liked to hear the old ones." As I told Cousin Katie, I knew I wasn't young, but I didn't like to have the fact rubbed in.

– Marion Ramsey Furness
Letter to her daughter Anita
– December 23, 1894

Membership increased steadily and impressively. In 1896, there were nearly 300 members (120 active, 230 associate, and 5 honorary). By 1914, there were 1,232 members, with about one-fifth student members and about one-tenth "active" (that is, performing) members. Around this time was added a special (lower-fee) non-voting category for "business women employed during the day, all school teachers and men [!]"

Fees for membership also increased. By 1930, the dues were up to $5 for Active and Associate members (students $3), and members could buy one "season guest ticket" for $5, enabling them to bring a husband or friend. In addition, a one-time $5 initiation fee (except for students) had been introduced in 1920. As the Depression continued, the $5 initiation fee was discontinued "as a concession to the general financial stringency."

In 1935, the Executive Committee enthusiastically explored the idea of opening up Active memberships to men, which would "add materially to the program and stimulate the interest of men in the club." However, when the committee realized that Active membership would entitle the men to vote and hold office, the motion for expanding membership to men was withdrawn.

In 1943, all concert seats were open to the public, although subscribers were still called members, and subscription income was referred to as "dues." In 1947, the five classes of membership were: Active, Associate, Student, Honorary, and Complimentary. Active members were the only ones who could vote.

USUAL FEE DROPPED BY SCHUBERT CLUB

Initiation Charge Suspended Temporarily While Enrolling New Members.

In tough financial times, The Schubert Club essentially made a half-price deal for new concert-going members. All the local newspapers ran articles about the dues price break, as shown in this *Pioneer Press* headline.

These women were not as formidable as they appear in this newspaper photograph from 1933. They eagerly recruited and welcomed new members.

In 1954, becoming a charter member of the new St. Paul Arts & Science Council accelerated The Schubert Club's shift to being a nonprofit organization, rather than a club. Hiring full-time staff in the late 1960s and acquiring more permanent office space completed the shift. Today, there are still Board committees that oversee the separate activities of the organization, but the office staff handles most of the administration.

In 1972, there was still an "Active Artist Section" —an echo of the early "Active Member" classification. These musicians were featured in monthly concerts at the Arts & Science Center (where The Schubert Club offices were then located) and in monthly "Impromptu Concerts" in the homes of Board members or the "Active Artists" themselves. By the 1980s, audition procedures had dropped, and the Sunday concert series with local performers was called simply "Metro Area Artists." That series ended in 2000.

The final vestige of official club membership was dropped in 2003 with the discontinuation of The Schubert Club's student membership, which had included performing opportunities, free tickets to the International Artist Series, and a discount on the Competition application.

Currently there is no way to be an official "Schubert Club member," but there certainly are many ways to be involved with The Schubert Club.

> *"Moved, seconded and carried that the secretary instruct delinquents from the Chorus Class that they must either pay an extra dollar and go on Associate List or forfeit membership."*
>
> Executive Committee Minutes, 1896

THE SCHUBERT CLUB begs to call attention to one of the features of the present season's work, namely, its STUDENT'S SECTION, which may be explained in part as follows:

1st. The Student's Section shall be composed of young girls or women, properly endorsed socially, who present certificates signed by a teacher to the effect that the applicant is a pupil in *actual study*. The membership fee is $3.00.

2nd. Three of the season's programs shall be given by and for the particular benefit of these student members.

For many years, student membership required certification from a teacher. More startling to modern sensibilities was the assumption that the young women be "properly endorsed socially."

An die Musik

The An die Musik Award is The Schubert Club's highest honor. It's presented annually to a classical music enthusiast whose outstanding dedication and commitment over many years has significantly furthered the work and mission of The Schubert Club. The award is named after Schubert's setting of Franz von Schober's poem.

2000 - Elizabeth Musser

2001 - Mary Ann Feldman

2002 - Gilman Ordway

2003 - Sarah-Maud Weyerhaeuser Sivertsen

2004 - George M. Reid

2005 - Dr. Arthur Kaemmer

2006 - Michael Steinberg

2006 - Eric Friesen

2006 - Jack Forsythe

2007 - Thelma Hunter

Art Kaemmer, 2005 winner

An die Musik D. 547

Du holde Kunst, in wieviel grauen Stunden,
Wo mich des Lebens wilder Kreis umstrickt,
Hast du mein Herz zu warmer Lieb' entzunden,
Hast mich in eine bess're Welt entrückt!

Oft hat ein Seufzer, deiner Harf' entflossen,
Ein süßer, heiliger Akkord von dir
Den Himmel bess'rer Zeiten mir erschlossen,
Du holde Kunst, ich danke dir dafür!

To Music D. 547

O blessed art, how often in dark hours,
when the savage ring of life tightens round me,
have you kindled warm love in my heart,
have transported me to a better world!

Often a sigh has escaped from your harp,
a sweet, sacred harmony of yours
has opened up the heavens to better times for me,
O blessed art, I thank you for that!

The Schubert Club: An American Wigmore Hall

Judith Kogan

A professional harpist, Judith Kogan has made several recordings, including collaborations with both voice and flute. A writer for the Harvard Crimson *while at college, she also holds a degree from the Juilliard School of Music, an experience that inspired her to write* Nothing But the Best: the Struggle for Perfection at the Juilliard School. *She is married to conductor Hugh Wolff, whose extensive conducting and recording experience includes eight years with The Saint Paul Chamber Orchestra. She was elected to The Schubert Club Board in 2007.*

Recorder player Cléa Galhano and Sharon Carlson (Assistant to The Schubert Club's Executive Director) stand beneath the inspirational canopy at Wigmore Hall in 2004.

WIGMORE HALL, LONDON. The very name elicits swoons of rapture or awed silence from music lovers the world over. Unrivalled in affection and respect, with an acoustic that is legendary. Artists claim there's no better place to give a recital; audience members claim there's no better place to hear one. The hall itself, a stone's throw from Oxford Street, in the heart of commercial London, bespeaks elegance and old world charm. The iron and glass canopy, which bears the hall's name, is like a beacon to concertgoers. Once inside, you walk down a red-carpeted corridor whose walls announce, via photos and programs, upcoming performances. Polished brass plates on the doors and a dedicated staff lend the venue the patina of a five-star hotel. Enter the hall, with just 580 seats; it feels more like a grand living room than a concert hall. Sunlight streams in through four curved leaded glass windows in the rounded ceiling. Verona marble with Brazilian mahogany paneling wrap around the entire room. The performers are close to the audience, but not suffocatingly so. The stage is set in a round-backed marble wall

The allegorical artwork in the cupola above the stage at Wigmore Hall.

with two mahogany doors through which artists enter and exit. Over the stage is an arts and crafts cupola with a bas-relief symbolizing the striving of humanity after the elusiveness of music. Wigmore is a shrine to music as much as it is an ambient concert hall.

A standard-bearer for the presentation and promotion of solo and chamber music recitals of the highest quality—Wigmore is the protector of an art form. One eye on the past, one on the future and a hand in the present, Wigmore Hall presents hundreds of events a year. It discovers, nurtures and promotes young talent, supports those on the brink of major careers, and commissions new works while preserving the memory and sanctity of our musical heritage. In this larger respect, The Schubert Club is something of an American Wigmore Hall. In their overlapping hundred year histories, they have grown to function quite similarly. That The Schubert Club, an entity that for most of its life didn't even have a space of its own, has come to function like Wigmore Hall, is worthy of exploration.

Wigmore Hall started life in 1901 as Bechstein Hall, sponsored by the German company that made one of Europe's most popular pianos. Because it was a hall for hire it held unusual concerts—accordion, hand bell, alpine yodeling—as well as the standard debuts. The Schubert Club, on the other hand, began in 1882 as an amateur organization dedicated to the presentation of musical recital by voice or instrument. It didn't have a regular venue so it met and presented concerts at homes, hotels and churches. Within a few years, The Schubert Club shed its amateurish trappings, created a club constitution and bylaws, and committed itself to promoting the culture of music in the City of Saint Paul. That meant upping the ante in almost every sphere of concert presentation and meant attracting artists of international renown. It established a series of "Five High Class Artists' Recitals" drawing talent from abroad and clearing enough profit to make the series viable.

The Schubert Club dealt with a population base quite different from that which filled the salons of European capitals, where classical music was part of the vernacular. In 1895, The Schubert Club's woman president, urging members to coax husbands, sons and brothers to attend concerts, wrote that "many of us have not waked up to the great importance of hearing fine music at every possible opportunity if we would become broadly cultured. Never mind if they [the men] grumble a little at first at being dragged to concerts and lectures and pronounce them a bore. They would unconsciously become musically educated in spite of themselves." Whether manipulation of the recalcitrant male population had anything to do with it, by the turn of the century, The Schubert Club had a stellar reputation. Saint Paul had become one of the most musical communities in the country.

Through the first decade of the twentieth century, both Wigmore Hall and The Schubert Club prospered. By 1914, The Schubert Club was the second largest music club in the U.S. But in 1915 a fire at the Saint Paul Public Library destroyed all the club's study materials, sheet music and manuscript records dating back to the club's inception.

The situation for Bechstein Hall was more dire. When World War I began in 1914, Bechstein, like all German businesses in Britain, was put into the hands of an official receiver, a status akin to bankruptcy. Bookings were cancelled and the disruptions of war affected the concerts that remained. There was a move to rid the Hall of any trace of things German—the hall, its studios, offices and Bechstein pianos were auctioned off. A nearby shop bought the hall; it was renamed Wigmore Hall after the street on which it stood.

By the second half of the twentieth century, both Wigmore and The Schubert Club were back up and running and newly committed to their missions of promoting classical music. And since then, from the planning of seasons to the promotion of events to the introduction of modern technology to pursue their goals, The Schubert Club and Wigmore Hall have come closer and closer to pursuing parallel courses.

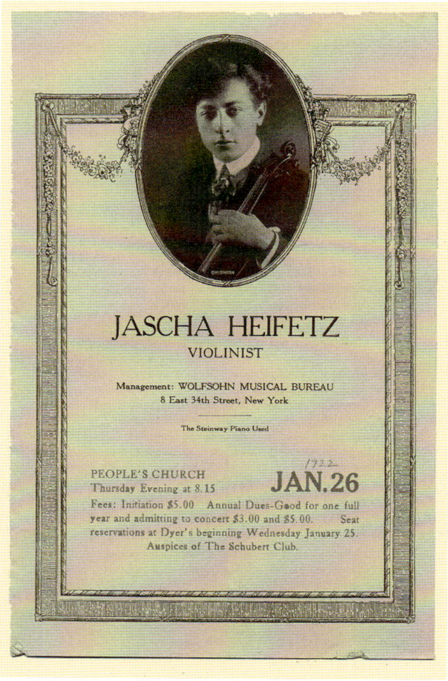

Advertisement for Heifetz's 1922 Schubert Club concert.

In their overlapping century of existence, Wigmore Hall and The Schubert Club have presented hundreds of recitals featuring the same legendary artists—Artur Rubinstein, Jascha Heifetz, Dietrich Fischer-Dieskau, Elisabeth Schwarzkopf, Cecilia Bartoli, and Alfred Brendel. Eugene Ysaÿe, the violinist who played Wigmore Hall's opening concert in 1901 appeared for The Schubert Club in 1895. Wigmore has lured top quality artists to its jewel of an intimate space in one of the great European capitals of the world. The Ordway Center for the Performing Arts, where the main Schubert Club series takes place, is a top-notch venue and artists are treated to first-class hospitality. With the dwindling number of recital presenters worldwide, The Schubert Club is more appreciated than ever.

At both organizations, concert seasons have been planned around themes. Wigmore has fashioned seasons around a single composer, type of composition, instrument and performer, but because it holds over four hundred concerts a year (compared to The Schubert Club's approximately fifty), it has generally maintained a balance in what it offers. One season, The Schubert Club built its International Artist Series at Ordway Center around a concept (pianists), but it has generally sought and achieved balance in its programming by presenting a variety of series (early music, art song) at different venues: Sundin Music Hall (at Hamline University), the James J. Hill House, Ted Mann Concert Hall, the Walker Art Center, the Mill City Museum, and the Raspberry Island Bandshell among them. Both Wigmore and The Schubert Club attempt to balance the old and new, recognizing the need to keep recital literature alive by promoting new works while satisfying the demand for the traditional repertoire, and both have ventured outside the western canon. Wigmore has presented jazz and folk fiddle concerts. The Schubert Club owns an Indonesian gamelan and has presented it in concert, and sponsors a jazz piano scholarship competition. The Schubert Club and Wigmore both have multiple series and different audiences for each. They also both have a lunchtime series, a boon to those who are housebound at night or want to hear live music in the middle of the day.

Wigmore and Schubert Club audiences tend to be loyal, knowledgeable and enthusiastic. The typical Wigmore/Schubert Club concertgoer is said to be so attentive you can hear him or her listening. The chatter before and after concerts makes evident the audience knows the repertoire. Audience members understand the tiny gesture from an artist: a flick of the wrist means wait until I've finished the set, a wave after a second encore means I'm done for the night. They understand protocol, too—they'll wince if someone applauds at the "wrong" time. They encounter each other outside of the hall, and nod; though they often don't know each other's names, they know where they sit at concerts. Like a brand name one returns to again and again, they know they can count on a Schubert Club or Wigmore concert for quality and interest. When you phone either office, you get a polite informed voice, not a series of electronic prompts. When you buy a ticket, the agent asks your name and phone number so the patron can be called if a concert is cancelled. You can phone either box office and ask, after giving your name, for "my normal seat." And when you get to a concert, if you discover you've left your ticket home, a new one will be printed.

Both Wigmore and The Schubert Club consider education and outreach to be fundamental to their missions. Early on at The Schubert Club, educational programs given by and for the members were considered as important as performances; music study sessions and lectures on a composer were part of the regular club activities. In the 1890s The Schubert Club broke ground by creating a student section with its own study activities. At both Wigmore and The Schubert Club, education and outreach programs have brought classical music into the lives of those who'd otherwise be without it, and to those seeking a depth of understanding unattainable just from attendance at a concert. Wigmore hosts Family Days and Family Concerts that enable young audience members to try instruments and coax them into the world of music through such media as painting and puppetry. For school groups there are age-appropriate presentations in the hall, and for adults, pre-concert talks and lecture recitals. The Schubert Club's outreach program dates back almost a hundred years. In 1908 the Club had an Altruistic Section, which provided free musical entertainment for the enjoyment of the culturally deprived, presenting programs at industrial plants, correctional facilities and orphan asylums. Later, it introduced concerts for the elderly in rest homes, and music therapy for handicapped children. There is also Project CHEER, a program for teaching music to underprivileged youngsters. The Club's philosophy has always been that music is a source of pleasure but also of giving, and that in this respect, it has a moral role to play. To promote the training and performing of young musicians, each spring The Schubert Club holds a student competition, giving students a public platform for performance, and a chance to win a portion of the over fifty thousand dollars in prize money. The Schubert Club sponsors master classes where students learn from each other as well as the visiting artist-coaches. While Wigmore doesn't sponsor master classes or competitions, its stage has been rented by independent arts organizations for that purpose.

A key component in Wigmore's impact across the United Kingdom is its longstanding relationship with BBC Radio 3. Like National Public Radio, the BBC is heard throughout the country. As Minnesota music lovers tune into Minnesota Public Radio, those in Britain keep their dials set at Radio 3. Wigmore's Monday lunchtime recitals are broadcast live on Radio 3, just as MPR used to air live the weekly noontime "Live from Landmark" series. Minnesota Public Radio also used to record and air all of the International Artist Series concerts; it still records and broadcasts fragments from them. MPR has also been a co-sponsor of The Schubert Club's Saint Paul Summer Song Festival. Both The Schubert Club and Wigmore now have recording labels as well. Over the last ten years, The Schubert Club has released a couple dozen studio recordings under its Ten Thousand Lakes label. Wigmore recently launched Wigmore Hall Live, through which it plans to release recordings of past and present concerts at a rate of twelve to sixteen discs per year.

Three times The Schubert Club has sponsored recitals by Minnesota musicians at Wigmore Hall: those of Janet Horvath, a cellist in the Minnesota Orchestra (1986), and of the recorder player Cléa Galhano (2004 and 2006). For Horvath's recital, The Schubert Club commissioned Minnesota composer Libby Larsen

to write a piece she titled *Juba*, an improvisatory work based on nineteenth century African-American slave dances. It incorporates in its hard-driving sections handclapping by both the cellist and pianist. Galhano's 2004 recital included a piece for recorder and harpsichord by Schubert Club composer-in-residence David Evan Thomas. Called *Rigadoons*, it is a medley of neo-baroque dances—part-homage, part-confection. Both *Juba* and *Rigadoons* were later performed in recital in Minnesota.

Eliminating the one remaining glaring difference between Wigmore Hall and The Schubert Club, The Schubert Club now has a recital space of its own—albeit a modest one. Since 1974, The Schubert Club has had offices in the Landmark Center, built in 1902 as a federal government building. On the southeast corner of the Landmark Center's second floor is an ample room with rounded bay corners, fifteen foot high ceilings, and windows that look out onto Rice Park and Fifth Street. Elegant but not precious, the room was appropriated by The Schubert Club and turned into a performance space that seats eighty. Situated next to four rooms that comprise The Schubert Club Museum's second-floor gallery, it is a jewel. Over the doorway outside the room is a steel, etched-glass marquee (what Bruce Carlson liked to call a "cantilevered-frieze") modeled on the canopy over the sidewalk at Wigmore Hall.

Getting permission to add the marquee was no small matter. Because the Landmark Center is on the National Register of Historic Places, any plan to alter its original design must be approved by Minnesota Landmarks. Bruce Carlson, trained as a lawyer, built a case to win permission to create a new entrance to the room, and to this end, took photographs of drinking fountains and other non-original features that violated the historic purity of the building. Permission granted, The Schubert Club hired an architect and steel

Executive Director Bruce Carlson standing below the new entryway with pianists Alexander Braginsky and Yefim Bronfman.

worker to design and build the marquee; it was installed on June 14, 2005. The Schubert Club now has a performance space it controls. Thus far the space has been used for concerts, master classes, rehearsals, receptions and museum exhibitions. The venue is without an official name. Originally Room 205 of the Landmark Center, in its new incarnation it is variously called Gallery 205 or simply 205. The generous arts patron and friend of The Schubert Club Judy Dayton has suggested Wigmore West. (And why not? The New York rock venue Fillmore East inspired some San Franciscans to dub their venue Fillmore West.)

The room has acoustics on the warm and "friendly" side—very clear for instruments and for sung and spoken diction, both when empty and full. At the concert that officially opened the space, artists soprano Maria Jette and pianist Irina Elkina were favorably impressed by it.

Though small, the room has an expansive feel, due in part to the high ceiling and decorative windows on two walls. It is possible for an artist to draw inspiration from something beautiful in the room; it reminded Elkina of a Russian palace. Its pillars and lilac-colored walls give it a stateliness that complements its musical centerpiece—an eight-foot Bechstein concert grand. Built in Berlin in 1878 and resting in Budapest before coming to United States, it has been played by Franz Liszt, Gustav Mahler, Johannes Brahms, Béla Bartók, Zoltán Kodály and Ernst von Dohnányi. It was owned most recently by the late Margaret Baxtresser, winner of the 1950 Naumburg Award.

Let's recall the role of Bechstein in the Wigmore Hall story. Wigmore Hall began as Bechstein Hall; naturally, the hall's piano was a Bechstein. With the arrival of Gallery 205's Bechstein, the links between The Schubert Club and Wigmore become ever more numerous. Should the parallels continue, we might find The Schubert Club one day renamed the Fifth Club, just as Bechstein Hall was renamed for the street on which it was situated. To get the tuning just right, it might want to call itself the Perfect Fifth Club.

An overhead view of the performing area in Gallery 205, showing The Schubert Club's 1878 Bechstein piano.

Through Two World Wars

In World War I, The Schubert Club added a War Service Committee to its operations. The efforts of this committee included distribution of the "Music Will Help Win the War" stamps. Its most strenuous work, however, was collecting records under the auspices of the National Phonograph Records Recovery Corps, operating under the slogan "Draft your slacker records." More than 3,000 records were sent to the soldiers at Fort Snelling. The committee also organized entertainment for military personnel at Fort Snelling, the Soldiers and Sailors Club, at "victory meetings," and other gatherings. They also gathered relief funds for the "American Friends of the Musicians in France."

There was also a Committee on Community Singing: "The immediate object of the committee is to provide opportunity for self expression, through singing, to every person in an audience. The outgrowing objects are the good feeling, the sense of fellowship, the reciprocal interest, the power and strength which come through mass movement, the doing of things together." For a Schubert Club program on French music, the singing included the Marseillaise, "Over There," and "There's a Long, Long Trail." For a student section presentation on *War Songs of the Past and Present*, those in attendance sang "Dixie," "Over There," and "The Star-Spangled Banner."

The Community Singing chairman reported in April 1919 that their autumn activities that year had suffered from the influenza epidemic, but they had made progress: "Business Schools have been canvassed and regular 'sings' started there (Nicolls School and Rasmussen have taken up community singing thru this influence). Factories have been visited and employers urged to introduce community singing for the employees."

On Community Singing

"Our music in the hearts of soldiers and civilians tones the system, heals the broken-hearted, urges action, restores balance, gives encouragement, injects 'pep', 'puts it over' and gives us the odds."

- from "Is Music an Essential?"
by Schubert Club President
Florence Briggs

In World War II, The Schubert Club again formed a War Service Committee. The organization sponsored several parties at induction centers, providing refreshments and musical entertainment. Unused concert tickets were distributed—free—through the USO Service Men's Center and the Officers' Club. And when it became obvious that someone needed to oversee the records in the Music Room at the Service Men's Center, Schubert Club workers took over. As the Executive Board determined, "It seems fitting that we take charge of this room—someone who will see to it that records are re-arranged, old ones taken out, new ones provided, etc." The Schubert Club understood that music may indeed be able to help win wars, for it certainly can build community spirit.

A Message in Time of War

THE SCHUBERT CLUB

IT has been urged at this time that the work of the Schubert Club is more necessary than ever,--as an educational force; as an agent to lighten heavy hearts; as an influence holding, so far as possible, to normal thinking and ways of doing; as an organization with a mind to the performance of its duty in contributing, through music, toward the permanence and solidarity of social life in its best sense.

Thus advised, the usual avenues of pleasant activity are held open. To these has been added the opportunity for mass singing. We would have a part in the great movement which is sweeping the country under the banner of "Community Music" and tending to create and sustain a unity of spirit, purpose and action which may be, and is, turned to constructive use at a time when so many destructive forces are at work in the world.

Believing such creative work, however humble and lowly may be its setting, or however elaborate, to be a patriotic and sacred duty, the President begs to be allowed to extend her greetings, to members of the Club and to those who will be, and invites a renewal and extension of associations, in a cause held close to the heart and in which duty and privilege walk hand in hand.

FLORENCE L. C. BRIGGS,
October 1st, 1917. President.

The Dunn Book

The Schubert Club's first hundred years were detailed in a well-researched book by James Taylor Dunn, *Saint Paul's Schubert Club: A Century of Music, 1882-1982.* He signed copies for eager customers at a reception in Landmark Center in 1983. Like the history published twenty-five years later (that is, the book in your hands now), the earlier one also contained an essay by Patricia Hampl.

The Schubert Club Film Series

After moving into the new Saint Paul Arts and Science Center in 1965, The Schubert Club participated in creating activities for the Center. Between 1971 and 1982 The Schubert Club sponsored a series of evening films in the auditorium. Commencing with Sir Kenneth Clark's *Civilisation* series of documentaries, this festival of old and 'recent' feature length films was most often presented in relation to a specific theme or concept. Although many included operas, musical theater and biographies of composers, the majority of films offered by The Schubert Club were not on the subject of music. Their themes ranged from Russian and French classics to Shakespeare tragedies to Katherine Hepburn. Films based on Agatha Christie novels, the Thin Man series and Charlie Chan were also among the large screen performances shown in the series.

Part-time Schubert Club administrative assistant Martha Von Blon did the art work for many of the Film Series posters.

Performers from Minneapolis's Southwest High School band brought their jazzy sound to the bandstand twice in the 2003-2004 season, playing in September and then in June as part of The Schubert Club's *Razzmatazz! on Raspberry Island* series that featured several local bands in Sunday afternoon performances.

A Jewel of Saint Paul: Raspberry Island Bandstand

Always in search of new ventures, The Schubert Club commissioned an elegant bandstand to be both a venue for musical events and to serve as a beautiful work of art. The bandstand occupies Raspberry Island on the Mississippi River where the river flows through downtown Saint Paul. Sharing the island is the Minnesota Boat Club, the oldest athletic organization in Minnesota and an appropriate neighbor for a project from Minnesota's oldest musical organization. The stainless steel and glass structure was designed by New York architect James Carpenter who, accommodating the wishes of Bruce Carlson, drew inspiration from the double-curved hull of Bruce's classic 1930s Chris-Craft boat.

Ground-breaking for the $2 million structure took place in October 2001, with the grand opening of the finished edifice on September 8, 2002. Officially named The Schubert Club Heilmaier Memorial Bandstand honoring the late Anna Heilmaier, a research librarian at the downtown Public Library and longtime friend of The Schubert Club, the modern 25-by-50 foot structure is a welcome addition to downtown's Saint Paul picturesque riverfront and has served for many local events, including one of the peak attractions of The Schubert Club's Saint Paul Summer Song Festival: the outdoor song picnic.

Inspiring Collaborations to Benefit our Community

The Schubert Club was formed to fulfill a need for musical activities in a growing community. One hundred and twenty-five years later, the organization is still motivated by the needs of our community.

Supporting the general level of musical activity and interest for this region has always been important, and not just to benefit The Schubert Club. For example, in 1920, Schubert Club leadership canvassed the members for contributions to fund a municipal organ for the St. Paul Auditorium. Later in the 1920s, Board President Florence Briggs sent a letter urging Schubert Club members to attend the local symphony concerts. She commented that "we should be the richer as individuals, as an organization, as a contributing element in the city's cultural life."

The history of collaborative efforts with the Saint Paul Public Library, an organization that also began in 1882, is a prime example of Schubert Club dedication to community. Schubert Club members gave free concerts in public libraries in the 1910s. A performance in 1917 of the Gilbert and Sullivan operetta *Iolanthe*—presented by Schubert Club students and other members, with assistance by the Mechanic Arts High School Boys' Glee Club—was given as a benefit for the music department of the Saint Paul Public Library. In the 1940s, The Schubert Club established a record listening room at the Saint Paul Public Library. More recently, The Schubert Club worked with the Library's Youth Services to create children's programs in the 1990s and a booklist for music lovers. A shared birthday celebration in downtown Saint Paul in September 2007 commemorated the long history the two organizations have in the community.

When the St. Paul Council of Arts and Sciences was established in 1954, The Schubert Club became a charter member. The organization's purpose was to focus attention on the arts and to coordinate the city's cultural organizations. That focus continued through the United Arts Council and exists today in the Arts & Culture Partnership.

Voice teacher Virginia Hardin Olson, here seen with baritone Gérard Souzay (who performed twice on the International Artist Series), provided a link from The Schubert Club to the opera community. She served as Schubert Club Board President in the 1960s and was one of the founders of Opera St. Paul (now Skylark Opera) in 1980.

In 1965, The Schubert Club collaborated with the St. Paul Opera Guild and the St. Paul Philharmonic Society to present the opera *The Ballad of Baby Doe* (which had premiered less than ten years earlier). The Women's Opera Guild and The Schubert Club created an "Opera Day" in 1971 at the Arts and Science Center, which included performances and lectures (and a sherry hour before the luncheon). Opera collaborations continued in the 1970s with weekly Brown Bag Operas, co-sponsored by The Schubert Club and the Opera Guild. Currently, The Schubert Club provides an annual award through the Metropolitan Opera National Council Regional Auditions.

The Schubert Club has a history of encouraging local emerging organizations, like the Minneapolis Symphony Orchestra (now the Minnesota Orchestra).

Educational institutions make superb partners, and The Schubert Club regularly co-sponsors concerts and master classes with the University of Minnesota, Hamline University, and other centers of learning. Through the years, there have been other notable musical co-sponsorships with Walker Art Center, Minnesota Public Radio, MacPhail Center for the Arts, and the Minnesota Historical Society, as well as partnerships with the City of Saint Paul and local schools. The Flint Hills International Children's Festival has become an annual collaboration where The Schubert Club shares a music-activity tent with the Minnesota Opera, The Saint Paul Chamber Orchestra, and The Saint Paul Conservatory of Music. Ordway Center, which organizes the Children's Festival and is the home for The Schubert Club International Artist Series, has been the focal point for a number of collaborative projects.

There have also been connections with smaller organizations. In the last fifty years, The Schubert Club collaborations have provided encouragement or stability for what were then emerging organizations such as the Minnesota Composers Forum (now the American Composers Forum), Music in the Park Series, The Rose Ensemble, and, most recently, the Indonesian Performing Arts Association of Minnesota (which grew out of Schubert Club gamelan activities). As a concert presenter, The Schubert Club also supports individual musicians and smaller ensembles through performance opportunities, commissions, and releases on its Ten Thousand Lakes recording label. It also maintains a directory of local classical music groups on its website. All of these activities foster the local musical community—as The Schubert Club was established to do.

Recorder player Cléa Galhano performing at United Hospital.

Music Therapy and Hospital Concerts

While The Schubert Club's Music Therapy division of the Student Section may not receive the public profile of the Scholarship Competition, this area has been a viable component of The Schubert Club's community outreach.

Music therapists are healthcare professionals who use music to meet the health and healing needs of the elderly, the emotionally or developmentally disabled and other individuals whose physical or mental capacities are impaired through illness. Quietly working in nursing homes, hospitals, hospices, institutions, and clinics around the country, trained music therapists serve a wide segment of the population.

Thanks to the early leadership of board members Adelaide Gordon, Jeanne Shepard, and Nancy Shepard, The Schubert Club in 1976 added a music therapy committee whose members promoted this relatively unknown profession. The committee increased awareness of this profession by awarding an annual scholarship in addition to providing workshops and vocational opportunities for students interested in pursuing careers in this field. For several years The Schubert Club funded a music therapist at the Bridgeview School in Saint Paul and at the Courage Center in Golden Valley and more recently funded concerts at Abbott Northwestern Hospital in Minneapolis.

In the spring of 2002, board member Hélène Houle urged The Schubert Club to sponsor a monthly concert series at the United Hospital in downtown Saint Paul. The thirty-minute program, still in place today, is held in the hospital's small interfaith chapel. The concerts are free and open to patients, doctors, hospital staff, guests, and all who might benefit from spending a few quiet minutes listening to music. Additionally, the concerts are broadcast over the hospital's closed-circuit television channel so the music is able to reach hundreds of patients in their rooms. The musicians are usually asked to perform quieter or meditative works. Violins, cellos, harps, guitars, flutes and recorders fit the bill nicely.

It is the hope of the Music Therapy Committee that The Schubert Club's efforts over the years have quietly raised the public's awareness of the value of music therapy in our community.

One Hundred and Twenty-Five Years of NEW Music

One wouldn't necessarily know it from looking at The Schubert Club's library where floor-to-ceiling shelves hold 18th century musician biographies, complete catalogue of Schubert's works, and small, seemingly unassuming books with titles like *Ancient Musics of the World* and *The Agony of Modern Music*. Nor would one necessarily guess from the renowned eight concert series it presents annually, which seem—to the uninitiated—to focus on programming early music, music for Indonesian gamelan, 19th century song, and classical-romantic keyboard music.

But The Schubert Club, this bastion of the tried and true, has a little-known—yet wildly influential—soft spot for living composers.

Whether it stems from the increasing nationalism of the 1890s, the need to keep up with the scope of so many other arts organizations in the 1900s, or even the Altruistic Committee of the 1910s, The Schubert Club has long understood that one way to achieve its mission of "promoting the art of music," is to strengthen our musical community through the creation and propagation of new works.

Without too much digging, one soon discovers The Schubert Club in such comprehensive roles as producing concert programs of living composers, organizing score study, sponsoring visiting lecturers on new music, releasing new music on their own record label, and, beginning in 1975, as a commissioning agent of more than 80 new works.

The Schubert Club has featured local composers prominently since at least 1896, when Duluth composer Gerard Tonning presented a concert of his manuscripts with assistance from the "Club Chorus" of Saint Paul.

1896

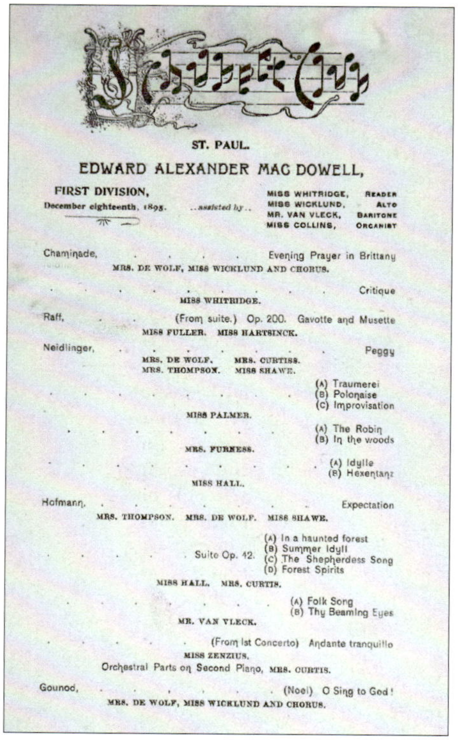

ST. PAUL.

EDWARD ALEXANDER MAC DOWELL,

FIRST DIVISION,
December eighteenth, 1895.

..assisted by..
MISS WHITRIDGE, READER
MISS WICKLUND, ALTO
MR. VAN VLECK, BARITONE
MISS COLLINS, ORGANIST

Chaminade, ... Evening Prayer in Brittany
MRS. DE WOLF, MISS WICKLUND AND CHORUS.

. . . . Critique
MISS WHITRIDGE.

Raff, . . (From suite.) Op. 200. Gavotte and Musette
MISS FULLER. MISS HARTSINCK.

Neidlinger, ... Peggy
MRS. DE WOLF. MRS. CURTISS.
MRS. THOMPSON. MISS SHAWE.

. . . . (A) Traumerei
(B) Polonaise
(C) Improvisation
MISS PALMER.

. . . . (A) The Robin
(B) In the woods
MRS. FURNESS.

. . . . (A) Idylle
(B) Hexentanz
MISS HALL.

Hofmann, ... Expectation
MRS. THOMPSON. MRS. DE WOLF. MISS SHAWE.

. . . . . Suite Op. 42. (A) In a haunted forest
(B) Summer Idyll
(C) The Shepherdess Song
(D) Forest Spirits
MISS HALL. MRS. CURTIS.

. . . . (A) Folk Song
(B) Thy Beaming Eyes
MR. VAN VLECK.

. . . . . (From Ist Concerto) Andante tranquillo
MISS ZENZIUS.
Orchestral Parts on Second Piano, MRS. CURTIS.

Gounod, ... (Noel) O Sing to God!
MRS. DE WOLF, MISS WICKLUND AND CHORUS.

1895

From 1895-1904, two of the most performed American composers on Schubert Club recitals were also accomplished pianists: the New Hampshire-born Amy Beach and New York native Edward MacDowell, who, still only in his thirties, was easily revered as the greatest American composer by his 1890s audience. This concert program from 1895 also includes the music of his teacher Joachim Raff.

In 1899, the music of Parisian composer Cécile Chaminade was causing quite a stir in America. By 1900, nearly 100 "Chaminade Clubs" had sprouted up around the country. This concert program, presented nine years before Chaminade would make her first concert tour to America, showed off her typically French musical wit and facile melodic gift. Still considered one of the most published women composers in history, her "Scarf Dance" (the final piece on this program) sold over five million copies during her lifetime.

1899

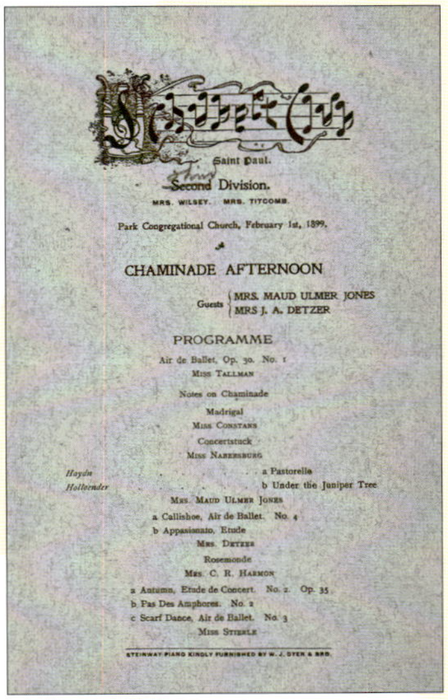

Schubert Club

Saint Paul.

~~Second~~ Third Division.

MRS. WILSEY. MRS. TITCOMB.

Park Congregational Church, February 1st, 1899.

CHAMINADE AFTERNOON

Guests { MRS. MAUD ULMER JONES / MRS J. A. DETZER

PROGRAMME

Air de Ballet, Op. 30. No. 1
Miss Tallman

Notes on Chaminade

Madrigal
Miss Constans

Concertstuck
Miss Nabersburg

Haydn . . . . . a Pastorelle
Hollaender . . . . . b Under the Juniper Tree
Mrs. Maud Ulmer Jones

a Callishoe, Air de Ballet. No. 4
b Appasionato, Etude
Mrs. Detzer

Rosemonde
Mrs. C. R. Harmon

a Autumn, Etude de Concert. No. 2. Op. 35
b Pas Des Amphores. No. 2
c Scarf Dance, Air de Ballet. No. 3
Miss Stierle

STEINWAY PIANO KINDLY FURNISHED BY W. J. DYER & BRO.

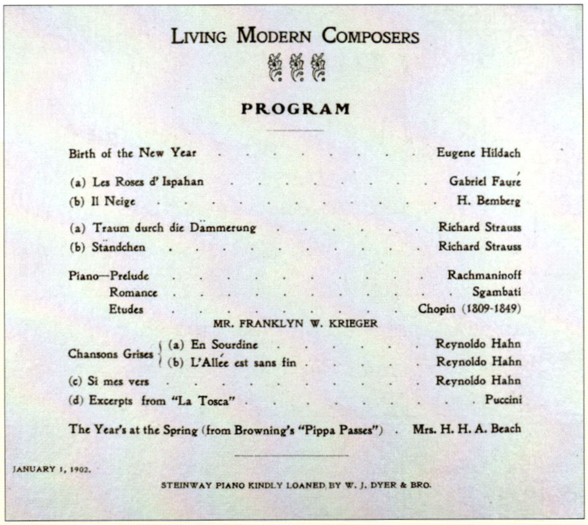

LIVING MODERN COMPOSERS

PROGRAM

Birth of the New Year	Eugene Hildach
(a) Les Roses d' Ispahan	Gabriel Fauré
(b) Il Neige	H. Bemberg
(a) Traum durch die Dämmerung	Richard Strauss
(b) Ständchen	Richard Strauss
Piano—Prelude	Rachmaninoff
Romance	Sgambati
Etudes	Chopin (1809-1849)
MR. FRANKLYN W. KRIEGER	
Chansons Grises (a) En Sourdine	Reynoldo Hahn
Chansons Grises (b) L'Allée est sans fin	Reynoldo Hahn
(c) Si mes vers	Reynoldo Hahn
(d) Excerpts from "La Tosca"	Puccini
The Year's at the Spring (from Browning's "Pippa Passes")	Mrs. H. H. A. Beach

JANUARY 1, 1902.

STEINWAY PIANO KINDLY LOANED BY W. J. DYER & BRO.

1902

Even early on, The Schubert Club was on top of new talent. This 1902 program entitled "Living Modern Composers" was performed by Katherine Richards Gordon and Franklin Krieger. It featured such European musical young 'uns as Rachmaninoff, who, at 28 years old, wouldn't make his U.S. debut for another 7 years. Puccini's *Tosca*, now so solidly positioned in opera repertory, had been given its U.S. premiere in New York less than a year before. And Fauré was so little known outside his native France that the young Aaron Copland felt it necessary to introduce the "Neglected Master" to the American audience in an article published in 1924–a whole twenty-two years after The Schubert Club first programmed Fauré's music.

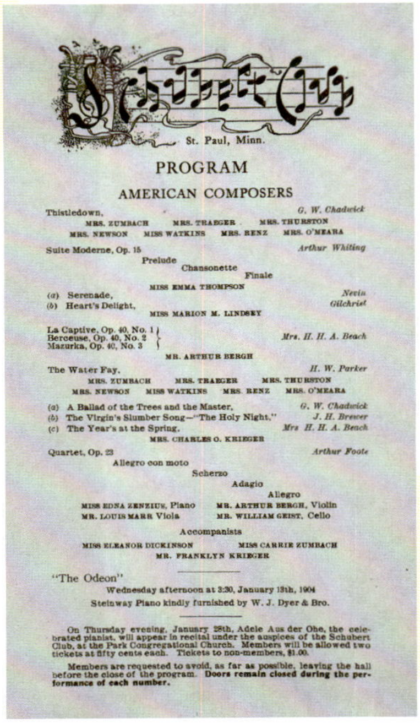

Schubert Club

St. Paul, Minn.

PROGRAM

AMERICAN COMPOSERS

Thistledown, — *G. W. Chadwick*
MRS. ZUMBACH MRS. TRAEGER MRS. THURSTON
MRS. NEWSON MISS WATKINS MRS. RENZ MRS. O'MEARA

Suite Moderne, Op. 15 — *Arthur Whiting*
Prelude
Chansonette
Finale
MISS EMMA THOMPSON

(*a*) Serenade, — *Nevin*
(*b*) Heart's Delight, — *Gilchrist*
MISS MARION M. LINDSEY

La Captive, Op. 40, No. 1
Berceuse, Op. 40, No. 2
Mazurka, Op. 40, No. 3 — *Mrs. H. H. A. Beach*
MR. ARTHUR BERGH

The Water Fay, — *H. W. Parker*
MRS. ZUMBACH MRS. TRAEGER MRS. THURSTON
MRS. NEWSON MISS WATKINS MRS. RENZ MRS. O'MEARA

(*a*) A Ballad of the Trees and the Master, — *G. W. Chadwick*
(*b*) The Virgin's Slumber Song—"The Holy Night," — *J. H. Brewer*
(*c*) The Year's at the Spring. — *Mrs H. H. A. Beach*
MRS. CHARLES O. KRIEGER

Quartet, Op. 23 — *Arthur Foote*
Allegro con moto
Scherzo
Adagio
Allegro
MISS EDNA ZENZIUS, Piano MR. ARTHUR BERGH, Violin
MR. LOUIS MARR Viola MR. WILLIAM GEIST, Cello

Accompanists
MISS ELEANOR DICKINSON MISS CARRIE ZUMBACH
MR. FRANKLYN KRIEGER

"The Odeon"
Wednesday afternoon at 3:30, January 13th, 1904
Steinway Piano kindly furnished by W. J. Dyer & Bro.

On Thursday evening, January 28th, Adele Aus der Ohe, the celebrated pianist, will appear in recital under the auspices of the Schubert Club, at the Park Congregational Church. Members will be allowed two tickets at fifty cents each. Tickets to non-members, $1.00.

Members are requested to avoid, as far as possible, leaving the hall before the close of the program. **Doors remain closed during the performance of each number.**

1904

This program featured four of the most influential American composers of the day: George Whitefield Chadwick, Amy Beach, Horatio Parker, and Arthur Foote. Known (along with Edward MacDowell and John Knowles Paine) as the "Boston Six," these composers were part of the Second New England School. But don't let the name fool you! It was still really the *first* crop of concert music composers to flourish in America, leaving behind a large body of work. Amy Beach, the youngest of the group, had been a child prodigy at the piano, but, forced by her husband to give only one concert per year, luckily turned to composition as her musical outlet. Horatio Parker made history by being Charles Ives's composition teacher. Arthur Foote (last on this program) was the uncle of the longtime minister of the same name at Unity Church in Saint Paul.

1924

"What Next in Music?" In 1924, classical music lovers around the world felt change coming. Earlier that year, George Gershwin had brought jazz into the concert hall with *Rhapsody in Blue*, and the premiere of Arnold Schoenberg's expressionist opera *Die glückliche Hand* had left audiences cold. Luckily, The Schubert Club "prepared" Saint Paul audiences for these new musical developments with Baltimore pianist and socialite Marion Rous, who, in a lecture-recital demonstrating atonality, polytonality and jazz, attempted to eliminate "the undue shock which naturally accompanies sudden changes."

SCHUBERT RECEPTION MUSIC WINS PRAISE

Mme. Metzger-Ziegler Sings Three Compositions by Dr. George Geist.

1933

Local composers have also enjoyed the limelight on Schubert Club events. In the 1930s, mezzo-soprano Mme. Maedy Metzger-Ziegler (say that three times fast) moved from Karlsruhs, Germany to Saint Paul, where she continued to sing professionally. For the annual meeting in 1933, she sang three songs by local surgeon Dr. George A. Geist, gathering glowing reviews! Needless to say, the Geist family has had season tickets ever since. And today Geist's grand-nephew, who works in downtown Saint Paul, spends many a long lunch break tickling the ivories in The Schubert Club Museum.

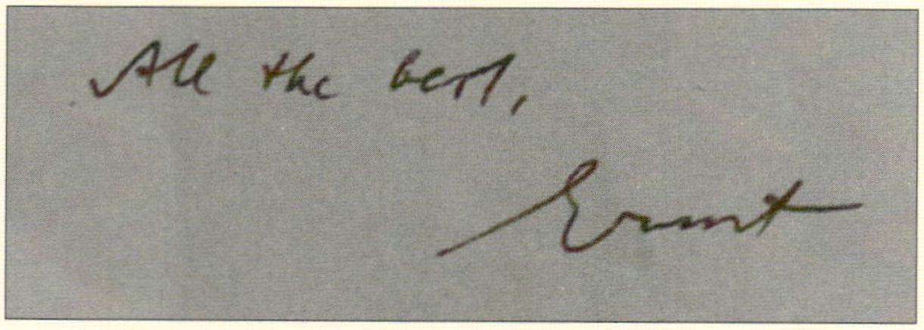

A note from composer Ernst Krenek is part of The Schubert Club Museum's Gilman Ordway Manuscript Collection.

1936-1945

Keeping Score… From the mid-1930s to '40s, the Manuscript Study Group and Manuscript Section provided an informal venue to study and discuss the craft of composition. The idea wasn't new—the Minnesota Manuscript Club had begun in 1893—but the diverse topics (including technique in piano composition, the role of inspiration, and writing incidental music for radio scripts) provided enough focus to attract local composers, university students, and their friends. Notable composer Ernst Krenek, then dean of the School of Fine Arts at Hamline University, served with Millie Loevinger to organize the sessions. Loevinger (or "Mrs. Gustavus," as she signed) must have set a marvelous tone for these meetings. Her 1941 report to the board is worth reprinting:

> *It is not the purpose of this group to serve as critic – our purpose is rather the two-fold one of giving to these composers… an audience which is both discriminating and appreciative, and of giving to that audience a continuity in the development of new music as it comes from its source.*

1940

On April 1, 1940, The Schubert Club sponsored an unprecedented event in Saint Paul: a feature concert entirely of music by Minnesota composers, performed by professional musicians. New music from neo-romantic to "the most advanced abstract modernism" was represented in works by Donald Ferguson, John Verrall, Dr. George Geist, Dr. John J. Becker, Donovan Winters, Johan Egilsrud, William Lindsay, and Winifred Reichmuth Bolle.

The three surviving newspaper clippings surrounding the event (such significant press couldn't possibly be due to the fact that music critic at the *Minneapolis Morning Tribune* was one of the featured composers?) give generally positive reviews. The concert was a "milestone in the chronicle of Minnesota music," with The Schubert Club deserving "a bright new feather for its bonnet." And even the criticism is written with typical Minnesotan reserve. Of John Becker's *Sonate for Violin and Piano, the Minneapolis Times-Tribune* wrote, "...as proof of quality, it remains for the future to decide. A present inability to enjoy it may be a part of our love for music."

The Schubert Club's 1940 concert of music by Minnesota composers came with a sort of warning label at the top of the program:

Foreword:—Today's concert is a cross-section of many types of expression. Therefore it is important that the listener approach the various works without bias, without a preconceived idea of what the music should be, but rather to discover what each composer had to say in his own peculiar idiom. Comparison of works written in different styles and with different objectives is insidious. Understanding of these works will grow out of the conviction that all were written sincerely, each in its own style and with its own individuality.

THE ST. PAUL SCHUBERT CLUB presents
its seventy-fourth annual concert series

Fifth Street between Seven Corners and Washington, St. Paul
THE ST. PAUL AUDITORIUM
THEATRE SECTION

SCHUBERT CONCERT SERIES

• Tuesday, OCTOBER 23 SOCIETA CORELLI Distinguished Italian Chamber Orchestra with Piano . . . fourteen gifted musicians . . . third American tour

• Thursday, NOVEMBER 1 DAVID LLOYD Minneapolis-born leading tenor of the New York City Opera Company . . . many appearances with Boston Symphony, Philadelphia Orchestra, New York Philharmonic and Minneapolis Symphony

• Tuesday, DECEMBER 4 GARY GRAFFMAN Gifted young American pianist . . . "Had his Town Hall audience shouting bravos" — *New York Journal-American*

• Thursday, JANUARY 31 FESTIVAL QUARTET Formed at Aspen Music Festival . . . four great instrumentalists . . .
SZYMON GOLDBERG . . . violin
WILLIAM PRIMROSE . . . viola
NIKOLAI GRAUDAN . . . cello
VICTOR BABIN . . . piano

• Tuesday, MARCH 19 THE LITTLE SINGERS OF PARIS Thirty-two voice Boys' Choir . . . "An experience unforgettable!" Virgil Thompson . . . *New York Herald-Tribune*

Painting by Paul Fetler . . . composer and faculty member of University of Minnesota

1956

After the 1955-56 season went down as one of the most successful in the Club's history, the stakes were high—perhaps that's why this 1956-57 season brochure was so bold! The artist, who happened to be the distinguished composer Paul Fetler, was new on the faculty of the University of Minnesota. Over a quarter century later, The Schubert Club would commission his Concerto for Piano and Orchestra.

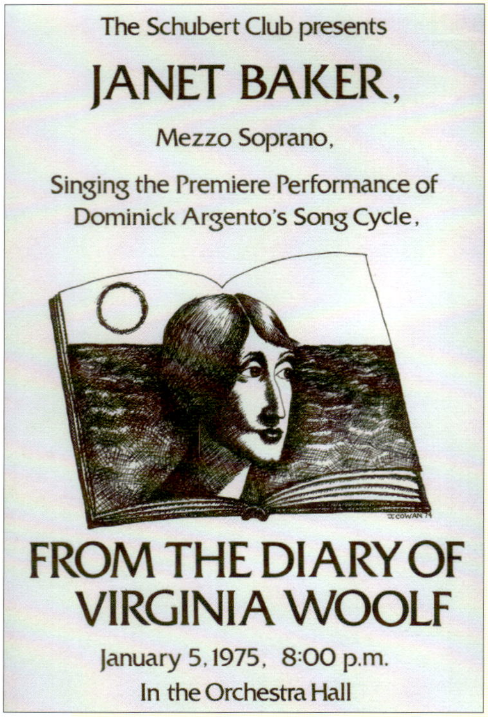

1975

One of the first official Schubert Club commissions, Dominick Argento's 35-minute song cycle *From the Diary of Virginia Woolf* won the illustrious Pulitzer Prize in 1975.

Late 1970s

Newly formed in 1973, the Minnesota Composers Forum moved in the late 1970s into a small corner of The Schubert Club's office space at Landmark Center, where The Schubert Club assisted the Forum with programming, marketing, and the procuring of commissions for new works by Forum members. The organization was later renamed the American Composers Forum and now enjoys its very own office space a few blocks away. This picture shows some of the founding members (left to right): Libby Larsen, Lila Jacobs, Randall Davidson, and Stephen Paulus.

1983

Standing with pianist Thelma Hunter and oboist Richard Killmer after the premiere of her *Genesis I* in 1983, composer Janika Vandervelde (far right) has since fulfilled two other commissions from The Schubert Club, as well as works for the Minnesota Orchestra, the Saint Paul Chamber Orchestra, the Guthrie Theater, The Minnesota Chorale, and Zeitgeist. Of this early work, Vandervelde writes:

> *My first memories of The Schubert Club go back to the early 80s, when I worked for the Minnesota Composers Forum doing odd jobs. In those days, the Forum was housed in the Landmark Center, in the offices of The Schubert Club. From my perch on the third floor, I caught glimpses of Bruce Carlson coming and going, but my first real encounter came on the day Bruce took me to lunch at the Saint Paul Hotel to discuss a commission. Still a student living from hand to mouth, I thought I had hit the big time.*
>
> *The commission turned into a piece for Richard Kilmer and Thelma Hunter. Thus was born my Genesis series of compositions and my career as a composer of chamber music.*

2004

With help from the HRK Foundation, The Schubert Club launches the Composer Mentorship Program in 2004. The program, headed up initially by composer-in-residence David Evan Thomas, provides free composition lessons, score study and guided listening opportunities to one lucky Twin Cities high school student. By 2007, the program has expanded to four students per year.

2006

In 2006, The American Composers Forum teamed up with The Schubert Club to co-sponsor their second ArtSong competition. The overwhelming response brought 290 manuscript submissions from American composers living in 33 states, Canada, and Europe. The first prize was awarded to Texas composer Karim Al-Zand for *The Secret of Your Heart*, a cycle of love songs on texts by Rabindranath Tagore.

2007

Composition was the theme for the 2007 Annual Meeting, where commissioned composers and long-time friends of The Schubert Club Libby Larsen (right) and Stephen Paulus (who was also the featured speaker) joined current composers-in-residence Abbie Betinis (left) and Edie Hill for a group pose.

Minnesota Composers Forum and The Schubert Club

Stephen Paulus

Prolific and versatile, Stephen Paulus, whose first Schubert Club commission was in 1976, has written more than 200 works, in a variety of genres. He was one of the composers commissioned to write a piece for The Schubert Club's centenary in 1982, and he was the featured speaker at the organization's Annual Meeting in May 2007.

I am not sure that I can even recall how it was that the Minnesota Composers Forum ended up being affiliated with Bruce Carlson and The Schubert Club. From participating in the piano competitions at an early age, I had known about Bruce and while I was a graduate student at the University of Minnesota I had asked him if The Schubert Club would support my building of a glass armonica. For a couple of years I was the pianist for The Schubert Club Boychoir and had a casual acquaintance with Bruce. Perhaps a few circumstances like these prompted him to take an interest in the Minnesota Composers Forum.

Bruce had already commissioned a few works from some of us on the local composer scene. Suddenly we found ourselves in a small office on the fourth floor of the St. Paul Building on Fifth Street and Wabasha Avenue (a temporary home for The Schubert Club at the time). Bruce took on this little parasite called the Minnesota Composers Forum and gave us a small corner office. It turned out that he provided much more than real estate though, as we found out soon enough. Bruce was able to advise us on everything from how to polish a grant request to helping us develop our visions for the future. Our relationship with him became a lifelong friendship in which music and a passion for the arts developed into a shared vision. For that and so much more we thank him.

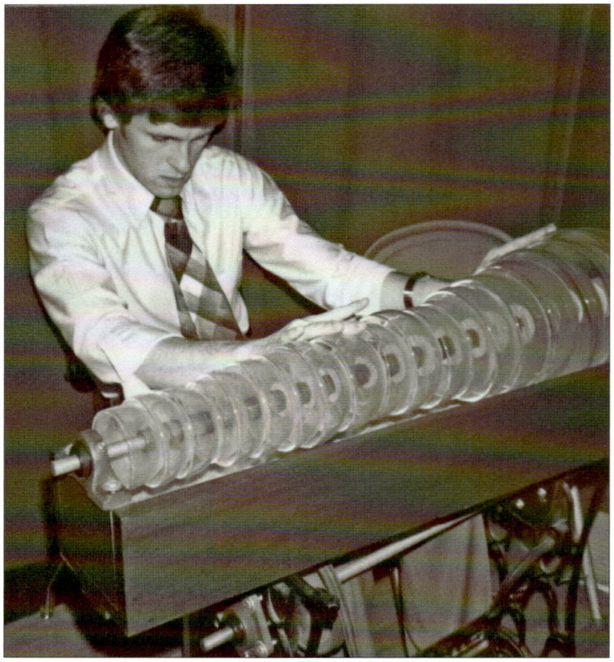

The glass armonica that Stephen Paulus constructed is now part of The Schubert Club Museum.

Libby Larsen

Libby Larsen, one of the most active and prolific composers working today, has written over 200 works spanning virtually every genre and is one of The Schubert Club's most often commissioned composers. An articulate and influential advocate for the arts, in 1973 she was a co-founder of the Minnesota Composers Forum (now the American Composers Forum), and recalls below The Schubert Club's role in its genesis.

We were twenty-four year-olds, the founding group of the Minnesota Composers Forum, and we knew one truth: we were composers. No doubt about it. Although we knew that fact, we weren't quite sure what it meant. We were just burning with desire to compose. We had a little non-profit group and an enormous passion to make it possible for people to hear our compositions. We needed all the advice we could find.

Bruce Carlson *found* us. I will always be grateful for Bruce and want to tell you that one of the most important moments in my life came when I met him for the first time. I asked him if he thought that we composers were doing anything worthwhile. He said, "Oh yeah. You guys are diamonds in the rough." Then he gave us an office space, a telephone line, and pointed us towards Sue Weil and Dolores Johnson—two of our first four board members. But most importantly, Bruce gave us his full confidence, enthusiasm, and advice—forever. Bruce provided us a future as composers. There is no greater gift than that. To say thank you is only one beautiful note in a symphony of gratitude.

For the Record

David Morrison

David Morrison, who works on Museum projects as well as graphics for The Schubert Club, has designed the covers and booklets for many of the CD and DVD recordings that The Schubert Club has released recently.

Thomas Edison's invention of the phonograph in 1877 predated The Schubert Club by only five years. Although Edison's initial interest was in recording speech, not music, it was not many years before recorded music became a popular form of entertainment. And soon thereafter the contest of "live" versus "canned" music arose. (The latter term was apparently a whimsical reference to the shape of the wax cylinders that the Edison phonograph played.)

The Schubert Club, always interested in promoting recital music, eventually saw recordings as a useful means to that end—although it took a hundred years! In the early 1980s pianist Peter Serkin was invited to record dances by the organization's namesake, Franz Schubert, on a Graf fortepiano owned by the The Schubert Club Museum. The recording was released on

Recording engineer Russ Borud adjusts the controls while Mary Therese Royal de Martinez listens. On the recording, she sang and accompanied herself on a copy of a Viennese fortepiano. Her daughter Marina, born shortly after *'Twas One of Those Dreams* was released in 1994 on the Ten Thousand Lakes label, still loves to hear her mother sing.

the ProArte Digital label on vinyl and cassette. Other Serkin recordings followed.

Significant among those early ProArte productions was a recording of music by young Minnesota composer Libby Larsen performed by local artists Janis Hardy and Dan Dressen. A focus on regional artists has characterized Schubert Club recordings since then, with some notable exceptions, such as Dame Janet Baker's release on the D'Note label of the Pulitzer prize-winning song cycle *From the Diary of Virginia Woolf.* That piece was a Schubert Club commission, and the recording was a point of pride.

After producing numerous recordings on ProArte and D'Note, Executive Director Bruce Carlson had a notion to create a recording label of The Schubert Club's own. At a particularly jolly lunch with composer Stephen Paulus, the Ten Thousand Lakes record label was born. Its first production was Paulus's *Carols for Christmas*.

Twenty-five compact discs have appeared on Ten Thousand Lakes since then. One of them, "O, Bell' Alma," by Michelle Frisch and Kathy Kienzle, was named best new recording from North America by Gramophone Magazine. The label's range is wide: from classical Javanese gamelan, through Belladonna Baroque Quartet, Piano e-Competition winners, and music of the Paris Conservatory, to brand new compositions by Minnesota composers such as David Evan Thomas, Randall Davidson, Cary John Franklin, and others. With more still to come, Schubert Club recordings are available on the web at ***www.schubert.org***.

An evening to remember at the Brilliant Corners Jazz Club. Wynton Marsalis puts down his trumpet while listening to Itzhak Perlman play jazz. Bruce Carlson, executive director of The Schubert Club, is seated next to Perlman.

What does an artist do following a Schubert Club recital?

If he's Itzhak Perlman, he gets in on a jam session with jazz trumpeter Wynton Marsalis.

Sharon Carlson

Most artists arrive by commercial planes, some come in cars, and a few get here by train. Itzhak Perlman chartered a private jet the last time he appeared on The Schubert Club International Artist Series, and Bruce hired a limo and driver and met his plane when it landed at Holmen Field in downtown Saint Paul.

It was October 2003—Perlman's first solo recital in the Twin Cities in fifteen years.

He began his program by ripping into his first piece, a Bach sonata, then surprised the audience by announcing the baseball score from the World Series—he'd been listening to the Game on the radio from his backstage dressing room before the concert started! The audience loved it. The Yankees were playing the Marlins that evening in the third game of the Series, and at the start of Perlman's concert, the Marlins had already scored one hit with the Yankees 0. Perlman pretended to snarl at that lousy score, though the audience chuckled and seemed to like the fact that Perlman was a baseball fan. By intermission the Game had picked up considerably, the Yankees scoring several runs, and the Marlins way behind. So by the end of the second half of the program, Perlman began giving regular updates on the game, as he went on and off the stage fetching his music between encores. He added some Chopin, Kreisler, Fauré, and

Tchaikovsky during this period, and the audience rose to its feet, giving him a standing ovation, then sat back down and clamored for more. The Yankees won 6-1.

As if this wasn't reason enough to remember Perlman's visit, it just so happened that Wynton Marsalis, the great jazz trumpeter, was in town the very same night and staying at the same hotel Perlman was. This popular jazz man had been invited to play a concert at a tiny club in downtown Saint Paul—a new jazz establishment called Brilliant Corners located on Sixth and Wabasha, site of the old Fanny Farmer candy store. Marsalis's appearance was a favor to the Club's owners and was meant to give the new venue a boost and some publicity. This it did, especially when Itzhak Perlman became involved after learning about the Marsalis gig and expressing interest in attending his concert. The way Perlman saw it—he not only wanted to attend the concert, he wanted to participate in a jam session!

That's where Bruce stepped in. I was with Bruce in the lobby of the Saint Paul Hotel when Perlman came riding through the lobby on his rented motor scooter after he'd finished having lunch at the Grill. Perlman spotted Bruce and, bursting to tell him the news that Marsalis was in town, wheeled right toward him and said emphatically, "I want to go to Marsalis's concert." Mind you, Perlman had his own concert that night— with The Schubert Club! One thing Bruce learned early on was when dealing with a superstar like Itzhak Perlman, you don't argue; you start putting a plan together.

So Bruce suggested that Perlman call Marsalis himself so as to make introductions and arrangements. Bruce would take it from there. So Bruce and I went over to the little Brilliant Corners Club and Bruce found the manager and explained how the situation was shaping up. Naturally this guy was thrilled at the prospect of not only presenting the great Wynton Marsalis—but having Itzhak Perlman drop by as well! So the plan was to bring Perlman over to Brilliant Corners following his Ordway recital, just in time to get in on Marsalis's last session.

In order to make this plan go smoothly, it occurred to Bruce that he might need a bodyguard to protect Perlman, anticipating a crowd of jazz enthusiasts congregating on the street near the club. Bruce spotted a gentleman sitting in the hotel lobby who seemed to fit the part. He was a nice looking man, bald and mustachioed, with lots of arm muscles who, as a matter of fact, closely resembled our former governor, Jesse Ventura. Bruce's instincts on this one were uncanny. The guy had been a bodyguard for the Rolling Stones! So this man listened to our story and agreed to meet us at 11:15 p.m., walk with Perlman, Bruce and me to Brilliant Corners, and handle the crowds if necessary.

So it was that exactly 11:15 p.m. we all traipsed over to Brilliant Corners—Perlman steering his motorized scooter, a pair of crutches resting on his leg, Bruce in his trenchcoat carrying Perlman's five-million-dollar Stradivarius, the Jesse Ventura look-alike walking beside Perlman's scooter—and me, weaving in and out of these guys trying to be helpful.

We arrived at the Club and encountered a crowd of shivering jazz nuts who were not able to fit inside, peering through the windows and waiting for Marsalis's last show to begin.

Suddenly, the four of us came into view as we made our way across the Wabasha intersection and headed toward the front door. A crowd of friendly people noticed us and one by one they began to recognize Itzhak Perlman.

We were let inside, greeted by the Club manager and then Perlman and Bruce took front row positions. Perlman sat in his scooter, and they brought a chair for Bruce. The house was completely packed, no seats anywhere. The bodyguard left after completing his walking assignment.

So the great Wynton Marsalis came out onto the tiny stage area and shook hands with the great Itzhak Perlman, then proceeded to perform a dazzling 45-minute show with his jazz quartet before calling upon Perlman to open his violin case and show his stuff! Perlman told Bruce during the show that he didn't know if he could play with them, the improvisation technique of jazz being so much different than the more secure notation of classical music, but somehow they landed on "Summertime" and the two masters proceeded to play, alternating solos, melody lines, improvisational deviations, and so on. Perlman's violin wailed in jazz-like fashion—even his facial contortions contributed to the atmosphere. The "back-up men" on piano, saxophone, and drums, along with Marsalis, had no trouble coming in and out, picking up the threads of the tune from one another, spinning off onto a variety of themes and solos. It was a magical night and the audience sensed that a little bit of history was taking place right there on the tiny stage of Brilliant Corners.

Sharon Carlson was assistant for many years to Schubert Club Executive Director Bruce Carlson. Her chapter on Office Observations appears in the Administration section.

Faint Praise?

In a 1965 *Minneapolis Tribune* article entitled "Culture Outdraws," writer Al McConagha noted that major cultural events in the Twin Cities had had an audience of 1,749,349, while Viking and Twins home games had about 200,000 less at 1,513,121. The Schubert Club is one of the organizations mentioned, with concert attendance of 8,000. The article went on to state boldly that attendance had been greater the previous year at Schubert Club concerts in Saint Paul than the total number of adults participating in the Minneapolis Park Board summer softball program.

The Press of Publicity

"The local press has been most encouraging and to it are we greatly indebted, not only for its words of commendation as to our efforts as an organization and to its grateful recognition of our artists, but even more, perhaps, to the inspiration coming from what it expects of us and which, perforce, we must live up to."

- Florence Briggs,
Schubert Club President's Report,
February 8, 1911

Looking through the old scrapbooks of The Schubert Club, one is struck by how much press coverage there used to be for everything to do with the organization. From 1910 through about 1970, the newspapers ran articles—or at least notices—about Schubert Club meetings, auditions, Board presidents, concerts, music lessons, afternoon teas, free community performances, and Competition winners.

It was common for each newspaper to have multiple articles about each major recital: one alerting readers to the performance, one interviewing the performer after he or she arrived in town, and then a review. Articles like "Opera Star Gives Inside Tips on Attaining Facial Beauty" (singer Rose Bampton in 1946) may have been fluff, but they were also good publicity. Violinist Nathan Milstein had several articles before his 1958 concert: one about his 1719 Stradivari violin, another where he advises parents to start their children's music education early, and a third about his non-musical hobbies. (He mentioned beating violinist Jascha Heifetz at ping-pong. "'And I beat him just after I had played the Mendelssohn Concerto with the New York Philharmonic under Toscanini,' he recalls with a grin.") The Schubert Club scrapbook from 1972 has six different articles about Beverly Sills's recital (two lead-up articles and four reviews).

There used to be more newspapers in the area, for one thing—including the German-language *Volkszeitung* that frequently published notices of Schubert Club events. There was not as much competition for the entertainment pages of the day–not just because there were fewer arts organizations, but also from television and video games that now receive column inches. Also, newspapers had "society" columns that reported on small concerts, lectures, member teas, and changes of leadership.

Here are some headlines from the past that we are unlikely to see in our local newspapers these days (and not just because there is no longer a Schubert Club membership):

NEW SCHUBERT CLUB MEMBERS FETED

SCHUBERT CLUB WILL HAVE ANNUAL MEETING WEDNESDAY

DEADLINE FOR SCHUBERT CLUB FILING FEBRUARY 17

TEA TO FOLLOW SCHUBERT CLUB MUSICAL EVENT

SCHUBERT CLUB UNUSED TICKET PLEA

2 CHANGES MADE IN RULES ON SCHUBERT CLUB TRYOUTS

SCHUBERT ARTISTS ENTERTAIN OLD FOLK

SCHUBERT CLUB NOT IN A RUT

Well, okay, maybe we could still see that last one (which appeared in 1959).

For more than fifty years, The Schubert Club had a vigorous Press Committee that produced articles and cultivated relationships with journalists. Several of the Board presidents wrote extensive regular columns for music journals. In the 1940s, The Schubert Club hired a paid publicist, Helen France. In the 1955-56 season, she reported submitting 207 news releases to Twin Cities and out-state newspapers. In addition, expanded publicity efforts (what we would today call "outreach") put different women in charge of making contacts with industry, clubs, church groups, and music teachers.

In the mid-1970s, as newspaper coverage was declining dramatically, The Schubert Club's own printed publication, *The Schubert Club Notes,* began. Now, with the Internet, there are additional possibilities for keeping people informed. The Schubert Club's *e-notes*, a monthly e-mail newsletter, began in 2004 (as *e-news*) and now features a drawing of Schubert at a (computer) keyboard. Visitors to the constantly-improving Schubert Club website can find concert information, order tickets, buy recordings, learn about the Museum of Musical Instruments, download application forms for the Scholarship Competition, make a contribution, and find links to reviews and other articles about The Schubert Club.

The website also includes a Directory of Twin Cities Classical Music organizations and an informal listing of private music instructors. There is even an online discussion forum available through The Schubert Club's website where concertgoers and museum visitors can comment on what they have seen or heard (or want to see and hear). So we are managing somehow without the preposterously-thorough press coverage of the early days.

www.schubert.org

Apparently, newspaper ads used to be inexpensive!

Reviewers

OVER THE YEARS, CERTAIN reviewers have produced so much commentary on Schubert Club concerts that they almost seem like part of the organization. Their praise, however, is never taken for granted, and their negative opinions are pondered carefully. Here are three whose long careers as newspaper critics and whose extensive coverage of Schubert Club activities have given them a substantial place in the organization's scrapbooks.

Frances Boardman – *St. Paul Pioneer Press*

For nearly thirty years, Frances Boardman reviewed Schubert Club concerts in the *St. Paul Pioneer Press*. Throughout the 1920s and 1930s, she built up a reputation as a trustworthy and intelligent critic who allowed glints of humor to come through in her writing.

John Harvey succeeded Francis Boardman as music critic at the *Pioneer Press* when she retired in 1945. When he, in turn, retired from the *Pioneer Press-Dispatch* in 1978, The Schubert Club honored him at their annual luncheon and meeting, where Mary Ann Feldman gave the "Tribute Address." In a 1952 article, Harvey had praised The Schubert Club's approach to engaging artists. He used the term "venturesome conservatism" to describe the policy that struck a middle ground between limiting the season to sure-fire box office draws or gambling with a group of unknowns. Half a century later, that phrase is still apt.

John Harvey of the *Pioneer Press and Dispatch* with Mary Ann Feldman at the Schubert Club's annual meeting.

Michael Anthony – *Minneapolis Star Tribune*

The earliest Michael Anthony reviews in The Schubert Club scrapbooks are from 1979, a year when he reviewed both Vladimir Horowitz and Beverly Sills for the *Minneapolis Tribune*. Twenty-five years later, he was still attending and reviewing Schubert Club concerts. In 2007, budget constraints prompted the *Star Tribune* to discontinue the position of classical music reviewer.

The year after *Hair*—billed as "the American tribal love/rock musical"—opened on Broadway amid a storm of controversy, The Schubert Club adapted one of its hit songs for publicity purposes. *The St. Paul Pioneer Press* even printed the punning verse that accompanied invitations to The Schubert Club's then annual "Fortissimo Luncheon" that kicked off the 1969-1970 season.

When the moon is in the Seventh House
And Schubert Club aligns with Mars,
Suite sounds will guide their season
A-chording to the stars.

The invitation included the signs of the zodiac with the names of associated composers.

The commissioning of "Nightshade Rounds" by The Schubert Club was a very meaningful experience for me. The piece was written for Sharon Isbin, one of the great guitarists of our time, and her performances and recording have been extraordinary. Since the premiere, the piece has been performed and recorded by numerous guitarists in Europe and the UK.

Over the course of my career I have held various administrative positions, including that of Dean of The Juilliard School. During that period, I had the honor of appointing Sharon Isbin to Juilliard to head up the first guitar program in the history of the School, a program she still heads with great distinction. So our initial project through The Schubert Club led to other interesting things indeed.

– Bruce MacCombie, composer

Bruce MacCombie has taught at Yale School of Music, the University of Massachusetts at Amherst, and served as Dean of the Juilliard School and School for the Arts at Boston University. His "Nightshade Rounds" for solo guitar is the title track on Sharon Isbin's EMI/Virgin Classics album named "Best Classical Album of the Year" in 1994 by Guitar Player *magazine.*

"I Guess This Means He's Going to be Famous"

In his delightfully candid *Catalogue Raisonné As Memoir* (2004), Pulitzer Prize-winning composer Dominick Argento credits "one Bruce Carlson, a law student at the university" for first comparing his music to that of Benjamin Britten in a letter to the editor which ran in the *Minneapolis Tribune*. A decade later, the two finally met, becoming fast friends and confidants. Dominick writes that Bruce was "as strong a champion of my music as there has ever been."

The Schubert Club has commissioned three major works from Argento, all extended song cycles. While each is entirely different, the ever-reflective composer finds some similarities in scope:

> *Without intending it, I now notice that all three cycles share certain characteristics: they are person-oriented and exhibit a seriousness of purpose not present in their other siblings … The greater weightiness of these cycles is a reflection of the commissioner they have in common and the specific audience that he has cultivated, perhaps the most discerning group of music lovers in this area.*

(We couldn't agree more.)

From the Diary of Virginia Woolf

Eight songs for medium voice and piano

Excerpted from *Catalogue Raisonné As Memoir* (University of Minnesota Press, 2004). Used by permission.

Bruce Carlson, manager of The Schubert Club, booked soprano Jessye Norman for a recital in 1974 and commissioned me to write a cycle for her. By the time I had searched for and found a suitable text to fit her unique talents (excerpts from Sappho), she canceled. . . . I can't remember why [Beverly] Sills also had to cancel, but to my good fortune she was replaced with British mezzo Janet Baker. . . .

For Janet. . . I looked up [Virginia Woolf's] *A Writer's Diary*. . . . The hardest part was picking which entries to use; I reduced my favorite but unwieldy dozen down to eight and arranged them chronologically from the earliest to the final entry, spacing the others in between about five years apart.

The finished score was sent off to Boosey, and both Baker and her accompanist, Martin Isepp, received a copy of it months before the date of the premiere. However, both were touring independently in different parts of Europe and North America, and they had had no opportunity to go over the piece together until they arrived in Minneapolis Thursday evening before the Sunday afternoon recital. They worked Friday and Saturday and requested that I not attend any rehearsal until Sunday morning.

When I arrived at the brand-new Orchestra Hall that Sunday morning, I was introduced to Janet and Martin, and they asked if they should go through one song at a time and then discuss it, or sing the cycle straight through. I said I preferred having them do the entire thing first without any interruptions from me. When they finished, I was speechless, utterly flabbergasted. It was perfection. Two days before, they had never done the piece, and now I had just heard a performance that to this day has never been surpassed. . . . Janet asked me to come up and give them my criticism. I went onstage and said, "I have nothing to tell you except that I'm a blubbering mass of gratitude and will never be able to thank you enough." I took my leave and let them go on to rehearse the rest of the program alone. Unbeknownst to them, the engineer, who was setting balances and microphone placements to tape the recital for a later radio broadcast, was surreptitiously recording the rehearsal. Janet is distinctly heard on that tape whispering to Martin as I walked offstage, "What a lovely man!"

That following April, weeks before the Pulitzers were announced, Hugo Weisgall phoned: inside information had it that Woolf had won. I didn't believe him. A week later Stuart Pope at Boosey called to say he, too, had heard the rumor. I still didn't believe it. He promised he would phone at 5 (Minneapolis time) the morning the *New York Times* published the winners' names. On the eve of announcement day, I sat by the phone all night, unable to sleep, reading Will Durant's *Story of Philosophy*. At 5, nothing. At 6, nothing. By 8, still nothing. Convinced I hadn't won, I went to bed. Soon after 9 a.m. the phone rang. I no longer remember what had delayed him, but Stuart said yes, it was true: Woolf had won…

By noon, vans from the four local TV stations were parked in front of our house with long black cables snaking across a small patch of lawn, onto the porch, in through the open front door, up a staircase on which half a dozen radio and newspaper reporters, plus stringers for the AP and UPI, were jostling for position…The following morning during a tremendous downpour our doorbell rang and Carolyn answered to find our postman in slicker and plastic-protected cap, rain streaming off his visor, down his glasses, face, chin, holding a tall stack of soggy letters, cards, and mailgrams. Smiling but bemused he handed her the pile and said, "I guess this means he's going to be famous."

Snow Dreams

"Even though that was quite a while ago, I do remember the premiere of "Snow Dreams" (1982) quite well. I had originally turned down the flute/guitar medium since I had no idea how to write for the guitar. But after I heard Sharon Isbin and Carol Wincenc perform, I said, "I have to do this. These players are just too good!" It was not an easy piece to write, but I am now happy to report that it is one of my most popular pieces, and is recorded on New World Records by Carol and Sharon. (I went on to write two more pieces for Carol and one more for Sharon.)

Thank you, Schubert Club!"

– Joan Tower, composer

Joan Tower, hailed as "one of the most successful woman composers of all time" by The New Yorker *magazine, wrote "Snow Dreams" as a Schubert Club centennial anniversary commission in 1982. A Professor of Music at Bard College, she won the prestigious Grawemeyer Award in Composition in 1990.*

Michael Barone, around 1973, in the KSJR music library (which doubled as his office) on the top floor of Wimmer Hall on the Saint John's University campus (the original home of Minnesota Public Radio).

Minnesota Public Radio Connections

J. Michael Barone

For several decades, radio announcer Michael Barone has been an informal advisor to The Schubert Club about organs, performers, and music in general.

A newcomer to the Minnesota cultural scene in 1967, Minnesota Public Radio began, an offshoot of Saint John's University, as station KSJR-FM in Collegeville. That original operation soon became independent of SJU, and as MPR gradually evolved into a statewide network during the late 1960s and early 1970s, relationships were sought with numerous community arts organizations, particularly in the Twin Cities. An obvious alliance was soon forged with The Schubert Club of Saint Paul.

I was hired as MPR's Music Director in August 1968, and remember conversing with Bruce in an ill-fated attempt to obtain an interview with ever-reticent Peter Serkin prior to Serkin's memorable Saint Paul Auditorium debut, a performance that included works by Messiaen presented in virtual darkness with a 'light show' backdrop. I also recorded a Schubert Club Organ Competition winner, possibly as early as 1969 or 1970 (long before PIPEDREAMS!).

Eventually, MPR was invited to broadcast concert recordings of Schubert Club International Artist Series events. Dennis D. Rooney was producer and host for much of that early work; Dennis engineered many of those recordings, often assisted by D. Michael Shields. Their 1975 recording (for MPR) of Dame Janet Baker's Orchestra Hall premiere of Dominick Argento's *From the Diary of Virginia Woolf* proved effective and timely, since that marvelous score, commissioned by The Schubert Club, went on to win a Pulitzer Prize, and our MPR concert recording later was issued on CD with Schubert Club sponsorship.

MPR has been involved with many other Schubert Club-sponsored performances, from new-music premieres to clavichord recitals. Live MPR broadcasts of Schubert Club Daytime Concerts from the little auditorium at the former Saint Paul Arts and Science Center (at 10th and Cedar) evolved into the "Live from Landmark" programs (precursors of today's Courtroom Concerts), co-produced by The Schubert Club and MPR in the basement theater of the Landmark Center. These fun programs combined a variety of classical music formats with congenial conversations.

As one of the primary presenters of classical music in the Twin Cities, The Schubert Club has been, and remains an organization with which the Classical Music Service of Minnesota Public Radio has enjoyed, and will continue to foster, a mutually beneficial collaborative and most friendly relationship.

On a more personal note, I always enjoyed dropping in on Bruce with some new "bright idea" of my own, or to catch up on the latest batch of his. During the formative days of the Keyboard Collection, I made a chance encounter with a unique Wurlitzer grand piano at the downtown Minneapolis Schmitt Music store. It had a rich, characterful tone, and a distinctive physical presence, with art deco styling, no lid, and a curved, plexiglass stand instead of the usual three legs. I suggested that Bruce "go take a look." He must have liked what he saw, since that piano is in The Schubert Club Keyboard Collection today.

One unresolved "pipe dream" concerns a pipe organ for the Landmark Center. With the fabulous Wanamaker Organ in Philadelphia in mind, I suggested to Bruce a similar lavish installation in Saint Paul. Bruce did not feel that the "time was right" for such a project, though he did engage me to bid on (and win, for The Schubert Club) an elegant, modest Kilgen tracker-action organ from a church in Sunburg, Minnesota. His original intention was to install it in an unrealized extension of the keyboard collection in the Landmark sub-basement. Later, we thought of putting it on a moving platform on the main floor. Unfortunately, that organ languished in the Landmark attic for several years until, realizing that 'the time' might never come, Bruce sold it to a congregation in Plymouth. Although you will find a small chamber organ in the Keyboard Collection, I still think a grand concert organ, playing into the Landmark Cortile, would be a remarkable addition to the Saint Paul cultural scene. Perhaps, some day, in Bruce's memory....

Artists-in-Residence

In the last twenty years, a number of local musicians have served as artists-in-residence for The Schubert Club. There is no standard job description, however. Some have worked in Landmark Center and distinguished themselves as excellent Museum guides, like pianists Roderick Kettlewell and Irina Elkina, and composers David Evan Thomas and Abbie Betinis. Some have been linked through performances—like Belladonna, a baroque quartet that is featured annually on the Early Music Series, or through broader programs—like gamelan musician Joko Sutrisno. Cung Tien and Cary John Franklin, composers-in-residence from the 1990s, had less direct involvement with specific Schubert Club programs than Edie Hill and Abbie Betinis, the current composers-in-residence. The one constant feature is that these excellent musicians became for a while a particular source of pride to the organization, a vital connection to music as it is being lived by performers and composers in our community.

[See photos next page]

In 2006, composers-in-residence Edie Hill (shown here amid 290 mailed-in manuscripts) and Abbie Betinis adjudicated the first round of compositions submitted for the ArtSong Competition, a collaboration between The Schubert Club and the American Composers Forum.

During his period as artist-in-residence, oboist Stanley King acquired two instruments for The Schubert Club Museum during a trip to Mongolia in 1999, including this dramatic *morin khuur* or horse-head fiddle.

For the Landmark Center premiere in 1998 of his piece "In the Country of Baseball," composer David Evan Thomas dressed appropriately for accompanying soprano Carol Eikum (except that the mitt had to be removed when he played the piano). His notes about the work say that, "While no stage directions are indicated in the score, the gestures of baseball are entirely appropriate, particularly in the Pitching and Fielding movements, provided they enhance the performance." David Evan Thomas served as Schubert Club composer-in-residence for eight years, ending in 2005.

Pianist Irina Elkina (left) served as a Museum docent as part of her position as artist-in-residence. In this photograph, she and her twin sister Julia (who as a duo-piano team have performed on The Schubert Club's International Artist Series) pay a visit to Landmark Center with their infant daughters.

Abbie Betinis, one of two current composers-in-residence, represented The Schubert Club at the Capitol as part of Arts Advocacy Day in 2007.

The Schubert Club
Commissioned Work, 1973-2007

Composer	Title of Piece and Instrumentation	Commission Year
Aderholdt, Sarah	In the Order They Were Taken From Us string quartet, 5 offstage speakers	1985
Argento, Dominick	A Few Words About Chekhov mezzo-soprano voice, baritone voice, piano	1996
Argento, Dominick	From the Diary of Virginia Woolf mezzo-soprano voice, piano	1974
Argento, Dominick	The Andrée Expedition baritone voice, piano	1982
Barnett, Carol	Apparizioni piano solo	1987
Bernstein, David S.	Late Autumn Moods and Images violin, cello, piano	1990
Betinis, Abbie	Some Glad Morning mixed chorus, violin, mandolin, banjo, cello	2006
Betinis, Abbie	Nattsanger soprano voice, cello, clarinet, piano	2007
Brief, Todd	Water Image piano solo	1990
Buys, Earl	Songs of Youth and Age baritone voice, piano	1985
Callahan, James	Sonus fortepiano solo	1995
Chalmiers, Harry	Night Voices violin, harp, narrator	1996
Childs, Mary Ellen	The Capacity of Calm Endurance piano solo	1989
Davidson, Randall	CoMix violin, piano, woodwinds, 2 percussion	1993
Davidson, Randall	Entrance soprano voice, piano	2004

Composer	Title of Piece and Instrumentation	Commission Year
Davidson, Randall	Kittyhawk violin, piano	1986
Davidson, Randall	Song and Dance cellos (3)	1984
Deak, Jon	Bye-Bye! flute (narrator), piano (narrator)	1986
Fetler, Paul	Concerto for Piano and Orchestra piano, orchestra	1983
Franklin, Cary John	An Emily Dickinson Cycle medium voice, piano	1987
Franklin, Cary John	Falls Flyer oboe, guitar	1999
Hall, Juliana	Night Dances high voice, piano	1987
Hall, Juliana	Winter Windows baritone voice, piano	1989
Hampl, Patricia	Libretto for Libby Larsen's Claire de Lune opera in 2 acts	1984
Harris, Matthew	Sonata for Cello and Piano cello, piano	1989
Heitzeg, Steve	Wild Songs voice (soprano), 2 percussionists, recorded Bonobo vocalizations	2006
Hemberg, Eskil	...In the earth mezzo-soprano voice, piano	1988
Hill, Edie	Bow Echo solo amplified cello solo	1997
Hill, Edie	Il Cantico Delle Creature mixed chorus, a cappella	2006
Hovda, Eleanor	Strings violin, piano	1989
Kechley, David	Voices from the Garden guitar quartet	1993
Kernis, Aaron Jay	Brilliant Sky, Infinite Sky baritone voice, violin, piano, percussion	1990

Composer	Title of Piece and Instrumentation	Commission Year
Kernis, Aaron Jay	String Quartet #2 (musica instrumentalis) string quartet	1997
Kim-Hwang, Yoon Hee	dharma-Dharma flute, harp	1989
Larsen, Libby	Before Winter baritone voice, organ	1982
Larsen, Libby	Fire and Brimstone MIDI grand piano	1996
Larsen, Libby	Juba cello, piano	1986
Larsen, Libby	Me (Brenda Ueland) soprano voice, piano	1987
Larsen, Libby	Raspberry Island Dreaming mezzo-soprano voice, orchestra	2002
Larsen, Libby	The Silver Fox: A Chamber Opera for the Young voices (6), flute, violin, piano	1979
Larsen, Libby	Traveling in Every Season mezzo-soprano voice, piano	1983
Lee, I-Chuun	Ton-Wha Street MIDI grand piano	1993
Lesniaski, David	Fortepiano Etudes fortepiano solo	2001
Lesniaski, David	Fortepiano Sonata fortepiano solo	1984
MacCombie, Bruce	Nightshade Rounds guitar solo	1979
MacKay, Jr., John	Three Songs of Reflection baritone voice, piano	1982
Maud, Arthur	In te Domine speravi (Psalm 31) mixed chorus, a capella	2001
McHugh, Charles	Calm Seas, Auspicious Gales violin, cello, piano	1984
Moriarty, Patrick	Jackson: Daytime Sky saxophone, trombone	1984

Composer	Title of Piece and Instrumentation	Commission Year
Mumford, Jeffrey	A landscape of interior resonances piano solo	2000
Olsen, David John	Cascades: Speaking in Tongues MIDI grand piano	1993
Olsen, David John	Crossovers piano solo	1989
Paulus, Stephen	Artsongs tenor voice, piano	1983
Paulus, Stephen	Fountain Of My Friends treble chorus, piano	1976
Paulus, Stephen	Mad Book, Shadow Book: Michael Morley's Songs tenor voice, piano	1976
Ratner, Richard	A Song for St. Cecilia's Day, 1687 soprano voice, piano	1990
Reese, Mona Lyn	Tombeau for Michael Collins harpsichord solo	1987
Reilly, Jim	Historic Songs treblec chorus, piano	1973
Rorem, Ned	Nine Episodes for Four Players clarinet, violin, cello, piano	2001
Rusche, Marjorie	Brenda soprano voice, violin, piano	1985
Rusche, Marjorie	Whales Weep Not! mezzo-soprano voice, piano	1984
Schoenfield, Paul	Five Days from the Life of a Manic-Depressive piano duet (4-hands)	1984
Schoenfield, Paul	Peccadilloes piano solo	1995
Schoenfield, Paul	Three Intermezzi piano solo	2004
Sergeyeva, Tatyana	Two Movements for Two Pianos piano duet (two pianos)	1996
Skrowaczewski, Stanislas	Musica a Quattro clarinet, violin, viola, cello	1998

Composer	Title of Piece and Instrumentation	Commission Year
Solum, Stephen	Excursions for the MIDI Grand Piano MIDI grand piano	1990
Solum, Stephen	Fantasy disklavier piano solo	1995
Thomas, David Evan	By Heart soprano voice, harp	2000
Thomas, David Evan	Greetings and a Farewell violin, piano	1997
Thomas, David Evan	Moonlight on a Midnight Stream: A Romantic Entertainment vocal quartet, piano	1994
Thomas, David Evan	O bell' Alma: concert paraphrase on themes from Donizetti's Lucia di Lammermoor flute, harp	2004
Thomas, David Evan	Sonata for Oboe and Guitar oboe, guitar	1999
Thomas, David Evan	String Quartet #2: "North of Spring" string quartet	2001
Thomas, David Evan	The Healing Fountain violin, cello, piano	2002
Thomas, David Evan	While All the World Made Merry high voice, piano	1995
Tower, Joan	Snow Dreams flute, guitar	1983
Vandervelde, Janika	Genesis I oboe, piano	1983
Vandervelde, Janika	Genesis III (Clockwork Rhapsody) piano solo	1985
Vandervelde, Janika	Henry's Fate tenor voice, clarinet, cello, piano, percussion	1983
Watson, D. John	Ring-ee-Tye treble chorus, orchestra	1985
Wolman, Amnon	Pedestrians' Crossing MIDI grand piano controlling live synthesizer or computer controlled sampler via MIDI	1993
Ying, Zhang	Spring Water stone xylophone (dan da) solo	1997

INDEX

Numbers in bold type refer to images. A complete list of artists who have appeared in the International Artists Series can be found on pages 31-37. A list of compositions commissioned by The Schubert Club can be found on pages 220-224. This information has not been incorporated into the index.

HAPPY
125th